THE
ALLOY OF LAW

**ALSO BY BRANDON SANDERSON
FROM GOLLANCZ:**

Mistborn
The Final Empire
The Well of Ascension
The Hero of Ages

The Stormlight Archive
The Way of Kings Part One
The Way of Kings Part Two

Elantris
Warbreaker

THE
ALLOY OF LAW

A MISTBORN NOVEL

BRANDON SANDERSON

GOLLANCZ
LONDON

Copyright © Dragonsteel Entertainment, LLC 2011
Interior illustrations copyright © Isaac Stewart, Ben McSweeney 2011
All rights reserved

The right of Brandon Sanderson to be identified as the
author of this work has been asserted by him in accordance
with the Copyright, Designs and Patents Act 1988.

First published in Great Britain in 2011 by Gollancz
An imprint of the Orion Publishing Group
Orion House, 5 Upper St Martin's Lane,
London WC2H 9EA
An Hachette UK Company

A CIP catalogue record for this book
is available from the British Library

ISBN 978 0 575 10580 5 (Cased)
ISBN 978 0 575 10582 9 (Trade Paperback)

3 5 7 9 10 8 6 4 2

Printed in Great Britain by Clays Ltd, St Ives plc

The Orion Publishing Group's policy is to use papers
that are natural, renewable and recyclable products and
made from wood grown in sustainable forests. The logging
and manufacturing processes are expected to conform to
the environmental regulations of the country of origin.

www.brandonsanderson.com
www.orionbooks.co.uk

FOR JOSHUA BILMES

Who is never afraid to tell me what is wrong with a book,

then fight for that same book no matter who else gives up on it.

ACKNOWLEDGMENTS

I first pitched the idea of later-era Mistborn novels to my editor back in 2006, I believe. It had long been my plan for Scadrial, the planet these books take place upon. I wanted to move away from the idea of fantasy worlds as static places, where millennia would pass and technology would never change. The plan then was for a second epic trilogy set in an urban era, and a third trilogy set in a futuristic era—with Allomancy, Feruchemy, and Hemalurgy being the common threads that tied them together.

This book isn't part of that second trilogy. It's a side deviation, something exciting that grew quite unexpectedly out of my planning for where the world would go. The point of telling you all of this, however, is to explain that it would be impossible to list all of the people who have helped me along the years. Instead, the best I can do is list some of the wonderful people who helped me with this specific book.

Alpha readers included, as always, my agent, Joshua Bilmes, and my editor, Moshe Feder. This book is dedicated to Joshua, actually. Professionally, he's believed in my work longer than anyone outside my writing group. He has been a wonderful resource and a good friend.

Other alphas were my writing group: Ethan Skarstedt, Dan Wells, Alan & Jeanette Layton, Kaylynn ZoBell, Karen Ahlstrom, Ben & Danielle Olsen, Jordan Sanderson (kind of), and Kathleen Dorsey. Finally, of course, there's the Inseparable Peter Ahlstrom, my assistant and friend, who does all kinds of important things for my writing and doesn't get nearly enough thanks for it.

At Tor Books, thanks go to Irene Gallo, Justin Golenbock, Terry

McGarry, and many others I couldn't possibly name—everyone from Tom Doherty to the sales force. Thank you all for your excellent work. Once again, I feel the need to give a special thanks to Paul Stevens, who goes above and beyond what I could reasonably expect to give aid and explanations.

Beta readers included Jeff Creer and Dominique Nolan. A special thanks to Dom for being a resource in regards to weaponry and guns. If you ever need anything shot properly, he's the one to call.

Note the lovely cover by Chris McGrath, whom I asked for specifically because of his work on the Mistborn paperback covers. Both Ben McSweeney and Isaac Stewart returned to provide interior art for this book, as their work on *The Way of Kings* was just plain awesome. They've continued in their awesomeness. Ben also provided equally awesome illustrations for the recently released Mistborn RPG from Crafty Games. Check it out at crafty-games.com, especially if you're interested in Kelsier's origin story.

Last of all I'd like to once again thank Emily, my wonderful wife, for her support, commentary, and love.

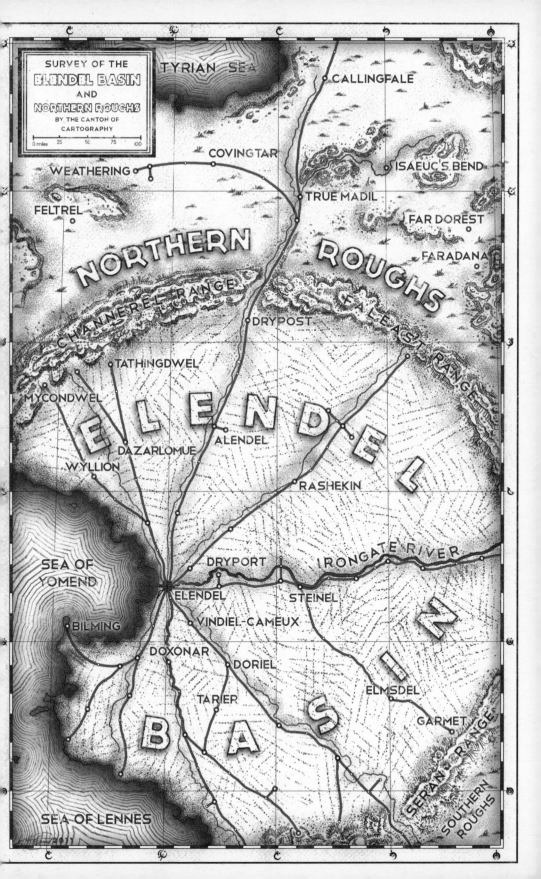

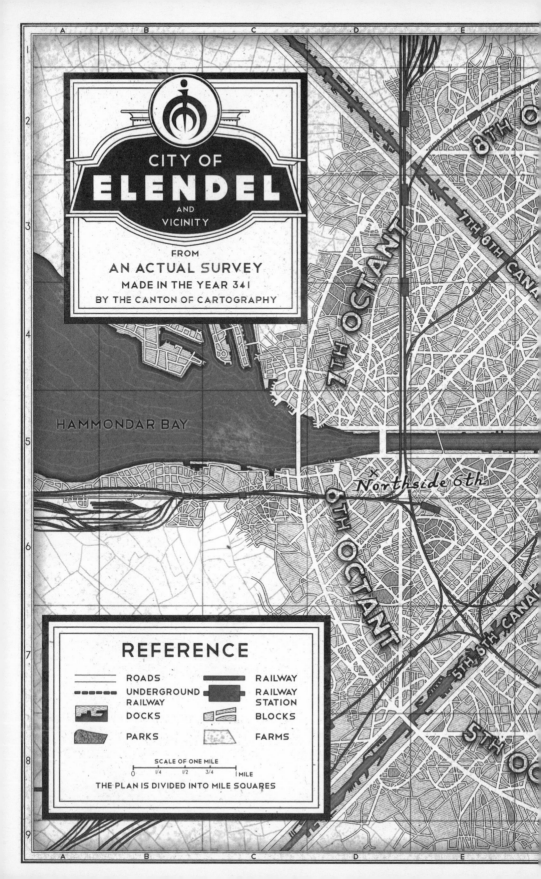

1ST OCTANT

2ND OCTANT

3RD OCTANT

4TH OCTANT

8TH 1ST CANAL

1ST 2ND CANAL

3RD 4TH CANAL

4TH 5TH CANAL

Madion Ways

Tekiel Manor

nner 7th

Field of Rebirth

ongard

IRONGATE RIVER

Ranette's House

Dampmere Park

Ladrian Mansion

4th Octant Constabulary Precinct Office

Ironspine Bldg

ekiel Tower   Yomen Manor

Cett Mansion

Demoux Promenade

My friend, annotated
with locations as per
your instructions.
~Nazh

G   H   I   J   K

1
2
3
4
5
6
7
8
9

2011

THE ALLOY
OF LAW

PROLOGUE

Wax crept along the ragged fence in a crouch, his boots scraping the dry ground. He held his Sterrion 36 up by his head, the long, silvery barrel dusted with red clay. The revolver was nothing fancy to look at, though the six-shot cylinder was machined with such care in the steel-alloy frame that there was no play in its movement. There was no gleam to the metal or exotic material on the grip. But it fit his hand like it was meant to be there.

The waist-high fence was flimsy, the wood grayed with time, held together with fraying lengths of rope. It smelled of age. Even the worms had given up on this wood long ago.

Wax peeked up over the knotted boards, scanning the empty town. Blue lines hovered in his vision, extending from his chest to point at nearby sources of metal, a result of his Allomancy. Burning steel did that; it let him see the location of sources of metal, then Push against them if he wanted. His weight against the weight of the item. If it was heavier, he was pushed back. If he was heavier, it was pushed forward.

In this case, however, he didn't Push. He just watched the lines to see if any of the metal was moving. None of it was. Nails holding together buildings, spent shell casings lying scattered in the dust, or horseshoes piled at the silent smithy—all were as motionless as the old hand pump planted in the ground to his right.

Wary, he too remained still. Steel continued to burn comfortably in his stomach, and so—as a precaution—he gently Pushed outward from himself in all directions. It was a trick he'd mastered a few years back; he didn't Push on any specific metal objects, but created a kind of defensive bubble around himself. Any metal that came streaking in his direction would be thrown slightly off course.

It was far from foolproof; he could still get hit. But shots would go wild, not striking where they were aimed. It had saved his life on a couple of occasions. He wasn't even certain how he did it; Allomancy was often an instinctive thing for him. Somehow he even managed to exempt the metal he carried, and didn't Push his own gun from his hands.

That done, he continued along the fence—still watching the metal lines to make sure nobody was sneaking up on him. Feltrel had once been a prosperous town. That had been twenty years back. Then a clan of koloss had taken up residence nearby. Things hadn't gone well.

Today, the dead town seemed completely empty, though he knew it wasn't so. Wax had come here hunting a psychopath. And he wasn't the only one.

He grabbed the top of the fence and hopped over, feet grinding red clay. Crouching low, he ran in a squat over to the side of the old blacksmith's forge. His clothing was terribly dusty, but well tailored: a fine suit, a silver cravat at the neck, twinkling cuff links on the sleeves of his fine white shirt. He had cultivated a look that appeared out of place, as if he were planning to attend a fine ball back in Elendel rather than scrambling through a dead town in the Roughs hunting a murderer. Completing the ensemble, he wore a bowler hat on his head to keep off the sun.

A sound; someone stepped on a board across the street, making it creak. It was so faint, he almost missed it. Wax reacted immediately, flaring the steel that burned inside his stomach. He Pushed on a group of nails in the wall beside him just as the crack of a gunshot split the air.

His sudden Push caused the wall to rattle, the old rusty nails straining in their places. His Push shoved him to the side, and he rolled across the ground. A blue line appeared for an eyeblink—the bullet, which hit the ground where he had been a moment before. As he came up from his roll, a second shot followed. This one came close, but bent just a hair out of the way as it neared him.

Deflected by his steel bubble, the bullet zipped past his ear. Another inch to the right, and he'd have gotten it in the forehead—steel bubble or no. Breathing calmly, he raised his Sterrion and sighted on the balcony of the old hotel across the street, where the shot had come from. The balcony was fronted by the hotel's sign, capable of hiding a gunman.

Wax fired, then Pushed on the bullet, slamming it forward with extra thrust to make it faster and more penetrating. He wasn't using typical lead or copper-jacketed lead bullets; he needed something stronger.

The large-caliber steel-jacketed bullet hit the balcony, and his extra power caused it to puncture the wood and hit the man behind. The blue line leading to the man's gun quivered as he fell. Wax stood up slowly, brushing the dust from his clothing. At that moment another shot cracked in the air.

He cursed, reflexively Pushing against the nails again, though his instincts told him he'd be too late. By the time he heard a shot, it was too late for Pushing to help.

This time he was thrown to the ground. That force had to go somewhere, and if the nails couldn't move, he had to. He grunted as he hit and raised his revolver, dust sticking to the sweat on his hand. He searched frantically for the one who'd fired at him. They'd missed. Perhaps the steel bubble had—

A body rolled off the top of the blacksmith's shop and thumped down to the ground with a puff of red dust. Wax blinked, then raised his gun to chest level and moved over behind the fence again, crouching down for cover. He kept an eye on the blue Allomantic lines. They could warn him if someone got close, but only if the person was carrying or wearing metal.

The body that had fallen beside the building didn't have a single line pointing to it. However, another set of quivering lines pointed to something moving along the back of the forge. Wax leveled his gun, taking aim as a figure ducked around the side of the building and ran toward him.

The woman wore a white duster, reddened at the bottom. She kept her dark hair pulled back in a tail, and wore trousers and a wide belt, with thick boots on her feet. She had a squarish face. A strong face, with lips that often rose slightly at the right side in a half smile.

Wax heaved a sigh of relief and lowered his gun. "Lessie."

"You knock yourself to the ground again?" she asked as she reached the cover of the fence beside him. "You've got more dust on your face than Miles has scowls. Maybe it's time for you to retire, old man."

"Lessie, I'm *three months* older than you are."

"Those are a long three months." She peeked up over the fence. "Seen anyone else?"

"I dropped a man up on the balcony," Wax said. "I couldn't see if it was Bloody Tan or not."

"It wasn't," she said. "He wouldn't have tried to shoot you from so far away."

Wax nodded. Tan liked things personal. Up close. The psychopath lamented when he had to use a gun, and he rarely shot someone without being able to see the fear in their eyes.

Lessie scanned the quiet town, then glanced at him, ready to move. Her eyes flickered downward for a moment. Toward his shirt pocket.

Wax followed her gaze. A letter was peeking out of his pocket, delivered earlier that day. It was from the grand city of Elendel, and was addressed to Lord Waxillium Ladrian. A name Wax hadn't used in years. A name that felt wrong to him now.

He tucked the letter farther into his pocket. Lessie thought it implied more than it did. The city didn't hold anything for him now, and House Ladrian would get along without him. He really should have burned that letter.

Wax nodded toward the fallen man beside the wall to distract her from the letter. "Your work?"

"He had a bow," she said. "Stone arrowheads. Almost had you from above."

"Thanks."

She shrugged, eyes glittering in satisfaction. Those eyes now had lines at the sides of them, weathered by the Roughs' harsh sunlight. There had been a time when she and Wax had kept a tally of who had saved the other most often. They'd both lost track years ago.

"Cover me," Wax said softly.

"With what?" she asked. "Paint? Kisses? You're already covered with dust."

Wax raised an eyebrow at her.

"Sorry," she said, grimacing. "I've been playing cards too much with Wayne lately."

He snorted and ran in a crouch to the fallen corpse and rolled it over. The man had been a cruel-faced fellow with several days of stubble on his cheeks; the bullet wound bled out his right side. *I think I recognize him,* Wax thought to himself as he went through the man's pockets and came out with a drop of red glass, colored like blood.

He hurried back to the fence.

"Well?" Lessie asked.

"Donal's crew," Wax said, holding up the drop of glass.

"Bastards," Lessie said. "They couldn't just leave us to it, could they?"

"You *did* shoot his son, Lessie."

"And you shot his brother."

"Mine was self-defense."

"Mine was too," she said. "That kid was *annoying.* Besides, he survived."

"Missing a toe."

"You don't need ten," she said. "I have a cousin with four. She does just fine." She raised her revolver, scanning the empty town. "Of course, she does look kind of ridiculous. Cover me."

"With what?"

She just grinned and ducked out from behind the cover, scrambling across the ground toward the smithy.

Harmony, Wax thought with a smile, *I love that woman.*

He watched for more gunmen, but Lessie reached the building without any further shots being fired. Wax nodded to her, then dashed across the street toward the hotel. He ducked inside, checking the corners for foes. The taproom was empty, so he took cover beside the doorway, waving toward Lessie. She ran down to the next building on her side of the street and checked it out.

Donal's crew. Yes, Wax had shot his brother—the man had been robbing a railway car at the time. From what he understood, though, Donal hadn't ever cared for his brother. No, the only thing that riled Donal was losing money, which was probably why he was here. He'd put a price on Bloody Tan's head for stealing a shipment of his bendalloy. Donal probably hadn't expected Wax to come hunting Tan the same day he did, but his men had standing orders to shoot Wax or Lessie if seen.

Wax was half tempted to leave the dead town and let Donal and Tan have at it. The thought of it made his eye twitch, though. He'd promised to bring Tan in. That was that.

Lessie waved from the inside of her building, then pointed toward the back. She was going to go out in that direction and creep along behind the next set of buildings. Wax nodded, then made a curt gesture. He'd try to hook up with Wayne and Barl, who had gone to check the other side of the town.

Lessie vanished, and Wax picked his way through the old hotel toward a side door. He passed old, dirty nests made by both rats and men. The town picked up miscreants the way a dog picked up fleas. He even passed a place where it looked like some wayfarer had made a small firepit on a sheet of metal with a ring of rocks. It was a wonder the fool hadn't burned the entire building to the ground.

Wax eased open the side door and stepped into an alleyway between the hotel and the store beside it. The gunshots earlier would have been heard, and someone might come looking. Best to stay out of sight.

Wax edged around the back of the store, stepping quietly across the red clay ground. The hillside here was overgrown with weeds except for the entrance to an old cold cellar. Wax wound around it, then paused, eyeing the wood-framed pit.

Maybe . . .

He knelt beside the opening, peering down. There had been a ladder here once, but it had rotted away—the remnants were visible below in a pile of old splinters. The air smelled musty and wet . . . with a hint of smoke. Someone had been burning a torch down there.

Wax dropped a bullet into the hole, then leaped in, gun out. As he fell, he filled his iron metalmind, decreasing his weight. He was Twinborn—a Feruchemist as well as an Allomancer. His Allomantic power was Steelpushing, and his Feruchemical power, called Skimming, was the ability to grow heavier or lighter. It was a powerful combination of talents.

He Pushed against the round below him, slowing his fall so that he landed softly. He returned his weight to normal—or, well, normal for him. He often went about at three-quarters of his unadjusted weight, making himself lighter on his feet, quicker to react.

He crept through the darkness. It had been a long, difficult road, finding where Bloody Tan was hiding. In the end, the fact that Feltrel had suddenly emptied of other bandits, wanderers, and unfortunates had been a major clue. Wax stepped softly, working his way deeper into the cellar. The scent of smoke was stronger here, and though the light was fading, he made out a firepit beside the earthen wall. That and a ladder that could be moved into place at the entrance.

That gave him pause. It indicated that whoever was making

their hideout in the cellar—it could be Tan, or it could be someone else entirely—was still down here. Unless there was another way out. Wax crept forward a little farther, squinting in the dark.

There was light ahead.

Wax cocked his gun softly, then drew a little vial out of his mistcoat and pulled the cork with his teeth. He downed the whiskey and steel in one shot, restoring his reserves. He flared his steel. Yes . . . there was metal ahead of him, down the tunnel. How long was this cellar? He had assumed it would be small, but the reinforcing wood timbers indicated something deeper, longer. More like a mine adit.

He crept forward, focused on those metal lines. Someone would have to aim a gun if they saw him, and the metal would quiver, giving him a chance to Push the weapon out of their hands. Nothing moved. He slid forward, smelling musty damp soil, fungus, potatoes left to bud. He approached a trembling light, but could hear nothing. The metal lines did not move.

Finally, he got close enough to make out a lamp hanging by a hook on a wooden beam near the wall. Something else hung at the center of the tunnel. A body? Hanged? Wax cursed softly and hurried forward, wary of a trap. It *was* a corpse, but it left him baffled. At first glance, it seemed years old. The eyes were gone from the skull, the skin pulled back against the bone. It didn't stink, and wasn't bloated.

He thought he recognized it. Geormin, the coachman who brought mail into Weathering from the more distant villages around the area. That was his uniform, at least, and it seemed like his hair. He'd been one of Tan's first victims, the disappearance that sent Wax hunting. That had only been two months back.

He's been mummified, Wax thought. *Prepared and dried like leather.* He felt revolted—he'd gone drinking with Geormin on occasion, and though the man cheated at cards, he'd been an amiable enough fellow.

The hanging wasn't an ordinary one, either. Wires had been used to prop up Geormin's arms so they were out to the sides, his head cocked, his mouth pried open. Wax turned away from the gruesome sight, his eye twitching.

Careful, he told himself. *Don't let him anger you. Keep focused.* He would be back to cut Geormin down. Right now, he couldn't afford to make the noise. At least he knew he was on the right track. This was certainly Bloody Tan's lair.

There was another patch of light in the distance. How long *was* this tunnel? He approached the pool of light, and here found another corpse, this one hung on the wall sideways. Annarel, a visiting geologist who had vanished soon after Geormin. Poor woman. She'd been dried in the same manner, body spiked to the wall in a very specific pose, as if she were on her knees inspecting a pile of rocks.

Another pool of light drew him onward. Clearly this wasn't a cellar—it was probably some kind of smuggling tunnel left over from the days when Feltrel had been a booming town. Tan hadn't built this, not with those aged wooden supports.

Wax passed another six corpses, each lit by its own glowing lantern, each arranged in some kind of pose. One sat in a chair, another strung up as if flying, a few stuck to the wall. The later ones were more fresh, the last one recently killed. Wax didn't recognize the slender man, who hung with hand to his head in a salute.

Rust and Ruin, Wax thought. *This isn't Bloody Tan's lair . . . it's his gallery.*

Sickened, Wax made his way to the next pool of light. This one was different. Brighter. As he approached, he realized that he was seeing sunlight streaming down from a square cut in the ceiling. The tunnel led up to it, probably to a former trapdoor that had rotted or broken away. The ground sloped in a gradual slant up to the hole.

Wax crawled up the slope, then cautiously poked his head out. He'd come up in a building, though the roof was gone. The brick walls were mostly intact, and there were four altars in the front, just to Wax's left. An old chapel to the Survivor. It seemed empty.

Wax crawled out of the hole, his Sterrion at the side of his head, coat marred by dirt from below. The clean, dry air smelled good to him.

"Each life is a performance," a voice said, echoing in the ruined church.

Wax immediately ducked to the side, rolling up to an altar.

"But we are not the performers," the voice continued. "We are the puppets."

"Tan," Wax said. "Come out."

"I have seen God, lawkeeper," Tan whispered. Where was he? "I have seen Death himself, with the nails in his eyes. I have seen the Survivor, who is life."

Wax scanned the small chapel. It was cluttered with broken benches and fallen statues. He rounded the side of the altar, judging the sound to come from the back of the room.

"Other men wonder," Tan's voice said, "but I know. I know I'm a puppet. We all are. Did you like my show? I worked so hard to build it."

Wax continued along the building's right wall, his boots leaving a trail in the dust. He breathed shallowly, a line of sweat creeping down his right temple. His eye was twitching. He saw corpses on the walls in his mind's eye.

"Many men never get a chance to create true art," Tan said. "And the best performances are those which can never be reproduced. Months, years, spent preparing. Everything placed right. But at the end of the day, the rotting will begin. I couldn't truly mummify them; I hadn't the time or resources. I could only preserve them long enough to prepare for this one show. Tomorrow, it will be ruined. You were the only one to see it. Only you. I figure . . . we're all just puppets . . . you see . . ."

The voice *was* coming from the back of the room, near some rubble that was blocking Wax's view.

"Someone else moves us," Tan said.

Wax ducked around the side of the rubble, raising his Sterrion.

Tan stood there, holding Lessie in front of him, her mouth gagged, her eyes wide. Wax froze in place, gun raised. Lessie was bleeding from her leg and her arm. She'd been shot, and her face was growing pale. She'd lost blood. That was how Tan had been able to overpower her.

Wax grew still. He didn't feel anxiety. He couldn't afford to; it might make him shake, and shaking might make him miss. He could see Tan's face behind Lessie; the man held a garrote around her neck.

Tan was a slender, fine-fingered man. He'd been a mortician. Black hair, thinning, worn greased back. A nice suit that now shone with blood.

"Someone else moves us, lawman," Tan said softly.

Lessie met Wax's eyes. They both knew what to do in this situation. Last time, he'd been the one captured. People always tried to use them against each other. In Lessie's opinion, that wasn't a disadvantage. She'd have explained that if Tan *hadn't* known the two of them were a couple, he'd have killed her right off. Instead, he'd kidnapped her. That gave them a chance to get out.

Wax sighted down the barrel of his Sterrion. He drew in the trigger until he balanced the weight of the sear right on the edge of firing, and Lessie blinked. One. Two. Three.

Wax fired.

In the same instant, Tan yanked Lessie to the right.

The shot broke the air, echoing against clay bricks. Lessie's head jerked back as Wax's bullet took her just above the right eye. Blood sprayed against the clay wall beside her. She crumpled.

Wax stood, frozen, horrified. *No . . . that isn't the way . . . it can't . . .*

"The best performances," Tan said, smiling and looking down at Lessie's figure, "are those that can only be performed once."

Wax shot him in the head.

1

Five months later, Wax walked through the decorated rooms of a large, lively party, passing men in dark suits with tailcoats and women in colorful dresses with narrow waists and lots of folds through long pleated skirts. They called him "Lord Waxillium" or "Lord Ladrian" when they spoke to him.

He nodded to each, but avoided being drawn into conversation. He deliberately made his way to one of the back rooms of the party, where dazzling electric lights—the talk of the city—produced a steady, too-even light to ward off the evening's gloom. Outside the windows, he could see mist tickling the glass.

Defying decorum, Wax pushed his way through the room's enormous glass double doors and stepped out onto the mansion's grand balcony. There, finally, he felt like he could breathe again.

He closed his eyes, taking the air in and out, feeling the faint wetness of the mists on the skin of his face. *Buildings are so . . . suffocating here in the city,* he thought. *Have I simply forgotten about that, or did I not notice it when I was younger?*

He opened his eyes, and rested his hands on the balcony railing to look out over Elendel. It was the grandest city in all the world, a metropolis designed by Harmony himself. The place of Wax's youth. A place that hadn't been his home for twenty years.

Though it had been five months since Lessie's death, he could still hear the gunshot, see the blood sprayed on the bricks. He had left the Roughs, moved back to the city, answering the desperate summons to do his duty to his house at his uncle's passing.

Five months and a world away, and he could still hear that gunshot. Crisp, clean, like the sky cracking.

Behind him, he could hear musical laughter coming from the warmth of the room. Cett Mansion was a grand place, full of expensive woods, soft carpets, and sparkling chandeliers. No one joined him on the balcony.

From this vantage, he had a perfect view of the lights down Demoux Promenade. A double row of bright electric lamps with a steady, blazing whiteness. They glowed like bubbles along the wide boulevard, which was flanked by the even wider canal, the still and quiet waters reflecting the light. An evening railway engine called a greeting as it chugged through the distant center of the city, hemming the mists with darker smoke.

Down Demoux Promenade, Wax had a good view of both the Ironspine Building and Tekiel Tower, one on either side of the canal. Both were unfinished, but their steelwork lattices already rose high into the sky. Mind-numbingly high.

The architects continued to release updated reports of how high they intended to go, each one trying to outdo the other. Rumors he'd heard at this very party, credible ones, claimed that both would eventually top out at over fifty stories. Nobody knew which would end up proving the taller, though friendly wagers were common.

Wax breathed in the mists. Out in the Roughs, Cett Mansion—which was three stories high—would have been as tall as a building got. Here, it felt dwarfed. The world had gone and changed on him during his years out of the city. It had grown up, inventing lights that needed no fire to glow and buildings that threatened to rise higher than the mists themselves. Looking down that wide street at the edge of the Fifth Octant, Wax suddenly felt very, very old.

"Lord Waxillium?" a voice asked from behind.

He turned to find an older woman, Lady Aving Cett, peeking out the door at him. Her gray hair was up in a bun and she wore rubies at her neck. "By Harmony, my good man. You'll take a chill out here! Come, there are some people you will wish to meet."

"I'll be along presently, my lady," Wax said. "I'm just getting a little air."

Lady Cett frowned, but retreated. She didn't know what to make of him; none of them did. Some saw him as a mysterious scion of the Ladrian family, associated with strange stories of the realms beyond the mountains. The rest assumed him to be an uncultured, rural buffoon. He figured he was probably both.

He'd been on show all night. He was *supposed* to be looking for a wife, and pretty much everyone knew it. House Ladrian was insolvent following his uncle's imprudent management, and the easiest path to solvency was marriage. Unfortunately, his uncle had *also* managed to offend three-quarters of the city's upper crust.

Wax leaned forward on the balcony, the Sterrion revolvers under his arms jabbing his sides. With their long barrels, they weren't meant to be carried in underarm holsters. They had been awkward all night.

He should be getting back to the party to chat and try to repair House Ladrian's reputation. But the thought of that crowded room, so hot, so close, sweltering, making it difficult to breathe. . . .

Giving himself no time to reconsider, he swung off over the side of the balcony and began falling three stories toward the ground. He burned steel, then dropped a spent bullet casing slightly behind himself and Pushed against it; his weight sent it speeding down to the earth faster than he fell. As always, thanks to his Feruchemy, he was lighter than he should have been. He hardly knew anymore what it felt like to go around at his full weight.

When the casing hit the ground, he Pushed against it and sent himself horizontally in a leap over the garden wall. With one hand on its stone top, he vaulted out of the garden, then reduced his weight to a fraction of normal as he fell down the other side. He landed softly.

Ah, good, he thought, crouching down and peering through the mists. *The coachmen's yard.* The vehicles everyone had used to get there were arranged here in neat rows, the coachmen themselves chatting in a few cozy rooms that spilled orange light into the mists. No electric lights here; just good, warmth-giving hearths.

He walked among the carriages until he found his own, then opened the trunk strapped to the back.

Off came his gentleman's fine dinner coat. Instead he threw on his mistcoat, a long, enveloping garment like a duster with a thick collar and cuffed sleeves. He slipped a shotgun into its pocket on the inside, then buckled on his gun belt and moved the Sterrions into the holsters at his hips.

Ah, he thought. *Much better.* He really needed to stop carrying the Sterrions and get some more practical weapons for concealment. Unfortunately, he'd never found anything as good as Ranette's work. Hadn't she moved to the city, though? Perhaps he could look her up and talk her into making him something. Assuming she didn't shoot him on sight.

A few moments later, he was running through the city, the mistcoat light upon his back. He left it open at the front, revealing his black shirt and gentleman's trousers. The ankle-length mistcoat had been divided into strips from just above the waist, the tassels streaming behind him with a faint rustle.

He dropped a bullet casing and launched himself high into the air, landing atop the building across the street from the mansion. He glanced back at it, the windows ablaze in the evening dark. What kind of rumors was he going to start, vanishing from the balcony like that?

Well, they already knew he was Twinborn—that was a matter of public record. His disappearance wasn't going to do much to help patch his family's reputation. For the moment, he didn't care. He'd spent almost every evening since his return to the city at one social function or another, and they hadn't had a misty night in weeks.

He needed the mists. This was who he was.

Wax dashed across the rooftop and leaped off, moving toward Demoux Promenade. Just before hitting the ground, he flipped a spent casing down and Pushed on it, slowing his descent. He landed in a patch of decorative shrubs that caught his coat tassels and made a rustling noise.

Damn. Nobody planted decorative shrubs out in the Roughs. He pulled himself free, wincing at the noise. A few weeks in the city, and he was already getting rusty?

He shook his head and Pushed himself into the air again, moving out over the wide boulevard and parallel canal. He angled his flight so he crested that and landed on one of the new electric lamps. There was one nice thing about a modern city like this; it had a *lot* of metal.

He smiled, then flared his steel and Pushed off the top of the streetlamp, sending himself in a wide arc through the air. Mist streamed past him, swirling as the wind rushed against his face. It was thrilling. A man never truly felt free until he'd thrown off gravity's chains and sought the sky.

As he crested his arc, he Pushed against another streetlight, throwing himself farther forward. The long row of metal poles was like his own personal railway line. He bounded onward, his antics drawing attention from those in passing carriages, both horse-drawn and horseless.

He smiled. Coinshots like himself were relatively rare, but Elendel was a major city with an enormous population. He wouldn't be the first man these people had seen bounding by metal through the city. Coinshots often acted as high-speed couriers in Elendel.

The city's size still astonished him. Millions lived here, maybe as many as *five* million. Nobody had a sure count across all of its wards—they were called octants, and as one might expect, there were eight of them.

Millions; he couldn't picture that, though he'd grown up here. Before he'd left Weathering, he'd been starting to think it was getting too big, but there couldn't have been ten thousand people in the town.

He landed atop a lamp directly in front of the massive Ironspine Building. He craned his neck, looking up through the mists at the towering structure. The unfinished top was lost in the darkness. Could he climb something so high? He couldn't Pull on metals, only Push—he wasn't some mythological Mistborn from the old stories, like the Survivor or the Ascendant Warrior. One Allomantic power, one Feruchemical power, that was all a man could have. In fact, having just one was a rare privilege—being Twinborn like Wax was truly exceptional.

Wayne claimed to have memorized the names of all of the different possible combinations of Twinborn. Of course, Wayne also claimed to have once stolen a horse that belched in perfect musical notes, so one learned to take what he said with a pinch of copper. Wax honestly didn't pay attention to all of the definitions and names for Twinborn; he was called a Crasher, the mix of a Coinshot and a Skimmer. He rarely bothered to think of himself that way.

He began to fill his metalminds—the iron bracers he wore on his upper arms—draining himself of more weight, making himself even lighter. That weight would be stored away for future use. Then, ignoring the more cautious part of his mind, he flared his steel and *Pushed*.

He shot upward. The wind became a roar, and the lamp was a good anchor—lots of metal, firmly attached to the ground—capable of pushing him quite high. He'd angled slightly, and the building's stories became a blur in front of him. He landed about twenty stories up, just as his Push on the lamp was reaching its limit.

This portion of the building had been finished already, the exterior made of a molded material that imitated worked stone. Ceramics, he'd heard. It was a common practice for tall buildings, where the lower levels would be actual stone, but the higher reaches would use something lighter.

He grabbed hold of an outcropping. He wasn't so light that the wind could push him away—not with his metalminds on his forearms and the weapons he wore. His lighter body did make it easier to hold himself in place.

Mist swirled beneath him. It seemed almost playful. He looked upward, deciding his next step. His steel revealed lines of blue to nearby sources of metal, many of which were the structure's frame. Pushing on any of them would send him away from the building.

There, he thought, noting a decent-sized ledge about five feet up. He climbed up the side of the building, gloved fingers sure on the complexly ornamented surface. A Coinshot quickly learned not to fear heights. He hoisted himself up onto the ledge, then dropped a bullet casing, stopping it with his booted foot.

He looked upward, judging his trajectory. He drew a vial from his belt, then uncorked it and downed the liquid and steel shavings inside it. He hissed through his teeth as the whiskey burned his throat. Good stuff, from Stagin's still. *Damn, I'm going to miss that when my stock runs out,* he thought, tucking the vial away.

Most Allomancers didn't use whiskey in their metal vials. Most Allomancers were missing out on a perfect opportunity. He smiled as his internal steel reserves were restored; then he flared the metal and launched himself.

He flew up into the night sky. Unfortunately, the Ironspine was built in set-back tiers, the upper stories growing progressively narrower as you went higher. That meant that even though he Pushed himself directly up, he was soon soaring in open darkness, mists around him, the building's side a good ten feet away.

Wax reached into his coat and removed his short-barreled shotgun from the long, sleevelike pocket inside. He turned—pointing it outward—braced it against his side, and fired.

He was light enough that the kick flung him toward the building. The boom of the blast echoed below, but he had spray shot in the shells, too small and light to hurt anyone when it fell dispersed from such a height.

He slammed into the wall of the tower five stories above where he'd been, and grabbed hold of a spikelike protrusion. The decoration up here really was marvelous. Who did they think would be looking at it? He shook his head. Architects were curious types.

Not practical at all, like a good gunsmith. Wax climbed to another shelf and jumped upward again.

The next jump was enough to get him to the open steelwork lattice of the unfinished upper floors. He strolled across a girder, then shimmied up a vertical member—his reduced weight making it easy—and climbed atop the very tallest of the beams jutting from the top of the building.

The height was dizzying. Even with the mists obscuring the landscape, he could see the double row of lights illuminating the street below. Other lights glowed more softly across the town, like the floating candles of a seafarer's ocean burial. Only the absence of lights allowed him to pick out the various parks and the bay far to the west.

Once, this city had felt like home. That was before he'd spent twenty years living out in the dust, where the law was sometimes a distant memory and people considered carriages a frivolity. What would Lessie have thought of one of these horseless contraptions, with the thin wheels meant for driving on a city's fine paved streets? Vehicles that ran on oil and grease, not hay and horseshoes?

He turned about on his perch. It was difficult to judge locations in the dark and the mists, but he did have the advantage of a youth spent in this section of the city. Things had changed, but not *that* much. He judged the direction, checked his steel reserves, then launched himself out into the darkness.

He shot outward in a grand arc above the city, flying for a good half a minute on the Push off those enormous girders. The skyscraper became a shadowed silhouette behind him, then vanished. Eventually, his impetus ran out, and he dropped back through the mists. He let himself fall, quiet. When the lights grew close—and he could see that nobody was below him—he pointed his shotgun at the ground and pulled the trigger.

The jolt punched him upward for a moment, slowing his descent. He Pushed off the birdshot in the ground to slow him further; he landed easily in a soft crouch. He noticed with dissatisfaction that he'd all but ruined some good paving stones with the shot.

Harmony! he thought. This place really was going to take some getting used to. *I'm like a horse blundering through a narrow marketplace,* he thought, hooking his shotgun back under his coat. *I need to learn more finesse.* Out in the Roughs, he'd been considered a refined gentleman. Here, if he didn't watch himself, he'd soon prove himself to be the uncultured brute that most of the nobility already assumed that he was. It—

Gunfire.

Wax responded immediately. He Pushed himself sideways off an iron gate, then ducked in a roll. He came up and reached for a Sterrion with his right hand, his left steadying the shotgun in its sleeve in his coat.

He peered into the night. Had his thoughtless shotgun blasts drawn the attention of the local constables? The guns fired again, and he frowned. *No. Those are too distant. Something's happening.*

This actually gave him a thrill. He leaped into the air and down the street, Pushing off that same gate to get height. He landed atop a building; this area was filled with three- and four-story apartment structures that had narrow alleyways between. How could people live without any space around them? He'd have gone mad.

He crossed a few buildings—it was handy that the rooftops were flat—and then stopped to listen. His heart beat excitedly, and he realized he'd been hoping for something like this. It was why he'd been driven to leave the party, to seek out the skyscraper and climb it, to run through the mists. Back in Weathering, as the town grew larger, he'd often patrolled at night, watching for trouble.

He fingered his Sterrion as another shot was fired, closer this time. He judged his distance, then dropped a bullet casing and Pushed himself into the air. He'd restored his weight to three-quarters and left it there. You needed some weight on you to fight effectively.

The mists swirled and spun, teasing him. One could never tell which nights would bring out the mists; they didn't conform to normal weather patterns. A night could be humid and chill, and yet not a wisp of mists would appear. Another night could begin dry as brittle leaves, but the mists would consume it.

They were thin this night, and so visibility was still good. Another crack broke the silence. *There,* Wax thought. Steel burning with a comfortable warmth within him, he leaped over another street in a flurry of mistcoat tassels, spinning mist, and calling wind.

He landed softly, then raised his gun in front of him as he ran in a crouch across the roof. He reached the edge and looked down. Just below him, someone had taken refuge behind a pile of boxes near the mouth of an alley. In the dark, misty night, Wax couldn't make out many details, but the person was armed with a rifle resting on a box. The barrel was pointed toward a group of people down the street who wore the distinctive domed hats of city constables.

Wax Pushed out lightly from himself in all directions, setting up his steel bubble. A latch on a trapdoor at his feet rattled as his Allomancy affected it. He peered down at the man firing upon the constables. It would be good to do something of actual value in this city, rather than just standing around chatting with the overdressed and the overprivileged.

He dropped a bullet casing, and his Allomancy pressed it down onto the rooftop beneath him. He Pushed more forcefully on it, launching himself up and through the swirling mists. He decreased his weight dramatically and pushed on a window latch as he fell, positioning himself so he landed right in the middle of the alleyway.

With his steel, he could see lines pointing toward four different figures in front of him. Even as he landed—the men muttering curses and spinning toward him—he raised his Sterrion and sighted on the first of the street thugs. The man had a patchy beard and eyes as dark as the night itself.

Wax heard a woman whimpering.

He froze, hand steady, but unable to move. The memories, so carefully dammed up in his head, crashed through and flooded his mind. Lessie, held with a garrote around her neck. A single shot. Blood on the redbrick walls.

The street thug jerked his rifle toward Wax and fired. The steel bubble barely deflected it, and the bullet tugged through the fabric of Wax's coat, just missing his ribs.

He tried to fire, but that whimpering . . .

Oh, Harmony, he thought, appalled at himself. He pointed his gun downward and fired into the ground, then Pushed on the bullet and threw himself backward, up out of the alleyway.

Bullets pierced the mists all around him. Steel bubble or not, he should have fallen to one of them. It was pure luck that saved his life as he landed on another roof and rolled to a stop, prone, protected from the gunfire by a parapet wall.

Wax gasped for breath, hand on his revolver. *Idiot,* he thought to himself. *Fool.* He'd never frozen in combat before, even when he'd been green. *Never.* This, however, was the first time he'd tried to shoot someone since the disaster in the ruined church.

He wanted to duck away in shame, but he gritted his teeth and crawled forward to the edge of the roof. The men were still down there. He could see them better now, gathering and preparing to make a run for it. They probably wanted nothing to do with an Allomancer.

He aimed at the apparent leader. However, before Wax could fire, the man fell to gunfire from the constables. In moments, the alleyway swarmed with men in uniforms. Wax raised his Sterrion beside his head, breathing deeply.

I could have fired that time, he told himself. *It was just that one moment where I froze. It wouldn't have happened again.* He told himself this several times as the constables pulled the malefactors out of the alley one at a time.

There was no woman. The whimpering he'd heard had been a gang member who'd taken a bullet before Wax arrived. The man was still groaning in pain as they took him away.

The constables hadn't seen Wax. He turned and disappeared into the night.

A short time later, Wax arrived at Ladrian Mansion. His residence in the city, his ancestral home. He didn't feel like he belonged there, but he used it anyway.

The stately home lacked expansive grounds, though it did have four elegant stories, with balconies and a nice patio garden out back. Wax dropped a coin and bounded over the front fence, landing atop the gatehouse. *My carriage is back,* he noticed. Not surprising. They were getting used to him; he wasn't certain whether to be pleased by that or ashamed of it.

He Pushed off the gates—which rattled at the weight—and landed on a fourth-story balcony. Coinshots had to learn precision, unlike their cousin Allomancers, Ironpullers—also known as Lurchers. Those would just pick a target and Pull themselves toward it, but they usually had to grind up the side of a building, making noise. Coinshots had to be delicate, careful, accurate.

The window was unlatched; he'd left it that way. He didn't fancy dealing with people at the moment; his abortive confrontation with the criminals had rattled him. He slipped into the darkened room, then padded across it and listened at the door. No sounds in the hallway. He opened the door silently, then moved out.

The hallway was dark, and he was no Tineye, capable of enhancing his senses. He felt his way with each step, being careful not to trip on the edge of a rug or bump into a pedestal.

His rooms were at the end of the hallway. He reached for the brass knob with gloved fingers. Excellent. He carefully pushed the door open, stepping into his bedroom. Now he just had to—

A door opened on the other side of his room, letting in bright yellow light. Wax froze in place, though his hand quickly reached into his coat for one of his Sterrions.

An aging man stood in the doorway, holding a large candelabrum. He wore a tidy black uniform and white gloves. He raised an eyebrow at Wax. "High Lord Ladrian," he said, "I see that you've returned."

"Um . . ." Wax said, sheepishly removing his hand from inside his coat.

"Your bath is drawn, my lord."

"I didn't ask for a bath."

"Yes, but considering your night's . . . entertainments, I thought it prudent to prepare one for you." The butler sniffed. "Gunpowder?"

"Er, yes."

"I trust my lord didn't shoot anyone too important."

No, Wax thought. *No, I couldn't.*

Tillaume stood there, stiff, disapproving. He didn't say the words he was undoubtedly thinking: that Wax's disappearance from the party had caused a minor scandal, that it would be even *more* difficult to procure a proper bride now. He didn't say that he was disappointed. He didn't say these things because he was, after all, a proper lord's servant.

Besides, he could say them all with a glance anyway.

"Shall I draft a letter of apology to Lady Cett, my lord? I believe she will expect it, considering that you sent one to Lord Stanton."

"Yes, that would be well," Wax said. He lowered his fingers to his belt, feeling the metal vials there, the revolver at each hip, the weight of the shotgun strapped inside his coat. *What am I doing? I'm acting like a fool.*

He suddenly felt exceedingly childish. Leaving a party to go patrolling through the city, looking for trouble? What was wrong with him?

He felt as if he'd been trying to recapture something. A part of the person he'd been before Lessie's death. He had known, deep down, that he might have trouble shooting now and had wanted to prove otherwise.

He'd failed that test.

"My lord," Tillaume said, stepping closer. "May I speak . . . boldly, for a moment?"

"You may."

"The city has a large number of constables," Tillaume said. "And they are quite capable in their jobs. Our house, however, has but one high lord. Thousands depend on you, sir." Tillaume nodded his head in respect, then moved to begin lighting some candles in the bedroom.

The butler's words were true. House Ladrian was one of the most powerful in the city, at least historically. In the city's government, Wax represented the interests of all of the people his house employed. True, they'd also have a representative based on votes in their guild, but it was Wax they depended on most.

His house was nearly bankrupt—rich in potential, in holdings, and in workers, but poor in cash and connections because of his uncle's foolishness. If Wax didn't do something to change that, it could mean jobs lost, poverty, and collapse as other houses pounced on his holdings and seized them for debts not paid.

Wax ran his thumbs along his Sterrions. *The constables handled those street toughs just fine,* he admitted to himself. *They didn't need me. This city doesn't need me, not like Weathering did.*

He was trying to cling to what he had been. He wasn't that person any longer. He couldn't be. But people did need him for something else.

"Tillaume," Wax said.

The butler looked back from the candles. The mansion didn't have electric lights yet, though workmen were coming to install them soon. Something his uncle had paid for before dying, money Wax couldn't recover now.

"Yes, my lord?" Tillaume asked.

Wax hesitated, then slowly pulled his shotgun from its place inside his coat and set it into the trunk beside his bed, placing it beside a companion he'd left there earlier. He took off his mistcoat, wrapping the thick material over his arm. He held the coat reverently for a moment, then placed it in the trunk. His Sterrion revolvers followed. They weren't his only guns, but they represented his life in the Roughs.

He closed the lid of the trunk on his old life. "Take this, Tillaume," Wax said. "Put it somewhere."

"Yes, my lord," Tillaume said. "I shall have it ready for you, should you need it again."

"I won't be needing it," Wax said. He had given himself one last night with the mists. A thrilling climb up the tower, an evening spent with the darkness. He chose to focus on that—rather than his failure with the toughs—as his night's accomplishment.

One final dance.

"Take it, Tillaume," Wax said, turning away from the trunk. "Put it somewhere safe, but put it away. For good."

"Yes, my lord," the butler said softly. He sounded approving.

And that, Wax thought, *is that.* He then walked into the washroom. Wax the lawkeeper was gone.

It was time to be Lord Waxillium Ladrian, Sixteenth High Lord of House Ladrian, residing in the Fourth Octant of Elendel City.

2

SIX MONTHS LATER

"How's my cravat?" Waxillium asked, studying himself in the mirror, turning to the side and tugging at the silver necktie again.

"Impeccable as always, my lord," Tillaume said. The butler stood with hands clasped behind his back, a tray with steaming tea sitting beside him on the serving stand. Waxillium hadn't asked for tea, but Tillaume had brought it anyway. Tillaume had a thing about tea.

"Are you certain?" Waxillium asked, tugging at the cravat again.

"Indeed, my lord." He hesitated. "I'll admit, my lord, that I've been curious about this for months. You are the first high lord I've ever waited upon who can tie a decent cravat. I'd grown quite accustomed to providing that assistance."

"You learn to do things on your own, when you live out in the Roughs."

"With all due respect, my lord," Tillaume said, his normally monotone voice betraying a hint of curiosity, "I wouldn't have thought that one would need to learn that skill in the Roughs. I wasn't aware that the denizens of those lands had the slightest concern for matters of fashion and decorum."

"They don't," Waxillium said with a smile, giving one final adjustment to the cravat. "That's part of why *I* always did. Dressing like a city gentleman had an odd effect on the people out there. Some immediately respected me, others immediately underestimated me. It worked for me in both cases. And, I might add, it was unspeakably satisfying to see the looks on the faces of criminals when they were hauled in by someone they had assumed to be a city dandy."

"I can imagine, my lord."

"I did it for myself too," Waxillium said more softly, regarding himself in the mirror. Silver cravat, green satin vest. Emerald cuff links. Black coat and trousers, stiff through the sleeves and legs. One steel button on his vest among the wooden ones, an old tradition of his. "The clothing was a reminder, Tillaume. The land around me may have been wild, but I didn't need to be."

Waxillium took a silver pocket square off his dressing stand, deftly folded it in the proper style, and slipped it into his breast pocket. A sudden chiming rang through the mansion.

"Rust and Ruin," Waxillium cursed, checking his pocket watch. "They're early."

"Lord Harms is known for his punctuality, my lord."

"Wonderful. Well, let's get this over with." Waxillium strode out into the hallway, boots gliding on the green velvet-cut rug. The mansion had changed little during his two-decade absence. Even after six months of living here, it still didn't feel like it was *his*. The faint smell of his uncle's pipe smoke still lingered, and the decor was marked by a fondness for deep dark woods and heavy stone sculpture. Despite modern tastes, there were almost no portraits or paintings. As Waxillium knew, many of those had been valuable, and had been sold before his uncle's death.

Tillaume walked alongside him, hands clasped behind his back. "My lord sounds as though he considers this day's duty to be a chore."

"Is it that obvious?" Waxillium grimaced. What did it say about him that he'd rather face down a nest of outlaws—outgunned and outmanned—than meet with Lord Harms and his daughter?

A plump, matronly woman waited at the end of the hallway, wearing a black dress and a white apron. "Oh, Lord Ladrian," she said with fondness. "Your mother would be so pleased to see this day!"

"Nothing has been decided yet, Miss Grimes," Waxillium said as the woman joined the two of them, walking along the balustrade of the second-floor gallery.

"She *did* so hope that you'd marry a fine lady someday," Miss Grimes said. "You should have heard how she worried, all those years."

Waxillium tried to ignore the way those words twisted at his heart. He *hadn't* heard how his mother worried. He'd hardly ever taken time to write his parents or his sister, and had only visited that one time, just after the railway reached Weathering.

Well, he was making good on his obligations now. Six months of work, and he was finally getting his feet under him and pulling House Ladrian—along with its many forgeworkers and seamstresses—from the brink of financial collapse. The last step came today.

Waxillium reached the top of the staircase, then hesitated. "No," he said, "I mustn't rush in. Need to give them time to make themselves comfortable."

"That is—" Tillaume began, but Waxillium cut him off by turning the other way and marching back along the balustrade.

"Miss Grimes," Waxillium said, "are there other matters that will need my attention today?"

"You wish to hear of them now?" she asked, frowning as she bustled to keep up.

"Anything to keep my mind occupied, dear woman," Waxillium said. Rust and Ruin . . . he was so nervous that he caught himself reaching inside his jacket to finger the grip of his Immerling 44-S.

It was a fine weapon; not as good as one of Ranette's make, but a proper, and small, sidearm for a gentleman. He'd decided he would be a lord, and not a lawman, but that didn't mean he was going to go about unarmed. That . . . well, that would just be plain insane.

"There is one matter," Miss Grimes said, grimacing. She was the Ladrian house steward, and had been for the last twenty years. "We lost another shipment of steel last night."

Waxillium froze on the walkway. "What? Again!"

"Unfortunately, my lord."

"Damn it. I'm starting to think the thieves are targeting only us."

"It's only our second shipment," she said. "House Tekiel has lost five shipments so far."

"What are the details?" he asked. "The disappearance. Where did it happen?"

"Well—"

"No, don't tell me," he said, raising a hand. "I can't afford to be distracted."

Miss Grimes gave him a flat look, since that was probably why she'd avoided telling him about it before his meeting with Lord Harms. Waxillium rested a hand on the railing, and felt his left eye twitch. Someone was out there, running an organized, highly efficient operation stealing the contents of entire railcars. They were being called the Vanishers. Perhaps he could poke around a little and . . .

No, he told himself sternly. *It is not my duty. Not anymore.* He would go to the proper authorities, perhaps hire some guards or personal investigators. He would not go chasing bandits himself.

"I'm sure the constables will find those responsible and bring them to justice," Waxillium said with some difficulty. "Do you think that's long enough to make Lord Harms wait? I think that's long enough. It hasn't been too long, has it?" Waxillium turned and walked back the way he'd come. Tillaume rolled his eyes as he passed.

Waxillium reached the stairs. A young man in a green Ladrian vest and a white shirt was climbing them. "Lord Ladrian!" Kip said. "Post has arrived."

"Any parcels?"

"No, my lord," the boy said, handing over a signet-sealed letter as Waxillium passed. "Only this. Looked important."

"An invitation to the Yomen-Ostlin wedding dinner," Miss Grimes guessed. "Might be a good place to have your first public appearance with Miss Harms."

"The details haven't been decided!" Waxillium protested as they stopped at the bottom of the staircase. "I've barely broached the topic with Lord Harms, yet you practically have us married. It's entirely possible that they will upend this entire matter, like what happened with Lady Entrone."

"It will go well, young master," Miss Grimes said. She reached up, adjusting the silk square in his pocket. "I've got a Soother's sense for these matters."

"You do realize I'm forty-two years old? 'Young master' doesn't exactly fit any longer."

She patted his cheek. Miss Grimes considered any unmarried man to be a child—which was terribly unfair, considering that *she* had never married. He refrained from speaking to her about Lessie; most of his family back in the city hadn't known about her.

"Right, then," Waxillium said, turning and striding toward the sitting room. "Into the maw of the beast I go."

Limmi, head of the ground-floor staff, waited by the doorway. She raised her hand as Waxillium approached, as if to speak, but he slid the dinner-party invitation between two of her fingers.

"Have an affirmative response drafted to this, if you would, Limmi," he said. "Indicate I'll be dining with Miss Harms and her father, but hold the letter until I'm done with my conference here. I'll let you know whether to send it or not."

"Yes, my lord, but—"

"It's all right," he said, pushing the door open. "I mustn't keep the . . ."

Lord Harms and his daughter were *not* in the sitting room. Instead, Waxillium found a lanky man with a round, sharp-chinned face. He was about thirty years of age, and had a few days of stubble on the chin and cheeks. He wore a wide-brimmed Roughs-style hat, the sides curving up slightly, and had on a leather duster. He was playing with one of the palm-sized upright clocks on the mantel.

"'Ello Wax," the man said brightly. He held up the clock. "Can I trade you for this?"

Waxillium swiftly pulled the door shut behind him. "Wayne? What are you *doing* here?"

"Looking at your stuff, mate," Wayne said. He held up the clock appraisingly. "Worth what, three or four bars? I've got a bottle of good whiskey that might be worth the same."

"You have to get out of here!" Waxillium said. "You're supposed to be in Weathering. Who's watching the place?"

"Barl."

"Barl! He's a miscreant."

"So am I."

"Yes, but you're the miscreant *I* chose to do the job. You could have at least sent for Miles."

"Miles?" Wayne said. "Mate, Miles is a right *horrible* human being. He'd rather shoot a man than bother actually finding out if the bloke was guilty or not."

"Miles keeps his town clean," Waxillium said. "And he's saved my life a couple of times. This is beside the point. I told *you* to watch over Weathering."

Wayne tipped his hat to Waxillium. "True, Wax, but you ain't a lawkeeper no longer. And me, I've got important stuff to be about." He looked at the clock, then pocketed it and set a small bottle of whiskey on the mantel in its place. "Now, sir, I'll need to be asking you a few questions." He pulled a small notepad and pencil from inside his duster. "Where were you last night at around midnight?"

"What does that—"

Waxillium was interrupted by chimes sounding at the door again. "Rust and Ruin! These are high-class people, Wayne. I've spent months persuading them that I'm not a ruffian. I need you *out* of here." Waxillium walked forward, trying to usher his friend toward the far exit.

"Now, that's right suspicious behavior, innit?" Wayne said, scrawling something on his notepad. "Dodging questions, acting all anxious. What are you hiding, sir?"

"Wayne," Waxillium said, grabbing the other man's arm. "Part of me is appreciative that you'd come all this way to aggravate me, and I *am* glad to see you. But *now is not the time.*"

Wayne grinned. "You assume I'm here for you. Don't you think that's a pinch arrogant?"

"What else would you be here for?"

"Shipment of foodstuffs," Wayne said. "Railway car left Elendel four days ago and arrived in Weathering with the entire contents of a single car empty. Now, I hear that you recently lost two shipments of your own to these 'Vanishers.' I've come to question you. Right suspicious, as I said."

"Suspicious . . . Wayne, I *lost* two shipments. I'm the one who got robbed! Why would that make me a suspect?"

"How am I to know how your devious, criminal genius mind works, mate?"

Footsteps sounded outside the room. Waxillium glanced at the door, then back at Wayne. "Right now, my criminal genius mind is wondering if I can stuff your corpse anywhere that wouldn't be too obvious."

Wayne grinned, stepping back.

The door opened.

Waxillium spun, looking as Limmi sheepishly held the door open. A corpulent man in a very fine suit stood there, holding a dark wooden cane. He had mustaches that drooped all the way down to his thick neck, and his waistcoat framed a deep red cravat.

". . . saying it doesn't matter whom he's seeing!" Lord Harms said. "He'll want to speak with me! We had an *appointment,* and . . ." Lord Harms paused, realizing the door was open. "Ah!" He strode into the room.

He was followed by a stern-looking woman with golden hair fixed into a tight bun—his daughter, Steris—and a younger woman who Waxillium didn't recognize.

"Lord Ladrian," Harms said, "I find it *very* unbefitting to be made to wait. And who is this that you're meeting with in my stead?"

Waxillium sighed. "It's my old—"

"Uncle!" Wayne said, stepping forward, voice altered to sound gruff and lose all of its rural accent. "I'm his uncle Maksil. Popped in unexpectedly this morning, my dear man."

Waxillium raised an eyebrow as Wayne stepped forward. He'd removed his hat and duster, and had plastered his upper lip with a realistic-looking fake mustache with a bit of gray in it. He was scrunching his face up just slightly to produce a few extra wrinkles at the eyes. It was a good disguise, making him look like he might be a few years older than Waxillium, rather than ten years younger.

Waxillium glanced over his shoulder. The duster sat folded on the floor beside one of the couches, hat atop it, a pair of dueling canes lying crossed beside the pile. Waxillium hadn't even noticed the swap—of course, Wayne had naturally done it while inside a speed bubble. Wayne was a Slider, a bendalloy Allomancer, capable of creating a bubble of compressed time around himself. He often used the power to change costumes.

He was also Twinborn, like Waxillium, though his Feruchemical ability—healing quickly from wounds—wasn't so useful outside of combat. Still, the two made for a very potent combination.

"Uncle, you say?" Lord Harms asked, taking Wayne's hand and shaking it.

"On the mother's side!" Wayne said. "Not the Ladrian side, of course. Otherwise I'd be running this place, eh?" He sounded nothing like himself, but that was Wayne's specialty. He said that three-quarters of a disguise was in the accent and voice. "I've wanted for a long time to come check up on the lad. He's had something of a rough-and-tumble past, you know. He needs a firm hand to make certain he doesn't return to such unpleasant ways."

"I've often thought the very same thing!" Lord Harms said. "I assume we're given leave to sit, Lord Ladrian?"

"Yes, of course," Waxillium said, covertly glaring at Wayne. *Really?* that glare said. *We're doing this?*

Wayne just shrugged. Then he turned and took Steris's hand and bowed his head politely. "And who is this lovely creature?"

"My daughter, Steris." Harms sat. "Lord Ladrian? You didn't tell your uncle of our arrival?"

"I was so surprised by his appearance," Waxillium said, "that I did not have an opportunity." He took Steris's hand and bowed his head to her as well.

She looked him up and down with a critical gaze, and then her eyes flicked toward the duster and hat in the corner. Her lips turned down. Doubtless she assumed they were his.

"This is my cousin Marasi," Steris said, nodding to the woman behind her. Marasi was dark-haired and large-eyed, with bright red lips. She looked down demurely as soon as Waxillium turned to her. "She has spent most of her life in the Outer Estates and is rather timid, so please don't upset her."

"I wouldn't dream of it," Waxillium said. He waited until the women were seated beside Lord Harms, then sat on the smaller sofa facing them, and facing the doorway. There was another exit from the room, but he'd discovered that there was a squeaky floorboard leading to it, which was ideal. This way, someone couldn't sneak up on him. Lawman or lord, he didn't fancy getting shot in the back.

Wayne primly settled himself in a chair directly to Waxillium's right. They all stared at one another for an extended moment. Wayne yawned.

"Well," Waxillium said. "Perhaps I should begin by asking after your health."

"Perhaps you should," Steris replied.

"Er. Yes. How's your health?"

"Suitable."

"So is Waxillium," Wayne added.

They all turned to him.

"You know," he said. "He's wearing a suit, and all. Suitable. Ahem. Is that mahogany?"

"This?" Lord Harms said, holding up his cane. "Indeed. It's a family heirloom."

"My lord Waxillium," Steris cut in, voice stern. She did not seem to enjoy small talk. "Perhaps we can dispense with empty prattle. We all know the nature of this meeting."

"We do?" Wayne asked.

"Yes," Steris said, voice cool. "Lord Waxillium. You are in the position of having an unfortunate reputation. Your uncle, may he rest with the Hero, tarnished the Ladrian name with his social reclusiveness, occasional reckless forays into politics, and blatant adventurism. You have come from the Roughs, lending no small additional measure of poor reputation to the house, particularly considering your insulting actions to various houses during your first few weeks in town. Above all this, your house is nearly destitute.

"We, however, are in a desperate circumstance of our own. Our financial status is excellent, but our name is unknown in the highest of society. My father has no male heir upon which to bestow his family name, and so a union between our houses makes perfect sense."

"How very logical of you, my dear," Wayne said, the upper-class accent rolling off his tongue as if he'd been born with it.

"Indeed," she said, still watching Waxillium. She reached into her satchel. "Your letters and conversations with my father have been enough to persuade us of your serious intent, and during these last few months in the city your public comportment has proven more promisingly sober than your initial boorishness. So I have taken the liberty of drawing up an agreement that I think will suit our needs."

"An . . . agreement?" Waxillium asked.

"Oh, I'm so eager to see it," Wayne added. He reached into his pocket absently and got out something that Waxillium couldn't quite discern.

The "agreement" turned out to be a large document, at least twenty pages long. Steris handed one copy to Waxillium and one to her father, and retained another for herself.

Lord Harms coughed into his hand. "I suggested she write

down her thoughts," he said. "And . . . well, my daughter is a very thorough woman."

"I can see that," Waxillium said.

"I suggest that you never ask her to pass the milk," Wayne added under his breath, so only Waxillium could hear. "As she seems likely to throw a cow at you, just to be certain the job is done thoroughly."

"The document is in several parts," Steris said. "The first is an outline of our courtship phase, wherein we make obvious—but not too speedy—progress toward engagement. We take just long enough for society to begin associating us as a couple. The engagement mustn't be so quick as to seem a scandal, but cannot come too slowly either. Eight months should, by my estimates, fulfill our purposes."

"I see," Waxillium said, flipping through the pages. Tillaume entered, bringing a tray of tea and cakes, and deposited it on a serving table beside Wayne.

Waxillium shook his head, closing the contract. "Doesn't this seem a little . . . stiff to you?"

"Stiff?"

"I mean, shouldn't there be room for romance?"

"There is," Steris said. "Page thirteen. Upon marriage, there shall be no more than three conjugal encounters per week and no fewer than one until a suitable heir is provided. After that, the same numbers apply to a two-week span."

"Ah, of course," Waxillium said. "Page thirteen." He glanced at Wayne. Was that a *bullet* the other man had taken from his pocket? Wayne was rolling it between his fingers.

"If that is not enough to satisfy your needs," Steris added, "the next page details proper mistress protocols."

"Wait," Waxillium said, looking away from Wayne. "Your document allows *mistresses*?"

"Of course," Steris said. "They are a simple fact of life, and so it's better to account for them than to ignore them. In the document, you will find requirements for your potential mistresses along with the means by which discretion will be maintained."

"I see," Waxillium said.

"Of course," Steris continued, "I will follow the same guidelines."

"You plan to take a mistress, my lady?" Wayne asked, perking up.

"I would be allowed my own dalliances," she said. "Usually the coachman is the object of choice. I would abstain until heirs were produced, of course. There mustn't be any confusion about lineage."

"Of course," Waxillium said.

"It's in the contract," she said. "Page fifteen."

"I don't doubt that it is."

Lord Harms coughed into his hand again. Marasi, Steris's cousin, maintained a blank expression, though she looked down at her feet during the conversation. Why had she been brought?

"Daughter," Lord Harms said, "perhaps we should move the conversation to less personal topics for a span."

"Very well," Steris said. "There *are* a few things I wanted to know. Are you a religious man, Lord Ladrian?"

"I follow the Path," Waxillium said.

"Hmmm," she said, tapping her fingers against her contract. "Well, that's a safe choice, if somewhat dull. I, for one, have never understood why people would follow a religion whose god *specifically* prohibits worshipping him."

"It's complicated."

"So Pathians like to say. With the same breath as you try to explain how simple your religion is."

"That's complicated too," Waxillium said. "A simple kind of complicated, though. You're a Survivorist, I assume?"

"I am."

Delightful, Waxillium thought. Well, Survivorists weren't *too* bad. Some of them, at least. He stood up. Wayne was still playing with that round. "Would anyone else like some tea?"

"No," Steris said with a wave of her hand, looking through her document.

"Yes, please," Marasi said softly.

Waxillium crossed the room to the tea stand.

"Those are very nice bookshelves," Wayne said. "Wish I had shelves like those. My, my, my. And . . . we're in."

Waxillium turned. The three guests had glanced at the shelves, and as they turned away, Wayne had started burning bendalloy and thrown up a speed bubble.

The bubble was about five feet across, including only Wayne and Waxillium, and once Wayne had it up he couldn't move it. Years of familiarity let Waxillium discern the boundary of the bubble, which was marked by a faint wavering of the air. For those inside the bubble, time would flow much more quickly than for those outside.

"Well?" Waxillium asked.

"Oh, I think the quiet one's kinda cute," Wayne said, his accent back in place. "The tall one is insane, though. Rust on my arms, but she is."

Waxillium poured himself some tea. Harms and the two women looked frozen as they sat on their couch, almost like statues. Wayne was flaring his metal, using as much strength as he could to create a few private moments.

These bubbles could be very useful, though not in the way most people expected. You couldn't shoot out of them—well, you could, but something about the barrier interfered with objects passing through it. If you fired a shot in a speed bubble, the bullet would slow as soon as it hit ordinary time and would be moved erratically off course. That made it nearly impossible to aim from within one.

"She's a very good match," Waxillium said. "It's an ideal situation for both of us."

"Look, mate. Just because Lessie—"

"This is *not* about Lessie."

"Whoa, hey." Wayne raised a hand. "No need to get angry."

"I'm not—" Waxillium took a deep breath, then continued more softly. "I'm not angry. But it's not about Lessie. This is about my duties."

Damn you, Wayne. I'd almost gotten myself to stop thinking about her. What would Lessie say, if she saw what he was doing? Laugh, probably. Laugh at how ridiculous it was, laugh at his discomfort. She hadn't been the jealous type, perhaps because she'd never had any reason to be. With a woman like her, why would Waxillium have wanted to look elsewhere?

Nobody would ever live up to her, but fortunately it didn't matter. Steris's contract actually seemed a good thing, in that regard. It would help him divide himself. Maybe help with a little of the pain.

"This *is* my duty now," Waxillium repeated.

"Your duties used to involve saving folks," Wayne said, "not marrying 'em."

Waxillium crouched down beside the chair. "Wayne. I can't go back to what I was. You sauntering in here, meddling in my life, isn't going to change that. I'm a different person now."

"If you were going to become a different person, couldn't you have chosen one without such an ugly face?"

"Wayne, this is *serious*."

Wayne raised his hand, spinning the cartridge between his fingers and proffering it. "So is this."

"What *is* that?"

"Bullet. You shoot folks with 'em. Hopefully bad ones—or at least ones what owes you a bar or two."

"Wayne—"

"They're turning back." Wayne set the cartridge on the tea-serving tray.

"But—"

"Time to cough. Three. Two. One."

Waxillium cursed under his breath, but pocketed the round and stood back up. He started coughing loudly as the speed bubble collapsed, restoring normal time. To the three visitors, only seconds had passed, and to their ears Waxillium and Wayne's conversation would be sped up to the point that most of it would be inaudible. The coughing would cover anything else.

None of the three visitors seemed to have noticed anything unusual. Waxillium poured the tea—it was a deep cherry color today, likely a sweet fruit tea—and brought a cup over to Marasi. She took it, and he sat down, holding his own cup in one hand, taking out and gripping the cartridge with the other. Both the casing and the medium-caliber bullet's jacket looked like steel, but the entire thing seemed too light. He frowned, hefting it.

Blood on her face. Blood on the brick wall.

He shivered, fighting off those memories. *Damn you, Wayne,* he thought again.

"The tea is delicious," Marasi said softly. "Thank you."

"You're welcome," Waxillium said, forcing his mind back to the conversation. "Lady Steris, I will consider this contract. Thank you for producing it. But really, I was hoping this meeting might allow me to learn more about you."

"I have been working on an autobiography," she said. "Perhaps I will send you a chapter or two of it by post."

"That's . . . very unconventional of you," Waxillium said. "Though it would be appreciated. But please, tell me of yourself. What are your interests?"

"Normally, I like plays." She grimaced. "At the Coolerim, actually."

"Am I missing something?" Waxillium asked.

"The Coolerim Playhouse," Wayne said, leaning forward. "Two nights ago, it was robbed in the middle of the performance."

"Haven't you heard?" Lord Harms asked. "It was in all the broadsheets."

"Was anyone harmed?"

"Not at the event itself," Lord Harms said, "but they did take a hostage as they escaped."

"Such a *horrid* thing," Steris said. "Nobody has heard from Armal yet." She looked sick.

"You knew her?" Wayne asked, his accent slipping faintly as he grew interested.

"Cousin," Steris said.

"Same as . . ." Waxillium asked, nodding toward Marasi.

The three regarded him with confused expressions for a moment, but then Lord Harms jumped in. "Ah, no. Different side of the family."

"Interesting," Waxillium said, leaning back in his chair, tea sitting ignored in his hand. "And ambitious. Robbing an entire playhouse? How many of the robbers were there?"

"Dozens," Marasi said. "Maybe as many as thirty, so the reports say."

"Quite a band. That means as many as another eight just to drive them away. And vehicles for escaping. Impressive."

"It's the Vanishers," Marasi said. "The ones stealing from the railway also."

"That hasn't been proven," Wayne replied, pointing at her.

"No. But one of the witnesses from a railway robbery described several men who were at the theater robbery."

"Wait," Waxillium said. "There were witnesses to one of the railway robberies? I thought they happened in secret. Something about a ghostly railcar appearing on the tracks?"

"Yes," Wayne said. "The railway engineers stop to investigate and—probably—panic. But the phantom railcar vanishes before they can investigate it. They continue on, but when they reach the end of the line, one of their train's cars is empty. Still locked, no signs of forced entry. But the goods are all gone."

"So nobody sees the culprits," Waxillium said.

"The recent ones have been different," Marasi said, growing animated. "They've started robbing passenger cars as well. When the train stops because of the phantom on the tracks, men jump into the cars and start going through, collecting jewelry and pocketbooks from the occupants. They take a woman hostage—threatening to kill her if anyone follows—and go. The freight car is still robbed as well."

"Curious," Waxillium said.

"Yes," Marasi said. "I think—"

"My dear," Lord Harms cut in. "You are bothering Lord Ladrian."

Marasi blushed, then looked down.

"It wasn't a bother," Waxillium said, tapping his teacup with his finger. "It—"

"Is that a *bullet* in your fingers?" Steris asked, pointing.

Waxillium looked down, realizing that he was rolling the cartridge between forefinger and thumb. He closed his fist around it before his memories could return. "It's nothing." He shot a glare at Wayne.

The other man mouthed something. *Push on it.*

"You are *quite* certain your unconventional past is behind you, Lord Ladrian?" Steris asked.

"Oh, he's certain," Wayne said, grimacing. "You don't have to worry about *him* being unconventional. Why, he's downright boring! Unbelievably, comically, nonsensically *boring.* You could squeeze more excitement out of a beggar waiting in line at the soup kitchen on rat meat day. It—"

"Thank you, *Uncle,*" Waxillium said dryly. "Yes, Steris, my past is just that. Past. I am committed to my duties as head of House Ladrian."

"Very well," she said. "We will need a formal entrance into high society as a couple. A public event of some sort."

"How about the Yomen-Ostlin wedding dinner?" Waxillium said absently. *Push on it.* "I received an invitation just this morning."

"An excellent idea," Lord Harms said. "We were invited as well."

Push on it. Waxillium reached into his left sleeve and covertly took a small pinch of steel shavings from the pouch he kept there. He dropped it into his tea and took a drink. That didn't give him much of a reserve, but it was enough.

He burned the steel, the familiar lines of blue springing up around him. They pointed to all nearby sources of metal.

Except the one in his fingers.

Aluminum, he realized. *No wonder it's light.*

Aluminum and a few of its alloys were Allomantically inert; you couldn't Push or Pull on them. It was also *very* expensive. It cost more than even gold or platinum.

The bullet was designed to kill Coinshots and Lurchers, men like Waxillium himself. That gave him a shiver, though he gripped the round more tightly. There were days when he'd have given his best gun for a few aluminum bullets, though he hadn't heard of an alloy that would produce a bullet with sound ballistics.

Where? he mouthed to Wayne. *Where did you find it?*

Wayne just nodded to the guests, who were looking right at Waxillium.

"Are you quite all right, Lord Ladrian?" Steris asked. "I know a good zinc counselor if you have need of some emotional aid."

"Er . . . no. Thank you. I am quite all right, and I think this has been a very productive meeting. Wouldn't you agree?"

"That depends," she said, rising, apparently taking that as an invitation to end the conversation. "The wedding party is on the morrow, I believe. I can count on you having reviewed the contract by then?"

"You can," Waxillium said, rising as well.

"*I* think this meeting was wonderful," Wayne said as he stood. "You're just what my nephew needs, Lady Steris! A firm hand. None of this rabble-rousing he's been used to."

"I agree!" Lord Harms said. "Lord Ladrian, perhaps your uncle can attend the dinner—"

"No," Waxillium said quickly before Wayne could say anything. "No, unfortunately, he has to return to his estates. Told me just earlier. He has a very important foaling to attend."

"Oh, well then," Lord Harms said, helping Marasi to her feet. "We will send you word of confirmation once we have accepted the Yomen invitation."

"And I will do likewise," Waxillium said, escorting them to the door of the room. "Farewell until then." Tillaume bowed to them there, then escorted them out. Their departure felt rushed to Waxillium, but he was relieved to see them go. Considering Wayne's sudden intrusion, that had actually gone pretty well. Nobody had ended up trying to shoot him.

"Nice bunch," Wayne said. "I now see what you're doing. With a wife and in-laws like those, you'll feel quite at home here—just like the jailhouse and its occupants back in Weathering!"

"Very nice," Waxillium said under his breath, waving one last time as the Harms family walked out the mansion doors. "Where did you get the bullet?"

"It was dropped at the theater robbery. Traded the constables for it this morning."

Waxillium closed his eyes. Wayne had a very liberal interpretation of what "trading" entailed.

"Oh, don't get that way," Wayne said. "I left them a nice cobblestone for it. I think Steris and her pop are convinced you're a loon, by the way." He grinned.

"That's nothing new. My association with you has been convincing people I'm insane for years now."

"Ha! And here I thought you'd lost your sense of humor." Wayne walked back into the room. He slid his pencil out of his pocket as he passed a table, trading it for one of Waxillium's pens.

"My humor isn't lost, Wayne," Waxillium said, "just strained. What I told you is true, and this bullet doesn't change anything."

"Maybe it doesn't," Wayne said, retrieving his hat, duster, and dueling canes. "But I'm still gonna see what I can find."

"It's not your job."

"And it wasn't your job to start hunting down criminals out in the Roughs. Doesn't change what needs to be done, mate." Wayne walked up to Waxillium, then handed him the hat. Once Waxillium took it, Wayne threw on his coat.

"Wayne . . ."

"People are being taken, Wax," he said, taking back his hat and putting it on. "Four hostages so far. None returned. Stealing jewelry is one thing. Taking food from Roughs towns is another. Kidnapping people . . . well, there's something goin' on here. I'm gonna find out what it is. With or without you."

"Without me."

"Fine." He hesitated. "But I need something, Wax. A place to look. You always did the thinking."

"Yes, having a brain helps with that, surprisingly."

Wayne narrowed his eyes at him. Then he raised his eyebrows, pleadingly.

"All right," Waxillium said, sighing and fetching his teacup. "How many robberies now?"

"Eight. Seven railway cars and, most recently, the theater."

"Four hostages?"

"Yeah. Across three of the latest robberies. Two were taken from one of the trains, then one from the robbery at the theater. All four hostages are women."

"Easier to overpower," Waxillium said idly, tapping his cup, "and more likely to make the men worry about getting them killed if they try to give chase."

"Do you need to know what was stolen?" Wayne said, reaching into the pocket of his duster. "I traded one of the constables for a list. . . ."

"It doesn't matter." Waxillium took a drink from his cup. "Or, at least, most of it probably doesn't. It's not about the robberies."

"It's . . . not?"

"No. Large gang. Well funded—too well funded." He pulled out the round and looked it over. "If they really wanted money, they'd be robbing gold transports or banks. The robberies are probably a distraction. If you want a man's horses, sometimes the best thing to do is let his hogs loose. While he's chasing them down, you ride off.

"I'd lay money on these Vanishers being after something else, something unlikely. Perhaps an item that is easy to overlook in all that has been taken. Or maybe it's really about extortion—and they plan to start asking for protection money from people in town. See if anyone's been contacted about that. I haven't, by the way.

"If that goes nowhere, look at the hostages. One of them might have been carrying something that was the *real* target of the robbery. I wouldn't be surprised if this turned out to be about clandestine blackmail."

"But they robbed a few trains before taking any hostages."

"Yes," Waxillium said. "And they got away with it. There was no reason to expose themselves by robbing passengers if they could make off with cargo unseen and unstopped. They're after something else, Wayne. Trust me."

"All right." The wiry man rubbed his face, then finally pulled off the fake mustache. He stuffed it into his pocket. "But tell me. Don't you even want to know? Doesn't it itch at you?"

"No." That wasn't completely true.

Wayne snorted. "I'd believe you if you could say that without your eye twitching, mate." He nodded toward the bullet. "I notice you didn't offer to give that back."

"I didn't." Waxillium pocketed it.

"And you still wear your metalminds," Wayne said, nodding to the bracers hidden mostly by the cuffs of Waxillium's sleeves. "Not to mention that you're still keeping steel inside your sleeve. I noticed a gun catalogue over on the table, too."

"A man must have hobbies."

"If you say so," Wayne said, then stepped forward, tapping Waxillium on the chest. "But you know what I think? I think you're looking for excuses to not let go. This thing, it's who you are. And no mansion, no marriage, and no mere *title* is going to change that." Wayne tipped his hat. "You're meant to be helping people, mate. It's what you do."

With that, Wayne left, his duster brushing against the doorframe as he walked out.

The Elen

Newsworthy Con

4th of Doxil, 341   Edition ꡒꡗꡙꡊꡛꡖꡌ

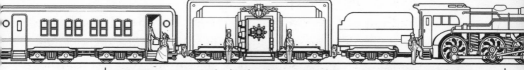

EXPLORING ...E PITS OF ...LTANIA"

...our exclusive series, ...ancer Jak continues his ...ts exploring the distant ...ns.

...this installment, he ...of the days he spent in ...famous Pits of Eltania, ...Koloss tribes rule the ...nd precious, unknown ...s can be discovered. ...story below the fold. ...hundred percent true ...om the pen of the ex- ...himself!

HOUSE TEKIEL UNVEILS THE "BREAKNAUGHT"

Claiming it will revolutionize security and transportation, Reshelle Tekiel announced her House's new vault-style train car, intended for the transportation and protection of valuable goods via railway. The car is on display for the public at the Evergall Trainyards until the 19th.

Designed specifically as a response to the terrible and ever-increasing rise in bandit attacks by such groups as the infamous "Vanishers," the new Breaknaught train car is fabricated from the finest steel, designed upon the latest modern lines and sealed by a massive door and lock identical to those found upon the vaults of Tekiel's own banking houses.

The timing mechanism of this scientifically advanced lock guarantees that once sealed, the railcar cannot be reopened until well after it has reached its destination. Thus the Breaknaught allows even the most concerned of gentlemen to rest secure in the certainty that their valued cargo may travel unmolested along the lines of the Elendel Basin and the lands beyond.

Indeed, this is a greater concern than ever in light of the recent attacks upon those traveling the railways near our fair Elendel itself. None are safe from the ravenous ways of the Vanishers, stripping ladies and lords of their precious valuables at gunpoint. While blood has yet to be spilled in their attacks, they have recently begun adding kidnapping to their list of sins, and it seems only a matter of time before injury results.

Rather than wait for the painfully slow machinations of other house lords to defend lives and goods from these thieves through Senate procedure, House Tekiel has stepped forward once again with an ingenious solution that takes an active hand in battling these villains.

THE PHANTOM RAILCAR!

Described by Witnesses!

In this harrowing report, three witnesses tell of the night their train was robbed by the Vanishers. One of them is the train engineer herself, and she explains in great detail the ghostly apparition. Discover the facts for yourself, and see why this phantom is too quiet, too bright, and too unworldly to be anything other than a force from beyond. Experts from the university compare train disasters to determine which is the apparition's origin, and the death lists give insight as to what the phantoms may desire. Exclusive reporting, only found here! Reverse side.

Reverse side.

...ion Leader ...bandons ...idarity with ...ade Union ...ty Members

...surprise switch from ...line position, Trade ...Leader Elors Durnsed ...nced his intention to

...greeted with near-violent derision from members of the Trade Union Party interviewed by this broadsheet. A Line Riveter at the site of the Ironspine Building who gave his name as Brill told this reporter that Mr. Durnsed should "bloody well keep his head clear of these parts if he knows what's what." Before he could expand upon this statement, his local union representative intervened

RELIEF FROM YOUR PAINS!

Mistress Halex, Allomancer, has opened a new Soothing Parlor. Within its relaxing confines, one can find relief from stress, anxiety, and concern—leaving with a light heart and a soaring mind. Our reporter visits the parlor to give a detailed report of what goes on. A luxurious massage, sweet scents, and a Soother on duty

Exploring the Pits of Eltania!

My dear editor, and by way of you, my dearest readers: I trust that my missive finds you well and in the possession of a willing ear, for the incredible events that trans-

3

Eight hours later, Waxillium stood at an upper window of his mansion. He watched the last broken fragments of a dying day. They dimmed, then grew black. He waited, hoping. But no mist came.

What does it matter? he thought to himself. *You're not going to go outside anyway.* Still, he wished the mists were out; he felt more at peace when they were out there, watching. The world became a different place, one he felt he better understood.

He sighed and crossed his study to the wall. He turned the switch, and the electric lights came on. They were still a wonder to him. Even though he knew the Words of Founding had given hints regarding electricity, what men had achieved still seemed incredible.

He crossed the room to his uncle's desk. His desk. Back in Weathering, Waxillium had used a rough, flimsy table. Now he had a sturdy, smoothly polished desk of stained oak. He sat down and began leafing through ledgers of house finances. It wasn't long, however, before his eyes started flicking toward the stack of broadsheets lying on his easy chair. He'd asked Limmi to go gather a few of them for him.

He usually ignored the broadsheets these days. Reports of crimes had a way of setting his mind running in circles and keeping him from focusing on his business. Of course, now that thoughts of the Vanishers had been planted in his mind, he'd have trouble letting go and doing anything productive, at least until he had scratched a few itches about what they'd been doing.

Perhaps just a little reading, he told himself. *To catch up on current events.* It wouldn't hurt to be informed; in fact, it might be important to his ability to entertain discussions with others.

Waxillium fetched the stack and returned to his desk. He easily found an account of the robberies in the day's paper. Other broadsheets in the stack had even more information. He'd mentioned the Vanishers to Limmi, and so she'd gathered a few broadsheets that were intended for people who wanted a collection of all of the recent stories on them. These reprinted articles from weeks or even months ago, with the original dates of the stories' publication. Those types of broadsheets were popular, he could tell, as he had three different ones from three different publishers. It seemed everyone wanted to stay up to date on items they'd missed.

By the dates listed on the reprinted articles, the first robbery had happened much earlier than he'd assumed. Seven months ago, just before he'd arrived back in Elendel. There had been a lapse of four months between the first railway cargo disappearance and the second. The name "Vanishers" hadn't started being used until this second attack.

The robberies were all similar, save for the one at the playhouse. A train was stopped because of a distraction on the tracks—early on, a fallen tree. Later, a ghostly phantom railcar that appeared from the mists, traveling directly at the train. The engineers stopped in a panic, but the phantom ahead vanished.

The engineers would start their train again. When it reached its destination, one of their cars was found to have been emptied of all goods. People were ascribing all kinds of mystical powers to the robbers, who seemed to be able to pass through walls and locked cargo cars without trouble. *But what goods were stolen?* Waxillium thought, frowning. The reports of the first theft didn't say, though it did mention the cargo had belonged to Augustin Tekiel.

Tekiel was one of the richest houses in the city, based over in the Second Octant, though it was building its new skyscraper in the financial district of the Fourth Octant. Waxillium read the articles over again, then searched through the broadsheets, scanning them for any further mention of the first robbery before the second occurred.

What's this? he thought, holding up a broadsheet that included a reprint of a letter Augustin Tekiel had written for publication a few months back. The letter denounced the Elendel constables for failure to protect or recover Tekiel's goods. The broadsheet had happily printed it, even made a headline of it: "Constables Incompetent, Tekiel Slams."

Three months. It had taken three months for Tekiel to say anything. Waxillium put aside these compilation broadsheets, then searched through the more recent broadsheets for other mentions. There was no shortage of them; the robberies were dramatic and mysterious, two things that sold a lot of papers.

The second and third robberies had been of steel shipments. Odd, that. An impractically heavy substance to take, and not as valuable as simply robbing the passenger cars. The fourth robbery had been the one that caught Wayne's attention: packaged foodstuffs from a train on its way to the northern Roughs. The fifth robbery had been the first to involve the passengers. The sixth and seventh had done so as well, the seventh being the only time the Vanishers had taken two hostages instead of one.

All three of the later robberies had involved stealing from a freight car as well as from passengers. Metals in two cases, foodstuffs in another case—at least, that was all the newspaper reported. With each case, the details had grown more interesting, as the cargo cars had been better secured. More sophisticated locks, guards riding along. The robberies happened incredibly quickly, considering the weight of goods taken.

Did they use a speed bubble, like Wayne makes? Waxillium thought.

But no. You couldn't move in or out of a speed bubble once one was up, and it would be impossible to make one large enough to facilitate this kind of robbery. So far as he knew, at least.

Waxillium continued reading. There were a great many articles with theories, quotes, and eyewitness reports. Many suggested a speed bubble, but editorials cut those to shreds. Too much manpower would be needed, more than could fit in a speed bubble. They thought it more likely that a Feruchemist who could increase his strength was lifting the heavy materials out of the cars and carrying them off.

But to where? And why? And how were they bypassing the locks and the guards? Waxillium cut out articles he found interesting. Few had any solid information.

A soft knock at the door interrupted him in the middle of spreading the articles out on his desk. He looked up to see Tillaume in the doorway holding a tray of tea and a basket, the handle over his arm. "Tea, my lord?"

"That would be wonderful."

Tillaume strode forward and set up a small stand beside the desk, getting a cup and a sharp white napkin. "Do you have a preference?" Tillaume could manufacture dozens of varieties of tea from the simplest of starting points, blending and making what he considered ideal.

"Whatever."

"My lord. There is *great* importance to tea. It should never merely be 'whatever.' Tell me. Are you planning to sleep soon?"

Waxillium looked over the array of cut-out reports. "Definitely not."

"Very well. Would you prefer something to help clear your mind?"

"That might be nice."

"Sweet or not?"

"Not."

"Minty or spicy?"

"Minty."

"Strong or weak?"

"Er . . . strong."

"Excellent," Tillaume said, taking several jars and some silver spoons from his basket. He began mixing powders and bits of herbs into a cup. "My lord looks very intent."

Waxillium tapped the table. "My lord is annoyed. Broadsheets make for *terrible* research opportunities. I need to know what was in the first shipment."

"The first shipment, my lord?"

"The first railcar that the thieves stole from."

"Miss Grimes would note that you seem to be slipping into old habits, my lord."

"Miss Grimes isn't here, fortunately. Besides, Lord Harms and his daughter seemed *aghast* that I didn't know about the robberies. I must keep abreast of events in the city."

"That's a very excellent excuse, my lord."

"Thank you," Waxillium said, taking the cup of tea. "I almost have myself completely persuaded." He took a sip. "Preservation's Wings, man! This is *good*."

"Thank you, my lord." Tillaume took out the napkin and snapped it in his hands, then folded it down the middle and laid it across the arm of Waxillium's chair. "And I *believe* that the first thing stolen was a shipment of wool. I heard it being discussed at the butcher's earlier in the week."

"Wool. That makes no sense."

"None of these crimes make much sense, my lord."

"Yes," Waxillium said. "Unfortunately, those are the most interesting kind of crimes." He took another sip of the tea. The strong, minty scent seemed to clear his nose and mind. "I need paper."

"What—"

"A large sheet," Waxillium continued. "As big as you can find."

"I will see what is available, my lord," Tillaume said. Waxillium caught a faint sigh of exasperation from the man, though he left the room to do as asked.

How long had it been since Waxillium had started his research?

He glanced at the clock, and was surprised at the time. Well into the night already.

Well, he was into it now. He'd never sleep until he'd worked it through. He rose and began to pace, holding his teacup and saucer before him. He stayed away from the windows. He was backlit, and would make an excellent target for a sniper outside. Not that he really thought there *would* be one, but . . . well, he felt more comfortable working this way.

Wool, he thought. He walked over and opened a ledger, looking up some figures. He grew so absorbed that he didn't notice the passing of time until Tillaume returned.

"Will this do, my lord?" he asked, bringing in an artist's easel with a large pad of paper clipped to it. "The old Lord Ladrian kept this for your sister. She did love to draw."

Waxillium looked at it, and felt his heart clench. He hadn't thought of Telsin in ages. They had been so distant most of their lives. Not by intent, like his distance from his uncle; Waxillium and the previous Lord Ladrian had often been at odds. No, his distance from Telsin had been one born more of laziness. Twenty years apart, only seeing his sister occasionally, had let him slide along without much contact.

And then she'd died, in the same accident as his uncle. He wished the news had been harder for him to hear. It *should* have been harder for him to hear. She'd been a stranger by then, though.

"My lord?" the butler asked.

"The paper is perfect," Waxillium said, rising and fetching a pencil. "Thank you. I was worried we'd have to hang the paper on the wall."

"Hang it?"

"Yes. I used to use some bits of tar."

That idea seemed to make Tillaume *very* uncomfortable. Waxillium ignored him, walking over and beginning to write on the pad. "This is nice paper."

"I'm pleased, my lord," Tillaume said uncertainly.

Waxillium drew a little train in the top left corner, putting in a track ahead of it. He wrote a date beneath it. "First robbery. Fourteenth of Vinuarch. Target: wool. Supposedly." In like manner, he added more trains, tracks, dates, and details down the paper.

Wayne had always mocked him when he'd sketched out crimes to help him think. But it worked, though he frequently had to put up with Wayne's playful additions of little stick-figure bandits or mistwraiths rampaging across the otherwise neat and orderly sketchwork and notes.

"Second robbery happened much later," Waxillium continued. "Metals. For the first robbery, Lord Tekiel didn't make any kind of fuss until months had passed." He tapped the paper, then crossed out the word "wool." "He didn't lose a shipment of wool. It was early summer then, and wool prices would be too low to justify the freight charges. As I recall, the rates were unusually high in Vinuarch because the eighteenth railway line was out of service. It would take a man with breadcrumbs for brains to pay a premium to ship out-of-season wares to people who didn't want them."

"So . . ." Tillaume said.

"Just a moment," Waxillium said. He walked over and pulled a few ledgers off the shelf beside his desk. His uncle had some shipping manifests here. . . .

Yes. The old Lord Ladrian had kept *very* good track of what his competitor houses had been shipping. Waxillium scanned the lists for oddities. It took him a little while, but he eventually came up with a theory.

"Aluminum," Waxillium said. "Tekiel was probably shipping aluminum, but avoiding taxes by claiming it as something else. In here, his stated aluminum shipments for the last two years are much smaller than they were for previous years. His smelters are still producing, however. I'd bet my best gun that Augustin Tekiel—with the help of some railway workers—has been running a nice, profitable little smuggling operation. That's why he didn't make a big commotion about the theft at first; he didn't want to draw attention."

Waxillium walked over and wrote some notations on his paper. He lifted his cup of tea to his lips, nodding to himself. "That also explains the long wait between the first and second robberies. The bandits were making use of that aluminum. They probably sold some of it on the black market to fund their operation, then used the rest to make aluminum bullets. But why would they *need* aluminum bullets?"

"For killing Allomancers?" Tillaume asked. He had been tidying the room while Waxillium read the ledgers.

"Yes." Waxillium drew in images of faces above three of the robberies, the ones where they'd taken hostages.

"My lord?" Tillaume asked, stepping up beside him. "You think the captives are Allomancers?"

"The names have all been released," Waxillium said. "All four are women from wealthy families, but none of them openly have Allomantic powers."

Tillaume remained quiet. That didn't mean everything. Many Allomancers among the upper crust were discreet about their powers. There were plenty of situations where that could be useful. For instance, if you were a Rioter or Soother—capable of influencing people's emotions—you wouldn't want people to suspect.

In other cases, Allomancy was flaunted. A recent candidate for the orchard-growers seat on the Senate had run solely on the platform that he was a Coppercloud, and was therefore impossible to affect with zinc or brass. The candidate won by a landslide. People hated thinking that someone might secretly be pulling their leaders' strings.

Waxillium started noting his speculations around the margins of the paper. Motives, possible ways they were emptying the freight cars so quickly, similarities and differences among the heists. As he wrote he hesitated, then added a couple of stick-figure bandits at the top, drawn in Wayne's sloppy style. Crazy though it was, he felt better having them there.

"I'll bet the captives were all Allomancers, secretly," Waxillium said. "The thieves had aluminum bullets to deal with Coinshots, Lurchers, and Thugs. And if we were able to catch any of the thieves, I'll bet good money that we'd find them wearing aluminum linings in their hats to shield their emotions from being Pushed or Pulled on." That wasn't uncommon among the city's elite as well, though the common men couldn't afford such luxury.

The robberies *weren't* about money; they were about the captives. That was why no bounty had been demanded, and why the bodies of the captives hadn't been discovered dumped somewhere. The robberies were meant to obscure the true motives for the kidnappings. The victims were not the spur-of-the-moment hostages they were meant to appear. The Vanishers were gathering Allomancers. And Allomantic metals—so far raw steel, pewter, iron, zinc, brass, tin, and even some bendalloy had been stolen.

"This is dangerous," Waxillium whispered. "Very dangerous."

"My lord . . ." Tillaume said. "Weren't you going to go over the house account ledgers?"

"Yes," Waxillium said distractedly.

"And the lease for the new offices in the Ironspine?"

"I can still get to that tonight too."

"My lord. When?"

Waxillium paused, then checked his pocket watch. Again, he was surprised to see how much time had passed.

"My lord," Tillaume said. "Did I ever tell you about your uncle's horse-racing days?"

"Uncle Edwarn was a gambler?"

"Indeed he was. It was a great problem to the house, soon after his rise to high lord. He would spend most of his days at the tracks."

"No wonder we're destitute."

"Actually, he was quite *good* at the gambling, my lord. He usually came out ahead. Far ahead."

"Oh."

"He stopped anyway," Tillaume said, collecting his tray and Waxillium's empty teacup. "Unfortunately, my lord, while he was winning a small fortune at the races, the house lost a *large* fortune in mismanaged business and financial dealings." He walked toward the door, but turned. His normally somber face softened. "It is not my place to lecture, my lord. Once one becomes a man, he can and must make his own decisions. But I do offer warning. Even a good thing can become destructive if taken to excess.

"Your house *needs* you. Thousands of families rely upon you. They need your leadership and your guidance. You did not ask for this, I understand. But the mark of a great man is one who knows when to set aside the important things in order to accomplish the vital ones."

The butler left, closing the door behind him.

Waxillium stood alone beneath the uncannily steady glow of the electric lights, looking at his diagram. He tossed the pencil aside, suddenly feeling drained, and fished out his pocket watch. It was two fifteen. He should be getting some sleep. Normal people slept at these hours.

He dimmed the lights to not be backlit, then walked to the window. He was still depressed not to see any mists, even though he hadn't expected them. *I never said daily prayers,* he realized. *Things have been too chaotic today.*

Well, it was better to arrive late than not at all. He reached into his pocket, fishing out his earring. It was a simple thing, stamped on the head with the ten interlocking rings of the Path. He slipped it into his ear, which was pierced for the purpose, and leaned against the window to stare out at the darkened city.

There was no specific prescribed posture for praying as a Pathian. Just fifteen minutes of meditation and pondering. Some liked to sit with legs crossed, eyes closed, but Waxillium had always found it *harder* to think in that posture. It made his back hurt and his spine tingle. What if someone sneaked around behind him and shot him in the back?

So, he just stood. And pondered. *How are things up there in the mists?* he thought. He was never sure how to talk to Harmony. *Life's good, I assume? What with you being God, and all?*

In response, he felt a sense of . . . amusement. He could never tell if he created those sensations himself or not.

Well, since I'm not God myself, Waxillium thought, *perhaps you could use that omniscience of yours to drum up some answers for me. It feels like I'm in a bind.*

A discordant thought. This wasn't like most of the binds he'd been in. He wasn't tied up, about to be murdered. He wasn't lost in the Roughs, without water or food, trying to find his way back to civilization. He was standing in a lavish mansion, and while his family was having financial troubles, it was nothing they couldn't weather. He had a life of luxury and a seat on the city Senate.

Why, then, did he feel like these last six months had been among the hardest he'd ever lived? An endless series of reports, ledgers, dinner parties, and business deals.

The butler was right; many *did* rely on him. The Ladrian house had started as several thousand individuals following the Origin, and had grown large in three hundred years, adopting under its protection any who came to work on its properties or in its foundries. The deals Waxillium negotiated determined their wages, their privileges, their lifestyle. If his house collapsed, they'd find employment elsewhere, but would be considered lesser members of those houses for a generation or two until they obtained full rights.

I've done hard things before, he thought. *I can do this one. If it's right. Is it right?*

Steris had called the Path a simple religion. Perhaps it was. There was only one basic tenet: Do more good than harm. There were other aspects—the belief that all truth was important, the requirement to give more than one took. There were over three hundred examples listed in the Words of Founding, religions that could have been. Might have been. In other times, in another world.

The Path was to study them, learn from their moral codes. A few rules were central. Do not seek lust without commitment. See the strengths in all flaws. Pray and meditate fifteen minutes a day. And don't waste time worshipping Harmony. Doing good *was* the worship.

Waxillium had been converted to the Path soon after leaving Elendel. He was still convinced that the woman he'd met on that train ride must have been one of the Faceless Immortals, the hands of Harmony. She'd given him his earring; every Pathian wore one while praying.

The problem was, it was hard for Waxillium to feel like he was doing anything useful. Luncheons and ledgers, contracts and negotiations. He knew, logically, that all of it was important. But those, even his vote on the Senate, were all abstractions. No match for seeing a murderer jailed or a kidnapped child rescued. In his youth, he'd lived in the City—the world's center of culture, science, and progress—for two decades, but he hadn't found himself until he'd left it and wandered the dusty, infertile lands out beyond the mountains.

Use your talents, something seemed to whisper inside of him. *You'll figure it out.*

That made him smile ruefully. He couldn't help wondering why, if Harmony really *was* listening, he didn't give more specific answers. Often, all Waxillium got from prayer was a sense of encouragement. Keep going. It's not as difficult as you feel it is. Don't give up.

He sighed, just closing his eyes, losing himself in thought. Other religions had their ceremonies and their meetings. Not the Pathians. In a way, its very simplicity made the Path much harder to follow. It left interpretation up to one's own conscience.

After meditating for a time, he couldn't help feeling that Harmony wanted him to study the Vanishers *and* to be a good house lord. Were the two mutually exclusive? Tillaume thought they were.

Waxillium glanced back at the stack of broadsheets and the easel with the drawing pad on it. He reached into his pocket, taking out the bullet Wayne had left.

And against his will, he saw in his mind's eye Lessie, head jerking back, blood spraying into the air. Blood covering her beautiful brown hair. Blood on the floor, on the walls, on the murderer who had been standing behind her. But that murderer hadn't been the one to shoot her.

Oh, Harmony, he thought, raising a hand to his head and slowly sitting down, back to the wall. *It really is about her, isn't it? I can't do that again. Not again.*

He dropped the round, pulled off his earring. He stood, walked over, cleaned up the broadsheets, and closed the drawing pad.

Nobody had been hurt by the Vanishers yet. They were robbing people, but they weren't harming them. There wasn't even proof that the hostages were in danger. Likely they'd be returned after ransom demands were met.

Waxillium sat down to work on his house's ledgers instead. He let them draw his attention well into the night.

4

Harmony's forearms," Waxillium mumbled, stepping into the grand ballroom. "This is what passes for a modest wedding dinner these days? There are more people in here than live in entire *towns* in the Roughs."

Waxillium had visited the Yomen mansion once in his youth, but that time, the grand ballroom had been empty. Now it was filled. Rows and rows of tables lined the hardwood floor of the cavernous chamber; there had to be over a hundred of them. Ladies, lords, elected officials, and the wealthy elite moved and chatted in a low hum, all dressed in their finest. Sparkling jewels. Crisp black suits with colorful cravats. Women with dresses after the modern fashion: deep colors, skirts that went down to the floor, thick outer layers with lots of folds and lace. Most women wore tight, vestlike coats over the top, and the necklines were much lower now than he remembered them being in his childhood. Perhaps he was simply more likely to notice.

"What was that, Waxillium?" Steris asked, turning to the side and letting him help off her overcoat. She wore a fine red dress that seemed calculatedly designed to be completely in fashion but not too daring.

"I was simply noting the size of this gathering, my dear," Waxillium said, folding her coat and handing it—along with his bowler hat—to a waiting attendant. "I've been to quite a number of functions since my return to the city, and none were this enormous. Practically half the city seems to have been invited."

"Well, this is something special," she said. "A wedding involving two very well-connected houses. They wouldn't want to leave anyone out. Except, of course, the ones they left out on purpose."

Steris held out her arm for him to take. He'd received a detailed lecture during the carriage ride on how, precisely, he was to hold it. His arm above hers, taking her hand lightly, fingers wrapping down under her palm. It looked horribly unnatural, but she insisted that it would convey the exact meaning they intended. Indeed, as they stepped down onto the ballroom floor, they drew a number of interested looks.

"You imply," Waxillium said, "that one purpose of this wedding dinner is not in who is invited, but who is *not*."

"Precisely," she said. "And, in order to fulfill that purpose, *everybody* else must be invited. The Yomens are powerful, even if they do believe in Sliverism. Horrid religion. Imagine, revering Ironeyes himself. Anyway, nobody will ignore an invitation to this celebration. And so, those to be slighted will not only find themselves without a party to attend, but unable to arrange their own diversions, as anyone they might have wanted to invite will be here. That leaves them to either associate with other uninviteds—therefore reinforcing their outcast status—or to sit alone at home, thinking about how they have been insulted."

"In my experience," Waxillium said, "that sort of unhappy brooding leads to a high probability of people getting shot."

She smiled, waving with calculated fondness to someone they passed. "This isn't the Roughs, Waxillium. It is the City. We don't do such things here."

"No, you don't. Shooting people would be too charitable for City folks."

"You haven't even seen the worst of it," she noted, waving to someone else. "You see that person turned away from us? The stocky man with the longer hair?"

"Yes."

"Lord Shewrman. An infamously dreadful party guest. He's a complete bore when not drunk and a complete buffoon when he is drunk—which is most of the time, I might add. He is probably the least likable person in all of upper society. Most people here would rather spend an hour amputating one of their own *toes* than spend a few moments chatting with him."

"So why is he here?"

"For the insult factor, Waxillium. Those who were snubbed will be even more aghast to learn that Shewrman was here. By including a few bad alloys like him—men and women who are utterly undesirable, but who don't realize it—House Yomen is essentially saying, 'We'd even prefer spending time with *these* people to spending it with you.' Very effective. Very nasty."

Waxillium snorted. "If you tried something that rude out in Weathering, it would end with you strung up by your heels from the rafters. If you're lucky."

"Hum. Yes." A servant stepped forward, gesturing for them to follow as she led them to a table. "You understand," Steris continued more softly, "that I am no longer responding to your 'ignorant frontiersman' act, Waxillium."

"Act?"

"Yes," she said distractedly. "You are a man. The prospect of marriage makes men uncomfortable, and they clutch for freedom. Therefore, you have begun regressing, tossing out savage comments to provoke a reaction from me. This is your instinct for masculine independence; an exaggeration meant, unconsciously, to undermine the wedding."

"You assume it's an exaggeration, Steris," Waxillium said as they approached the table. "Maybe this is what I am."

"You are what you choose to be, Waxillium," she said. "As for these people here, and choices made by House Yomen, I did not make these rules. Nor do I approve of them; many are inconvenient. But it is the society in which we live. Therefore, I make of myself something that can survive in this environment."

Waxillium frowned as she released his arm and fondly kissed cheeks with a few women from a nearby table—distant relatives, it seemed. He found himself clasping hands behind his back and nodding with a civil smile to those who came to greet Steris and him.

He'd made a good showing for himself these last months while moving among upper society, and people treated him far more amiably than they once had. He was even fond of some of those who approached. However, the nature of what he was doing with Steris still made him uncomfortable, and he found it difficult to enjoy much of the conversation.

In addition, this many people in one place still made his back itch. Too much confusion, too difficult to watch the exits. He preferred the smaller parties, or at least the ones spread across a large number of rooms.

The bride and groom arrived, and people rose to clap. Lord Joshin and Lady Mi'chelle; Waxillium didn't know them, though he did wonder why they were speaking with a scruffy man who looked like a beggar, dressed all in black. Fortunately, it didn't seem Steris intended to drag him over to wait with those intent upon congratulating the newlyweds at the earliest possible moment.

Soon, the first tables were served their meals. Silverware began to clatter. Steris sent for a servant to prepare their table; Waxillium passed the time by inspecting the room. There were two balconies, one at each shorter end of the rectangular ballroom. There appeared to be space for dining up there, though no tables had been set up. They were being used for musicians today, a group of harpists.

Majestic chandeliers hung from the ceiling—six enormous ones down the center, outfitted with thousands of sparkling pieces of crystal. Twelve smaller ones hung at their sides. *Electric lights,* he noted. *Those chandeliers must have been a horrible pain to light before the conversion.*

The sheer cost of a party like this numbed his senses. He could have fed Weathering for a year on what was being spent for this single evening. His uncle had sold the Ladrian ballroom a few years back—it had been a separate building, in a different neighborhood from the mansion. That made Waxillium happy; from what he remembered, it had been as large as this one. If they'd still owned it, people might have expected him to throw lavish parties like this.

"Well?" Steris asked, holding out her arm for him again as the servant returned to lead them to their table. He could see Lord Harms and Steris's cousin Marasi sitting at the table already.

"I'm remembering why I left the City," Waxillium said honestly. "Life is so damn *hard* here."

"Many would say that of the Roughs."

"And few of them have lived in both," Waxillium said. "Living here is a different kind of hard, but it's still hard. Marasi is joining us again?"

"Indeed."

"What *is* going on with her, Steris?"

"She's from the Outer Estates and badly wanted the chance to attend university here in the City. My father took pity on her, as her own parents haven't the means to support her. He is allowing her to reside with us for the duration of her studies."

A valid explanation, though it seemed to roll out of Steris's mouth far too quickly. Was it a practiced excuse, or was Waxillium assuming too much? Either way, further discussion was interrupted as Lord Harms rose to greet his daughter.

Waxillium shook hands with Lord Harms, took Marasi's hand and bowed, then sat. Steris began speaking with her father about the people she'd noted to be attending or absent, and Waxillium rested elbows on the table, listening with half an ear.

Hard room to defend, he thought absently. *Snipers on those balconies would work, but you'd need some on each one, watching to make sure nobody gets beneath the other.* Anyone with a strong enough gun—or the right Allomantic powers—could take out snipers from below. The pillars below the balconies would also be good shelter, though.

The more cover there was, the better the situation for the one who was outnumbered. Not that you ever wanted to be outnumbered, but he'd rarely been in any fight where he wasn't. So he looked for cover. In the open, a gunfight came down to who could field the most men with weapons. But once you could hide, skill and experience started to compensate. Maybe this room wouldn't be too bad a place to fight after all. He—

He hesitated. What was he doing? He'd *made* his decision. Did he have to keep remaking it every few days?

"Marasi," he said, forcing himself into conversation. "Your cousin tells me you've entered into university studies?"

"I'm in my final year," she said.

He waited for a further reply, and didn't get one.

"And how go your studies?"

"Well," she said, and looked down, holding her napkin.

That was productive, he thought with a sigh. Fortunately, it looked like a server was approaching. The lean man began pouring wine for them. "The soup will be along presently," he explained with a faint Terris accent, lofty vowels, and a slightly nasal tone.

The voice froze Waxillium stiff.

"Today's soup," the server continued, "is a delightfully seasoned prawn bisque with a hint of pepper. You shall find it quite enjoyable, I think." He glanced at Waxillium, eyes twinkling in amusement. Though he wore a false nose and a wig, those were Wayne's eyes.

Waxillium groaned softly.

"My lord doesn't like prawns?" Wayne asked with horror.

"The bisque is quite good," Lord Harms said. "I've had it at a Yomen party before."

"It's not the soup," Waxillium said. "I've just recalled something I forgot to do." *It involves strangling someone.*

"I shall return shortly with your soup, my lords and ladies," Wayne promised. He even had a fake line of Terris earrings in his

ears. Of course, Wayne *was* part Terris, as was Waxillium himself—as evidenced by their Feruchemical abilities. That was rare
in the population; though nearly a fifth of the Originators had been
Terris, they weren't prone to marrying other ethnicities.

"Does that server look familiar?" Marasi asked, turning and watching him go.

"He must have served us last time we were here," Lord Harms
said.

"But I wasn't with you last—"

"Lord Harms," Waxillium jumped in, "has anything been heard
of your relative? The one who was kidnapped by the Vanishers?"

"No," he said, taking a sip of his wine. "Ruin those thieves. This
kind of thing is *absolutely* unacceptable. They should confine such
behavior to the Roughs!"

"Yes," Steris said, "it does somewhat undermine one's respect
for the constabulary when things like this occur. And the robbery
inside the city! How terrible."

"What was it like?" Marasi suddenly asked. "Lord Ladrian? Living where there was no law?" She seemed genuinely curious, though
her comment earned a glare from Lord Harms, likely for bringing up
Waxillium's past.

"It was difficult sometimes," Waxillium admitted. "Out there,
some people just believe they can take what they want. It would actually *surprise* them when someone stood up to them. As if I were some
spoiler, the only one who didn't understand the game they were all
playing."

"Game?" Lord Harms said, frowning.

"A figure of speech, Lord Harms," Waxillium said. "You see, they
all seemed to think that if you were skilled or well armed, you could
take whatever you want. I was both, and yet instead of taking, I
stopped them. They found it baffling."

"It was very brave of you," Marasi said.

He shrugged. "It wasn't bravery, honestly. I just kind of fell into
things."

"Even stopping the Surefires?"

"They were a special case. I—" He froze. "How did you know about *that?*"

"Reports trickle in," Marasi said, blushing. "From the Roughs. Most of them get written up by someone. You can find them at the university or at the right bookshop."

"Oh." Uncomfortable, he picked up his cup and drank some wine.

As he did, something slipped into his mouth. He nearly spat out the entire mouthful in surprise. He contained himself. Barely.

Wayne, I really am *going to throttle you.* He moved the object into his hand, covering the act with a cough.

"Well," Steris said, "hopefully the constables will soon deal with these ruffians and we can return to peace and law."

"Actually," Marasi said, "I don't think that's likely."

"Child," Lord Harms said sternly. "That's quite enough."

"I'd like to hear what she has to say, my lord," Waxillium said. "For the sake of conversation."

"Well . . . all right . . . I suppose."

"It's simply a theory I had," Marasi said, blushing. "Lord Ladrian, when you were lawkeeper in Weathering, what was the population of the city?"

He fingered the item in his hand. A spent bullet casing that had been capped with a dab of wax. "Well, it started to grow rapidly in the last few years. But for most of the time, I'd say it was around fifteen hundred."

"And the surrounding area?" she asked. "All the places you'd patrol, but didn't have their own lawkeepers?"

"Maybe three thousand total," Waxillium said. "Depending. There are a lot of transients out in the Roughs. People looking to find a mineral claim or to start up a farmstead. Workers moving from place to place."

"Let's say three thousand," Marasi said. "And how many of you were there? Those who helped you keep the law?"

"Five or six, depending," he said. "Wayne and I, and Barl most of the time. A few others on and off."

And Lessie, he thought.

"Let's say six per three thousand," she said. "Gives us an easy number to work with. One lawman per five hundred people."

"What is the point of this?" Lord Harms asked sufferingly.

"The population of our octant is around six hundred thousand," she explained. "By the same ratio Lord Ladrian described, we should have roughly twelve hundred constables. But we don't. It's somewhere closer to six hundred, last I looked over the numbers. So, Lord Ladrian, your 'savage' wildlands actually had *double* the number of lawmen watching over it as we have here in the city."

"Huh," he said. *Odd information for a young woman of means to have.*

"I'm not trying to diminish your accomplishments," she said quickly. "You more likely had a higher percentage of lawbreakers as well, since the reputation of the Roughs draws that type. But I think it's a matter of perception. As you said, out of the city, people expect to get away with their crimes.

"Here, they are more circumspect—and many of the crimes are smaller in scope. Instead of the bank getting robbed, you get a dozen people being robbed on their way home at night. The nature of the urban environment makes it easier to hide if you keep your crimes below a certain level of visibility. But I wouldn't say life is really *safer* in the city, despite what people think.

"I'll bet more people are murdered here, by percentage of the population, than out in the Roughs. There is so much more going on in the City, however, that people pay less attention to it. By contrast, when a man is murdered in a small town, it's a very disruptive event—even if it's the only murder that's happened in years.

"And all of this isn't even counting the fact that much of the wealth in the world is concentrated in a few places inside the city. Wealth draws men looking for opportunity. There are a whole *host* of reasons why the City is more dangerous than the Roughs. It's just that we pretend that it isn't."

Waxillium folded his arms in front of him on the table. *Curious.* Once she started talking, she didn't seem shy at all.

"You see, my lord," Harms said. "This is why I tried to still her."

"It would have been a shame if you had," Waxillium said, "as I believe that's the most interesting thing anyone has said to me since I returned to Elendel."

Marasi smiled, though Steris just rolled her eyes. Wayne returned with the soup. Unfortunately, the area right around them was crowded—Wayne wouldn't be able to create a speed bubble around just Waxillium and himself. It would catch someone else, and anyone caught in it would have time sped up for them as well. Wayne couldn't shape the bubble or choose whom it affected.

While the others were distracted by the soup, Waxillium broke the wax off the sealed shell casing and found a small rolled-up piece of paper inside. He glanced at Wayne, then unrolled it.

You were right, it read.

"I usually am," he muttered as Wayne placed a bowl in front of him. "What are you up to, Wayne?"

"One seventy, thank you," Wayne said under his breath. "I've been lifting weights and eating steak."

Waxillium gave him a flat stare, but got ignored as Wayne proceeded to explain—with his slight Terris accent—that he'd soon return with a bread basket and more wine for the group.

"Lord Ladrian," Steris said as they began eating, "I suggest that we begin compiling a list of conversational topics we can employ when in the company of others. The topics should not touch on politics or religion, yet should be memorable and give us opportunities to appear charming. Do you know any particularly witty sayings or stories that can be our starting point?"

"I once shot the tail off a dog by mistake," Waxillium said idly. "It's kind of a funny story."

"Shooting dogs is hardly appropriate dinner conversation," Steris said.

"I know. Particularly since I was aiming for its balls."

Marasi just about spat her soup across the table.

"Lord Ladrian!" Steris exclaimed, though her father seemed amused.

"I thought you said I couldn't shock you any longer," he said to Steris. "I was merely testing your hypothesis, my dear."

"Honestly. You *will* eventually overcome this rural lack of decorum, won't you?"

He stirred his soup to make sure Wayne hadn't hidden anything in it. *I hope he at least washed that bullet casing.* "I suspect that I will, indeed, eventually overcome it," he said, raising the spoon to his lips. The soup was good, but too cold. "The amusing thing is that when I was in the Roughs, I was considered to be highly refined—so much so, in fact, that they thought me haughty."

"Calling a man 'refined' by Roughs standards," Lord Harms said, raising a finger, "is like saying a brick is 'soft' by building-material standards—right before you smash it into a man's face."

"Father!" Steris said. She glared at Waxillium, as if the comment were his fault.

"It was a perfectly legitimate simile," Lord Harms said.

"We will have no further talk of hitting people with bricks or of shootings, *regardless* of the target!"

"Very well, cousin," Marasi said. "Lord Ladrian, I once heard that you threw a man's own knife at him and hit him right through the eye. Is the story true?"

"It was actually Wayne's knife," Waxillium said. He hesitated. "And the eye was an accident. I was aiming for the balls that time too."

"Lord Ladrian!" Steris said, nearly livid.

"I know. That's quite off target. I've got *really* bad aim with throwing knives."

Steris looked at them, growing red as she saw that her father was snickering, but trying to cover it up with his napkin. Marasi met her gaze with innocent equanimity. "No bricks," Marasi said, "and no guns. I was making conversation as you requested."

Steris stood. "I'm going to see myself to the women's washroom while you three compose yourselves."

She stalked away, and Waxillium felt a stab of guilt. Steris was stiff, but she seemed earnest and honest. She did not deserve mockery. It was very hard not to try provoking her, however.

Lord Harms cleared his throat. "That was uncalled for, child," he said to Marasi. "You must not make me regret my promise to start bringing you to these functions."

"Don't blame her, my lord," Waxillium said. "I was the primary offender. I'll offer a suitable apology to Steris when she returns, and will guard my tongue for the rest of the evening. I shouldn't have allowed myself to go so far."

Harms nodded, sighing. "I'll admit, I've been tempted to such lengths myself a time or two. She's much as her mother was." He gave Waxillium a pitying look.

"I see."

"This is our lot, son," Lord Harms said, standing. "To be lord of a house requires certain sacrifices. Now, if you'll excuse me, I see Lord Alernath over at the bar and I think I'll grab a nip of something harder with him before the main course. If I don't go before Steris gets back, she'll bully me into staying. I shouldn't be long." He nodded to the two of them, then waddled toward a group of higher-built tables off to the side, next to an open bar.

Waxillium watched him go, idly thinking and rolling Wayne's note in his fingers. Previously, he'd assumed Lord Harms had driven Steris to be as she was, but it appeared he was more under *her* thumb than vice versa. *Another curiosity,* he thought.

"Thank you for your defense of me, Lord Ladrian," Marasi said. "It appears that you are as quick to come to a lady's aid with words as you are with pistols."

"I was merely stating the truth as I saw it, my lady."

"Tell me. Did you really shoot off a dog's tail when aiming for his . . . er . . ."

"Yes," Waxillium said, grimacing. "In my defense, the damn thing was attacking me. Belonged to a man I hunted down. The aggressiveness wasn't the dog's fault; the poor thing looked like it hadn't been fed in days. I was trying to shoot it somewhere nonlethal, scare it off. That part about the man I hit in the eye was fabricated, though. I wasn't actually aiming for any body part in particular—I was just hoping I'd hit."

She smiled. "Might I ask you something?"

"Please."

"You looked crestfallen when I spoke of the statistics dealing with lawman ratios. I didn't mean to offend or downplay your heroics."

"It's all right," he said.

"But?"

He shook his head. "I'm not sure if I can explain it. When I found my way out to the Roughs, when I started bringing in the warranted, I started to . . . Well, I thought I'd found a place where I was needed. I thought I'd found a way to do something that no-body else would do."

"But you did."

"And yet," he said, stirring his soup, "it appears that all along, the place I left behind might have needed me even more. I'd never noticed."

"You did important work, Lord Ladrian. *Vital* work. Besides, I understand that before you arrived, nobody was upholding the law in that area."

"There was Arbitan," he said, smiling, remembering the older man. "And, of course, the lawkeepers over in Far Dorest."

"A distant city and with a short reach," she said, "which had a single capable lawman to serve a large population. Jon Deadfinger had his own problems. By the time you had built things up, Weathering was protected better than those in the City—but it did not start that way."

He nodded, though—again—he was curious about how much she knew. Were people *really* telling stories about him and Wayne all the way over here in the city? Why hadn't he heard of them before now?

Her statistics *did* bother him. He hadn't thought of the City as dangerous. It was the Roughs, wild and untamed, that needed rescuing. The City was the land of plenty that Harmony had created to shelter mankind. Here, trees grew fruit in abundance and cultivated lands had water without need for irrigation. The ground was always fertile, and somehow never got farmed out.

This land was supposed to be different. Protected. He'd put away his guns in part because he'd convinced himself that the constables could do their jobs without help. *But don't the Vanishers prove that might not be the case?*

Wayne returned with the bread and a bottle of wine, then stopped, looking at the two empty seats. "Oh dear," he said. "Did you grow so tired of waiting that you *devoured* your two companions?"

Marasi glanced at him and smiled.

She knows, Waxillium realized. *She recognizes him.*

"If I may note something, my lady," Waxillium said, drawing her attention back. "You are far less unassuming than you were at our first meeting."

She winced. "I'm not very good at being shy, am I?"

"I wasn't aware it was something that required practice."

"I try all the time," Wayne said, sitting down at the table and taking the baguette out of his basket. He took a healthy bite. "Nobody gives me any credit for it. 'S because I'm misunderstood, I tell you." His Terris accent had vanished.

Marasi looked confused. "Should I pretend to be aghast at what he's doing?" she asked Waxillium in a hushed tone.

"He saw that you'd recognized him," Waxillium said. "Now he's going to sulk."

"Sulk?" Wayne started eating Steris's soup. "That's right unkind, Wax. *Ugh.* This stuff is far worse than I was telling you guys. Sorry 'bout that."

"It will reflect in my tip," Waxillium said dryly. "Lady Marasi, I was serious in my inquiry. To be frank, it seems that you've been trying to act with exaggerated timidity."

"Always looking down after you speak," Wayne agreed. "Raising the pitch of your tone a little too much with questions."

"Not the type to be studying at the university at her own re-quest," Waxillium noted. "Why the act?"

"I'd rather not say."

"You'd rather not," Waxillium said, "or Lord Harms and his daugh-ter would rather you not?"

She blushed. "The latter. But please. I would really prefer to leave the topic."

"Ever charming, Wax," Wayne said, taking another bite from the loaf of bread. "See that? You've pushed the lady almost to tears."

"I'm not—" Marasi began.

"Ignore him," Waxillium said. "Trust me. He's like a rash. The more you scratch him, the more irritating he gets."

"Ouch," Wayne said, though he grinned.

"Aren't you worried?" Marasi asked softly of Wayne. "You're wearing a waiter's uniform. If they see you sitting at the table and eating . . ."

"Oh, that's a good point," Wayne said, tipping his chair back. The person behind him had left, and with Lord Harms gone, Wayne had just enough room to—

—and there it was. He leaned his chair forward again, clothing changed back to a duster with a loose button-down shirt and thick Roughs trousers underneath. He spun his hat on his finger. The earrings were gone.

Marasi jumped. "Speed bubble," she whispered, sounding awed. "I thought I'd be able to see something from outside!"

"You could, if you were watching closely," Waxillium said. "A blur. If you look at the next table over, the sleeve of his waiter's coat is sticking out from where he tossed it. His hat folds—though the sides are stiff, you can compress it between your hands. I'm still trying to figure out where he had the duster."

"Under your table," Wayne said, sounding very self-satisfied.

"Ah, of course," Waxillium said. "He had to know beforehand which table would be ours so he could be assigned as our waiter." *I really should have looked under the table before we sat,* Waxillium thought. *Would that have seemed too paranoid?* He didn't feel paranoid; he didn't lie awake at nights, worried that he'd be shot, or think that conspiracies were trying to destroy him. He just liked to be careful.

Marasi was still looking at Wayne; she seemed bemused.

"We aren't what you expected," Waxillium said. "From the reports you read?"

"No," she admitted. "The accounts usually omitted matters of personality."

"There are stories 'bout us?" Wayne asked.

"Yes. Many."

"Damn." He sounded impressed. "Do we get royalties for them or something? If we do, I want Wax's share, seeing as to how I did all the stuff they say he did. Plus he's already rich and all."

"They are news-style reports," Marasi said. "Those don't pay royalties to their subjects."

"Filthy cheats." Wayne paused. "I wonder if any of the other fine ladies in this establishment have heard of my outrageously heroic and masculine exploits. . . ."

"Lady Marasi is a student at the university," Waxillium said. "I'm assuming she read reports that are collected there. Most of the public won't be familiar with them."

"That is true," she said.

"Oh," Wayne said, sounding disappointed. "Well, maybe Lady Marasi herself might be interested in hearing more of my outrageously—"

"Wayne?"

"Yes."

"Enough."

"Right."

"I do apologize for him," Waxillium said, turning to Marasi. She still wore the bemused expression on her face.

"He does that a lot," Wayne said. "Apologizing. I think it's one of his personal failings. I try to help him out by being damn near perfect, but so far, that hasn't been enough."

"It's quite all right," she said. "I do wonder if I should write something for my professors describing how . . . unique it was to meet you two."

"What is it, exactly, that you are studying at the university?" Waxillium asked.

She hesitated, then blushed deeply.

"Ah, see!" Wayne said. "Now, *that's* how to act shy. You're getting much better! Bravo."

"It's just that . . ." She raised a hand to shade her eyes and looked down in embarrassment. "It's just . . . Oh, all right. I'm studying legal justice and criminal behavioristics."

"That's something to be ashamed of?" Waxillium said, sharing a confused look with Wayne.

"Well, I've been told it's not very feminine," she said. "But beyond that . . . well, I'm sitting with you two . . . and . . . well, you know . . . you're two of the most famous lawkeepers in the world, and all . . ."

"Trust me," Waxillium said. "We don't know as much as you might think."

"Now, if you were studying buffoonery and idiotic behavior," Wayne added, "*that* is something we're experts on."

"That's two things," Waxillium said.

"Don't care." Wayne continued eating the bread. "So where *are* the other two? I'm assuming you didn't really devour them. Wax only eats people on the weekend."

"Both will likely be returning soon, Wayne," Waxillium said. "So if you had a purpose to your visit, you may wish to be on with it. Unless this is just normal, run-of-the-mill tormenting."

"I told you what it was about," Wayne said. "You didn't accidentally eat my note, did you?"

"No. It didn't say much."

"It said enough," Wayne said, leaning in. "Wax, you told me to look at the hostages. You were right."

"They're all Allomancers," Waxillium guessed.

"More than that," Wayne said. "They're all relatives."

"It's only been three hundred years since the Originators, Wayne. We're *all* relatives."

"Does that mean you'll take responsibility for me?"

"No."

Wayne chuckled, pulling a folded piece of paper from his duster pocket. "It's more than that, Wax. Look. Each of the women kidnapped was from a particular line. I did some *researchin'*. Real, serious stuff." He paused. "Why do they call it *re*search if I've only done it this one time?"

"Because I'll bet you had to look things up twice," Waxillium said, taking the paper and studying it. It was written awkwardly, but was decipherable. It explained the basic lines of descent of each of the women kidnapped.

Several things stood out. Each of them could trace back to the Lord Mistborn himself. Because of that, most of them *also* had a strong heritage of Allomancy in their past. They were all fairly closely related, third or fourth cousins, some first.

Waxillium looked up, and noticed Marasi smiling broadly, regarding him and Wayne.

"What?" Waxillium asked.

"I *knew* it!" she exclaimed. "I knew you were in town to investigate the Vanishers. You showed up to become house lord only one month after the first robbery happened. You're going to catch them, aren't you?"

"Is *that* why you insisted that Lord Harms bring you to meetings with me?"

"Maybe."

"Marasi," Waxillium said, sighing. "You're jumping to conclusions. Do you think the deaths in my family, making me house lord, were fabrications?"

"Well, no," she said. "But I was surprised that you'd accepted the title until I realized that you probably saw it as a chance to find out what is going on with these robberies. You have to admit, they *are* unusual."

"So is Wayne," Waxillium said. "But I wouldn't uproot myself, change my entire lifestyle, and accept responsibility for an entire house just to study him."

"Look, Wax," Wayne jumped in—ignoring the barb, which was unusual for him. "Please tell me you brought a gun with you."

"What? No, I didn't." Waxillium folded up the paper and handed it back. "Why would you care?"

"Because," Wayne said, snatching the paper from his hand and leaning in. "Don't you see? The thieves are looking for places they can rob where the wealthy upper class of Elendel can be found— because *among* those wealthy upper-class types, they find their targets. People with the right heritage. Those types, rich types, have stopped traveling on the railway."

Waxillium nodded. "Yes, if the women really *are* the true targets, the high-profile robberies will make potential future targets much less likely to travel. A valid connection. That must be why the thieves attacked the theater."

"And where else are there wealthy individuals with the right heritage?" Wayne asked. "A place where people wear their finest jewelry, which will let you rob them as a distraction? A place where you can find the right hostage to take as the real prize?"

Waxillium's mouth grew dry. "A large wedding reception."

The doors at both ends of the ballroom suddenly burst open.

5

The bandits didn't look like the kind Waxillium was used to. They didn't mask their faces with kerchiefs or wear dusters and wide-brimmed Roughs hats. Most of them wore vests and bowler-style city hats, dull trousers, and loose, buttoned shirts that were rolled to the elbows. They weren't *better* dressed, really, just different.

They were well armed. Rifles held at shoulders for many, pistols in the hands of others. People throughout the ballroom noticed immediately, silverware clanking and curses sounding. There were at least two dozen bandits, perhaps three. Waxillium noticed with dissatisfaction that some more were coming in from the right, through the doors to the kitchens. They would have left men behind to watch the staff and keep them from running for help.

"Hell of a time to leave your guns," Wayne said. He moved off his seat and crouched beside the table, slipping his twin hardwood dueling canes out from underneath.

"Put those down," Waxillium said softly, counting. Thirty-five men he could see. Most were congregated at the two ends of the rectangular ballroom, directly in front of and behind Waxillium. He was in almost the very center of the room.

"What?" Wayne said sharply.

"Put the canes down, Wayne."

"You can't mean—"

"Look at this room!" Waxillium hissed. "How many bystanders are there in here? Three hundred, four? What will happen if we provoke a firefight?"

"You could protect them," Wayne said. "Push them out of the way."

"Maybe," Waxillium said. "It would be very risky. So far, none of these robberies have turned violent. I won't have you turning this one into a bloodbath."

"I don't have to listen to you," Wayne said sullenly. "You're not in charge of me anymore, Wax."

Waxillium met his eyes and held them as the room filled with cries of alarm and concern. Looking reluctant, Wayne slid back up into his seat. He didn't put down the dueling canes, but he did keep his hands under the tablecloth, hiding them from view.

Marasi had turned, watching the thieves begin to move through the room, her eyes wide and her rose lips parted. "Oh my." She spun around, digging out her pocketbook with trembling fingers. She whipped out a small notepad and a pencil.

"What are you doing?" Waxillium asked.

"Writing down descriptions," she said, her hand shaking. "Did you know that, statistically, only one out of two witnesses can accurately describe a criminal who assaulted them? Worse, seven out of ten will pick the wrong man out of a lineup if a similar but more threatening man is presented. In the moment, you are far more likely to overestimate the height of an assailant, and you will often describe him as being similar to a villain from a story you've recently heard. It's vital, if you are witnessing a crime, to pay special attention to the details of those involved. Oh, I'm babbling, aren't I?"

She looked terrified, but she started writing anyway, jotting down descriptions of every criminal.

"We never needed to do stuff like that," Wayne said, eyeing the thieves as they leveled guns at the partygoers, silencing them.

"Seein' as to how if we witness a crime, the guys doing it are usually dead by the end." He shot Waxillium a glare.

Several thieves began forcing cooks and servers out of the kitchens to join the guests. "If you please!" one of the robbers bellowed, shouldering a shotgun. "Sit down! Remain calm! And *be quiet*." He had a faint Roughs accent and a solid—though not tall—build, with bulging forearms and a mottled, grayish complexion, almost as if his face were made of granite.

Koloss blood, Waxillium thought. *Dangerous.*

People quieted save for a few whimperings from the overtaxed. The bride's mother appeared to have fainted, and the wedding party was hunkered down, the groom looking angry, with a protective arm over his new wife.

A second Vanisher stepped forward. This one, in contrast to the others, wore a mask: a knit cloth covering his face, with a Roughs hat atop it. "That's better," he said in a firm, controlled voice. Something about that voice struck Waxillium.

"If you're sensible, we'll be done with this in a matter of moments," the masked Vanisher said calmingly, walking amid the tables as about a dozen of the bandits began to fan through the room, opening large sacks. "All we want is your jewelry. Nobody needs to get hurt. It would be a shame to spoil such a fine party as this with bloodshed. Your jewelry isn't worth your life."

Waxillium glanced toward Lord Harms, who was still sitting by the bar. He'd begun patting his face with a handkerchief. The men with the sacks quickly fanned out through the room, stopping at each table and gathering necklaces, rings, earrings, pocketbooks, and watches. Sometimes the items were tossed in readily, sometimes reluctantly.

"Wax . . ." Wayne said, voice strained.

Marasi continued writing, pen and paper down in her lap.

"We need to get through this alive," Waxillium said softly. "Without anyone getting hurt. Then we can give our reports to the constables."

"But—"

"I will *not* be the cause of these people dying, Wayne," Waxillium snapped, voice much louder than he'd intended.

Blood on the bricks. A body in a leather coat, slumping to the ground. A grinning face, dying with a bullet in the forehead. Winning, even as he died.

Not again. Never again.

Waxillium squeezed his eyes closed.

Never again.

"How *dare* you!" a voice suddenly yelled. Waxillium glanced to the side. A man at a nearby table had stood up, shaking off the hand of the stout woman beside him. He had a thick, graying beard and wore a suit of an older cut, tails in the back reaching all the way down to his ankles. "I will *not* stay quiet, Marthin! I am a constable of the Eighth Guard!"

This drew the attention of the bandit leader. The masked man strolled toward the outspoken man, shotgun resting easily on his shoulder. "Ah," he said, "Lord Peterus, I believe it is." He waved to a pair of bandits, and they rushed forward, weapons trained on Peterus. "Retired chief of the Eighth constabulary. We'll be needing you to give up your weapon."

"How dare you commit a robbery here, at a wedding celebration," Peterus said. "This is *outrageous*! You should be ashamed of yourself."

"Ashamed?" the bandit leader said as his minions patted down Peterus and pulled a pistol—Granger model 28, optional thick grip—out of his shoulder holster. "*Ashamed?* To rob these? After what you people have done to the Roughs all these years? This isn't shameful. This here, this is *payback*."

There is *something about that voice*, Waxillium thought, tapping the table. *Something familiar. Quiet down, Peterus. Don't provoke them!*

"In the name of the law, I will see you hunted down and hanged for this!" Peterus cried.

The outlaw leader smacked Peterus across the face, knocking him to the ground. "What know your sort of the law?" the bandit leader growled. "And be careful about warning people you're going to see them executed. That gives them less reason to hold back. Rust and *Ruin,* you people sicken me."

He waved for his lackeys to resume gathering riches. The bride's mother had recovered, and was sobbing as her family was shaken down for its cash, including even the bridal necklace.

"The bandits really *are* interested in the money," Waxillium said softly. "See? They make each person at the table speak, to find jewelry hidden in mouths. Notice how they make each one stand up and then do a quick check of their pockets and around their seats."

"Of course they're interested in the money," Marasi whispered back. "That's the expected motive for robbery, after all."

"It's the hostages too, though," Waxillium said. "I'm sure of it." Originally, he'd assumed the robberies were just a cover for the bandits' real purpose. If that were the case, however, they wouldn't be so thorough about the money. "Hand me your notebook."

She glanced at him.

"Now," he said, sprinkling steel dust into his wine, then reaching under the table. She hesitantly handed over the notebook as a bandit walked toward their table. It was the gray-skinned one with the thick neck.

"Wayne," Waxillium said, "bat on the wall."

Wayne nodded curtly, sliding over his dueling canes. Waxillium drank his wine, and pressed the spiral-bound notebook and the dueling canes against his side of their square table. He slipped a small metal rod from his sleeve and pressed it against the canes, then burned steel.

Lines sprang up around him. One pointed toward the rod, and another to the notebook's wire coil. He lightly Pushed against them, then let go. The canes and the notebook remained pressed against the table's side, obscured by the tablecloth, which draped down over them. He had to be careful not to Push too hard, lest he move the table.

The bandit came to their table, proffering his sack. Marasi was forced to take off her small pearl necklace, the only jewelry she was wearing. With shaking hands, she searched in her pocketbook for any bills, but the bandit just snatched the entire thing and dumped it into his sack.

"Please," Waxillium said, making his voice shake. "Please, don't hurt us!" He pulled out his pocket watch, then dumped it to the table, as if in haste. He yanked its chain free of his vest and threw it in the sack. Then he got out his pocketbook and tossed it in, conspicuously pulling out both of his pockets with shaking hands to show he had nothing else. He began patting his coat pockets.

"That'll do, mate," the koloss-blooded man said, grinning.

"Don't hurt me!"

"Sit back down, you rusting git," the bandit said, looking back at Marasi. He leered, then patted her down, making her speak so he could check her mouth. She bore it with a deep blush, particularly when the patting down turned into a few solid gropes.

Waxillium felt his eye begin to twitch.

"Nothing else," the bandit said with a grunt. "Why'd I get the poor tables? And you?" He glanced at Wayne. Behind them, another of the bandits found Wayne's servant's coat under the table, holding it up with a confused expression.

"Do I *look* like I've got anything of value, mate?" Wayne asked, dressed in his duster and Roughs trousers. He'd turned up his Roughs accent. "I'm just 'ere by mistake. Was begging in the kitchen when I heard you blokes come in."

The bandit grunted, but patted Wayne's pockets anyway. He found nothing, then checked under the table and made them all stand up. Finally he swore at them for being "too poor" and snatched Wayne's hat off his head. He threw away his own hat— he was wearing a knit cap underneath, aluminum peeking through the holes—then walked off, sticking Wayne's hat on his head over the cap.

They sat back down.

"He took my lucky hat, Wax," Wayne growled.

"Steady," Waxillium said, handing Marasi back her notebook so she could return to taking covert notes.

"Why didn't you hide your pocketbook," she whispered, "as you did the notebook?"

"Some of the bills in it are marked," Waxillium said distractedly, watching the masked leader. He was consulting something in his hand. Looked like a couple of crinkled-up sheets of paper. "That'll allow the constables to track where they get spent, if they do get spent."

"Marked!" Marasi said. "So you *did* know we'd be robbed!"

"What? Of course I didn't."

"But—"

"Wax always carries some marked bills," Wayne said, eyes narrowing as he noticed what the leader was doing. "Just in case."

"Oh. That's . . . very unusual."

"Wax is his own special brand of paranoid, miss," Wayne said. "Is that bloke doing what I think he's doing?"

"Yes," Waxillium said.

"What?" Marasi asked.

"Comparing faces to drawings in his hand," Waxillium said. "He's looking for the right person to take as a hostage. Look how he's strolling through the tables, checking every woman's face. He's got a few others doing it too."

They fell silent as the leader strolled past them. He was accompanied by a fine-featured fellow with a scowl on his face. "I'm tellin' you," the second man said, "the boys are gettin' jumpy. You can't give 'em all this and never let 'em fire the bloody things."

The masked leader was silent, studying everyone at Wax's table for a moment. He hesitated briefly, then moved on.

"You're gonna have to let the boys loose sooner or later, boss," the second man said, his voice trailing off. "I think . . ." They were soon too far for Waxillium to make out what they were saying.

Nearby, Peterus—the former constable—had gotten back up into his seat. His wife was holding a napkin to his bleeding head.

This is the best way, Waxillium told himself firmly. *I've seen their faces. I'll be able to track down who they are when they spend my money. I'll find them, and fight them on my own terms. I'll . . .*

But he wouldn't. He'd let the constables do that part, wouldn't he? Wasn't that what he kept telling himself?

A sudden disturbance from the far side of the chamber drew his eyes. A few bandits led a couple of frazzled-looking women into the hall, one of them Steris. It looked like they'd finally thought to sweep the ladies' room. The other bandits were making pretty good time gathering goods. There were enough of them that it didn't take too long, even with this large crowd.

"All right," the boss called out. "Grab a hostage."

Too loud, Waxillium thought.

"Who should we take?" one of the bandits yelled back.

They're making a show of it.

"I don't care," the boss said.

He wants us to think he's picking one at random.

"Any of them will do," the boss continued. "Say . . . that one." He waved at Steris.

Steris. One of the previous abductees was her cousin. Of course. She was in the same line.

Waxillium's eye twitching grew worse.

"Actually," the boss said. "We'll take two this time." He sent his koloss-blooded lackey running back toward the tables of people. "Now, nobody follow, or they'll get hurt. Remember, a few jewels aren't worth your life. We'll cut the hostages loose once we're sure we aren't being followed."

Lies, Waxillium thought. *What do you want with them? Why are you—*

The koloss-blooded man who had stolen Wayne's hat stepped up to Wax's table and grabbed Marasi by the shoulder. "You'll do," he said. "You're coming for a ride with us, pretty."

She jumped as he touched her, dropping her notepad.

"Here now," another bandit said. "What's this?" He picked it up, looking through it. "All it's got is words, Tarson."

"Idiot," the koloss-blooded man—Tarson—said. "You can't read, can you?" He craned over. "Here, now. That's a description of *me*, isn't it?"

"I . . ." Marasi said. "I just wanted to remember, for my journal, you see. . . ."

"I'm sure," Tarson said, tucking the notebook into a pocket. His hand came out with a pistol, which he lowered at her head.

Marasi grew pale.

Waxillium stood up, steel burning in his stomach. The other bandit's pistol was trained at his head a second later.

"Your lady will be just fine with us, old boy," Tarson said with a smile on his grayish lips. "Up you go." He pulled Marasi to her feet, then pushed her before him toward the northern exit.

Waxillium stared down the barrel of the other bandit's pistol. With a mental Push, he could send that gun with a snap back into its owner's face, perhaps break his nose.

The bandit looked like he wanted to pull the trigger. He looked eager, excited by the thrill of the robbery. Waxillium had seen men like that before. They were dangerous.

The bandit hesitated, then glanced at his friends, and finally broke off, jogging toward the exit. Another was shoving Steris toward the door.

"Wax!" Wayne hissed.

How could a man of honor watch something like this? Every instinct of justice Waxillium had *demanded* he do something. Fight.

"Wax," Wayne said softly. "Mistakes happen. Lessie wasn't your fault."

"I . . ."

Wayne grabbed his dueling canes. "Well, *I'm* going to do something."

"It's not worth the cost of lives, Wayne," Waxillium said, shaking out of his stupor. "This isn't just about me. It's true, Wayne. We—"

"How *dare* you!" a familiar voice bellowed. Lord Peterus, the former constable. The aging man removed the napkin from his head, stumbling to his feet. "Cowards! *I* will be your hostage, if you require one."

The bandits ignored him, most jogging toward the exits of the room, waving their guns about and enjoying making the dinner-goers cringe.

"Cowards!" Peterus yelled. "You are *dogs*, each and every one of you. I'll see you hanged! Take me instead of one of those girls, or it will happen. I swear it by the Survivor himself!" He stumbled after the retreating boss, passing lords, ladies, and the wealthy—most of whom had gotten down and were hiding under their tables.

There goes the only man in this room with any courage, Waxillium thought, suddenly feeling a powerful shame. *Him and Wayne.*

Steris was almost to the door. Marasi and her captor were catching up to the boss.

I can't let this happen. I—

"COWARD!"

The masked bandit leader suddenly spun, hand snapping out, a gunshot cracking the air, echoing across the large ballroom. It was over in a heartbeat.

The aged Peterus collapsed in a heap. Smoke curled in the air over the bandit boss's pistol.

"Oh . . ." Wayne said softly. "You just made a bad mistake, mate. A *very* bad mistake."

The boss turned away from the body, holstering his gun. "Fine," he yelled, walking toward the door. "You can have some fun, boys. Burn it out of your blood quickly and meet me outside. Let's—"

Everything froze. People stopped in place. The curling smoke hung motionless. Voices quieted. Whimpering halted. In a circle around Waxillium's table, the air rippled just faintly.

Wayne stood up, shouldering his dueling canes, inspecting the room. He was placing each and every one of the bandits, Waxillium knew. Judging distances, preparing himself.

"As soon as I drop the bubble," Wayne said, "this place is going to erupt like an ammunition store in a volcano."

Waxillium calmly reached into his jacket and slid a hidden pistol from beneath his arm. He set it on the table. His twitch had vanished.

"Well?" Wayne asked.

"That's a terrible metaphor. How would an ammunition store get into a volcano?"

"I don't know. Look, are you going to fight or not?"

"I've tried waiting," Waxillium said. "I gave them a chance to leave. I *tried* giving this up."

"You gave it a good show, Wax." He grimaced. "Too good a show."

Waxillium rested his hand on the pistol. Then he picked it up. "So be it." With his other hand, he poured out his entire pouch of steel into his wine cup, then downed it.

Wayne grinned. "You owe me a pint for lying to me, by the way."

"Lying?"

"You said you hadn't brought a gun."

"I didn't bring *a* gun," Waxillium said, reaching to the small of his back and sliding a second pistol out. "You know me better than that, Wayne. I never go anywhere with only one. How much bendalloy do you have?"

"Not as much as I'd like. The stuff's damn expensive here in town. I've got maybe enough for five minutes' extra time. My metalminds are pretty much full, though. Spent a good two weeks sick in bed after you left." That would give Wayne some healing power, should he get shot.

Waxillium took a deep breath; the coldness inside him melted away and became a flame as he burned steel that pinpointed each and every source of metal in the room.

If he froze again . . .

I won't, he told himself. *I cannot.* "I'll get the girls. You keep the bandits on the south side off me. Our priority is to keep the bystanders alive."

"Gladly."

"Thirty-seven armed baddies, Wayne. In a room full of innocents. This is going to be *tough*. Stay focused. I'll try to clear some space as we start. You can catch a ride, if you want."

"Perfect as Preserves," Wayne said, turning and putting his back to Waxillium's. "You wanna know why I *really* came to find you?"

"Why?"

"I thought of you happy in a comfy bed, resting and relaxing, spending the rest of your life sipping tea and reading papers while people bring you food and maids rub your toes and stuff."

"And?"

"And I just couldn't leave you to a fate like that." Wayne shivered. "I'm too good a friend to let a mate of mine die in such a terrible situation."

"Comfortable?"

"No," Wayne said. "*Boring.*" He shivered again.

Waxillium smiled, then raised thumbs to hammers and cocked his pistols. When he'd been young and sought the Roughs, he'd ended up going where he'd been needed. Well, maybe that had happened again.

"Go!" he yelled, leveling his guns.

6

Wayne dropped the speed bubble.

First step, Waxillium thought as he took aim, *draw their attention.* He began gently Pushing away from himself in the way that created a steel bubble of force to interfere with bullets. It wouldn't protect him completely, but it would help. Unless they fired aluminum bullets.

Best to be careful. And best to shoot first.

The robbers were eagerly raising their weapons. He could see the lust for destruction in their eyes. They had been armed to the teeth, but so far, their robberies had occurred without a single shot being fired.

Rather than kill a lot of people, most of them probably just wanted to shoot the place up a little, but such situations easily grew more violent than expected. If they weren't stopped, the Vanishers would leave behind more than shattered windows and broken tables.

Waxillium quickly chose a bandit with a shotgun and dropped him with a bullet to the head. A second followed. Those shotguns were least dangerous to Waxillium, but they'd be deadly to the cowering bystanders.

His shots boomed in the cavernous chamber and the guests screamed. Some took the chance to run for the edges of the room. Most got down beside their tables. In the confusion, the bandits didn't spot Waxillium at first.

He dropped another man with a bullet to the shoulder. The smart thing to do from here would have been to crouch down beside a table and continue to fire. It would take the bandits precious moments to discover who was attacking them in a room so large and crowded.

Unfortunately, the men behind him opened fire, whooping in delight. They hadn't noticed what he was doing, though the men in front of him on the other side of the hall had seen their friends fall and were scattering for cover. In moments, the room would be a storm of lead and gunsmoke.

Taking a deep breath, Waxillium flared his steel and tapped his iron metalmind. Filling it made him lighter, but tapping it made him heavier—much heavier. He increased his weight a hundred-fold. There was a proportional increase in the strength of his body, or so he'd guessed, as he didn't crush himself with his own weight.

He raised his guns high over his head to keep them out of the radius, then Pushed outward from himself in a ring. He started carefully, gradually increasing its strength. When you Pushed, it was your weight against that of the object—in this case, the metal screws and bolts in the tables and chairs. They were swept away from him.

He became the epicenter of an expanding ring of force. Tables toppled, chairs scraped against the floor, and people screamed in surprise. Some were caught up in it, shoved away from him. Not so hard that they were hurt, he hoped, but it was better to suffer a few bruises than remain in the center of the room with what was coming.

Just to the side, he saw Wayne—who had been moving carefully toward the back of the room—leap up onto an overturned table, holding to its rim and grinning as he rode it in a rush toward the bandits back there.

Waxillium eased off on the Push. He stood alone in a large empty space at the center of the dining hall, surrounded by patches of spilled wine, food, and fallen dishes.

Then the firing started in earnest, the bandits in front of him letting loose with a barrage. He met the onslaught of bullets with another strong Push. The bullets stopped in the air, rebuffed in a wave. Given their speed, he could stop bullets that way only if he was expecting them.

He let the bullets fly back at their owners, but didn't Push too hard, lest he strike an innocent partygoer. It was enough to send the bandits scrambling, however, and yelling that there was a Coinshot in the room.

He was in real danger now. Quick as an eyeblink, Waxillium switched from tapping his metalmind to filling it, making himself far lighter. He pointed his revolver down and shot a bullet into the floor just behind himself and Pushed off it, launching into the air. Wind rushed in his ears as he threw himself over the barricade of furniture he'd made, where some of the guests still huddled. Luckily, many were realizing that the perimeters of the room would be much safer, and were scrambling that way.

Waxillium dropped right in the middle of the bandits, who had started taking cover behind the pile of tables and chairs. Men cursed as he spread his arms, guns pointed in opposite directions, and started firing. He spun, dropping four men with a quick spray of bullets.

Some bandits fired on him, but the bullets were off aim, and swerved away from his steel bubble. "Aluminum bullets!" one of the bandits was yelling. "Get out your bloody aluminum!"

Wax spun and fired two shots into that man's chest. Then he leaped to the side, rolling up next to a table that had been beyond his initial Push. A quick Push against the nails in the top overturned it, giving him cover as the bandits opened fire. He caught blue lines from some of the bullets, moving too quickly for him to Push out of the way.

Other bandits were reloading their guns. He was in luck; it

seemed from the curses of the bandit leaders that the men were supposed to have aluminum bullets loaded already, at least in some of the chambers. Shooting aluminum was like shooting gold, however, and many of the bandits appeared to have kept the aluminum in their pockets rather than wanting to have it in the guns, where they might end up firing it by accident.

A bandit ducked around the side of his table, aiming a pistol. Waxillium reacted by reflex, Pushing on the gun, slapping it back into his face. Waxillium dropped him with a bullet to the chest.

Empty, he thought to himself, counting the bullets he'd shot. He had just two left in the other gun. He glanced over the edge of his shelter, noting the locations of two reloading bandits who had hidden behind overturned tables. He took aim quickly, increased his weight, then fired and *Pushed* with everything he had on the bullet leaving his gun.

The bullet cracked in the air, driving forward into the table shelter and drilling right through it, hitting the bandit on the other side. Waxillium repeated, taking down the other bandit, who was stupefied to see the thick oak table penetrated by a simple revolver bullet. Then Waxillium threw himself over the top of his own table, getting to the other side just as the men behind him got around the wounded and started firing at him.

Bullets snapped against his shelter, but it held. This time, none of them gave off blue lines. Aluminum. He breathed deeply, dropping his revolvers and pulling out the Terringul 27 he had strapped to the inside of his calf. Not the largest-caliber gun, but its long barrel made it precise.

He spared a glance for Wayne, and counted four Vanishers down. His friend was gleefully leaping off a table toward a man with a shotgun. The two became a blur as Wayne activated a speed bubble. In an instant he was in a different place—bullets zipping through the area he'd left—hiding behind an overturned table, the bandit with the shotgun limp on the ground.

Wayne's favorite tactic was to get close, then catch one person in the speed bubble and fight them alone. He couldn't move the speed bubble after putting it up, but he could move around inside of it. So when he released the bubble after fighting his chosen foe one-on-one, he'd be standing in a different place than expected. Foes found him incredibly difficult to track and aim at.

But in a long fight, they'd eventually catch on and hold their fire until just after Wayne dropped a bubble. It took a couple of seconds between dropping one and putting up another, the time when Wayne was most vulnerable. Of course, even when the bubble was up, Wayne wasn't completely safe. It could be nerve-racking to know that his friend was fighting alone, enclosed by a bubble of accelerated time. If Wayne got into trouble while inside, Waxillium couldn't help. Wayne would be shot and bleeding before the bubble collapsed.

Well, Waxillium had his own troubles. With those aluminum bullets, his own protective bubble was useless. He let it drop. More bullets pelted his table and the floor around him, the pops of gunfire echoing in the grand hall. Fortunately, he could still see blue lines pointing to the ordinary steel of the bandits' guns, including those of a group of men attempting to flank him.

No time to deal with them, he thought. The bandit boss had sent Steris out with one of his men, but had paused by the door himself. He didn't seem surprised by the resistance. Something about the way he stood there, imperious and in control . . . Something about the way his eyes—the only visible part of his masked face—found Wax, and locked on to him . . . Something about that voice . . .

Miles? The thought was a shock.

Screams. Marasi's screams. Wax turned away from the bandit leader, feeling an unfamiliar sense of panic. Steris needed him, but Marasi did too, and she was closer. The koloss-blooded man named Tarson had her; he held her with one arm around the neck, towing her toward the door and cursing. His two companions looked about anxiously, as if expecting constables to come pouring in at any moment.

Marasi had gone limp. Tarson was shouting, and he jammed his revolver in her ear, but she had her eyes squeezed shut and refused to respond. She knew she wasn't some simple hostage; they wanted her specifically, and therefore wouldn't shoot her.

Good girl, Waxillium thought. It couldn't be easy, hearing the Vanisher shout, feeling the barrel on her temple. A few guests hid nearby, a well-dressed woman and her husband holding their hands to their ears and whimpering. The gunfire was loud, chaotic, though he barely noticed these things any longer. He should have slipped his earplugs in, regardless. Too late now.

Waxillium ducked to the side and fired two shots into the wooden floor to cause those flanking him to duck for cover. The Terringul was loaded with hollow-point bullets specifically designed to lodge in wood, giving him a good anchor when he needed one. They also happened to lodge in flesh, reducing the chances of a through-and-through shot that could injure bystanders, which suited him just fine.

He dashed forward in a crouch and leaped onto a large serving platter. He pressed one foot against the lip of the platter, and Pushed on the bullets behind him. The maneuver threw him forward in a skid across the polished wooden floor. He broke out of the tables into open space just before the steps out of the room, then kicked the platter out from under him and increased his weight, hitting the ground and stopping.

The platter flipped out in front of him, and the startled bandits began firing. Metal pinged against metal as some of the bullets hit the platter; Waxillium responded, dropping the men on either side of Tarson with two quick shots. Then he flared his steel and Pushed toward Tarson's gun to try knocking it away from Marasi.

Only then did Waxillium realize there was no blue line pointing to the man's gun. Tarson grinned, his ashy face topped by Wayne's hat. Then he whipped around, placing himself behind Marasi, whom he gripped by the neck with one hand, holding the gun steady against her head with the other.

No blue lines. *Rust and Ruin . . . an entire* gun *made of aluminum?*

Waxillium and Tarson both fell still. The bandits behind hadn't noticed Waxillium's floor-level escape on the platter; they were closing on the area where he'd been hiding. The boss still stood in the doorway, looking toward Waxillium. Wax *had* to be wrong about who he was. People could look alike, sound alike. That didn't mean . . .

Marasi whimpered. And Waxillium found himself unable to move, unable to raise his hand to fire. The shot he'd made to save Lessie played again and again in his mind.

I can make a shot like that, he thought to himself, angry. *I've done it a dozen times.*

He'd only missed once.

He couldn't move, couldn't think. He kept seeing her die again and again. Blood in the air, a smiling face.

Tarson apparently realized that Waxillium wouldn't fire. So he swung his gun away from Marasi's head and toward Waxillium.

Marasi went rigid. She locked her legs and slammed her head upward into the Vanisher's chin. Tarson's shot went wild and he stumbled backward, holding his mouth.

With Marasi mostly out of the way, Waxillium's mind cleared, and he found himself able to move again. He shot Tarson, though he couldn't bring himself to aim for the chest, not with Marasi stumbling nearby. He settled on dropping Tarson with a shot to the arm. Marasi raised her hand to her mouth in horror, watching him fall.

"He's over there!" Voices from behind, the three bandits he'd been fighting among the tables. An aluminum bullet split the air just beside him.

"Hold on," Waxillium said to Marasi, leaping forward and grabbing her around the waist. He raised his gun and shot the last bullet in his gun toward the doorway, hitting the masked leader of the Vanishers in the head.

The man collapsed in a heap.

Well, there goes that theory, Waxillium thought. Miles wouldn't have fallen to a mere bullet. He was a Twinborn of a particularly dangerous variety.

Tarson was rolling over, holding his arm and groaning. No time.

Guns empty. Waxillium dropped the gun and Pushed on it while holding tightly to Marasi. The Push hurled the two of them into the air; a hail of bullets sprayed through the space where they'd been. Unfortunately, they missed Tarson, who was rolling on the floor.

Marasi cried out, clinging to him as they flew up toward the brilliant chandeliers. Waxillium pushed off one of them, causing it to rock back and forth. That Push threw him and Marasi toward the nearby balcony, which was occupied by a group of cowering musicians.

Waxillium landed hard on the balcony; he was off-balance from carrying Marasi, and hadn't had time to judge the Push precisely. They rolled in a bundle of red and white fabric. When they came to a rest, Marasi clung to him, shaking and gasping for breath.

He sat up, and held her for a moment. "Thank you," she whispered. "Thank you."

"Don't mention it," he said. "That was very brave, stopping the bandit as you did."

"Seven out of ten kidnappings can be foiled by appropriate resistance on the part of the target," she said, words tumbling out of her mouth. She squeezed her eyes closed again. "Sorry. That was just very, *very* unsettling."

"I—" He froze.

"What?" she asked, opening her eyes.

Waxillium didn't respond. He rolled to the side, pulling loose from her grip as he noticed the blue lines moving to the left. Someone was coming up the steps to the balcony.

Waxillium came up beside a large harp as the balcony door burst open to reveal two Vanishers—one with a rifle, the other with a pair of pistols. Waxillium increased his weight by tapping his metalmind, then heaved with a desperate flare of steel, Pushing against the harp's metal mountings, nails, and strings. The instrument crashed into the wooden doorway and smashed the men against the wall. They slumped down, dropping to the stairs under the broken harp.

Waxillium ran to check their vitals. Convinced they wouldn't be dangerous any time soon, he grabbed the handguns and dashed back to the edge of the balcony, scanning the room below. The furniture he'd Pushed out of the way made a strange perfectly circular open space on the ballroom floor. Partygoers were making for the kitchens in increasingly large numbers. He looked for Wayne, but saw only the broken bodies of fallen bandits where he'd been.

"Steris?" Marasi asked, crawling up beside him.

"I'll go after her right now," Waxillium said. "Some men towed her outside, but they won't have had time to . . ." He trailed off as he noticed a blur beside the far door. It stopped, and suddenly Wayne was lying on the ground, blood pooling around him. A bandit stood above him looking quite pleased with himself, holding a smoking pistol.

Damn! Waxillium thought, feeling a spike of fear. If Wayne had been hit in the head . . .

Steris or Wayne?

She'll be safe, he thought. *They took her for a reason; they need her.*

"Oh no!" Marasi said, pointing at Wayne. "Lord Ladrian, is that—"

"He'll be all right if I can get to him," Waxillium said, hastily shoving a pistol into Marasi's hands. "Can you use one of these?"

"I—"

"Just start firing it if someone threatens you. I'll come." He leaped up onto the balcony railing. His way was mostly blocked by the chandeliers; he couldn't make a direct jump to Wayne. He'd have to jump down, then up again, and bound to—

No time. Wayne was dying.

Go!

Waxillium threw himself off the balcony. As soon as his feet were free, he tapped his metalmind and drew forth as much weight as he could. That didn't tow him to the ground; an object fell at the same speed, no matter its weight. Only air resistance mattered.

However, weight did matter a great deal when Pushing—which Waxillium did, throwing everything he had against the chandeliers. They ripped apart in a line, the metal inside them twisting upon itself, crystal exploding outward in a shower. That gave him plenty of room along the upper portion of the room to jump in an arc toward Wayne.

In a heartbeat, Waxillium stopped tapping his metalmind and started filling it instead, decreasing his weight to almost nothing. He Pushed on the broken harp behind, and a simultaneous quick Push against the nails in the floor kept him high.

The result was that he soared across the room in a graceful arc, passing through the space the large chandeliers had occupied. The glittering smaller chandeliers continued to shine on either side of him while crystal showered beneath, each tiny piece splintering the light into a spray of colors. His suit coat flapped, and he lowered the single revolver in his hand as he fell, pointing it at the bandit standing over Wayne.

Waxillium emptied six chambers at the thief. He couldn't afford to take chances.

The pistol was slick in Waxillium's hand as he hit the ground, Pushing on the floor nails to keep from breaking his legs. The thief slumped back against the wall, dead.

Just as Waxillium reached Wayne, a speed bubble sprang up around them. Waxillium exhaled in relief as Wayne stirred; he knelt to turn his friend face upward. Wayne's shirt was soaked with blood, a bullet hole visible in his belly. As Waxillium watched, it slowly closed up, healing itself.

"Damn," Wayne said, groaning. "Gut wounds *hurt.*"

Wayne couldn't have kept the bubble up while the bandit was alive—that would have told him Wayne wasn't dead. Outlaws and lawmen alike were accustomed to Metalborn; if the bubble had stayed up, the bandit would have quickly shot Wayne in the head.

So Wayne had been forced to drop the bubble and play dead. Luckily, the bandit hadn't turned him over to check his vitals and noticed that the wound was healing. Wayne was a Bloodmaker, a type of Feruchemist who could store health in the way that Waxillium stored weight. If Wayne spent some time being sickly and weak—his body healing itself much more slowly than normal—he could store up the health and healing ability in a metalmind. Then, when he tapped it, he healed at a greatly increased rate.

"How much do you have left in your metalmind?" Waxillium asked.

"That was the second bullet wound of the night," Wayne said. "I can maybe heal one more." Wayne stood as Waxillium pulled him to his feet. "Took me a good two weeks in bed to store up that much. Hope that girl of yours is worth it."

"Girl of *mine*?"

"Oh, c'mon, mate. Don't think I didn't see how you were looking at her during dinner. You always did like 'em smart." He grinned.

"Wayne," Waxillium said. "Lessie hasn't even been gone a year."

"You have to move on eventually."

"I'm done with this conversation," Waxillium said, looking over the nearby tables. Vanisher bodies lay strewn about, bones broken by Wayne's dueling canes. Waxillium spotted a few living ones hiding behind tables for cover, as if they hadn't realized yet that Wayne didn't carry guns.

"Five left?" Waxillium asked.

"Six," Wayne said, picking up and spinning his dueling canes. "There's another in the shadows over there. I brought down seven. You?"

"Sixteen, I think," Wax said distractedly. "Haven't been counting carefully."

"Sixteen? Damn, Wax. I was hoping you'd have rusted a bit, was thinkin' maybe I'd be able to catch you this time."

Waxillium smiled. "It's not a competition." He hesitated. "Even if I am winning. Some men got out the door with Steris. I shot the guy who took your hat, though he lived. He's probably gone by now."

"You didn't grab the hat for me?" Wayne asked, sounding offended.

"I was a *little* busy being shot at."

"Busy? Aw, mate. It doesn't take any effort at all to get shot at. I think you're just makin' excuses on account of being jealous of my lucky hat."

"That's it entirely," Waxillium said, fishing in his pocket. "How much time you have left?"

"Not much," Wayne said. "Bendalloy's almost gone. Maybe twenty seconds."

Waxillium took a deep breath. "I'm going for the three on the left. You go right. Get ready to jump."

"Got it."

"Go!"

Wayne ran forward and leaped onto a table in front of them. He dropped the speed bubble right as he launched himself off, and Waxillium braced himself by increasing his weight, then Pushed on Wayne's metalminds, sending the man soaring through the air in an arc toward the bandits. Once Wayne was airborne, Waxillium flipped from tapping his metalmind to filling it, then Pushed on some nails, launching himself into the air in a slightly different trajectory.

Wayne hit first, probably landing so hard he had to heal himself as he rolled between a pair of hiding bandits. He came up to his feet and slammed his dueling canes down on one bandit's arm. He then spun and smashed a cane into the second man's neck.

Waxillium tossed his gun as he fell, Pushing it hard into the face of a startled thief. He landed, then tossed the empty cartridge that Wayne had given him earlier—the one that had contained the message—at a second man. Pushing on it, he turned the casing into an improvised bullet, slamming it into the man's forehead and piercing his skull.

Waxillium shoved on the casing hard enough that it tossed him to the side. He plowed his shoulder into the chest of the man he'd thrown his gun at. The man stumbled back, and Waxillium slammed his forearm—and its metalmind bracer—into the man's head, dropping him.

One more, he thought. *Behind me to the right.* It was going to be close. Waxillium kicked the gun he'd dropped, intending to Push it toward the final bandit.

A gunshot sounded.

Waxillium froze, anticipating the pain of a bullet hitting him. Nothing happened. He spun to find the final bandit slumped over a table, bleeding, a gun dropping from his fingers.

What by the Survivor's scars . . . ?

He looked up. Marasi knelt on the balcony where he'd left her. She'd fetched the rifle from the bandit he'd crushed, and she obviously knew how to use it. Even as he watched, she fired again, dropping the bandit in the shadows Wayne had mentioned.

Wayne stood up from finishing off his two assailants. He looked confused until Waxillium pointed toward Marasi.

"Wow," Wayne said, stepping up to him. "I'm liking her more and more. Definitely the one of the two *I'd* pick if I were you."

The one of the two.

Steris!

Waxillium cursed and leaped forward, throwing himself in a Steelpush across the room toward the other exit. He hit the ground running, noting with concern that the boss's body wasn't where he'd dropped it. There was blood in the entryway. Had they dragged him away?

Unless . . . Maybe his theory wasn't wrong after all. But *damn it*, he couldn't be facing Miles. Miles was a lawman. One of the best.

Waxillium burst out into the night—this ballroom exit led directly to the street. Some horses stood here tied to a fence, and what looked like a group of grooms lay gagged and bound on the ground.

Steris, and the bandits who had carried her out, were gone. He did find a large group of constables riding into the courtyard, however.

"Great timing, chaps," Waxillium said, sitting down on the steps, exhausted.

"I don't care *who* you are or how much money you have," Constable Brettin said. "This is a total mess you've created, sir."

Waxillium sat on his stool, listening with only half an ear as he rested with his back against the wall. He was going to ache in the morning. He hadn't pushed his body so hard in months. He was lucky he hadn't twisted anything or thrown out a muscle.

"This *isn't* the Roughs," Brettin continued. "You think you can do anything you want? You think you can just pick up a gun and take the law into your own hands?"

They sat in the kitchens of Yomen Manor, in a side area that the constables had partitioned off for interviews. It hadn't been long since the end of the fight. Just long enough for the trouble to begin.

Though his ears still rang from the noise of the gunfire, Waxillium could also hear moans and cries from the ballroom as the partygoers were seen to. Beyond that, he could hear the clopping of hooves and the racket of the occasional automobile out in the mansion courtyard as the city's elite fled in groups as they were released. The constables would be speaking to each person, making certain they were well and checking their names off the guest list.

"Well?" Brettin demanded. He was the constable-general, head of the constabulary in their octant. He was probably feeling *very* threatened by the robberies happening under his watch. Waxillium could imagine what it would be like in his position, getting thunder each day from powers above him who were not pleased.

"I'm sorry, constable," Waxillium said calmly. "Old habits make for strong steel. I should have restrained myself, but would you have done any different? Would you have watched women being kidnapped and done nothing?"

"I have a legal right and responsibility you do not."

"I have a moral right and responsibility, constable."

Brettin harrumphed, but the calm words mollified him somewhat. He glanced to the side as a brown-suited constable wearing one of their domelike hats entered and saluted.

"Well?" Brettin asked. "What's the news, Reddi?"

"Twenty-five dead, Captain," the man said.

Brettin groaned. "You see what you've caused, Ladrian? If you'd just kept your head down like everyone else, then those poor folks would still be alive. Ruination! This is a mess. I could *hang* for this—"

"Captain," Reddi interrupted. He stepped in and spoke softly. "Excuse me, sir. But those were the *bandit* casualties. Twenty-five of them dead, sir. Six captured alive."

"Oh. And how many civilians killed?"

"Just one, sir. Lord Peterus. He was shot before Lord Ladrian started fighting back. Sir." Reddi was regarding Waxillium with a mixture of awe and respect.

Brettin glanced at Waxillium, then grabbed his lieutenant by the arm and towed him a little farther off. Waxillium closed his eyes, breathed softly, and caught some of the conversation.

"You mean . . . two men . . . thirty-one *by themselves*?"

"Yes, sir."

". . . else wounded . . . ?"

". . . broken bones . . . not too serious . . . bruises and scrapes . . . going to open fire . . ."

There was silence, and Waxillium opened his eyes to find the constable-general staring at him. Brettin waved Reddi away, then walked back.

"Well?" Waxillium asked.

"You appear to be a lucky man."

"My friend and I drew their attention," Waxillium said. "And most of the partygoers already had their heads down when the shooting began."

"You still broke bones with your Allomantic stunt," the constable-general said. "There will be bruised egos and angry lords. They'll come to *me* when they complain."

Waxillium said nothing.

Brettin crouched down before Waxillium, getting in close. "I know about you," he said softly. "I knew eventually I'd be having this talk with you. So let me be clear. This is my city, and I have the authority here."

"Is that so?" Waxillium asked, feeling very tired.

"It is."

"So where were you when the bandits started shooting people in the head?"

Brettin's face grew red, but Waxillium held his eyes.

"I'm not threatened by you," Brettin said.

"Good. I haven't said anything threatening yet."

Brettin hissed softly, then pointed at Waxillium, tapping a finger against his chest. "Keep your tongue civil. I've half a mind to toss you into jail for the night."

"Then do it. Maybe by morning you'll have found the *other* half of your mind, and we'll be able to have a reasonable conversation."

Brettin's face grew even redder, but he knew—as Waxillium did— that he wouldn't dare throw a house lord into jail without significant justification. Brettin finally broke away, waving a dismissive hand at Waxillium and stalking out of the kitchen.

Waxillium sighed, standing up and taking his bowler off the counter where he'd left it. *Harmony protect us from small-minded men with too much power.* He donned the hat and walked out into the ballroom.

The room had been mostly cleared of guests, the wedding party itself taken in Lord Yomen's carriage to a place where they could recover from the ordeal. The ballroom swarmed with an almost equal number of constables and physicians. The wounded were sitting on the raised wooden floor just before the exit; there looked to be about twenty or thirty people there. Waxillium noticed Lord Harms sitting at a table off to the side, staring down with a morose expression, Marasi trying to comfort him. Wayne was at the table too, looking bored.

Waxillium walked over to them, removing his hat, and sat down. He found that he didn't exactly know what to say to Lord Harms.

"Hey," Wayne whispered. "Here." He handed Waxillium something under the table. A revolver.

Waxillium looked at him, confused. It wasn't his.

"Figured you'd want one of these."

"Aluminum?"

Wayne smiled, eyes twinkling. "Snatched it out of the collection the constables made. Apparently there were *ten* of these. Figured you could sell it. I spent a lot of bendalloy fighting these gits. Need some money to replace it. But don't worry, I left a real nice drawing I did in the gun's place when I took it. Here."

He handed over something else. A handful of bullets. "Grabbed these too."

"Wayne," Waxillium said, fingering the long, narrow cartridges, "you realize these are rifle rounds?"

"So?"

"So they won't fit a revolver."

"They won't? Why not?"

"Because."

"Kind of a dumb way to make bullets, innit?" He seemed baffled. Of course, most things about guns baffled Wayne, who was generally better off throwing a gun at someone than trying to fire it at them.

Waxillium shook his head in amusement, but didn't turn the gun down. He *had* wanted one. He slipped the revolver into one of his shoulder holsters and turned to Lord Harms.

"My lord," Waxillium said. "I have failed you."

Harms dabbed his face with his handkerchief, looking pale. "Why would they take her? They'll let her go, won't they? They said they would."

Waxillium fell silent.

"They won't," Lord Harms said, looking up. "They haven't let any of the others go, have they?"

"No," Waxillium said.

"You *have* to get her back." Harms took Waxillium's hand. "I care nothing for the money or jewelry they took from me. It can be replaced, and most of it was insured anyway. But I'll pay *any* price for Steris. Please. She is to be your fiancée! You have to find her!"

Waxillium looked into the older man's eyes, and saw fear there. Whatever bravado this man had shown in earlier meetings, it was an act.

Funny, how quickly someone can stop calling you a miscreant and a rogue when they want your help, Waxillium thought. But if there was something he couldn't ignore, it was a sincere request for help.

"I'll find her," Waxillium said. "I promise it, Lord Harms."

Harms nodded. Then, he slowly pushed himself to his feet.

"Let me help you to the carriage, my lord," Marasi said.

"No," Harms said, waving her down. "No. Just let me . . . just let me go and sit by myself. I won't leave without you, but please give me some time alone." He walked away, leaving Marasi standing with her hands clasped.

She sat back down, looking sick. "He wishes it were she you had rescued and not me," she said softly.

"So, Wax," Wayne butted in. "Where did you say that bloke was who had my hat?"

"I told you that he got away after I shot him."

"I was hoping he'd dropped my hat, you know. Getting shot makes people drop stuff."

Waxillium sighed. "He still had it on when he left, I'm afraid."

Wayne started cursing.

"Wayne," Marasi said. "It's only a hat."

"Only a hat?" he asked, aghast.

"Wayne's a little attached to that hat," Waxillium said. "He thinks it's lucky."

"It *is* lucky. I ain't never died while wearing that hat."

Marasi frowned. "I . . . I'm not sure I know how to respond."

"That's a common reaction to Wayne," Waxillium said. "I did want to thank you for your timely intervention, by the way. Do you mind if I ask where you learned to shoot like that?"

Marasi blushed. "Ladies' target club at the university. We're quite well ranked against other clubs in the city." She grimaced. "I don't suppose . . . either of those fellows I shot pulled through?"

"Nah," Wayne said. "You plugged them right good, you did. The one near me left brains all over the door!"

"Oh dear." Marasi grew pale. "I never expected . . ."

"It's what happens when you shoot someone," Wayne pointed out. "At least, usually someone has the good sense to get dead when you go to all the trouble to shoot them. Unless you miss anything vital. That bloke what took my hat?"

"I hit him in the arm," Waxillium said. "But it should have brought him down better than it did. He has koloss blood for sure. Might be a Pewterarm as well."

That quieted Wayne. He was probably thinking the same thing as Waxillium—a band like this, with these numbers and such nice weapons, was likely to have at least a couple of Allomancers or Feruchemists among them.

"Marasi," Waxillium said, as something occurred to him, "is Steris an Allomancer?"

"What? No. She isn't."

"You certain?" Waxillium asked. "She might have been hiding it."

"She's not an Allomancer," Marasi said. "Nor a Feruchemist. I can promise it."

"Well, there's a theory rusted away," Wayne said.

"I need to think," Waxillium said, tapping the table with his fingernail. "Too much about these Vanishers doesn't make sense." He shook his head. "But, for now, I should bid you a good evening. I'm exhausted, and if I may be bold enough to say it, you look the same."

"Yes, of course," Marasi said.

They stood, walking toward the exit. The constables didn't stop them, though some did shoot Waxillium hostile looks. Others seemed disbelieving. A few looked awed.

This night, like the four previous, lacked any mists. Waxillium and Wayne walked Marasi to her uncle's carriage. Lord Harms sat inside, staring straight ahead.

As they arrived, Marasi took Waxillium's arm. "You really should have gone for Steris first," she said softly.

"You were closer. Logic dictated I save you first."

"Well, whatever the reason," she said, voice even more soft, "thank you for what you did. I just . . . Thank you." She looked like she wanted to say more, staring up into his eyes, then went onto her tiptoes and kissed him on the cheek. Before he could react, she turned away and climbed into the carriage.

Wayne stepped up to him as the carriage moved off into the dark street, horses' shoes clattering on the paving stones. "So," Wayne said, "you're going to marry her cousin?"

"Such is the plan."

"Awkward."

"She is an impulsive young woman half my age," Waxillium said. *An apparently brilliant, beautiful, intriguing young woman who also happens to be an excellent shot.* Once, that combination would have left him completely smitten. Now, he barely gave it a passing thought.

He turned away from the carriage. "Where are you staying?"

"Not sure yet," Wayne said. "I found this house where the folks who lives there is away, but I think they might be back tonight. Left 'em some bread as a thanks."

Waxillium sighed. *I should have guessed.* "I'll give you a room, assuming you promise not to steal too much."

"What? I *never* steal, mate. Stealing's bad." He ran a hand through his hair and grinned. "Might need to trade you for a hat to wear till I get my other one back, though. Do you need any bread?"

Waxillium just shook his head, waving for his carriage to drive them back to Ladrian Mansion.

7

The morning after the assault on the wedding dinner, Marasi stood before the imposing mansion at Sixteen Ladrian Place, holding her handbag before her in both hands. She always liked to grip something before herself when she was nervous, a bad habit. As Professor Modicarm said, "Obvious visual tells must be assiduously avoided by a practitioner of the law, lest he inadvertently give criminals an insight into his emotional state."

Thinking over quotes from her professors was another of her nervous habits. She continued to stand on the stone-paved sidewalk, indecisive. Would Lord Waxillium find it odd or invasive of her to come? Did he think her a silly girl with a silly hobby who foolishly assumed she could be of use to a seasoned lawman?

She should probably just go up and knock. But didn't she have a right to be nervous when confronting a man such as Waxillium Ladrian? A living legend, one of her personal heroes?

A young gentleman passed on the sidewalk behind her, walking an eager dog. He tipped his hat to her, though he spared a brief distrustful glance for Ladrian Mansion.

The building didn't seem to deserve such scrutiny; the venerable structure was built of stately, vine-bedecked stone, with large windows and an old iron gate. Three mature apple trees spread limbs over the front garden, and a member of the grounds staff was lazily sawing off a few dead branches. City law established by the Lord Mistborn himself required that even ornamental trees provide food.

What would it be like to visit the Roughs, she thought idly, *where the trees are scraggly and short?* The Roughs must be a fascinating place. Plants here in the Elendel Basin grew bountifully with little need for care or cultivation. A final gift of the Survivor, his munificent touch upon the land.

Stop fidgeting, she told herself. *Be firm. Control your surroundings.* That was something Professor Aramine had said just last week, and—

Damn it! She strode forward, through the open gate, up the steps, and to the door. She slammed the knocker down on the door three times.

A long-faced butler answered. He looked her up and down with dispassionate eyes. "Lady Colms."

"I was hoping I might see Lord Ladrian?"

The butler raised an eyebrow, then swung the door open the rest of the way. He said nothing, but a lifetime growing up around servants such as him—servants trained after the ancient Terris ideal—had taught her to read his actions. He did not think she should be visiting Waxillium, and particularly not alone.

"The sitting room is currently unoccupied, my lady," the butler said, pointing a stiff hand—palm up—toward a side chamber. He began stalking toward the staircase, moving with a sense of . . . inevitability. Like an ancient tree swaying in the wind.

She strolled into the room, forcing herself to hold her handbag at her side. Ladrian Mansion was decorated in a classical mode; the rugs had intricate patterns in dark shades, and the ornately carved picture frames were painted gold. Odd, that so many should favor frames that seemed to be trying to outdo the art they held.

Did it seem there was less art hanging in the mansion than

there should be? Several spots on the walls were conspicuously empty. In the sitting room, she looked up at a wide painting of a field of grain, clasping her hands behind her back.

Good. She was containing her nervousness now. There was no reason for it at all. Yes, she had read report after report about Waxillium Ladrian. Yes, stories of his bravery had been part of what inspired her to study law.

However, he was far more amiable than she'd imagined. She had always pictured him as gruff and stoic. Discovering that he spoke like a gentleman had been a surprise. And, of course, there was the relaxed—if acerbic—way he interacted with Wayne. Five minutes around the two of them had destroyed years' worth of youthful illusions about the calm, quiet lawman and his intense, devoted deputy.

Then the attack had come. The gunfire, the screaming. And Waxillium Ladrian, like a bolt of intense, bright lightning in the middle of a dark and chaotic tempest. He had saved her. How many days during her youth had she fondly dreamed of something like that happening?

"Lady Colms?" the butler said, stepping up to the doorway of the room. "I apologize, but the master says that he cannot spare the time to come down and converse with you."

"Oh," she said, feeling an immediate sinking in her stomach. So she'd made a fool of herself after all.

"Indeed, my lady," the butler said, lips turning down even farther. "You are to accompany me to his study so he can converse with you there."

Oh. Well, she hadn't expected that.

"This way please," the butler said. He turned around and lurched up the stairs, and she followed. At the top floor, they twisted through a few hallways—passing some serving and cleaning staff, who bobbed in respect to her—until they reached a room that dominated the far western side of the mansion.

The butler gestured for her to enter. The room beyond was much more cluttered than she'd anticipated. The shutters were closed and the shades drawn, and the large desk that dominated the far wall had been set up with tubes, burners, and other scientific-looking apparatus.

Waxillium stood to the side, holding something up with a pair of tongs and studying it intently. He wore a pair of black goggles, and had on a white shirt with sleeves rolled to the elbows. His suit coat lay draped over a chair at the side of the room, bowler hat topping it, leaving him in a diagonally checkered vest of black and gray. The room smelled of smoke and, oddly, sulfur.

"My lord?" the butler said.

Waxillium turned, goggles still on. "Ah! My lady Marasi. Come in, come in. Tillaume, you may leave us."

"Yes, my lord," the butler said with a suffering tone.

Marasi stepped into the room, glancing to the side where a large sheet of paper lay on the floor, folded upon itself and covered with cramped writing. Waxillium twisted a dial, and a small metal tube on the desk shot out a thin tongue of intense flame. He briefly held his tongs in the fire, then pulled them back out and dropped their contents into a small ceramic cup. He eyed it, then grabbed a glass tube from a rack on the desk and shook it.

"Here," he said, holding it up for her to study. There was a clear liquid in it. "Does this look blue to you?"

"Er . . . no? Should it?"

"Apparently not," he said. He shook the tube again. "Huh." He set the tube aside.

She stood silently. It was so hard not to recall the sight of him breaking through the line of tables, gun in hand as he expertly felled two of the men trying to haul her out into the night. Or the sight of him soaring through the air—gunshots exploding up from beneath, the chandeliers shattering and crystal spraying light around him—as he shot a man from midair and dropped to rescue his friend.

She was talking to a legend. And he was wearing a pair of very silly goggles.

Waxillium raised them to his forehead. "I'm trying to figure out what alloy they used in those guns."

"The aluminum ones?" she asked, curious.

"Yes, but they're not pure aluminum. They're something stronger, and the grain is wrong. I've never *seen* this alloy before. And the bullets must be yet another new alloy; I'll need to test those next. As a side note, I'm not certain if you appreciate the advantages you possess living in the City."

"Oh, I'd say I'm aware of many of them."

He grinned. Oddly, he looked *younger* today than he had on their previous meetings. "I suppose that perhaps you do. I was referring specifically to the ease of shopping you enjoy here."

"Shopping?"

"Yes, shopping! Marvelous convenience. Out in Weathering, if I wanted a gas burner that could reach the high temperatures required for testing alloys, I had to special-order it and wait for the right railway cars to come. *Then* I had to hope the equipment arrived without being damaged or broken.

"Here, however, I merely needed to send a few lads out with a list. In hours, I could set up an entire lab." He shook his head. "I feel so spoiled. And *you* seem hesitant about something. Is it the sulfur? I needed to test the gunpowder in the bullets, you see . . . and, well, I suppose I should open a window."

I will not *be nervous around him.* "It's not that, my lord Ladrian."

"Please, feel free to call me 'Wax' or 'Waxillium,'" he said, walking over to a window. She noticed that he stood to the side as he opened it, never standing directly in the line of sight of anyone outside. The cautious behavior was natural to him, and he didn't even seem to notice what he was doing. "There's no need to be formal with me. I have a rule—saving my life entitles you to use my given name."

"You saved mine first, I believe."

"Yes. But I was already in your debt, you see."

"Because?"

"Because you gave me an excellent excuse to shoot things," he replied, sitting down at his desk and making a few notations on a pad there. "That seems to be something I'd been needing for quite some time." He looked up and smiled at her. "The hesitance?"

"Should we be alone in the room, Lord Waxillium?"

"Why not?" he said, sounding genuinely confused. "Is there a mass murderer hiding in the wardrobe that I somehow missed?"

"I was actually referring to propriety, my lord."

He sat for a moment, then smacked his forehead. "I apologize. You'll have to forgive me for being a buffoon. It's been a long time since I've had to . . . Never mind. If you're uncomfortable, I'll go call Tillaume back." He rose, striding past her.

"Lord Waxillium!" she said. "*I'm* not uncomfortable. I assure you. I simply didn't want to put you in an awkward position."

"Awkward?"

"Yes." Now she felt like a right fool. "Please. I didn't mean to make a fuss."

"Very well, then," he said. "To be honest, I really *had* forgotten about things like this. It's basically nonsense, you realize."

"Propriety is nonsense?"

"Too much in high society is built around the idea of making certain you don't need to trust anyone," Waxillium said. "Contracts, detailed operating reports, not being seen alone with an eligible member of the opposite gender. If you remove the foundation of trust from a relationship, then what is the point of that relationship?"

This from someone who is marrying Steris for the express purpose of exploiting her wealth? She felt bad for the thought. It was very difficult not to feel bitter sometimes.

She moved on quickly. "So . . . the alloy?"

"Yes, the alloy," he said. "Likely a tangent I shouldn't be indulging in. An excuse to dig up an old hobby. But since I know where the aluminum itself came from—the first theft—I wondered if, perhaps, they might be using an alloy that includes components I could trace." He walked back over to his desk, where he picked up the revolver Wayne had given him the night before. She could see that he'd shaved some of the metal off the outside of the grip.

"Do you know much of metallurgy, Lady Marasi?" he asked.

"I'm afraid not," she said. "I probably should."

"Oh, don't feel that way. As I said, this is an indulgence of mine. There are many metallurgists in the city; I could probably have sent these shavings to one of them and gotten a report more quickly, and more accurately." He sighed, sitting back down in his chair. "I'm just accustomed to doing things myself, you see."

"Out in the Roughs, you often didn't have another choice."

"True enough." He tapped the gun against the table. "Alloys are remarkable things, Lady Marasi. Did you realize you can make an alloy with a metal that reacts to magnetism, but end up with one that doesn't? Mix it with an equal part of something else, and you don't get something that's half as magnetically reactive—you get something that's not reactive at all. When you make an alloy, you don't just mix two metals. You make a *new* one.

"That's a fundamental of Allomancy, you see. Steel is just iron with a pinch of carbon in it, but that makes all the difference. This aluminum has something else in it too—less than one percent. I think it might be ekaboron, but that's really just a hunch. A little pinch. It works for men too, oddly. A tiny change can result in creating an entirely new person. How like metals we are. . . ." He shook his head, then waved for her to take a seat in a chair against the wall. "But you didn't come to hear me blather. Come, tell me, what can I do for you?"

"It's actually what I can do for you," she said, sitting. "I've spoken to Lord Harms. I thought that because of your . . . Well, because House Ladrian is currently lacking in liquid assets, you see, I thought that you may not have the tools you need to seek Lady Steris. Lord Harms has agreed to bankroll you for whatever you need as you pursue her rescue."

Waxillium seemed surprised. "That's wonderful. Thank you." He paused, then looked at his desk. "Do you think he'd mind paying for this . . . ?"

"Not at all," she said quickly.

"Well, that's a relief. Tillaume nearly fainted when he saw what I'd spent. I think the old man's afraid we'll run out of tea if I keep this up. It's so incredible that I can be the source of employment for some twenty thousand people, own two to three percent of the land in the city, and yet still be so poor in ready cash. What an odd world business is." Waxillium leaned forward, clasping his hands, looking thoughtful. In the light of the open window, she could now see that he had bags under his eyes.

"My lord?" she asked. "Have you slept at all since the kidnapping?"

He didn't reply.

"Lord Waxillium," she said sternly. "You mustn't neglect your own well-being. Running yourself to rust will do no good for anyone."

"Lady Steris was taken on my watch, Marasi," he said softly. "I didn't lift a finger. I had to be *goaded* into it." He shook his head, as if to drive away bad thoughts. "But you needn't worry about me. I wouldn't have been able to sleep anyway, so I might as well be productive."

"Have you come to any conclusions?" she asked, genuinely curious.

"Too many," he said. "Often, the problem is not coming up with solutions—it's deciding which of them actually happened and which are pure fancy. Those men, for instance. They weren't professionals." He paused. "I'm sorry, that probably doesn't make any sense."

"No, it does," she said. "The way they kept itching to shoot the building up, they way their boss let himself be goaded into shooting Peterus . . ."

"Exactly," he said. "They had experience as thieves, certainly. But they weren't *refined* at it."

"A simple way to determine the type of criminal is by whom they kill and when," Marasi said, quoting a line from one of her textbooks. "Murders end with a hanging; thievery alone can mean escaping death. Those men, if they'd really known what they were doing, would have left quickly, glad they hadn't needed to do any shooting."

"So they're street toughs," Waxillium said. "Common criminals."

"With *very* expensive weapons," Marasi said, frowning. "Which implies an outside backer, doesn't it?"

"Yes," Waxillium said, growing eager and leaning in. "At first, I was very confused. I was *convinced* this was all about the kidnappings, the thievery just a front to disguise that. Then the men last night were genuinely interested in what they were taking. It baffled me. Judging by the price of aluminum, and how much they had to spend forging those guns, they've spent a fortune to make a lesser amount from last night's robbery. It didn't make sense."

"Unless we're dealing with two groups working together," Marasi said, understanding. "Someone has given funds to the bandits, allowing them to pull off these robberies. The backing group, however, demands that they kidnap certain people, making it seem like the result of random hostage-takings."

"Yes! He—whoever the backer is—wants the kidnapped women. And the Vanishers, they get to keep whatever they steal, or perhaps a percentage of it. It *is* all meant to use the robberies as a cover-up, but it's possible the bandits themselves don't understand how they're being used."

Marasi frowned, biting her lip. "But that means . . ."

"What?"

"Well, I'd hoped that this was mostly over with," she explained. "Your initial count of the thieves was just under forty, and you and Wayne killed or incapacitated thirty or so of them."

"Thirty-one," he said absently.

"I had assumed those remaining might cut their losses and flee. Killing three-quarters of a group should be enough to disband them, one would think."

"It would, in my experience."

"But this is different," she said. "The bandit boss has an outside backer offering wealth and weaponry." She frowned. "The boss spoke of 'payback,' as I recall. Could he be both the boss and the backer?"

"Perhaps," Waxillium said. "But I doubt it. Part of the point of all this would be to have someone else doing the dangerous work for you."

"Agreed," she said. "But the boss *does* seem to have his own ideology. Perhaps he was chosen because of it. Criminals often use basic rationalization skills to justify what they are doing, and a man who could capitalize on that—along with promising riches and lots of fun shooting things—would be ideal as a 'middle manager,' so to speak."

Waxillium smiled broadly.

"What?" she asked.

"You realize I spent all night coming to those conclusions? You just reached them in all of . . . what? Ten minutes?"

She sniffed. "I had some modest help from you."

"It might be said that I had modest help from myself, technically."

"The voices whispering to you as a result of sleep deprivation do *not* count, my lord."

His smile grew, and then he stood. "Come. Tell me what you make of this."

Curious, she followed him to the front of the room, where she'd noticed the heap of paper. He pulled it straight, revealing a long—perhaps five-foot—piece of paper that was several feet wide. Waxillium knelt on the ground, but she had a harder time, being in skirts. So she just bent down, looking over his shoulder.

"Genealogies?" she asked, surprised. It appeared that he'd traced each of the kidnapped women back to the Origin, starting with their names at the left of the long sheet, then working backward. It didn't list every relative, but it included the direct ancestors and a few notable names in each generation for each hostage.

"Well?" he asked.

"I'm beginning to suspect that you are an odd man, my lord," she said. "You spent all night doing this?"

"It did take a great deal of my time, though Wayne's paper gave me a good head start. Fortunately, my uncle's library had extensive genealogical resources. It was a hobby of his. But what do you *think*?"

"That it is a good thing you're soon to be engaged, for a good wife would have seen that you got your rest, rather than writing all night by candlelight. That's bad for your eyes, you know."

"We have electricity," he said, waving upward. "Besides, I doubt Steris will care about my sleeping habits. It's not in the contract, you see." There was a touch of bitterness in his tone—faint, but recognizable.

She'd said most of that to stall him for a few moments so she could read more of the names. "Allomancers," she said. "You analyzed the family lines for Allomantic powers in their heritage. They all converge on the Lord Mistborn. Didn't Wayne speak of this?"

"Yes," he said. "I believe that the one behind all this is looking for Allomancers. He's building an army. He picks the people he does because he suspects that they're secretly Allomancers. The fact that they aren't open about it makes it harder to recognize what he's doing."

"But Steris *isn't* an Allomancer. I promise it."

"That worried me for a time," he said. "But it's not a large issue. See, he's picking people he thinks are *probably* Allomancers, but he's bound to get it wrong a few times." Waxillium tapped the paper. "That does make me worry for her. Once the backer discovers that she's not what he thought she was, she'll be in greater danger."

Hence why you stayed up all night, she realized. *You think there isn't time.*

All of this, for a woman he obviously didn't love. It was difficult not to be jealous.

What? she thought. *You'd have had yourself be taken? Foolish girl.*

She did note that her own name was one of those listed. "You have my genealogy?" she said, surprised.

"Had to send out for it," he said. "Made some clerks quite angry in the middle of the night, I'm afraid. You're very odd."

"Excuse me?"

"Oh. Um, I mean on the list. You see here? You're second cousins with Steris."

"And?"

"And, that means you're . . . well, this is awkward to explain. You're, essentially, a sixth cousin to the main bloodline here. All of the others, including Steris, were much better connected—you have bloodlines on your father's side that dilute your connections. That makes you an odd target, compared to the others. I'm wondering if they picked you because they wanted to take someone random to break up their pattern and keep us guessing."

"Possible," she said carefully. "They didn't know Steris had been sitting with us, after all."

"Very true. But . . . here's where it gets speculative. You see? I can come up with plenty of reasons why Steris was targeted. The history of Allomancers isn't the only connection—because of the propinquity of high society, there are *many* other connections.

"In fact, as I look at it, the Allomancy factor is tenuous. If you're going to train fighters, why take only women? Why bother with Allomancers in the first place, when you have the funds and means to steal all of this aluminum? They could have stopped there and been rich. And I can't find anything to indicate, with certitude, that the other women taken were indeed Allomancers."

They're taking just women, Marasi thought, looking at the long lists, tying back to the Lord Mistborn. The most powerful Allomancer who ever lived. A nearly mythological figure, someone who had *all sixteen* Allomantic powers in one body. How powerful would he have been?

And suddenly, it made sense. "Rust and Ruin," she whispered.

Waxillium looked up at her. He'd probably have seen it, if he hadn't pushed himself so long through the night.

"Allomancy is genetic," she said.

"Yes. Which is why it shows up so much in these lines."

"Genetic. Taking all women. Waxillium, don't you see? They're not intending to build an army of Allomancers. They're intending to *breed* one. They're taking the women with the most direct Allomantic lines back to the Mistborn."

Waxillium stared at his large paper, then blinked. "By the Survivor's spear . . ." he whispered. "Well, at least this means Steris isn't in immediate danger. She's valuable to him even without being an Allomancer."

"Yes," Marasi said, feeling sick. "But if I'm right, then she'll be in a different kind of danger."

"Indeed," Waxillium said, subdued. "I should have seen this. Wayne will never let me live it down, once he finds out."

"Wayne," she said, realizing she hadn't asked after him. "Where is he?"

Waxillium checked his pocket watch. "He should be back soon. I sent him out to cause a little mischief."

...s There ...fe Across ...e Ocean?

...years ago, the coastal ...ation vessel the *Iron-* ...was taken by a terrible ...and blown into the ...deeps. Out of sight ...d, there was no way to ...ate properly, and the ...sailors found them- ...praying for their lives ...y sailed back eastward ...hopes of striking land. ...mony favored them, ...ey eventually found ...a strange island filled ...nusual animals. There ...lso found a refugee, a ...urvivor with a terrible ...f his ship being taken ...range seafaring people. ...y, long after their loved ...had given them up ...ad, the sailors have ...ed to civilization, bear- ...th them this refugee. ...ory is one of fright, ..., and wonder. Read ...we uncover the truths ...people of the oceans ...eir mystical Unknown ...s. Full story, reverse

HORSELESS CARRIAGES ARE A MENACE!

Horseless Carriages are a danger to our city and our way of life. These soulless contraptions haven't the common sense of a horse and coachman, both of whom are trained through years of practice and licensing to protect their passengers from danger. Statistics show that wrecks and fatalities are common with motorcars. Do not put your life, or the lives of your loved ones, at the mercy of something cold, steel, and lifeless. Stand up for what is right!

DENOUNCE HORSELESS CARRIAGES

Paid for by the coachman's union. The words of this advertisement do not reflect the opinions of the editors or staff of this broadsheet.

Ironeyes Sightings on the Rise!

Reports are flooding the city: sightings of Ironeyes himself. When Death stalks the streets of Elendel, how can you know that you are safe? Printed here are sixteen tips proven to keep Ironeyes from your home. Wards are included to make him pass over you while sleeping, and to frighten him if the worst happens and you encounter him in person. Exclusive report on the back, fourth column. Don't be one of the few left without proper protection! Read on, or else!

"The Faceless Immortals Saved My Life!"

A woman in the Fifth Octant suffered a harrowing experience when a fire broke out in her tenement. She and her children were saved by a shadowy figure she swore was wearing the face of her departed husband. A sighting of one of the Faceless Immortals? Delusion? Simple fancy? You decide. Story on the reverse, in the fifth column.

8

Wayne strode up the steps into the Fourth Octant constabulary precinct offices. His ears felt way too hot. Why was it that conners wore such uncomfortable hats? Maybe that was why they were so grouchy all the time—walking about the city, picking on respectable folk. Even after just a few weeks in Elendel, Wayne knew that was basically what constables did.

Bad hats. A bad hat could make a man right disagreeable, and that was the truth.

He burst through the double doors, slamming them open. The room inside basically looked like a big cage. A wooden railing in the front to keep people separated from the conners, desks behind for eating food or lounging and talking. His entrance caused a few of the brown-uniformed conners to sit bolt upright, some reaching for revolvers at their hips.

"Who's in charge of this place!" Wayne bellowed.

The astounded conners stared at him, then jumped to their feet, straightening uniforms and hastily sticking on their hats. He wore one of those uniforms himself. He'd traded for it at a precinct up in the Seventh Octant. He'd left a right good shirt as a replacement, as fair a trade as any man could ask. After all, that shirt had been *silk*.

"Sir!" one of the conners said. "You'll want Captain Brettin, sir!"

"Well where the hell is he?" Wayne yelled. He'd picked up the right accent from listening to just a few conners. People, they misunderstood the word "accent." They thought accents were those things everybody *else* had. But that wasn't it at all. Every person had an individual accent, a blend of where he'd lived, what he did for a living, who his friends were.

People thought Wayne imitated accents. He didn't. He outright stole them. They were the only things he was still allowed to steal, seeing as to how he'd turned to doing good with his life and stuff like that.

Several of the conners, still confused by his arrival, pointed toward a door at the side of the room. Others saluted, as if that were really the only thing they knew how to do. Wayne huffed through his thick, drooping fake mustache and stalked over to the door.

He acted as if he were just going to throw it open, but then pretended to hesitate and knocked instead.

Brettin would outrank him, barely. *Really unfortunate,* Wayne thought. *Here I am, twenty-five years as a constable, and still only a three-bar.* He should have been promoted ages ago.

As he raised his hand to knock on the door again, it flew open, revealing Brettin's lean face. He looked annoyed. "What is this racket and yelling—" He froze as he saw Wayne. "Who are you?"

"Captain Guffon Trenchant," Wayne said. "Seventh Octant."

Brettin's eyes flicked to Wayne's insignia, then back to his face. There was a moment of confusion, and Wayne could see panic in Brettin's eyes. He was trying to decide if he should remember Captain Guffon or not. The City was a big place, and—from what Wayne had overheard—Brettin was always mixing up people's names.

"I . . . of course, Captain," Brettin said. "Have . . . er, we met?"

Wayne blew out his mustaches. "We sat at the same table at the chairman's dinner last spring!" He was feeling pretty good about this accent. It was a mixture of seventh-son lord and foreman of an ironworks, with just a *hint* of canal captain. Speaking with it felt like he'd stuffed cotton in half of his mouth and had borrowed the voice from an angry dog.

But he'd spent weeks in the city now, listening in pubs in different octants, visiting the railway tracks, chatting with people in parks. He'd collected a good number of accents, adding them to the ones he'd already stolen. Even when living in Weathering, he'd taken trips to the city to gather accents. You found the best ones here.

"I . . . oh, of course," Brettin said. "Yes. Trenchant, I recognize you now. It has been a while."

"Never mind that," Wayne blustered. "What's this about you having *prisoners* from the Vanishers Gang? Good steel, man! We had to learn about it from the *broadsheets*!"

"We have jurisdiction here, as the event—" Brettin hesitated, looking at the room full of intrigued constables studiously pretending not to be listening. "Step inside."

Wayne eyed the watching men. Not a one of them had questioned him. Act like you were important, act like you were angry, and people just wanted to get out of your way. Basic psychology, that was. "Very well," he said.

Brettin closed the door, speaking quickly and authoritatively. "They were captured in our octant and the crime they were committing was here. We have jurisdiction flat-out. I did send you all a missive."

"A missive? Rust and Ruin, man! You know how many of those we get a day?"

"Well perhaps you should hire someone to sort through them," Brettin said testily. "That's what I eventually did."

Wayne blew out his mustache. "Well, you could have sent someone over to inform us," he said lamely.

"Next time, perhaps," Brettin said, sounding satisfied for having won the argument and disarmed an angry rival. "We *are* rather busy with those prisoners."

"Well and good," Wayne said. "When are you sending them to us?"

"*What?*" Brettin said.

"We have prior claim! You have jurisdiction for the initial inquest, but *we* have prosecution rights. First robbery happened in our octant." Wax had written that out for him. Bloke could be right useful, on occasion.

"You have to give us a written request for that!"

"We sent a missive," Wayne said.

Brettin hesitated.

"Earlier today," Wayne said. "You didn't get it?"

"Er . . . We get a lot of missives . . ."

"Thought you said you hired someone to read them."

"Sent him out for scones earlier, you see . . ."

"Ah. Well then." Wayne hesitated. "Can I have one?"

"Of the scones or the prisoners?"

Wayne leaned in. "Look, Brettin, let's melt this down and forge it. We both know you can stall for months with those prisoners while we complete proper transfer paperwork. That is basically worthless to both of us. You get a lot of hassle, and we lose any chance we had of catching the rest of these fellows. We need to move *quick*."

"And?" Brettin asked, suspicious.

"I want to question a few of the prisoners," Wayne said. "Chief sent me specifically. You let me in, give me a few minutes, and we'll stop all transfer requests. You can prosecute, but we get to keep hunting for their boss."

The two locked gazes. According to Wax, prosecuting the Vanishers would be good for careers—very good. But the real prize, the boss of the gang, was still at large. Getting him would mean glory, promotions, and maybe an invitation to join the upper crust. The late Lord Peterus himself had done it, when he'd captured the Copper Strangler.

Letting a rival constable interview the prisoners would be risky. Potentially losing the prisoners completely—as Brettin chanced doing—was even more so.

"How long?" Brettin said.

"Fifteen minutes each," Wayne said.

Brettin's eyes narrowed just slightly. "Ten minutes with two of the prisoners."

"Fine," Wayne said. "Let's do it."

It took longer to set things up than it should have. Constables tended to take their time about anything unless it involved burning buildings or murders in the streets—and they ran for those two only if someone rich was involved. Eventually, they had a room set up for him and pulled one of the bandits in.

Wayne recognized him. The fellow had tried to shoot him, so Wayne had broken his arm with a dueling cane. Downright rude, trying to shoot like that. When a fellow pulls out a dueling cane, you should respond with one of your own—or at least a knife. Trying to shoot Wayne was like bringing dice to a card game. What was the world coming to?

"Has he said anything so far?" Wayne asked Brettin and several of his minions, standing outside the door and looking in at the tubby, scraggly-haired bandit. He had his arm in a dirty sling.

"Not much," Brettin said. "Actually, none of them have given us much of anything. They seem . . ."

"Afraid," one of the other constables said. "They're afraid of something—or, at least, more afraid of talking than they are of us."

"Bah," Wayne said. "You just need to be *firm* with them! No coddling."

"We haven't been—" the constable began, but Brettin raised a hand to quiet him. "Your time is slipping away, Captain."

Wayne sniffed, then sauntered into the room. It was small, practically a closet, with only the one door. Brettin and the others left it open. The bandit sat in a chair, manacled hands linked by chains to his feet and both locked to the floor. There was a table between them.

The bandit watched him resentfully. He didn't seem to recognize Wayne. It was probably the hat.

"So, son," Wayne said. "You're in a heap of trouble."

The bandit didn't reply.

"I can get you off easy. No hangman's noose for you, if you are willing to be smart."

The bandit spat at him.

Wayne leaned in, hands on the table. "Here now," he said very softly, changing his speech to the natural, fluid accent that the bandits had been using. A cup of canal worker for authenticity, a healthy dose of bartender for trust, and the rest Sixth Octant, north side, where most had sounded like they'd come from. "Is that the way to speak to the bloke who killed a conner and took his uniform, all to get you outta here, mate?"

The bandit's eyes opened wide.

"Don't do that, now," Wayne said softly. "You're looking too eager. That'll make 'em suspicious. Damn it all. You're gonna have to spit on me again."

The man hesitated.

"Do it!"

He spat.

"Ruination!" Wayne bellowed, swapping back to the constable accent. He pounded the table. "I'll tear your ears off, boy, if you do that again."

The bandit looked at him. "Er . . . should I?"

Ah, good. Got the right neighborhood. "Like hell," Wayne hissed. "I really will rip yer ears off if you do." He leaned in, speaking in the street-tough accent, low enough so those outside couldn't hear. "The conners say you haven't talked. Good job on that. The boss'll be pleased."

"You're gonna get me out?"

"What do you think? Can't leave you to sing. It's either get you out or see you shaking hands with Ironeyes."

"I won't talk," the man said urgently. "No need to kill me. I *won't talk.*"

"And the others?"

The man hesitated. "I don't think they will either. Except maybe Sindren. He's new, and all."

Good, Wayne thought. "Sindren. Blond fellow, with the scar?"

"No. He's the short guy. Big ears." The robber squinted at Wayne. "Why don't I recognize you?"

"Why do you think?" Wayne said, standing back and resuming his constable voice. "Now, no more griping! Where is your base of operations? Where are you men working from? I want *answers!*" He leaned in again. "You don't recognize me because I'm too valuable to be seen by the common men. They might give me away. I work with your boss. Tarson."

"Tarson? He's not boss of anything. He just hits stuff."

Also good. "I meant his boss."

The bandit frowned. He was growing more suspicious.

"Your attitude is going to get you hanged, mate," Wayne said softly. "Who recruited you? I want to . . . speak with him."

"Who . . . Clamps does *all* the recruitment. You should know that." His eyes grew hostile.

Excellent, Wayne thought. "Done!" he said, turning around. "This one won't talk. Closed-mouthed git." He walked out of the room to join Brettin and the others.

"Why were you whispering so much?" Brettin demanded. "You said we could listen."

"I said you could listen," Wayne said, "but not that I'd say anything you could hear. You've got to speak low and threateningly with these types. Have any of the men given you names, yet?"

"Aliases," Brettin said, dissatisfied.

"Any of them give the name Sindren?"

Brettin looked at his men. They shook their heads.

Excellent. "I want to see the other men. I'm going to pick which one to interview next."

"That wasn't part of the deal," Brettin said.

"And I can still march on home and start up paperwork for a transfer . . ."

Brettin stewed for a moment, then led Wayne to the cells. Sindren was easy to pick out. The large-eared man looked young; he was wide-eyed as he watched the conners look into his cell.

"Him," Wayne said. "Let's go."

They grabbed him and brought him to an interrogation room. Once Sindren was chained down, Brettin and his men waited in the room.

"A little space to breathe, please," Wayne said, glaring at them.

"Fine," Brettin said. "But no more whispering. I want to hear what you have to ask him. He *is* still our prisoner."

Wayne glared at them, and they shuffled out, but left the door open. Brettin stood outside with his arms folded, looking at Wayne expectantly.

All right then, Wayne thought. He turned to the captive and leaned in. "Hello, Sindren."

The boy actually jumped. "How do you—"

"Clamps sent me," Wayne said softly in a street-tough accent. "I'm working on a way to get you out. I need you to remain perfectly still."

"But—"

"Still. Don't move."

"No whispering!" Brettin called in. "If you say—"

Wayne put up a speed bubble. It wasn't going to last long; he hadn't been able to scrounge up much bendalloy. He'd have to make it work.

"I'm an Allomancer," Wayne said, holding perfectly still. "I've sped up time for us. If you move, they'll notice the blur and know what happened. Do you understand? *Don't* nod yes. Just say so."

"Um . . . yes."

"Good," Wayne said. "As I said, Clamps sent me, and I'm here to get you out. Seems the boss worries you fellows will talk."

"I won't!" the youth said, voice nearly a squeak as he obviously worked hard to keep himself from moving.

"I'm sure you won't," Wayne said, moving his accent subtly to match the area this youth was from, Inner Seventh. He tossed in a sprinkle of millworker, which he caught in this lad's dialect. Probably from his father. "If you did, Tarson would have to break some of your bones. You know how he likes that, eh?"

The boy started to nod, but caught himself. "I know."

"But we'll get you out," Wayne said. "Don't worry. I don't recognize you. You new?"

"Yes."

"Clamps recruited you?"

"Just two weeks back."

"Which base were you working out of?"

"Which one?" the lad said, frowning.

"We have several stations of operation," Wayne said. "But of course you don't know that, do you? The boss only shows one to new kids, in case they get caught. Wouldn't want you to accidentally lead people to us, eh?"

"That would be awful," Sindren agreed. He eyed the door, but kept himself still. "He put me in the old foundry over in Longard. I thought we were the only ones!"

"That's the idea," Wayne said. "We can't let a simple mistake stop us from getting payback."

"Er, yes."

"You don't believe in all that, do you?" Wayne said. "It's okay. I think the boss gets a little crazy with that stuff too."

"Yeah," the youth said. "I mean, most of us just want the money, you know? Payback's nice. But . . ."

". . . money's better."

"Yeah. Boss is always talking about how things will be better when he's in charge, and how the city betrayed him, and stuff. But the city betrays everyone. That's how life is." The youth glanced again at the constables outside the door.

"Don't worry," Wayne said. "They think I'm one of them."

"How'd you do it?" the boy asked softly.

"Just gotta talk their language, son. Surprising how many people never figure that out. You're sure they never told you about any of the other bases? I need to know which ones are in danger."

"No," the youth said. "I only ever went to the foundry. Stayed there pretty much all the time, except when we went out on runs."

"Can I give you some advice, son?" Wayne asked.

"Please."

"Get out of this business of robbing folks. You aren't meant for it. If you ever do get free, go back to the mills."

The boy frowned.

"Takes a special type to be a proper criminal," Wayne explained. "You ain't that type. You see, in this conversation, I tricked you into confirming the name of the guy who recruited you and giving the location of your base."

The youth grew pale. "But . . ."

"Don't worry," Wayne said. "I'm on your side, remember? You're just lucky that I am."

"Yeah."

"All right," Wayne said, lowering his voice, remaining still. "I don't know if I can get you out by force. Face it, kid, you're not worth it. But I *can* help you. I want you to talk to the constables."

"*What?*"

"Give me until evening," Wayne said. "I'll go back to the base and clear the place out. Once that's done, you can sing to the conners, tell them everything you know. Don't worry, you weren't told enough to get us into real trouble. Our contingency plans will protect us. I'll tell the boss I told you to do it, and so you'll be all right.

"But don't talk to them until they promise to let you go free in return. Get a solicitor into the room; ask for one by the name of Arintol. He's supposed to be honest." At least, that was what people on the streets had told Wayne. "Get the conners to promise you freedom with Arintol in the room. Then, tell them everything you know.

"Once you're out, get away from the City. Some of the gang may not believe that I told you to talk, so it could be dangerous for you. Go to the Roughs and become a millworker. Nobody will care, there. Either way, kid, stay out of crime. You'll just end up getting someone killed. Maybe you."

"I . . ." The youth looked relieved. "Thank you."

Wayne winked. "Now, resist everything I ask you from here out." He started coughing and dropped the speed bubble.

"—that I can't hear," Brettin said, "I'm stopping this right here."

"Fine!" Wayne yelled. "Boy, tell me who you work for."

"I ain't giving you anything, conner!"

"You'll talk, or I'll have your toes!" Wayne yelled back.

The kid got into it, and Wayne gave the constables a good five minutes of arguing before throwing up his hands and storming out.

"I told you," Brettin said.

"Yeah," Wayne said, trying to sound dejected. "Guess you'll just have to keep working on them."

"It won't work," Brettin said. "I'll be dead and buried before these men talk."

"We could only be so lucky," Wayne said.

"What was that?"

"Nothing," Wayne said, sniffing the air. "I believe that the scones have arrived. Excellent! At least this trip won't be a complete waste."

9

So we aren't sure yet what happened," Waxillium said, sitting on the floor beside the long sheet of paper covered with his genealogical results. "The Words of Founding included a reference to two more metals and their alloys. But the ancients believed in sixteen metals, and the Law of Sixteen holds so strongly in nature that it can't be disregarded. Either Harmony changed the way that Allomancy itself works, or we never really understood it."

"Hmmm," Marasi said, sitting on the floor with her knees to the side. "I would not have expected that from you, Lord Waxillium. Lawman I had anticipated. Metallurgist, perhaps. But philosopher?"

"There is a link between being a lawman and a philosopher," Waxillium said, smiling idly. "Lawkeeping and philosophy are both about questions. I was drawn to law by a need to find the answers nobody else could, to capture the men everyone considered uncatchable. Philosophy is similar. Questions, secrets, puzzles. The human mind and the nature of the universe—the two great riddles of time."

She nodded thoughtfully.

"What was it for you?" Waxillium asked. "One does not often meet a young woman of means studying law."

"My means are not so . . . meaningful as they may seem at first," she said. "I would be nothing without my uncle's patronage."

"Still."

"Stories," she said, smiling wistfully. "Stories of the good and the evil. Most people you meet, they aren't quite either one."

Waxillium frowned. "I'd disagree. Most people seem basically good."

"Well, perhaps by one definition. But it seems that either one— good or evil—has to be pursued for it to be significant. People today . . . it seems they are good, or sometimes evil, mostly by *inertia*, not by choice. They act as their surroundings prepare them to act.

"It's like . . . well, think of a world where everything is lit with the same modest light. All places, outside or inside, lit by a uniform light that cannot be changed. If, in this world of common light, someone suddenly produced a light that was significantly brighter, it would be remarkable. By the same token, if someone managed to create a room that was dim, it would be remarkable. In a way, it doesn't matter how strong the initial illumination was. The story works regardless."

"The fact that most people are decent does not make their decency any less valuable to society."

"Yes, yes," she said, blushing. "And I'm not saying I wish that everyone were less decent. But . . . those bright lights and those dim places fascinate me, Lord Waxillium—particularly when they're dramatically out of order. Why is it that in one instance, a man raised in a basically good family—surrounded by basically good friends, with good employment and satisfactory means—starts strangling women with copper wires and sinking their bodies in the canals?

"And conversely, consider that most men who go to the Roughs adapt to the general climate of lax sensibilities there. But some others—a few remarkable individuals—determine to bring civilization with them. A hundred men, convinced by society that 'everybody does it this way,' will go along with the most crude and despicable of acts. But one man says no."

"It's really not as heroic as all that," Waxillium said.

"I'm certain it doesn't look that way to you."

"Have you ever heard the story of the first man I brought in?"

She blushed. "I . . . yes. Yes, let's just say that I've heard it. Peret the Black. A rapist and an Allomancer—Pewterarm, I believe. You walked into the lawkeeper station, looked at the board, ripped his picture off and took it with you. Came back three days later with him over the saddle of your horse. Of all the men on the board, you picked the most difficult, most dangerous criminal of the bunch."

"He was worth the most money."

Marasi frowned.

"I looked at that board," Waxillium said, "and I thought to myself, 'Well, any of these blokes is right likely to kill me. So I might as well pick the one worth the most.' I needed the money. I hadn't had anything to eat in three days but jerky and a few beans. And then there was Taraco."

"One of the great bandits of our era."

"With him," Waxillium said, "I figured I could get some new boots. He'd robbed a cobbler just a few days earlier, and I thought if I brought the man in, I might manage to get a new pair of boots out of it."

"I thought you'd picked him because he'd shot a lawkeeper over in Faradana the week before."

Waxillium shook his head. "I didn't hear that until after I brought him in."

"Oh." Then, remarkably, she smiled in eagerness. "And Harrisel Hard?"

"A bet with Wayne," Waxillium said. "You don't look disappointed."

"This just makes it more real, Lord Waxillium," she said. Her eager eyes glittered in an almost *predatory* way. "I need to write these down." She fished in her handbag, pulling out a pad and pencil.

"So that's what motivated you?" Waxillium asked as she scribbled notes. "You study out of a desire to be a hero, like in the stories?"

"No, no," she said. "I just wanted to learn about them."

"Are you sure?" he said. "You could become a lawkeeper, go out to the Roughs, live these same stories. Don't think that you can't because you're a woman; high society might lead you to believe that, but it doesn't matter out beyond the mountains. Out there, you don't have to wear lacy dresses or smell like flowers. You can belt on some revolvers and make your own rules. Don't forget, the Ascendant Warrior herself was a woman."

She leaned forward. "Can I admit something to you, Lord Waxillium?"

"Only if it's salacious, personal, or embarrassing."

She smiled. "I *like* the lacy dresses and smelling like flowers. I *like* living in the city, where I can demand modern conveniences. Do you realize I can send for Terris food at *any hour* of the night, and have it delivered?"

"Incredible." It actually was. He hadn't realized that was possible.

"As much as I like reading about the Roughs, and though I may like to visit, I don't think I'd take well to living there. I don't mix well with dirt, grime, and an overall lack of personal hygiene." She leaned in. "And, to be perfectly honest, I have no problem at all letting men like you be the ones to belt on revolvers and shoot people. Does that make me a terrible traitor to my sex?"

"I don't think so. You *are* pretty good at shooting things, though."

"Well, shooting *things* is okay. But people?" She shivered. "I know the Ascendant Warrior is a model for self-actualized women. We have classes on it at the university, for Preservation's sake, and her legacy is written into the law. But I don't really want to put on trousers and be her. I feel like a coward for admitting it sometimes."

"It's all right," he said. "You have to be yourself. But none of that explains why you are studying law."

"Oh, I do want to change the city," she said, growing eager. "Though I feel that tracking down every criminal and punching holes in them with pieces of metal moving at high speeds is a terribly inefficient way to do it."

"Sure can be fun, though."

"Let me show you something." She dug in her handbag a little more, and came out with some folded-up sheets of paper. "I spoke of how people generally act in response to their surroundings. Remember our discussion about the Roughs, and how there are often *more* lawkeepers per person there than here? And yet, crime is more prevalent. That's the result of environment. Look here."

She handed over some of the pages. "This is a report," she said. "I'm putting it together myself. It's about the nature of crime as related to environment. See here, this discusses the major factors that have decreased crime in some sections of the city. Hiring more constables, hanging more criminals, that sort of thing. They are of medium efficacy."

"What's this at the bottom?" Waxillium asked.

"Renovation," she said with a deep smile. "This case is where a wealthy man, Lord Joshin himself, purchased several parcels of land in one of the less reputable areas. He began renovating and cleaning up. Crime went way down. The people didn't change, just their environment. Now that area is a safe and respectable section of the city.

"We call it the 'broken windows' theory. If a man sees a broken window in a building, he's more likely to rob or commit other crimes, since he figures nobody cares. If all the windows are maintained, all the streets clean, all the buildings washed, then crime goes down. Just as a hot day can make a person irritable, it appears that a run-down area can make an ordinary man into a criminal."

"Curious," Waxillium said.

"Of course," she said, "this isn't the only answer. There will always be people who don't respond to their surroundings. They fascinate me, as I've mentioned. Anyway, I've always been good with numbers and figures. I see patterns like this and wonder. Cleaning up a few streets can be cheaper than employing more constables—but can actually decrease crime to a greater degree."

Waxillium looked over the reports, then back at Marasi. She had a flush of excitement in her cheeks. There was something captivating about her. How long had they been here? He hesitated, then pulled out his pocket watch.

"Oh," she said, glancing at the watch. "We shouldn't be chatting like this. Not with poor Steris in their hands."

"We can't do more until Wayne returns," Waxillium said. "In fact, he should have been back by now."

"He is," Wayne's voice said from the hallway outside.

Marasi jumped, letting out a faint yelp.

Waxillium sighed. "How long have you been out there?"

Wayne's head poked around the corner, wearing a constable's hat. "Oh, a little while. Seemed like you two were having some kind of 'smart people' moment. Didn't want to interfere."

"Wise of you. Your stupidity can be infectious."

"Don't use your fancy words 'round me, son." Wayne strolled in. Though he wore the constable's hat, he was otherwise normally dressed in his duster and trousers, dueling canes at his hips.

"Did you succeed?" Waxillium asked, standing up, then reaching down to help Marasi to her feet.

"Sure did—I got some scones." Wayne grinned. "And the dirty conners even paid for them."

"Wayne?"

"Yes?"

"*We're* dirty conners."

"Not no more," he said proudly. "We're independent citizens with a mind toward civic duty. And eating the scones of dirty conners."

Marasi grimaced. "They don't sound that appetizing when described that way."

"Oh, they were good." Wayne reached into the pocket of his

duster. "Here, I brought you some. Got a little mushed up in my pocket, though."

"No, really," she said, paling.

Wayne, however, chuckled and brought out a paper that he waved at Waxillium. "Location of the Vanishers' hideout in the city. Along with the name of their recruiter."

"Really?" Marasi said eagerly, rushing over to take the paper. "How did you do this?"

"Whiskey and *magic*," Wayne said.

"In other words," Waxillium said, walking up and reading the paper over Marasi's shoulder, "Wayne did a lot of fast talking. Nice work."

"We need to get going!" Marasi said, urgent. "Go there, get Steris, and—"

"They won't be there anymore," Waxillium said, taking the paper. "Not after having several of their members captured. Wayne, did you manage to get this without the constables hearing?"

He looked offended. "What do you think?"

Waxillium nodded, rubbing his chin. "We *should* probably go soon. Get to the scene before it gets too cold."

"But . . ." Marasi said. "The constables . . ."

"We'll drop them an anonymous tip once I've seen the place," Waxillium said.

"Won't be needed," Wayne added. "I set a fuse."

"For when?"

"Nightfall."

"Nice."

"You can show your appreciation with a big fat nugget of a rare and expensive metal," Wayne said.

"On the desk," Waxillium said, folding the paper and sliding it into his vest pocket.

Wayne walked over, glancing at the apparatus set up on the desk. "I'm not sure if I want to touch any of this, mate. I'm rather fond of all of my fingers."

"It's not going to explode, Wayne," he said dryly.

"You said that—"

"It happened *once*," Waxillium said.

"Do you know how bloody annoying it is to regrow fingers, Wax?"

"If it's on par with your complaining, then it's likely appalling indeed."

"I'm just sayin'," Wayne said, scanning the desk until he found the bottle of bendalloy flakes. He snatched that, then backed away warily. "The most innocent-looking of things have a tendency to explode around you. A bloke has to be cautious." He shook the bottle. "This isn't much."

"Don't act spoiled," Waxillium said. "That's far more than I could have gotten you on short notice if we'd been out in the Roughs. Drop the hat. Let's go look at this foundry your notes mention."

"We can use my carriage, if you like," Marasi said. To the side, Tillaume walked in, carrying a basket in one hand and a tray with tea in the other. He set the basket beside the door, then set the tray on the table and began pouring tea.

Waxillium eyed Marasi. "You want to come? I thought you said you wanted to leave the shooting to men like me."

"You said they won't be there," she replied. "So there's really no danger."

"They still want you," Wayne noted. "They tried to grab you at the dinner. It'll be dangerous for you."

"And they'd likely shoot either one of you without blinking," she said. "So how will it be any less dangerous for you?"

"I suppose it ain't," Wayne admitted.

Tillaume walked over, bringing a cup of tea for Waxillium on a small tray. Wayne plucked it off with a grin, though Tillaume tried to pull the tray away.

"How convenient," Wayne said, holding the teacup. "Wax, why didn't you ever get me one of these chaps back in Weathering?" The butler shot him a scowl, then hurried back to the table to prepare another cup.

Waxillium considered Marasi. There was something he was

missing, something important. Something about what Wayne had said . . .

"Why *did* they take you?" Waxillium asked Marasi. "There were better targets at that party. Women closer to the bloodlines they wanted."

"You said she might have been a decoy to throw us off," Wayne said, dumping some bendalloy into his teacup, then downing the entire thing in one draught.

"Yes," Waxillium said, looking into her eyes and seeing a flash of something there. She turned away. "But if that were the case, they'd have wanted to take someone that wasn't close to the same bloodline at all, not one who was a near cousin." He pursed his lips, and then it clicked. "Ah. You're illegitimate, then. Steris's half sister, by Lord Harms, I assume."

She blushed. "Yes."

Wayne whistled. "Wonderful show, Wax. Usually *I* wait to call someone a bastard until the second date." He eyed Marasi. "Third if she's pretty."

"I . . ." Waxillium felt a sudden burst of shame. "Of course. I didn't mean . . ."

"It's quite all right," she said softly.

It made sense. Marasi and Lord Harms had grown so uncomfortable when Steris had spoken of mistresses. And then there was the specific clause about them in the contract; Steris was accustomed to infidelity on the part of a lord. That also explained why Harms was paying for the education and housing of Steris's "cousin."

"Lady Marasi," Waxillium said, taking her hand. "Perhaps my years in the Roughs affected me more than I'd assumed. There was a time when I gave *thought* to my words before speaking them. Forgive me."

"I am what I am, Lord Waxillium," she said. "And I have grown comfortable with it."

"It was still crude of me."

"You needn't apologize."

"Huh," Wayne said thoughtfully. "Tea's poisoned."

With that, he toppled to the ground.

Marasi gasped, immediately going to his side. Waxillium spun, looking at Tillaume just as the butler turned from his supposed tea preparations and leveled a pistol at Waxillium.

There was no time for thought. Waxillium burned steel—he kept it in him when he thought he might be in danger—and Pushed on the third button of his vest. He always wore one made of steel there, to use either for restoring his metal reserves or as a weapon.

It burst from his vest, streaking across the room and striking Tillaume in the chest just as he pulled the trigger. The shot went wild. Neither the bullet nor the gun registered as metal to Waxillium's Allomantic senses. Aluminum, then.

Tillaume stumbled to the side and dropped the gun, pulling himself along the bookshelf in an attempt to flee. He left a line of blood on the floor before collapsing at the door.

Waxillium dropped to his knees beside Wayne. Marasi had jumped at the gunshot, and was staring at the gasping butler.

"Wayne?" Waxillium said, lifting his friend's head.

Wayne's eyes fluttered open. "Poison. I *hate* poison. Worse than losin' a finger, I tell you."

"Lord Waxillium!" Marasi said, alarmed.

"Wayne will be fine," Waxillium said, relaxing back. "So long as he can talk and he has some Feruchemical reserves, he can pull through just about anything."

"I'm not talking about him. The butler!"

Waxillium looked up with a start, realizing that the dying Tillaume was fiddling with the basket he'd brought in—the man reached a bloodied hand into it and pulled on something.

"Wayne!" Waxillium cried. "Bubble. *Now!*"

Tillaume fell back. The basket erupted in a blossoming ball of fire.

And then froze.

"Aw, hell," Wayne said, rolling over to look at the explosion in progress. "I warned you. I *said* things are always blowing up around you."

"I refuse to take responsibility for this one."

"He's *your* butler," Wayne said, coughing and crawling to his knees. "Blarek! It wasn't even *good* tea."

"It's getting bigger!" Marasi said, alarmed as she pointed at the explosion.

The fire blast had vaporized the basket before Wayne got his bubble up. The blast wave was slowly expanding outward, burning away the carpet, destroying the doorframe and the bookshelves. The butler himself had already been engulfed.

"Damn," Wayne said. "That's a big one."

"Probably meant to look like an accident with my metallurgy equipment," Waxillium said. "Burning our bodies, covering the murder."

"Shall we go out the windows, then?"

"That blast is going to be hard to outrun," Waxillium said thoughtfully.

"You could do it. Just gotta Push hard enough."

"Against what, Wayne? I don't see any good anchors in that direction. Besides, if I launch us backward that fast, going out the window is going to shred us and rip our bodies apart."

"Gentlemen," Marasi said, voice growing frantic, "it's getting *bigger*."

"Wayne can't stop time," Waxillium said. "Just slow it greatly. And he can't move the bubble once he's made it."

"Look," Wayne said. "Just blow the wall out. Push against the nails in the window frames and blast open the side of the building. Then you can shoot us out that direction without us running into anything."

"Do you even listen to yourself when you say these things?" Waxillium asked, hands on hips as he regarded his friend. "That's *brick* and *stone*. If I Push too hard, I'll just throw myself backward into the explosion."

"It's getting *really, really* close!" Marasi said.

"So make yourself heavier," Wayne said.

"Heavy enough so that I don't move when an entire *wall*—a well-built, extremely heavy one—is ripped off a building?"

"Sure."

"The floor would never be able to take it," Waxillium said. "It would shatter, and . . ."

He trailed off.

Both of them looked down.

Snapping into motion, Waxillium grabbed Marasi, pulling her over with a yelp. He rolled onto his back, holding her tightly atop him.

The explosion was taking up most of their field of vision now, having consumed a large portion of the room. It swelled closer and closer, glowing with angry yellow light, like a bubbling, bursting pastry expanding in an enormous oven.

"What are we—" Marasi said.

"Hold on!" Waxillium said.

He amplified his weight.

Feruchemy didn't work like Allomancy. The two categories of power were often lumped together, but in many ways, they were opposites. In Allomancy, the power came from the metal itself, and there was a limit to how much you could do at once. Wayne couldn't compress time beyond a certain amount; Waxillium could Push only so hard on a piece of metal.

Feruchemy was powered by a sort of cannibalism, where you consumed part of yourself for later use. Make yourself weigh half as much for ten days, and you could make yourself one and a half times as heavy for a near-equal amount of time. Or you could make yourself twice as heavy for half that time. Or four times as heavy for a quarter of that time.

Or extremely heavy for a few brief moments.

Waxillium drew into himself weight he'd stored in his metalminds across days spent going around at three-quarters weight. He became heavy as a boulder, then as heavy as a building, then *heavier.* All this weight was focused on one small section of the floor.

The wood crunched, then burst, exploding downward. Waxillium dropped out of Wayne's bubble of speed and hit real time, the shift jostling him. The next few moments were a blur. He heard the awesome sound of the explosion above—it hit with a wave of force. He released his metalmind and Pushed against the nails in the floor below them, trying to slow himself and Marasi.

He didn't have enough time to do it well. They crashed into the floor of the next story down, and something heavy landed on them, driving the breath from Waxillium's lungs. There was glaring brightness and a burst of heat.

Then it was over.

Waxillium lay dazed, ears ringing. He groaned, then realized that Marasi was clinging to him, shaking. He held her close for a moment, blinking. Were they still in danger? What had fallen on them?

Wayne, he thought. He forced himself to move, rolling over and setting Marasi aside. The floor beneath them had been crushed practically to splinters, the nails flattened to little disks. Part of his downward Push must have been while he still had the increased weight.

They were covered with chips of wood and plaster dust. The ceiling was a wreck, sections of wood smoldering, bits of ash and debris wafting down. There was nothing left of the hole he'd broken; the blast had consumed it and the floor around it.

Wincing, he moved Wayne. His friend had fallen on them and blocked the brunt of the explosion from above. His duster had been shredded, his back exposed, blackened and burned, blood dribbling down his sides.

Marasi raised a hand to her mouth. She was still trembling, her dark brown hair tangled, eyes wide.

No, Waxillium thought, uncertain if he should try to turn his friend over or not. *Please, no.* Wayne had used a portion of his health to recover from the poison. And last night, he'd said he only had enough left for one bullet wound. . . .

Anxious, he felt at Wayne's neck. There was a faint pulse. Waxillium closed his eyes and let out a deep breath. As he watched, the wounds on Wayne's back began to draw closed. It was a slow process. A Bloodmaker using Feruchemical healing was limited by how fast he wanted the power to work—recovering quickly required a much greater expenditure of health. If Wayne didn't have much left, he'd need to work at a slow pace.

Waxillium left him to it. Wayne would be suffering great pain, but there was nothing he could do. Instead, he took Marasi's arm. She was still trembling.

"It's all right," Waxillium said, his voice sounding odd and muffled because of the explosion's effect on his hearing. "Wayne is healing. Are you injured?"

"I . . ." She looked dazed. "Two in three sufferers of great trauma are unable to correctly identify their own injuries as a result of stress or the body's own natural coping mechanisms covering the pain."

"Tell me if any of this hurts," Waxillium said, feeling at her ankles, then legs, then arms for breaks. He carefully prodded her sides for broken ribs, though it was difficult through the thick cloth of her dress.

She slowly came out of her daze, then looked at him and pulled him close, tucking her head against his chest. He hesitated, then wrapped his arms around her and held her as she steadied her breath, obviously trying to get hold of her emotions.

Behind them, Wayne started coughing. He stirred, then groaned and lay still, letting the healing continue. They'd fallen into a spare bedroom. The building was burning, but not too badly. Likely the constables would soon be called.

Nobody has come running, Waxillium thought. *The other staff. Are they all right?*

Or were they part of it? His mind was still trying to catch up. Tillaume—a man who, as far as he knew, had served his uncle faithfully for decades—had tried to kill him. Three times.

Marasi pulled back. "I think I . . . I think I've composed myself. Thank you."

He nodded to her, pulling out his handkerchief and handing it over, then knelt by Wayne. The man's back was crusted with blood and burned skin, but it had been lifted and raised as scabs, new skin forming underneath.

"Is it bad?" Wayne asked, eyes still closed.

"You'll pull through."

"I meant the duster."

"Oh. Well . . . you're gonna need a *really* big patch this time."

Wayne snorted, then pushed himself up and moved into a sitting position. He winced several times during the process, then finally opened his eyes. Trails of tears were running down the side of his face. "I told you," Wayne said. "Innocent things are *always* exploding around you, Wax."

"You kept your fingers this time."

"Great. I can still strangle you."

Waxillium smiled, resting his hand on his friend's arm. "Thanks."

Wayne nodded. "I apologize for havin' to fall on you two."

"I'll forgive you, under the circumstances." Waxillium glanced at Marasi. She sat with her arms wrapped around herself, hunched forward, face pale. She saw his scrutiny, then lowered her arms, as if forcing herself to be strong, and began to stand up.

"It's all right," Waxillium said. "You can take more time."

"I'll be well," she said, though it was hard to make out the words, as his hearing was still dulled. "I just . . . I'm unaccustomed to people trying to kill me."

"You don't ever get accustomed to it," Wayne said. "Trust me." He took a deep breath, then pulled off the remnants of his duster and shirt. Then he turned his burned back to Waxillium. "You mind?"

"You may want to turn away, Marasi," Waxillium said.

She frowned, but didn't look away. So he grabbed the burned layer at Wayne's shoulder and—with a jerk—ripped the skin off his back. It came free in almost a single complete sheet. Wayne grunted.

New skin had formed underneath, pink and fresh, but it couldn't finish healing properly until the old, stiff, burned layer had been removed. Waxillium tossed it aside.

"Oh, *Lord of Harmony*," Marasi said, raising a hand to her mouth. "I think I might be sick."

"I warned you," Waxillium said.

"I thought you were referring to his burns. I didn't realize you were going to tear off his *entire back*."

"It feels much better now." Wayne rolled his arms in his shoulders, now shirtless. He was lean and muscled, and he wore a pair of gold metalmind bracers on his upper arms. His trousers had been singed, but were mostly intact. He reached down, pulling one of his dueling canes out of the wreckage. The other was still at his waist. "Now they owe me a hat *and* a duster. Where's the rest of the house staff?"

"I've been wondering that myself," Waxillium said. "I'll do a quick search and see if anyone's hurt. You get Marasi out the back. Sneak through the grounds and out the garden gate; I'll meet you there."

"Sneak?" Marasi asked.

"Whoever hired that bloke to kill us," Wayne said, "will be expecting that explosion to mean we've gone to meet Ironeyes."

"Right," Waxillium said. "We'll have an hour or two while the house is searched and Tillaume is identified—if there's enough left to identify. During that time, we'll be thought dead."

"It'll give us a little time to think," Wayne said. "Come on. We should move quick."

He led Marasi down the back stairs toward the grounds. She still seemed dazed.

Waxillium's ears felt like they were stuffed with cotton. He suspected the three of them had been shouting their conversation. Wayne was right. You never got used to people trying to kill you.

Waxillium began a quick search of the house, and started refilling his metalminds as he did. He became much lighter, about half his normal weight. Any more than that and it became difficult to walk normally, even with clothing and guns weighing him down. He was practiced at it, though.

During his search, he found Limmi and Miss Grimes unconscious, but alive, in the pantry. A glance out the window showed the coachman, Krent, standing with his hands on his head and looking at the burning building with eyes wide. Of the other house staff—the maids, the errand boys, the cook—there was no sign.

They might have been close enough to the blast to be caught in it, but Waxillium didn't think that likely. Probably, Tillaume—who had charge over household staff—had sent away everyone that he reasonably could, then had drugged the others and stuffed them someplace safe. It indicated a desire to ensure that nobody was hurt. Well, nobody but Waxillium and his guests.

In two quick trips, Waxillium carried the unconscious women out into the back garden—being careful not to be seen. Hopefully, they would soon be discovered by Krent or the constables. After that, Waxillium fetched a pair of revolvers from the closet on the main floor and got a shirt and jacket from the laundry for Wayne. He wished he could look for his old trunk, with his Sterrions, but there wasn't time.

He slipped out the back door and crossed the garden on too-light feet. Each step of the way, he was increasingly bothered by what had happened. It was horrible for someone to try to kill you; it was worse when the attack came from someone you knew.

It seemed implausible that the bandits would have been able to contact and bribe Tillaume so quickly. How could they have even known that an aging butler would be amenable? The groom or gardener would have been a far safer choice. Something more was going on here. From Waxillium's first day in the city, Tillaume had been trying to discourage him from getting involved in local lawkeeping.

On the night before the ball, he'd pointedly tried to get Waxillium to drop the subject of the robberies.

Whoever was behind this, the butler had been working with them for some time. And that meant they'd been watching Waxillium all along.

10

The carriage rattled on the paving stones as it rolled in a cautiously circuitous route toward the Fifth Octant. Marasi looked out at the busy street, her arms folded. Horses and carriages passed, and people flowed down sidewalks like the little blood cells through veins she'd looked at under a microscope at the university. They got clogged at corners or at sections where the paving stones were being replaced.

Lord Waxillium and Wayne sat on the other side of the carriage. Waxillium looked distracted, lost in his thoughts. Wayne was napping, head tipped back, eyes closed. He'd found a hat somewhere—a flimsy cap, of the type broadsheet boys liked to wear. After fleeing the mansion, they'd rounded the street corner and cut through Dampmere Park. On the other side, Waxillium had waved them down a carriage.

By the time they'd piled in, Wayne had been pulling on the cap, whistling softly to himself. She had no idea where he'd gotten it. Now he was snoring softly. After they'd nearly been killed, after he'd had the skin on his back seared off, he was sleeping. She could still smell the pungency of burned cloth, and her ears were ringing.

This was what you wanted, she reminded herself. *You're the one who insisted Lord Harms bring you along to meet Waxillium. You came to the mansion today of your own accord. You put yourself into this.*

If only she'd made a better show of herself. She was riding in a carriage with the greatest lawman that the Roughs had ever known—but at every occasion, she'd proven herself to be a helpless girl, prone to bursts of useless emotion. She started to sigh, but cut herself off. No. No sulking. That would only make things worse.

They were paralleling one of the great spoke-canals that divided the eight parts of the city. She'd seen reproductions of pages from the Words of Founding, which had included drawings and plans for Elendel, though the name of the city had been chosen by the Lord Mistborn. There was a large round park at the center where flowers bloomed year-round, the air warmed by a hot spring underneath. The canal spokes radiated from it, extending out into the bountiful hinterlands, and the river divided around it. Streets and blocks were laid out in an orderly way, with large streets—wider than anyone would once have assumed they'd need. Yet now they almost seemed insufficient.

The carriage was approaching the bridge to the Field of Rebirth; the blanket of green grass and blooming Marewill flowers rose in a gradual hillside slope. The statues of the Last Emperor and the Ascendant Warrior dominated the top, capping their tomb. There was a museum there. Marasi had been there several times as a girl to look at the relics of the World of Ash that had been saved by the Originators, those who had been nurtured in wombs of the earth and reborn to build society.

The carriage turned along the tree-shaded drive around the Field of Rebirth. Asphalt paving was used here instead of stones to quiet the clatter of steel-shod hooves, and also smoothed the way for the occasional motorcar. Those were still rare, but one of her professors claimed that they would eventually replace horses.

She tried to keep her mind on their task. There was more to the Vanishers than just the kidnappings and the robberies. What of the way the trains' cargo disappeared so abruptly, giving the Vanishers their name? And what of the extremely well-made weapons? And then there was the major effort to kill Waxillium, both with poison and that bomb.

"Lord Waxillium?" she said.

"Yes?"

"How did your uncle die?"

"Carriage accident," he said, looking thoughtful. "He, his wife, and my sister were riding in the Outer Estates. This was mere weeks after my cousin—the heir—had succumbed to disease. The trip was supposed to help ease their grief.

"Uncle Ladrian wanted to visit a particular peak to get a view of the landscape, but my aunt was too weak for the hike. They took a carriage. Along the way, the horse bolted. The hitchings snapped. The carriage went off the cliffside."

"I'm sorry."

"I am as well," he said softly. "I hadn't been to see any of them in years. I feel a strange guilt, as if I should be more crushed to lose them."

"I think that story involves enough crushed people already," Wayne murmured.

Waxillium gave him a glare, though Wayne didn't see it, as his eyes were still closed, the cap resting on his face.

Marasi kicked him in the shin, causing him to yelp. Then she blushed. "Be respectful of the dead," she said.

Wayne rubbed his leg. "Already she starts orderin' me around. Women." He put his cap back on his face and settled back.

"Lord Waxillium," she said. "Did you ever wonder if . . ."

"If someone might have killed my uncle?" Waxillium asked. "I am a lawkeeper. I wonder, if just briefly, about *every* death I hear of. But the reports I received indicated nothing suspicious. One of the things I learned early in my career was that sometimes, accidents simply *do* happen. My uncle was a risk taker. His gambling youth led to a middle age where he sought thrills. I eventually dismissed the tragedy as an accident."

"And now?"

"And now," Waxillium said, "I wonder if the reports sent to me were a little *too* clean. In retrospect, everything might have been carefully crafted not to arouse my suspicions. Beyond that, Tillaume was there, though he remained behind at the manor house the day of the accident."

"Why would they kill your uncle?" Marasi asked. "Shouldn't they have been worried about bringing you, an experienced law-keeper, back to town? Removing your uncle and accidentally putting Waxillium Dawnshot onto them . . ."

"Waxillium *Dawnshot*?" Wayne asked, cracking an eye. He sniffled softly and wiped his nose with his handkerchief.

She blushed. "Sorry. But it's what the reports call him."

"That's what they should call me," Wayne said. "I'm the one who likes a good shot of whiskey in the morning."

"'Morning' to you is well past noon, Wayne," Waxillium said. "I doubt you've ever seen the dawn."

"That's right unfair. See it all the time, when I stay up too late. . . ." He grinned underneath his hat. "Wax, when are we going to go see Ranette?"

"We're *not*," Waxillium said. "What makes you think we will?"

"Well, we're in town. She's in town too—moved here before you did, and all. Our house exploded. We could go see her, you know. Be all friendly, like."

"No," Waxillium said. "I wouldn't even know where to find her. The City is a big place."

"She lives over in the Third Octant," Wayne said absently. "Red-brick house. Two stories."

Waxillium gave Wayne a flat stare, which Marasi found curious. "Who is this person?"

"Nobody," Waxillium said. "How are you with a pistol?"

"Not good," she admitted. "The target club uses rifles."

"Well, a rifle doesn't fit in a handbag," Waxillium said, taking a pistol out of his shoulder holster. It was small, with a slim barrel. The entire weapon was only about as long as her hand.

She took the gun hesitantly.

"The trick to shooting with a pistol is to be steady," Waxillium said. "Use both hands, find low cover if you can and set your arms on it. Don't shake, take your time, and be sure to sight. Pistols are much harder to hit with, but that's partially because people tend to be wilder with them. The very nature of a rifle encourages you to take aim, while people's first impulse with a pistol seems to be to just point vaguely and pull the trigger."

"Yes," she said, hefting the gun. It was deceptively heavy. "Eight of ten of constables firing a handgun at a criminal ten feet away miss."

"Really?"

She nodded.

"Well," Waxillium said, "I guess Wayne doesn't need to feel so bad."

"Hey!"

Waxillium eyed her. "I once saw him try to shoot someone three paces away. He ended up hitting the wall *behind* himself."

"'S not my fault," Wayne grumbled. "Bullets are devious buggers. They shouldn't be allowed to bounce. Metal don't bounce, and that's true as titanium."

She checked the small revolver to make sure the safety was on, then tucked it into her singed handbag.

The Vanishers' hideout turned out to be an innocent-looking building near a canal dock. Two stories tall, it was flat-topped and wide, with numerous chimneys. Piles of dark ashes and slag were heaped along one wall of the building, and the windows looked like they hadn't been cleaned since the Final Ascension.

"Lady Marasi," Waxillium asked, checking the sights on his revolver, "would you be terribly offended if I suggested you wait in the carriage while we reconnoiter? The place is likely abandoned, but I wouldn't be surprised to find a few traps left behind."

"No," she said, shivering. "I wouldn't mind. I think that would be just fine."

"I'll wave when we're certain the place is clear," he said, then raised his handgun and nodded to Wayne. They ducked out of the carriage, running in a low squat to the side of the building. They didn't go to the door. Instead, Wayne jumped—and Waxillium must have Pushed him, for the wiry man leaped a good twelve feet and landed on the roof. Waxillium followed, jumping more gracefully, landing without a sound. They moved over to the far corner, where Wayne swung down and kicked in a window. Waxillium swung in after him.

She waited a few tense minutes. The coachman didn't say a word about any of it, though she heard him muttering "none of my business" to himself. Waxillium had paid him enough that he'd better stay quiet.

No gunshots sounded. Eventually, Waxillium opened the door to the building and waved. She hurriedly climbed from the carriage and approached.

"Well?" she asked.

"Two tripwires," Waxillium said, "rigged with explosives. Nothing else dangerous we could find. Other than Wayne's body odor."

"That's the smell of *incredibleness*," Wayne called from inside.

"Come on," Waxillium said, holding the door open for her.

She stepped in, then hesitated in the doorway. "It's empty."

She'd expected forges and equipment. Instead, the cavernous room was vacant, like a classroom during winter holiday. Light shone in through windows, though it was very dim. The chamber smelled of coal and fire, and there were blackened areas on the floor.

"Sleeping quarters up there," Waxillium said, pointing at the other side of the foundry. "The main chamber here is double height for half the building, but the other side has a second story. Looked like they could house some fifty men in there, men who could act like foundry workers during the days to maintain the front."

"Aha!" Wayne said from the darkness on the left side of the chamber. She heard a rattling, then light flooded the room as he pushed back the wall. It opened there, rolling to give large-scale access to the canal.

"How easily did that open?" Waxillium asked, trotting over. Marasi followed.

"I dunno," Wayne said, shrugging. "Easy enough."

Waxillium inspected the door. It slid on wheels in a small channel cut into the floor. He rubbed his fingers in the trench and brought them out, rubbing grease between them.

"They've been using it," Marasi said.

"Exactly," Waxillium said.

"So?" Wayne asked.

"If they were doing illegal things in here," Marasi said, "they wouldn't be wanting to open the entire side of the building with any frequency."

"Maybe they did it to keep up the act," Waxillium said, rising.

Marasi nodded, thoughtful. "Oh! Aluminum."

Wayne pulled out his dueling canes, spinning. "What? Where? Who's shooting?"

Marasi felt herself blush. "Sorry. I meant, we should check and see if we can find any aluminum droplets on the ground. You know, from forging or casting guns. That will tell us if this place is *really* the hideout, or if Wayne's source was trying to lead us to a bad alloy."

"He was honest," Wayne said. "I got a sense for that sort of thing." He sneezed.

"You believed that Lessie really was a dancer, the first time we met her," Waxillium said, rising.

"That's different. She was a woman. Good at lying, they are. The God Beyond made'm that way."

"I'm . . . not certain how I should take that," Marasi said.

"With a pinch of copper," Waxillium said. "And a healthy dose of skepticism. Just like anything Wayne says." He held out his hand.

Marasi frowned, raising her palm. He dropped something into it. Some bits of metal that looked like they'd been scraped off the floor, where they'd cooled. They were silvery, light, and dirty black around the edges.

"I found them on the floor over there," Waxillium said. "Near one of the blackened sections."

"Aluminum?" she asked eagerly.

"Yes," he said. "At least, I can't Push them with Allomancy, which along with their appearance is sufficient indication." He studied her. "You've got a good mind for this sort of thing."

She blushed. *Again. Rust and Ruin!* she thought. *I'm going to have to find a way to deal with that.* "It's about deviations, Lord Waxillium."

"Deviations?"

"Numbers, patterns, movements. People seem erratic, but they actually follow patterns. Find the deviations, isolate the reason why they deviated, and you'll often learn something. Aluminum on the floor. It's a deviation."

"And are there others, here?"

"The opening door," she said, nodding to the side. "Those windows. They're smeared with too much soot. If I were to guess, it was put there by burning a candle close to the glass to blacken it so nobody could peek in."

"Maybe it was natural," Waxillium said. "From forging."

"Why would the windows be *closed* during the heat of forging? Those windows can open easily, and they open outward—so there wouldn't be any soot on them. Not so much, at least. Either they left them closed while working in order to hide what was in here, or they darkened them intentionally."

"Clever," Waxillium said.

"So the question is," she said, "what have they been moving in and out of the building through that large side door? Something important enough that they'd open it, even after going through so much trouble with the windows."

"That part, at least, is easy," Waxillium said. "They've been robbing freight cars, so they've been moving the cargo in."

"Which implies they've been shipping it after stealing it . . ." Marasi said.

"Which gives us a lead," Waxillium said with a nod. "They've been moving things in and out of this location via the canals. In fact, the canals might be connected to how they're getting the cargo out of the railway cars so easily." He strode away toward the door.

"Where are you going?" she asked.

"I'm going to go sniff around outside," he said. "You two go look through the sleeping quarters. Tell me if you see any . . . deviations, as you put it." He hesitated. "Let Wayne go in first. We might have missed a trap or two. Better for him to explode than you."

"Hey!" Wayne said.

"I mean it with all fondness," Waxillium said, slipping out through the open side of the building. Then he leaned back in. "And maybe it will blow your face off, and spare us having to look at that mug of yours." With that, he left.

Wayne smiled. "Damn. Sure is good to see him acting more like himself again."

"So he wasn't always so solemn?"

"Oh, Wax has always been solemn," Wayne said, wiping his nose with his handkerchief. "But when he's at his best, there's a smirk underneath. C'mon."

He led her to the back part of the building. There was a small box by the wall, the explosives they had discovered and disarmed, she assumed. The ceiling was lower here. Wayne climbed up a stairwell, gesturing for her to wait.

She poked around, looking for anything that had been discarded, but succeeded only in making herself jump a few times when she thought she saw something from the corner of her eye. This side of the chamber was very dim.

Was Wayne taking too long? She fidgeted, then finally decided to climb the stairwell.

It was *dark* inside. Not pitch dark, just dark enough that she thought she should be able to see what she was doing—but couldn't. She hesitated halfway up the stairs, then decided she was a fool and pushed forward.

"Wayne?" she said, nervous as she peeked out of the stairwell. The upper floor was lit by a few windows, darkened by soot, despite being in an area where there would be no forging or casting. That reinforced her theory. And her nervousness.

"He is dead, young lady," an aged, distinguished voice said from the darkness. "I am sorry for your loss."

Her heart just about stopped.

"Yes," the voice continued, "he was simply too handsome, too clever, and too immensely remarkable in all aspects of his existence to allow to live." Someone pushed open a window, letting in light and revealing Wayne's face. "I'm afraid it took a hundred men to bring him down, and he killed all but one. His last words were, 'Tell Wax . . . that he's a total git . . . and he still owes me five notes.'"

"*Wayne,*" she hissed.

"Couldn't help myself, mate," he said, switching back to his own voice, which was completely different. "Sorry. But you shouldn't have come up here." He nodded to the corner, where a few sticks of something lay against the wall.

"More explosives?" she said, feeling faint.

"Yeah. We missed them on the first pass. Were rigged to blow when the latch was opened on a chest in the corner."

"Was there anything *in* the chest?"

"Yeah. Explosives. Weren't you listening?"

She gave him a flat stare.

"No," he said, chuckling. "I don't know what Wax expects us to find in this place. Swept it clean, they did."

By the light of the open window, she could make out a low-ceilinged room. Well, more of a loft. She and Wayne could walk in it without bending over, but him just barely. Waxillium would have to stoop.

The floorboards were warped and there were nails sticking out in places. She had images of prying one up and finding some stash of hidden clues, but as she felt across the floor, she realized she could see between the boards to the floor below. There wasn't really any space for hiding things.

Wayne poked through some cupboards built into the wall, checking for explosives, then knocking for hidden compartments. Marasi looked around, but quickly determined that there wasn't anything to find here. Other than, perhaps, the explosives.

Explosives.

"Wayne, what kind of explosives are those?"

"Hum? Oh, ordinary stuff. They call it dynamite, used for blowing holes in rock out in the Roughs. Pretty easy to get, even in the city. These are smaller sticks than I've seen, but basically the same stuff."

"Oh." She frowned. "Were they in anything?"

He hesitated, then looked back at the trunk. "Huh." He reached in and held up something. "They weren't *in* anything, but someone used this to prop up the fuse and the detonator."

"What is it?" she asked, hurrying over.

"Cigar box," he said, letting her see it. "Citizen Magistrates. Expensive brand. Very expensive."

She looked over the box. The top was painted gold and red, with the brand splayed across in large letters. There weren't any cigars left, though it *did* look like some numbers had been scribbled across the inside of the lid in pencil. The sequence didn't make any sense to her.

"We'll show it to Wax," Wayne said. "This is just the sort of thing he likes. It'll probably lead him to some grand theory about how our boss smokes cigars, and that'll somehow let him pick the guy out of a crowd. He's always doing stuff like that, ever since we started working together." Wayne smiled, taking the cigar box back, then returned to poking around the cupboards.

"Wayne," Marasi said. "How *did* you end up with Waxillium, anyway?"

"That wasn't in your reports?" he asked, knocking at the side of a cupboard.

"No. It's considered a bit of a mystery."

"We don't talk about it much," Wayne said, voice muffled, head inside the cupboard. "He saved my life."

She smiled, sitting down on the floor, resting her back against the wall. "That's probably a good story."

"It's not what you're thinking," he said, pulling his head out. "I was to be hanged over in Far Dorest, by the lawkeeper there."

"Wrongfully, I assume?"

"Depends on your definition of that particular word and all," Wayne said. "I shot a man. Innocent one."

"Was it an accident?"

"Yeah," Wayne said. "I only meant to rob him." He paused, looking at the cupboard, seeming distant. He shook his head, then crawled inside, pushing hard and breaking in the back wall.

That wasn't what she'd expected to hear. She sat back, hands around her legs. "You were a criminal?"

"Not a very capable one," Wayne said from inside the cupboard. "I've always had a problem not taking things. I just grab stuff, you know? And then it's there, in my fingers. Anyway, I was getting good at it, and I had some friends . . . they convinced me that I should go a little farther. Really take hold of my destiny, they said. Start going for coin, get into robbing with guns and the like. So I tried it out. Left a man dead. Father of three."

He pulled out of the broken cupboard, then held something up. It looked like cards of some sort.

"Clues?" she asked eagerly.

"Nudes," he said, flipping through them. "Old ones. Probably from before our bandits bought this place." He flipped through a few more, then tossed them back into the hole. "At least it will give the conners something fun to find." He looked back at her, seeming . . . haunted, his eyes lying in shadow, face lit on one side by the open window.

"So what happened?" she asked softly. "With you, I mean. Unless you don't want to tell."

He shrugged. "I didn't really know what I was doing, and I panicked. I think maybe I wanted to be caught. Never wanted to shoot that bloke. Just wanted his purse, you know? Old Deadfinger caught me easy. He didn't even have to beat a confession out of me." Wayne was quiet for a moment. "I cried the whole time. I was sixteen. Just a kid."

"Did you know you were an Allomancer?" she asked.

"Sure. That was kinda why I was in the Roughs in the first place, but that's another story. Anyway, bendalloy is hard to make.

Bismuth and cadmium aren't the kinds of metals you find in your corner store. Didn't know much about Feruchemy yet, though my father was a Feruchemist, so I had an idea. But storing health, it takes gold."

He walked over, sitting down on the floor beside her. "Still don't know why Wax saved me. I shoulda hanged, you know. Killed a good man. He wasn't even rich. He was a bookkeeper. Did charity work for anyone who needed it—wills drawn up, letters read. Every week, he transcribed letters for the mine workers who couldn't write, so they could send them home to their families in the city. Found out a lot about him in the trial, you see. Got to see his kids crying. And his wife . . ."

Wayne reached into his pocket, then unfolded something. A sheet of paper. "Got a letter from them a few months back."

"They write you *letters?*" Marasi said.

"Sure. I send them half of what I make. Keeps the kids fed, you know. Figure it makes sense, seein' as to how I killed their daddy. One went to university." He hesitated. "They still hate me. Write me the letters to let me know they haven't forgiven me, that no money will bring back their daddy. They're right. But they do take the money, so that's something."

"Wayne . . ." Marasi said. "I'm so sorry."

"Yeah. Me too. Some mistakes, though, you can't fix by being sorry. Can't fix them, no matter what you do. Guns and me, we haven't gotten along ever since. My hand starts shaking when I hold one, wobbling about like a damn fish dumped on the docks. Ain't that the funniest thing? Like my hand thinks by itself."

The sound of footsteps came from the stairwell and a few moments later Waxillium walked in. He raised an eyebrow at the two of them sitting there on the floor.

"See now," Wayne said. "We're having a heart-to-heart, here. Don't go stomping in and making a mess of things."

"I wouldn't dream of it," Waxillium said. "I spoke with the local beggars. The Vanishers *have* been moving something large in and out of the building and onto a canal boat. They did it on several occasions, always at night. It seems to have been bigger than just cargo; some kind of machinery, I suspect."

"Huh," Wayne said.

"Huh indeed," Waxillium said. "You?"

"Found a box," Wayne said, holding out the cigar box. "Oh, and some more dynamite. In case you want to blast out a new canal or something."

"Bring it," Waxillium said. "Might be useful." He took the cigar box.

"There's some nudie pictures too," Wayne noted, pointing at the cupboard. "They're so faded you can barely make out the good parts, though." He hesitated. "The ladies ain't wearing any guns, so you probably wouldn't be interested anyway."

Waxillium snorted.

"The cigar box is of an expensive variety," Marasi said, standing up. "Unlikely to be from one of the common thieves, unless they took it from someone. But look. Someone wrote some numbers on the inside."

"Indeed," Waxillium said. He narrowed his eyes, then looked at Wayne, who nodded.

"What?" she said. "You know something?"

Waxillium tossed the box back to Wayne, who tucked it away inside the pocket of his coat. It was large enough that it hung out. "Have you ever heard the name Miles Dagouter?"

"Sure," she said. "Miles Hundredlives. He's a lawkeeper, out in the Roughs."

"Yes," Waxillium said somberly. "Come on. I think it's time for us to take a trip. While we go, I'll tell you a few stories."

11

M iles stood by the railing and lit his cigar. He puffed on it a few times to get it going, then slowly released a stream of pungent smoke from between his lips.

"They've been spotted, boss," Tarson said as he walked up. Tarson's arm was in a sling; most men would still be in bed after taking a shot like he had. But Tarson was a Pewterarm and koloss-blooded. He'd heal quickly.

"Where?" Miles asked, looking down and surveying the setup of the new hideout. Besides Tarson, the only one up here with him was Clamps, third-in-command.

"They're at the old foundry," Tarson said. He was still wearing Wayne's hat. "Were talking to the beggars there."

"Should have dumped the lot of them in the canal," Clamps grumbled, scratching at the scar on his neck.

"I'm not going to start killing beggars, Clamps," Miles said softly. He wore a pair of aluminum revolvers; they gleamed in the electric lights of the large chamber. "You'd be surprised at how quickly something like that can backfire; turn the city's underclass against us, and all *kinds* of inconvenient information will find its way to the constables."

"Yeah, sure," Clamps said. "Of course. But, I mean, those beggars . . . they saw things, boss."

"Wax would have figured it out regardless," Miles said. "He is like a rat. Wherever you least wish him to be, there you will find him. In a way, that makes him predictable. I assume your explosive traps—foolproof though you promised they would be—were ineffective?"

Clamps coughed into his hand.

"Pity," Miles said. He took his silver lighter, still in his hand from lighting the cigar, and put it back in his pocket. It bore the seal of the lawkeepers of True Madil. It made the other men uncomfortable to see that. Miles kept it anyway.

The space before them was completely windowless. Big, glaring electric lights hung from the ceiling, and men were setting up forging and casting equipment. Miles was skeptical. A foundry below the ground? But Mister Suit promised that his ducts and electric fans would pull the smoke away and circulate the air. It helped that there was a lot less smoke with the electric furnaces they'd be using down here.

This room was very curious. A large tunnel led off into darkness on the left side of the chamber, and railway tracks were set into it. The beginnings, Mister Suit said, of an *underground* railway line in the city. How would it cut through the canals? It would have to run under them, he guessed. A strange image.

As of now, that tunnel was only a test. It led a short distance to a large wooden building, where Miles could quarter the rest of his men. He had another thirty or so. At the moment, they were bringing in boxes of supplies and what was left of their aluminum. There wasn't much. In one blow, Wax had all but upended the Vanishers.

Miles puffed on his cigar, thoughtful. As always, he was drawing upon his goldmind, invigorating himself, refreshing his body. He never felt sick, never lacked energy. He still had to sleep, and he still grew old, but other than that, he was practically immortal. So long as he had enough gold.

That was the problem though, wasn't it? Smoke curled in front of him, twisting upon itself like the mists.

"Boss?" Clamps asked. "Mister Suit is waiting. Aren't you going to go meet with him?"

Miles blew out smoke. "In a moment." Suit did *not* own him. "How is recruitment, Clamps?"

"It's . . . I'll need more time. One day ain't enough, 'specially following half of us getting slaughtered."

"Watch your tone," Miles said.

"Sorry."

"Wax was bound to enter the game eventually," Miles said softly. "He changes the rules, and it is true that we lost far more men than I would have liked. We are fortunate at the same time, however. Now that Waxillium has entered, we can anticipate him."

"Boss," Tarson said, leaning in, "there's talk among the men. That you and Wax . . . that you two set us all up." He cringed back, as if expecting a violent reaction.

Miles puffed on his cigar, and managed to contain his initial burst of anger. He was getting better at that. A little. "Why would they say that?"

"You were once a lawkeeper, and all . . ."

"I still am," Miles said. "What we do, it is not outside the law. Not the *true* law. Oh, the rich will make their own codes, will force us to live by them. But our law is the law of humanity itself.

"Men who work for me, they are given the dispensation of reform. Their work here washes away their previous . . . infractions. Tell them I am proud of them, Clamps. I realize we've been through something traumatic, but we did survive. We will face tomorrow with greater strength."

"I'll tell 'em, boss," Clamps said.

Miles covered a grimace. He couldn't decide if the words were the right ones or not; he wasn't meant for preaching. But the men needed conviction from him, so conviction he would display. "Fifteen years," he said softly.

"Boss?"

"Fifteen years I spent out in the Roughs, trying to protect the weak. And you know what? It never got better. All that effort, it meant nothing. Children still died, women were still abused. One man wasn't enough to change things, not with the corruption here at the heart of civilization." He took a puff on his cigar. "If we're going to change things, we need to change them here, first."

And Trell help me if I'm wrong. Why had Trell made men like him, if not to see wrongs righted? The Words of Founding had even included a lengthy explanation of Trellism and its teachings, which proved men like Miles were special.

He turned and moved along the walkway. It hung like a balcony on the north side of the large chamber. Tarson and Clamps stayed behind; they knew he liked to be alone when he faced Mister Suit.

Miles pulled open the door at the end of the walk, and entered Mister Suit's office. Why he needed an office here, Miles didn't know; perhaps he'd be keeping a closer eye on operations at this new base. Mister Suit had wanted them here from the beginning. It annoyed Miles that he'd finally had to accept the offer—it put him more closely under his backer's thumb.

Enough good robberies, and we won't need him any longer, Miles told himself. *Then we can move somewhere else.*

Mister Suit was a round-faced man with a full gray-streaked beard. He sat at his desk sipping a cup of tea and wearing an extremely stylish and expensive suit of black silk with a turquoise vest. As Miles entered, he was studying a broadsheet.

"You know I don't like the smell of those," Mister Suit said without looking up.

Miles puffed his cigar anyway.

Mister Suit smiled. "Did I hear that your old friend has *already* located your previous base of operations?"

"Men were captured," Miles said simply. "It was only a matter of time."

"They aren't very loyal to your cause."

Miles had no response to that. They both knew that most of his men worked for the money, and not for any greater purpose.

"Do you know why I like you, Miles?" Mister Suit asked.

I don't particularly care if you do or not, Miles thought, but held his tongue.

"You're careful," Mister Suit continued. "You have a goal, you believe in it, but you don't let it cloud your vision. In fact, your cause is not so different from that of my associates and me. I think it is a worthy goal, and you a worthy leader." Mister Suit turned over his broadsheet. "The shootings at the last robbery threaten to undermine my confidence in that assessment."

"I . . ."

"You lost your temper," Mister Suit said, voice growing cold, "and you therefore lost control of your men. *That* is why this disaster occurred. There was no other reason."

"Yes there was. Waxillium Ladrian."

"You should have been ready for him."

"He wasn't supposed to be there."

Mister Suit sipped his tea. "Come now, Miles. You wore a mask on your face. You knew there was a chance he'd come."

"I wore a mask," Miles said, keeping his temper with some effort, "because I am a man of some renown. Wax wasn't the only one who could have recognized me."

"A valid point, I suppose. But then, with how dramatic you insist on being—cargo that vanishes, rather than just being stolen, it makes me wonder why you avoid being recognized."

"The drama serves a purpose," Miles snapped. "I've told you. So long as the police are baffled by how we're getting the cargo, it will keep them making mistakes."

"And the drama?" Suit said idly, turning over a newspaper on his desk. "The 'Vanishers,' Miles?"

He said nothing. He'd explained his reasons before, the ones he let Suit know of. There was more to it, of course. He needed to be dramatic, needed to capture the public's attention. Miles was out to change the world. You couldn't do that if people thought of you as common thieves. Mystery, power, a pinch of magic . . . that could work wonders for his cause.

"No comment," Suit said. "Well, your reasoning has proven valid in the past. Except when it comes to Waxillium. I'll admit, Miles, that part of me wonders. Is there some ancient grudge between the two of you I should be aware of? Something that, perhaps, would have caused you to act recklessly?" Mister Suit's eyes were as cold as iron. "Something that would have made you try to *goad* him into attacking during that party? So you could fight him?"

Miles held that gaze, then leaned down, hands on the table, fingers gripping his cigar. "I have no grudge against Waxillium Ladrian. He is one of the finest men this world has known. A finer man than you or I, or practically anyone else in this city."

"And this is supposed to comfort me? You all but say that you won't fight him."

"Oh, I'll fight him. Kill him, if I have to. Wax chose the wrong side. Men like him, men like me, we have a choice. Serve the people or serve the wealthy. He abandoned his right to protection the moment he returned to this city and started mingling with them."

"Curious," Suit said. "I'm also one of *them*, you know."

"I work with what I have. And besides, you have . . . other things recommending you. Especially since you did renounce your claim to privilege."

"Not to privilege," Suit said. "Merely to title. And I still think you intended to provoke Waxillium. That's why you shot Peterus."

"I shot Peterus because he was an impostor," Miles snapped. "He pretended to seek justice, and everyone praised him for it, but all the while he was pandering to the elite and the corrupt. In the end, they let him come play at their parties, like a favored dog. I put him down."

Mister Suit nodded slowly. "Very well."

"I *will* clean this city up, Suit. Even if I have to rip out its blackened heart with my fingernails, I'll do it. But you're going to need to get me more aluminum."

"I am setting things in motion," Suit said. He opened a drawer in his desk and took out a rolled sheet of paper. He set it in front of Miles.

Miles took off the string and unrolled the paper. Schematics. "Tekiel's new 'unrobbable' freight car?"

Suit nodded.

"It will take time to—" Miles began.

"I've had people working on this for some time now. Your job is not the planning, Miles. Your job is the execution. I will see that you have the resources you need."

Miles looked over the blueprint. Suit was connected. Powerful. Miles couldn't help feeling that he'd gotten himself entangled in something far beyond his control. "My men are still holding the latest captive," he said. "What do you want done with her?"

"That will be arranged," Suit said. He took a sip of his tea. "If I had been paying closer attention, I would have removed that one from the list. Waxillium will not stop seeking her. It would have been so much easier if the explosion had worked. Now we must contemplate more direct action."

"I'll deal with him personally," Miles said. "Today."

"Miles Dagouter is Twinborn," Waxillium said, leaning forward in their train car. "A particularly dangerous variety of Twinborn."

"Double gold," Wayne said with a nod, reclining on the cushioned bench opposite Waxillium. Outside, the outer suburbs of Elendel passed in a blur.

Marasi sat on the bench near Wayne. "Gold Allomancers aren't particularly dangerous, from what I've read."

"No," Waxillium said. "They aren't. But it's the Compounding that makes Miles so powerful. If your Allomancy and Feruchemy share a metal, you can access its power tenfold. It's complicated. You store an attribute inside the metal, then *burn* it to release the power. It's called Compounding. By the legends, it's the way the Sliver gained immortality."

Marasi frowned. "I'd assumed stories of Miles's extraordinary healing abilities to be exaggerations. I assumed he was just a Bloodmaker, like Wayne."

"Oh, he's a Bloodmaker all right," Wayne said, spinning a dueling cane around his wrist and catching it again. "Except *he* doesn't ever run out of health."

Waxillium nodded, thinking back to years ago, when he'd first met Miles. The man had always made him uncomfortable, but he'd also been an excellent lawkeeper. For the most part.

Noting Marasi's confused look, Waxillium explained, "Normally a Feruchemist has to be sparing. It can take months to store up health or weight. I've been walking around at half weight since breaking us through the floor, trying to recover some of what I expended. I've barely filled my metalmind to a fraction of what I lost. It's even harder for Wayne."

Wayne wiped his nose. "I'll have to spend a few weeks in bed after this, feeling wretched. Otherwise, I'll be unable to heal myself. Hell, I'm already storing as much as I can and still move about normally. By the end of the day, I'll barely have enough to heal a scratch."

"But Miles . . ." Marasi said.

"Near-infinite healing ability," Waxillium said. "The man's virtually immortal. I heard he once took a shotgun blast to the face point-blank and walked away from it. We worked together out in the Roughs. He was the lawkeeper over in True Madil. There were three of us that had a kind of alliance going, during the good years. Miles, me, and Jon Deadfinger from Far Dorest."

"Miles doesn't like me much," Wayne noted. "Well . . . neither of them do, actually."

"Miles did good work," Waxillium said. "But he was judgmental and harsh. We respected one another, though mostly from a distance. I wouldn't call us friends. But out in the Roughs, anyone who stands up for what is right is an ally."

"It's the first law of the Roughs," Wayne said. "The more alone you are, the more you need a man you can trust at your side."

"Even if their methods go beyond what you'd choose yourself," Waxillium said.

"He doesn't sound like the type to take up a life of crime," Marasi said.

"No," Waxillium said softly. "He doesn't. But I was almost certain it was him behind the mask at the wedding, and that box of cigars, they're his favorites. I can't be sure it's him, but . . ."

"But you think it is."

Waxillium nodded. *Harmony helps us, but I do.* Lawkeepers were a special alloy. There was a code. Never give in, never let yourself be tempted. Working with criminals day in, day out could change a man. You began to see things the way they did. You started to think like them.

They all knew this job could twist you if you weren't careful. They didn't speak of it, and they didn't give in. Or they weren't supposed to.

"I'm not surprised," Wayne said. "Did you ever hear how he spoke of people in Elendel, Wax? He's a brutal man, Miles is."

"Yes," Waxillium said softly. "I hoped he'd stay focused on keeping order in his town and let his demons slumber."

The train passed beyond the suburbs, heading into the Outer Estates—the broad ring of orchards, fields, and pastures that fed Elendel. The landscape changed from city blocks to open expanses of tan and green, the canals shimmering blue as they cut the land.

"Does this change things?" Marasi asked.

"Yes," Waxillium said. "It means all this is far more dangerous than I'd thought."

"Delightful."

Wayne grinned. "Well, we wanted you to have the full experience. You know, for science and all."

"Actually," Waxillium said, "I've been thinking of how best to send you someplace safe."

"You want to be rid of me?" she asked. She widened her eyes to look heartbroken, her voice softening in a pitiful kind of betrayed way. He was half tempted to think she'd been learning from Wayne. "I thought I was being of help to you."

"You are," Waxillium said. "But you also have little practical experience in what we are doing."

"A woman must gain experience somehow," she said, lifting her head. "I've already survived a kidnapping and an assassination attempt."

The doors of the passenger car rattled as they rounded a bend. "Yes, but Lady Marasi, the presence of a Twinborn on the other side changes things. If it comes to a fight, I don't think I can defeat Miles. He's crafty, powerful, and determined. I'd rather you were somewhere safe."

"Where?" she asked. "Any of your estates would be obvious, as would those of my father. I can't very well hide in the underground of the city; I *highly* doubt I'd be inconspicuous there! I hasten to suggest that the safest place for me is near you."

"Odd," Wayne said, "I usually find the safest places in life are everywhere *but* near Wax. Have I mentioned the likelihood of explosions?"

"Perhaps we should just go to the constables," Marasi said. "Lord Waxillium . . . this kind of private investigation is technically illegal—at least insofar as we have important facts that the constables don't. We are required to bring what we know to the authorities."

"Don't get him thinking!" Wayne said. "I was just starting to get him to stop saying stuff like that!"

"It's all right, Wayne," Waxillium said softly. "I've made a promise. I told Lord Harms I'd return Steris to him. And I will. That is that."

"Then I will remain and help," Marasi said. "That is that."

"And I could really use some food," Wayne added. "Fat is fat."

"Wayne . . ." Waxillium said.

"I'm serious," Wayne said. "Ain't had nothing to eat since those scones."

"We'll get something at our stop," Waxillium said. "First, I would like to know something from Lady Marasi."

"Yes?"

"Well, assuming you are to remain with us, I'd like to know what kind of Allomancer you are."

Wayne sat up with a start. "Huh?"

Marasi blushed.

"You carry a pouch of metal shavings in your handbag," Waxillium said. "And you are always anxious to keep the handbag close. You know little about Feruchemy, but seem to understand Allomancy. You weren't surprised when Wayne stopped time in a bubble around us—in fact, you stepped right up to the barrier, as if familiar with them. And you come from a hereditary line that is being hunted precisely because it includes a lot of Allomancers."

"I . . ." she said. "Well, there really wasn't a good opportunity . . ." She blushed more furiously.

"I'm surprised, and a little disappointed," Wayne said.

"Well," she said quickly, "I—"

"Oh, not at you," Wayne said. "At Wax. I'd have expected that he'd put this sort of thing together on your first meeting."

"I'm growing slow in my old age," Waxillium said dryly.

"It's not really very useful," she said, looking down. "When I saw Wayne using his Slider ability, I started to get self-conscious. You see, I'm a Pulser."

As he'd suspected. "I think that could be very useful."

"Not really," she said. "Speeding up time . . . that is amazing. But what can one do with slowing it down, and only for myself? It's useless in a fight. Everyone else would move with great speed around me. My father was ashamed of the power. Told me to keep it quiet, much like my parentage."

"Your father," Waxillium said, "is someone that I'm increasingly certain is a fool. You have access to something useful. No, it won't fit every situation, but no tool does."

"If you say so," she said.

A merchant came down the train aisle, selling pretzels, and Wayne all but leaped out of his chair to get one. Waxillium settled back, looking out the window, thinking.

Miles. No, he couldn't be sure it was him. When Waxillium had shot the Vanisher boss in the face and dropped him, he'd assumed that he'd mistaken the voice. Miles wouldn't drop to a gunshot.

Unless he'd known that he had to feign a wound, lest Waxillium recognize him. Miles was crafty enough for something like that.

It is him, Waxillium thought. He'd known it from the first time the Vanisher boss had spoken. He just hadn't wanted to admit it.

This complicated things immensely. And, oddly, Waxillium found himself feeling overwhelmed. Twenty years as a lawkeeper, and this situation was already messier than any he'd investigated. He'd assumed that the Roughs made him strong, but there'd also been a simplicity to life out there, a simplicity he'd gotten used to.

Now he came charging in, guns raised, assuming he could handle a problem built on Elendel's scale. He assumed he could take down a team that was so well funded it could field men with guns made of something so expensive it might as well have been gold.

Maybe we should take it to the constables, Marasi had said. But could he?

He fingered the earring in his pocket. He'd felt that Harmony wanted him to do this, to investigate. But what was Harmony but an impression in Waxillium's mind? Confirmation bias, they called it. He felt what he expected to. That was what his logical brain said.

I wish I could feel the mists, he thought. *It's been weeks since I've been able to go out in them.* He always felt stronger in the mists. He felt like someone was watching, when he was out in them.

I have to continue with this, he told himself. He'd tried abstaining, and it had led to Lord Peterus being shot. Waxillium's usual method was to just take command and do what needed to be done. It was the way a lawman learned to work, out in the Roughs. *We aren't so different, Miles and I,* he thought. Perhaps that was what had always frightened him so much about the man.

The train slowed, pulling into their station.

12

Wayne stepped out of the carriage, following Waxillium and Marasi. He looked up to the carriage man, tossing him a coin. "We'll need you to wait a spell, mate. I trust it won't be a problem."

The carriage man looked at the coin and raised an eyebrow. "No problem at all, mate."

"That's quite the hat," Wayne said.

The carriage man wore a round cap of stiff felt, conical, but with a flat top and a feather on it. "We all wear 'em," he said. "Mark of Gavil's Carriages, you see."

"Huh. Wanna trade?"

"What? Trade hats?"

"Sure," Wayne said, tossing up his flimsy knit cap.

The man caught it. "I'm not sure . . ."

"I'll throw in a pretzel," Wayne said, fishing it out of his pocket.

"Er . . ." The man looked down at the coin in his hand, which was quite substantial. He pulled off his cap and tossed it down to Wayne. "No need. I guess . . . I'll just buy another."

"Mighty nice of you," Wayne said, taking a bite from the pretzel as he sauntered after Waxillium. He put the cap on. It wasn't a terribly good fit.

He hurried to catch up to the other two, who had stopped on a small hill. Wayne breathed in, smelling the humidity of the canal, the scents of wheat in the fields and flowers at their feet. Then he sneezed. He hated filling his metalmind when he was out doing stuff. He preferred to fill it in large chunks. That made him very sick, but he could sleep it off and drink a lot to pass the time.

This was worse. Filling his metalmind as much as he dared, storing up health as they went about, meant he got sick. Fast. He sneezed a lot more, his throat grew sore, and his eyes watered. He felt tired and groggy, too. But he'd need that health, so he did it.

He walked across the grass. The Outer Estates were an odd place. The Roughs were dry and dirty. The City was densely populated and—in places—grimy. Out here, things were just . . . nice.

A little too nice. Made his shoulders itch. This was the kind of place where a man would work in the field during the day, then go home and sit on his porch, drinking lemonade and petting his dog. Men died of boredom in places like that.

Odd, that in a place so open, he could feel even more anxious and confined than when locked in a cell.

"The last railway robbery happened here," Waxillium said. He held out his hand to the tracks—which rounded a bend just to their left—then moved his hand along their path, as if seeing something Wayne wasn't. He often did things like that.

Wayne yawned, then took another bite of his pretzel. "What whasdat, sir? What whazzat sir? What whassat, sir?"

"Wayne, what are you babbling about?" Waxillium turned, inspecting the canal to the right. It was wide and deep here, intended for carrying barges full of food into the city.

"Practicing my pretzel guy," Wayne said. "He had a great accent. Must have been from one of the new rim towns, right by the southern mountains."

Waxillium glanced at him. "That hat looks ridiculous."

"Fortunately, I can change hats," Wayne said in the pretzel-guy accent, "while you, sir, are stuck with that face."

"You two sound a lot like siblings," Marasi said, watching curiously. "Do you realize that?"

"So long as I'm the handsome one," Wayne said.

"The tracks here bend toward the canal," Waxillium said. "The other robberies all happened near canals as well."

"As I recall," Marasi noted, "most of the railway lines parallel the canals. The canals were here first, and when the tracks were laid, it made sense to follow the established paths."

"Yes," Waxillium said. "But it's especially striking here. Look how close the tracks get to the canal."

His accent is changing, Wayne thought. *Only six months back in the city, and it already shows. It's more refined in some ways, less formal in others.* Did people see how their voices were like living things? Move a plant, and it would change and adapt to the environment around it. Move a person, and the way they talked would grow, adapt, evolve.

"So that machinery the Vanishers are using," Marasi said, "you're thinking they can't move it far on land? They have to ship it up the canal, and pick a place near the tracks to set it up and carry out their robbery?"

Her accent . . . Wayne thought. *She uses more elevated diction around him than around me.* She tried so hard to impress Wax. Did he see it? Probably not. The man had always been oblivious about women. Even Lessie.

"Yes," Waxillium said, hiking down the hillside. "The question is, how did this thing—whatever it is—empty the freight cars so quickly and efficiently?"

"Why is that so odd?" Wayne said, following him. "If I'd been a Vanisher, I'd have brought a whole heap of men. That would let me finish the work faster."

"This isn't a question of simple manpower," Waxillium said. "The train cars were locked, and some of the later ones had guards inside. When the cars arrived at their destination, they were still locked, but empty. Beyond that, from one of the cars, many heavy ingots of iron were stolen. There's a bottleneck at the car door—beyond a certain point, more men wouldn't have helped. There is no way they unloaded hundreds of ingots in under five minutes using just manpower."

"A speed bubble?" Marasi asked.

"Could have helped," Wax said, "but not much. You'd have the same bottleneck, and you can't fit many people in a speed bubble. Let's say you could have six workers inside, which would be really tight. They'd have to move the iron ingots up to the edge of the speed bubble, then drop the bubble and create another—you can't move the bubbles once they're up—and repeat."

Wax shook his head, hands on hips. "The cost in bendalloy would be incredible. With one nugget worth about five hundred notes, Wayne can compress about two minutes into fifteen external seconds. To compress time equal to five minutes on the outside—gaining you enough time on the inside to move all of those iron bars—you'd need to spend *ten thousand* notes. The bars would be worth just a fraction of that; Harmony, you could buy your own *train* for that kind of money. I don't believe it. Something else is happening here."

"Machinery of some sort," Marasi said.

Wax nodded, walking down the hillside, scanning the ground. "Let's see if we can find any traces they may have left behind. Maybe the machinery had wheels that left ruts or tracks."

Wayne shoved his hands in his pockets and walked about, making a show of looking, but the whole reason he'd come to get Waxillium involved in this investigation was because he was good at this kind of stuff. If there were people involved, Wayne was quite handy. But flowers and dirt . . . not so much.

After a few minutes, Wayne was bored, so he wandered over to where Marasi was looking. She glanced at him. "I do have to say, Wayne . . . that hat *does not* fit you very well."

"Yeah. I just want to keep reminding Wax he owes me a new one."

"Why? You were the one who let the man take your old one from you."

"He convinced me not to fight back," Wayne grumbled. Seemed obvious to him. "And then, he *shot* the guy wearing it, and the guy walked away!"

"He couldn't have known the man would survive."

"He shoulda grabbed my hat," Wayne said.

She smiled, looking bemused.

Most people, they didn't understand hats, and Wayne didn't really blame them. Until you'd had a good, lucky hat, you wouldn't understand the value of it. "It's actually all right," Wayne said softly, kicking around in the weeds. "But don't tell Wax."

"What?"

"I *needed* to lose that hat," Wayne admitted. "Otherwise, it would have been blown up in the explosion, see? It was lucky it got stolen. It could have ended up like my duster."

"You're a very unique individual, Wayne."

"Technically, we all are," he said. Then he hesitated. "Except for twins, I guess. Anyway, there's something I've been wanting to ask you. It's a little personal, though."

"How personal?" she asked.

"Well, you know, about yourself and all. The personal kind of personal. I guess."

She looked at him, frowning, then blushed. Seemed the girl did that a lot, which was just fine by Wayne. Girls were pretty with a bit of color on them. "You don't mean about me . . . and you . . . I mean . . ."

"Oh, Harmony!" Wayne laughed. "It's not anythin' like that, mate. Don't worry. You're pretty enough, particularly through the coppers, if you know what I mean."

"The coppers?"

"Sure. Word with a lot of curves, like you. You have a pretty accent too, and some nice bounce to you in the cloud area."

"Dare I ask what that is?"

"The white, puffy things that float high above the fruitful land where the seeds are planted."

She blushed even further. "Wayne! That might be the most crude thing anyone has ever said to me."

"I strives for excellence, mate. I strives for excellence. But don't worry—like I said, you're right nice, but you ain't got enough punch for me. I like women what could take my face *clean* off with a good roundhouse."

"You prefer women who could beat you up?"

"Sure. It's a thing. Anyway, what I was talkin' about was your Allomancy. See, you and I, we have opposite powers. I speed up time, you slow it. So what happens if we *both* use it at the same time? Eh?"

"It's been documented," Marasi said. "They cancel one another out. Nothing happens."

"Really?"

"Yes."

"Huh," he said, wiping his nose with his handkerchief. "Most expensive 'nothing' a person could find, what with us both burning rare metals."

"I don't know," she said with a sigh. "My power is pretty good at doing nothing on its own. I don't think I really understood how pathetic being a Pulser was until I saw what your power could do."

"Oh, yours ain't so bad."

"Wayne, any time I use my ability—*any* time—I'll be left frozen in place, looking stupid while everyone else is able to run about. You can use your power to gain extra time. I can only use mine to lose time."

"Sure, but maybe sometime you want a certain day to come along sooner. You want it real badly, right? So you can burn some chromium, and poof, it's here!"

"I've . . ." She looked embarrassed. "I've actually done that. Chromium burns way more slowly than bendalloy."

"See! Advantages. How big can your bubbles get?"

"I can make one the size of a small room."

"That's *way* bigger than mine," Wayne said.

"Multiply zero by a thousand, and you still get zero."

He hesitated. "You do?"

"Er, yes," she said. "It's basic mathematics."

"I thought we were talking about Allomancy. When did it become about mathematics?"

That made her blush too. You expected that out of a girl when you talked about her more attractive body parts, but not when you mentioned mathematics. She was an odd alloy, this one.

She glanced to the side, toward Waxillium. He was crouching down beside the canal.

"Now *him*," Wayne said. "*He* likes 'em smart."

"I have no intentions toward Lord Ladrian," she said quickly. Too quickly.

"Pity," Wayne said. "I think he likes you, mate."

That might have been an exaggeration. Wayne wasn't certain what Wax was thinking in regards to Marasi—however, the man needed to get his mind off Lessie. Lessie had been a great girl. Wonderful, and all that. But she was dead, and Wax still had that . . . hollow look to him. The same one he'd displayed in the weeks after Lessie's death. It was softer now, but still there.

A new love would help a lot. Wayne was certain of it, so he found himself quite pleased with himself as Marasi started moving, eventually wandering over to where Wax was working. She touched his arm, and he pointed at something on the ground beside the canal. Together, they inspected it.

Wayne strolled over.

". . . perfectly rectangular," Marasi was saying. "From something mechanical."

The ground here was pressed down as if by something heavy in a square patch. It was apparently the only kind of track in the area, and didn't seem what Wax had been intending to find. He knelt beside it, frowning, and pressed his hand into the dirt, probably to check how compact it was. He looked up at the tracks again.

"Not enough footprints," Wax said softly. "There's no way this was carried out with manpower. Even if there was a speed-bubble."

"I think you're right," Marasi said. "If the robbery happened right there, a machine could have remained in the canal and still reached the tracks."

Waxillium stood and dusted his hands off. "Let's head back. I need time to think."

Waxillium walked down the center of the passenger car, hands wet from scrubbing them in the washroom. The car thumped beneath him, fields speeding by outside.

Where would Miles be hiding? Waxillium's mind went in loops. The City offered too many places to hide, and Miles wasn't a typical criminal. He was a former lawkeeper. Waxillium's normal instincts would be off.

He'll want to scale back, Waxillium decided. *He's careful. Judicious. He spent months between stealing the aluminum and making his next robbery.*

Miles had lost men and resources. He'd hide for a time. But *where?* Waxillium leaned against the corridor wall. This first-class railcar was made up of private compartments. He could faintly hear people talking in the one beside him. Children. It had been a long walk through six railcars to find the one with an available washroom. Wayne and Marasi were in a compartment several cars farther along.

If Marasi was right about the intended function of the kidnapped women, then a grim fate awaited them. Miles could afford to step back, let the trail grow cold. Each hour delayed would make him that much more difficult to find.

No, Waxillium thought. *He'll need one more heist.* A quick one, perhaps without any hostages, to get more aluminum. Waxillium had looked over the original theft reports, and had managed to make an accurate assessment of the amount of aluminum Tekiel had been smuggling. It would have barely been enough to outfit thirty or forty men. That would leave Miles needing one more heist before going to ground; that way, he could use the downtime to make more guns and ammunition.

That left Waxillium with one more opportunity to catch him. If he could set it up right. He—

The scream was faint, but Waxillium had trained himself to be vigilant for such things. Always alert, especially when he was busy thinking. He immediately threw himself to the side, which saved his life as the bullet ripped through the glass window at the end of the railcar.

Waxillium twisted, pulling a revolver from its holster. A figure in black stood in the next car, looking through the broken window. He wore the mask again, eyes exposed, knit covering the rest of his features. The build was right, though—and the height, even the way he held his gun.

Idiot! Waxillium thought. His instincts *had* been off. An ordinary criminal would have gone to ground. But not Miles. He was a former lawman, accustomed to hunting rather than being hunted.

And if you caused a twist in his plans, he'd come looking for you.

Union Leader Abandons Solidarity with Trade Union Party Members

In a surprise switch from party line position, Trade Union Leader Elors Durnsed announced his intention to set aside any objection to the closure of further negotiations between representatives of the United Tradeworkers Union and the Noble Houses Collective in their ongoing agreement disputes. Rumors of a series of secret meetings taking place between the Union Leader and private citizens whose interests are aligned with the Houses remain a matter of speculation, with all questions on the matter brushed aside.

The announcement was greeted with near-violent derision from members of the Trade Union Party interviewed by this broadsheet. A Line Riveter at the site of the Ironspine Building who gave his name as Brill told this reporter that Mr. Durnsed should "bloody well keep his head clear of these parts if he knows what's what." Before he could expand upon this statement, his local union representative intervened and gave assurances that the man was speaking metaphorically. However, the mood of the assembled Line Riveters and Shovelmen was decidedly against Mr. Durnsed.

The decision by the Union Leader means that the contract as written holds now through the remainder of the financial quarter. Subsequent to this revelation, industry stocks were trading generally higher, and even recently depressed Tekiel shares began to show positive activity.

RELIEF FROM YOUR PAINS!

Mistress Halex, Allomancer, has opened a new Soothing Parlor. Within its relaxing confines, one can find relief from stress, anxiety, and concern—leaving with a light heart and a soaring mind. Our reporter visits the parlor to give a detailed report of what goes on. A luxurious massage, sweet scents, and a Soother on duty to give a unique "Emotional Massage" leave you feeling as good on the inside as you do on the outside. Read the report on the back, column seven.

Feltri Proven to Be Rioter!

Alloran Feltri, long favored to win the Canalworkers 2nd Seat in this fall's elections, is rumored to have been using Allomantic abilities to create supporters. In a scandal sure to rock the city to its foundations, a former mistress has come forward to expose all. Complete story on reverse side, third column.

Allomancers for Hire.

All varieties. Coinshots, Pewterarms for industrial work or protection. Temporal Allomancers for time manipulation. Soothers, Rioters for dinner party amusement. Some Feruchemists available with advance warning. Metalurgistics Allied, Carronberry Square, 7th Oct. Are you Metalborn and wish to earn what you deserve? Call in person; ask for Jarrington.

Explori the Pits Eltania

My dear editor, and of you, my dearest rea trust that my missive you well and in the p sion of a willing ear, incredible events that pired in my recent expe may strike you with in lity and shock. I vow in earnest assertion th and every word I write is true and factual. I liv tales so that you may of the Roughs and th cinating people who l here beyond the mou beyond the law, and b cultured reason.

When I wrote my pr missive, I was certai my end had come. I I was captured and h the brute koloss of th of Eltania, and had told that on the mor would be executed a flesh feasted upon. I a gruesome end, and admit that I found m earnest prayer to the vor that very night! If needed the protection Who Lived, it was I!

You may assume my writing here that escaped. Well, in part true; but I have not l camp of the blue-skin loss. Indeed, I write y letter from the very ch where I was held to ecuted on that night now, it is not a prison, stead a grand palace! A so do the savages hold consider it. To me, it r merely a mud-floore Sleeping beneath th would be more pref especially if I could ha Miss Dramali by m But my quest to locate she has been taken wi to wait for later.

The koloss do try to my accommodatio They have brought m animals to feast upo have built me a fire, that they consider me of grand attention. Ar have given me severa ons of their own constr As I have mention fore, those weapons incredibly fine make thought creatures s

OH NO WORRIES, SIR! I AM QUITE CERTAIN WE SHALL FIND A PLACE FOR YOU. PERHAPS AT THE CHILDREN'S TABLE?

FAIR PAY

EQUAL RIGHTS

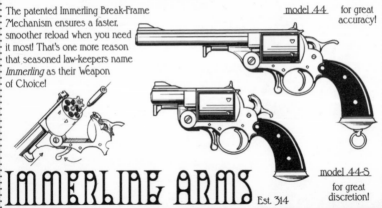

13

Waxillium didn't have time to raise his weapon. He instantly increased his weight and flared his steel as he Pushed forward on the doors between the railcars. The glass windows exploded as the doors bent and ripped free, blocking the bullets as Miles fired three times in quick succession.

The car lurched as the train began a turn. Heads popped out of compartments, wide eyes searching for the cause of the noise. Miles again took aim down the corridor at Waxillium. Children nearby were crying.

I can't risk bystanders, Waxillium thought. *I have to get out.*

As the gun fired, Waxillium threw himself forward. A bullet ricocheted near his head, spraying sparks. He couldn't sense it Allomantically. It was aluminum.

Waxillium burst out into the space between railcars, wind roaring and tugging on his clothing. As Miles fired his sixth shot, Waxillium Pushed on the couplers below and launched himself upward.

He soared into the air above the railcars. The wind caught him, pushing him backward as he fell. He landed with a thump on the roof several cars to the rear, going down on one knee and steadying himself with his free hand, wind blasting his hair and catching his jacket. He raised his revolver.

Miles was here. On the train.

I could stop him now. End this.

The next thought was immediate. How in the *world* was he going to stop Miles Hundredlives?

A masked figure rose between the train cars just ahead—maybe only ten feet away—holding a big-bore pistol. Miles always had preferred firepower to accuracy. He'd once said that he'd rather miss a few times knowing that when he *did* hit, the person he shot wouldn't be getting up again.

Waxillium cursed and filled his metalmind, dropping his weight to almost nothing, then rolled to the right, off the roof and over the side of the railcar. Gunshots followed. He grabbed the rim of a window, pressing himself against the side of the car and wedging one foot down into a slot in the metal along the car's side. His decreased weight allowed him to hold himself there easily, though his light body was buffeted by the wind.

Far ahead, the engine belched cinders and black smoke; below, the tracks were a-thunder. Waxillium raised his revolver in his right hand and waited as he clung to the side of the car with one hand and leg.

Miles's masked head soon poked out between the cars. Waxillium fired a single quick shot, Pushing the bullet forward with Allomancy for extra speed against the howling wind. He nailed Miles right in the left eye socket. The man's head snapped backward, and blood sprayed against the side of the railcar behind him. He stumbled, and Waxillium shot again, hitting him in the forehead.

The man reached up and ripped off his mask, revealing a hawk-like face with short black hair and prominent eyebrows. It *was* him. Miles. A lawkeeper, a man who should have known better. A Twinborn Compounder of awesome power. His eye grew back, and the head wound was gone in an eyeblink. Golden metal glimmered on his arms, deep within the sleeves. His metalminds; they were spikes he wore driven through the skin of his lower arm, like bolts. Metal that pierced skin was extremely difficult to touch with Steel-pushing.

Rust and Ruin! Even getting shot in the *eye* hadn't slowed him much. Waxillium sighted on an approaching tree and fired, then let go of the train and made himself as light as he could. He blew backward in the wind, and as the tree whipped past, he Pushed on the bullet lodged in it, shoving himself to the side, between two train cars. He crouched there, gasping, heart pounding as another of Miles's bullets ricocheted off the corner near him.

How did you fight someone who was virtually immortal?

Skirting some low hills, the railway rounded another curve. Verdant farms and placid orchards rolled past in the near distance. Waxillium grabbed the car's ladder and pulled himself up, carefully peeking over the edge of the roof.

Miles was charging toward him at full speed along the top of the railcar. Waxillium cursed, raising his gun as Miles did the same. Waxillium got his shot off first, and managed to hit Miles, who was only a few steps away by that point.

Waxillium aimed for the gun hand.

The bullet ripped into the flesh and bone, causing Miles to curse, dropping his gun. The weapon bounced once on the roof, then disappeared over the side. Waxillium smiled in satisfaction. Miles growled, then leaped forward off the top of the railcar and slammed into him.

Waxillium's head cracked back against the metal behind him, pain sending a flash of white across his vision. He grunted, dazed. *Idiot!* Most men would never have jumped like that; it was too likely to toss both of them off the moving train. That wouldn't bother Miles.

They had both fallen into the space between railcars, standing on the precarious footing there. Miles grabbed Waxillium by the vest with both hands, lifting him and slamming him back against the railcar behind. Waxillium reflexively fired again and again into

Miles's gut at point-blank range, but the bullets ripped out of Miles's back without even giving him pause. He pulled Waxillium forward and punched him across the face.

Pain flashed, and Waxillium's vision swam. He almost stumbled off and fell onto the speeding tracks just below. Desperate, Waxillium tried to Push himself up into the air. Miles was ready for this, and as soon as Waxillium started to rise, the other man hooked his foot under the bottom ladder rung and held on. Waxillium lurched, still feeling dazed, but didn't go into the air. He Pushed harder, but Miles hung on, eyes determined.

"You can rip the tendons in my foot, Wax," Miles yelled over the racket of wheels on the rails below and the howl of the wind, "but they'll reknit immediately. I think your body will give out before mine does. Push harder. Let's see what happens."

Waxillium let go, dropping back to the landing between cars. He tried to grab Miles in a headlock as he came down, but the other man was younger, faster, and a better brawler. Miles ducked—still holding on to Waxillium's vest—then pulled. Waxillium stumbled, off balance, as he lurched into Miles, who drove his fist into Waxillium's gut.

Waxillium gasped at the pain. Miles grabbed Waxillium on the shoulder and pulled him forward, moving to bury his fist in Waxillium's belly again.

So Waxillium increased his weight tenfold.

Miles stumbled, suddenly pulling against something incredibly heavy. His eyes went wide. He was used to dealing with Coinshots—they were one of the most common types of Allomancer, particularly among criminals. Feruchemists were far more rare. Miles knew what Waxillium was, but knowing about a power and anticipating it were different things.

Still aching and breathless from the punch, Waxillium threw his shoulder into Miles's chest, using his enormous weight to press Miles backward. The man cursed, then let go of Wax and swung away, quickly climbing up the ladder back to the railcar's roof.

Wax stopped tapping his metalmind and Pushed, throwing

himself upward. He landed on the other car, facing Miles across the small gap. Wind played with their clothing and fields passed on either side. The train swayed as it crossed a switch, and the un-steady footing made Waxillium wobble. He bent down on one knee, pressing one hand against the rooftop and increasing his weight to steady himself. Miles stood tall, obviously indifferent to the shaky footing.

Indistinctly, Waxillium could hear people crying out, probably as they moved into other cars, trying to get away from the fighting. With luck the disturbance would draw Wayne.

Miles reached for the gun at his other hip. Waxillium reached for his other gun as well; he'd dropped the first—the better of the two—in the fighting. His vision was still fuzzy, his heart racing, but he still got his gun leveled at almost exactly the same instant as Miles. Each fired.

A bullet grazed Wax's side, cutting through his coat and draw-ing blood. His own shot took Miles in the kneecap, making him stumble, knocking his next shot wild. Wax took careful aim, then shot Miles in the hand, again blasting apart flesh and bone. Miles's body immediately began to regrow itself, bone reassembling, sinew springing back like rubber, skin appearing like ice growing over a pond. But the gun dropped.

Miles reached for it. Wax casually lowered his gun and shot the other weapon, knocking it backward and off the shaking top of the train.

"Dammit!" Miles swore. "Do you know how much those things are worth?"

Still on one knee, Wax raised his gun beside his head, the wind of the train's motion blowing the smoke away from the barrel.

Miles rose to his feet again. "You know, Wax," he yelled over the wind, "I used to wonder if I'd have to face you. A part of me always thought your softness would cause it—I thought you'd let someone go that you shouldn't have. I wondered if I'd have a chance to hunt you down for it."

Waxillium didn't respond. He maintained a level gaze, face

impassive. On the inside, he was smarting, trying to catch his breath from the beating he'd taken. He raised his hand to his side, pressing it against the wound. Blessedly, it wasn't too bad, but it still wet his fingers with blood. The train swayed, and he quickly lowered his hand to the rooftop again.

"What was it that broke you, Miles?" Waxillium called. "The lure of wealth?"

"You know very well this isn't about money."

"You need gold," Waxillium yelled. "Don't deny it. You've always needed it, for your constant Compounding."

Miles didn't reply.

"What happened?" Waxillium yelled. "You were a lawkeeper, Miles. A damn good one."

"I was a dog, Wax. A hound, kept in line with false promises and stern orders." Miles backed up a few paces, then ran forward, leaping over the gap between them.

Waxillium stood warily and backed up.

"Don't tell me you never felt it," Miles yelled, snarling. "You worked *every day* to fix the world, Wax. You tried to end the pain, the violence, the robberies. It never worked. The more men you put down, the more troubles arose."

"It's the life of a lawkeeper," Waxillium said. "If you gave up, fine. But you didn't have to join the other side."

"I was already *on* the other side," Miles said. "Where do the criminals come from? Was it the shopkeeper next door who started rampaging and murdering? Was it the boys who grew up near town, working their father's dry farm?

"No. It was the mine workers, shipped out from the City to dig into the depths and exploit the latest rich find—then be abandoned once it was exhausted. It was the fortune hunters. It was the rich fools from the City who wanted adventure."

"I don't care who it was," Waxillium said, still backing up. He was on the next-to-last car. He was running out of space to retreat. "I served the law."

"I served it too," Miles called. "But now I serve something better. The essence of the law, but mixed with real justice. An alloy, Wax. The best parts of both made into one. I do something better than chase the filth sent to me from the city.

"You can't tell me you never noticed it. What of Pars the Deadman, your 'great catch' of the last five years? I remember you hunting him, I remember your nights without sleep, your anxiety. The blood on the dirt in the center of Weathering when he left old Burlow's daughter dead for you to find. Where did *he* come from?"

Waxillium didn't reply. Pars had been a murderer from the City, a butcher who had been caught killing beggars. He'd fled out into the Roughs, and there he had again worked to sate his grisly obsession.

"They didn't stop him," Miles spat, stepping forward. "They didn't send you help. They didn't care about the Roughs. Nobody cares about the Roughs—they barely seem to notice us save as a place to deposit their trash."

"So you rob them," Wax called. "Kidnap their daughters, murder any who stand in your way?"

Miles took another step forward. "I do what needs to be done, Wax. Isn't that the code of the lawkeeper? I haven't stopped being one; you never stop being a lawkeeper. It gets in you. You do what nobody else will. You stand up for the downtrodden, make things better, stop the criminals. Well, I've just decided to set my sights on a more powerful brand of criminal."

Waxillium shook his head. "You've let yourself become a monster, Miles."

"You say that," Miles said, wind whipping at his short hair, "but your eyes, Wax . . . they show the truth. I can see it. You *do* get what I'm saying. You've felt it too. You *know* that I'm right."

"I'm not going to join you."

"I'm not asking you to," Miles said, voice growing softer. "You've always been the good hound, Wax. If your master beats you, you just whimper and wonder how to better serve. I don't think we'd work well together. Not in this."

Miles lunged forward.

Waxillium dumped all of his weight into his metalmind and hopped backward, letting the wind grab and drag him a good twenty feet away. He increased his weight and landed on the last railcar. They were approaching the suburbs; the flora of the Outer Estates dwindled.

"Go ahead and run!" Miles called. "I'll just wander back and take little Lady Harms the bastard! And Wayne. I've long been wanting an excuse to put a bullet in that man's head." He turned and began to stroll in the other direction.

Waxillium cursed, dashing forward. Miles turned, his lips spreading in a cold smile. He reached down, pulling a long-bladed knife out of the back of his boot. It was aluminum; he didn't have a single Allomantically reactive piece of metal on his body that Waxillium could see.

I need to throw him off the train, Wax thought. He couldn't beat Miles here, not for good. He needed a more controlled environment. And he needed time to plan.

As he got close, Wax raised his gun and tried to blast the knife out of Miles's hand—but the other man spun the knife and rammed it through his own left forearm, jamming it right down through the flesh so it stuck out the bottom. He didn't even flinch. Stories told all around the Roughs claimed that after suffering hundreds of wounds that should have killed him, Miles had grown completely oblivious to pain.

Miles held his hands out, ready to grab Waxillium—but he'd also be able to whip out that knife in a flash. Waxillium got out his own knife and held it in his left hand. The two circled for a moment, Wax's increased weight helping to steady him atop the thumping train car. It still wasn't terribly sure footing, and sweat trickled down his brow, blown sideways by the wind.

A few fools poked their heads up between distant cars, trying to watch the action. Unfortunately, none of those fools was Wayne. Wax feinted forward with a quick step, but Miles didn't take the bait. Wax was only a fair knife fighter, and Miles was known as one of the best. But if Wax could roll them both off the train . . .

At this speed, it will end me, but not him, he thought. *Unless I can get a Push underneath me. Rusts. This is going to be hard.*

He had only one chance, and that was to end the fight quickly.

Miles came in to seize him. Wax took a breath and stepped into it, which Miles seemed to find surprising, though he still managed to grab Wax's arm. With his other hand, Miles pulled the knife free from his own arm, preparing to thrust it toward Wax. In desperation, Wax increased his weight and threw his shoulder into Miles's chest.

Unfortunately, Miles anticipated that move. He dropped to the roof, rolling, and kicked Wax in the legs.

In the blink of an eye, Wax was tumbling through the air toward the gravel and rock beside the railway tracks. Some primal part of him knew what to do. He Pushed on the knife in his hand, ripping it free and plunging it into the earth directly below him. That bounced him into the air as he simultaneously shed his weight. The wind caught him. He was spinning, and he lost all sense of direction.

He hit and rolled into a heap, slamming against something hard. He stopped moving, but his vision continued to lurch. The sky spun.

All grew still. His vision slowly returned to normal. He was alone in the middle of a weedy field. The train was puffing away down the tracks.

He groaned and rolled over. *A man my age shouldn't be doing this kind of thing,* he thought, stumbling to his feet. He hadn't started feeling his age until the last few years, but he was over forty now. That was ancient by Roughs standards.

He stared after the escaping railway train, shoulder aching. The thing was, Miles had said one thing that was right.

You never stopped being a lawkeeper.

Wax gritted his teeth and dashed forward. He scooped up the gun he'd dropped when falling—it was easy to find with his Allomancy—then jumped without breaking stride and landed atop the tracks.

He Pushed, throwing himself into the air. He reached a good

height, then Shoved on the rails behind him, shooting forward. A careful Push below, a continuous Push behind. The wind roared around him, his clothing a noisy flurry, blood seeping from the wound at his side.

There was a thrill to this, the flight of a Coinshot. It was a freedom no other Allomancer could know. When the air became his, he felt the same exhilaration he had years ago, when he'd first sought his fortune in the Roughs. He wished that he were wearing his mistcoat and that the mists were around him. Everything always seemed to work better in the mists. They were said to protect the just.

He caught up to the train in moments, then threw himself in a powerful arc over it. A small figure was walking along the tops of the railcars, making his way toward Wayne and Marasi.

Wax Pushed downward to keep himself from hitting too hard, but increased his weight at the same time, slamming into the train's roof and denting it into a crater around him. He stood up straight, then flipped his revolver open, as if to reload. The casings and unspent rounds flipped up into the air and he caught one.

Miles spun. Wax tossed the cartridge at him.

Looking startled, Miles snatched it out of the air.

"Goodbye," Wax said, then slammed as powerful a Push as he could into that cartridge.

Miles's eyes opened wide. His hand jerked backward into his chest, and then he was flung free of the train, the Push on the cartridge effectively transferred to him. The train rounded a bend as Miles soared through the air and crashed into the rocky ground beyond.

Wax sat down, then lay back, eyes toward the sky. He breathed in deeply, aching, and pressed his hand to the wound at his side. He rode all the way to the next stop before climbing down.

"We had orders, m'lord," the railway engineer said. "Even when I heard there was gunfire back in the passenger cars. We ain't to stop for *anything*. The Vanishers get you when you stop."

"It is just as well," Waxillium said, gladly taking a cup of water from a young man in an apprentice engineer's vest. "If you had stopped, it likely would have meant my death."

He sat in a small room at the station, which—by tradition—was owned and operated by a minor member of the house that owned the land nearby. The lord himself was out, but the steward had immediately sent for the local surgeon.

Waxillium had his coat, vest, and shirt off, and was holding a bandage to his side. He wasn't certain he had time to wait for that surgeon. It would take Miles about an hour of running to reach this station. Fortunately, he wasn't a steel Feruchemist, capable of increasing his speed.

An hour, likely, but it was best to plan for the worst. If Miles found a horse, he could arrive sooner. And Waxillium wasn't certain exactly how Miles's Compounding would affect his stamina. Perhaps he might be capable of running longer distances than he should be able to.

"We almost have your men out, m'lord," another apprentice said, entering. "Those locks aren't supposed to be this hard to open!"

Waxillium drank his water. Miles had planned his trap well. Wayne and Marasi had been confined in their car—along with all the others who happened to be there—by lengths of metal jammed into locking mechanisms on the outer doors. Miles had waited until Waxillium left his room, then had quietly trapped the others before hunting him.

There was some luck to that, at least. Miles hadn't simply killed them. It made sense that he hadn't, however. It would have been risky, going in to try to kill Wayne—who could heal himself—and risk drawing Waxillium back, then facing one on either side. Miles was too careful for that. Waxillium had been the real target. The others were better locked away until the primary goal was accomplished.

"You need to get your train going again," Waxillium said to the engineer. He was a heavyset man with a dark brown beard and a flat-topped cap. "You are in danger from the Vanishers. We need to ride the train all the way into the heart of the City. We can't delay."

"But your wound, m'lord!"

"It will be fine," Waxillium said. Out in the Roughs, he'd often had to go days or weeks with a wound before a surgeon could tend it.

"We—"

The door burst open and Marasi stumbled through. Her blue dress was still singed from the explosion at the mansion, but she wore it well, despite the folds of lace underneath the glistening outer layer. The blue vest that pulled closed around the bodice was missing a button on the bottom, probably ripped free in the fall. He hadn't noticed that before.

She raised her hands to her mouth at the sight of the bloody bandage, then immediately turned beet red at seeing him with his shirt off. He did have a moment of pride in the fact that, though he had some gray in his hair, he still had the lean muscles of a much younger man.

"Oh, *Harmony!*" she said. "Are you all right? Is that your blood? And should I be in here? I can go. I should probably go, shouldn't I? Are you sure you're all right?"

"He'll live," Wayne said, peeking in behind her. "Wha'd you do, Wax? Trip on the way out of the washroom?"

"Miles found me," Waxillium said, removing the bandage. It looked like the wound had mostly stopped bleeding. He took another bandage from one of the apprentices, then prepared to tie it in place.

"Is he dead?" Marasi asked.

"I killed him a few more times," Waxillium said, "and it was about as effective as what everyone else has tried."

"You need to get his metalminds off of 'im," Wayne said. "It's the only way."

"He keeps thirty different ones," Waxillium said, "all piercing his skin, all with enough healing to bring him back from practically any wound." A Pewterarm, or even a lesser Bloodmaker like Wayne, could be killed with a direct shot to the head. Miles could heal so quickly even that wouldn't kill him. He was said to keep the healing running constantly. From what Waxillium knew of Compounding, it could be very dangerous to stop once you'd started.

"Sounds like a challenge!" Wayne said.

Marasi lingered in the doorway for a moment longer, then apparently made a decision and rushed forward. "Let me see the wound," she said, kneeling beside Waxillium's bench.

He frowned, but stopped tying the bandage straps and let her peel back the cloth. She inspected the wound.

"You know something of surgery, m'lady?" the engineer said, shifting from foot to foot. He seemed a little anxious at her presence in the room.

"I go to university," she said.

Ah, that's right, Waxillium thought.

"So?" Wayne asked.

Marasi prodded at the wound. "University rules, set by Harmony himself, dictate a broad education."

"Yeah, I know they have to take girls," Wayne said.

Marasi paused. "Er . . . not that meaning of broad, Wayne."

"Students have to be trained in a little of everything," Waxillium said, "before they can choose a specialty."

"That includes basic healing and some small amount of surgery," Marasi said. "As well as complete anatomy courses."

Wayne frowned. "Wait. Anatomy. Meaning, *all* parts of anatomy."

Marasi blushed. "Yes."

"So—"

"So it was very popular in class to watch my reactions, apparently," she said, still blushing. "And I'd rather not dwell on that at the moment, Wayne, thank you. This needs stitches, Waxillium."

"Can you do it?"

"Er . . . I've never worked on anyone *alive* before . . ."

"Eh," Wayne said, "I spent *months* training with dueling canes on dummies before beating up my first real person. It's pretty much the same thing."

"I'll be all right, Marasi," Waxillium said.

"So many scars," she said quietly, as if not noticing what he'd said. She was staring at his chest and sides, and seemed to be counting the old bullet wounds.

"There are seven," he said softly in reply, replacing the bandage and tying it tight.

"You've been shot *seven* times?" she asked.

"A lot of gunshots aren't lethal, if you know how to care for them," Waxillium said. "They don't really—"

"Oh," she said, raising a hand to her lips. "I meant, we only have records of five. I really will need to hear about the other two some-time."

"Right," he said, grimacing and standing. He waved for his shirt.

"Oh, bother," she said. "That didn't come out very well, did it? I really am impressed that you have been shot so often. Really."

"Getting hit's not really that impressive," Wayne noted. "It don't take much skill to get shot. It's *avoiding* the bullets that's tough."

Waxillium snorted, pulling his arm through a sleeve.

Marasi stood. "I'll turn around so you can dress," she said, be-ginning to spin.

"Turn around," Waxillium said flatly.

"Um, yes."

"So I can dress."

"A little silly, I guess."

"A little," he said, smiling and pulling his other sleeve on. He began doing the buttons. Wayne looked so amused he was having trouble standing up.

"All right," she said, raising her hands to the sides of her face. "I *realize* that I get a little flustered sometimes. I'm just not used to things exploding, people getting shot at, and finding my friends sit-ting and bleeding with their shirts off when I walk in! This is all very new to me."

"It's all right," Waxillium said, laying a hand on her shoulder. "There are much worse things to be than genuine, Marasi. Besides, Wayne wasn't much better when he was new to all of this. Why, he used to get so nervous that he would start—"

"Hey," Wayne said, "no use bringin' *that* up."

"What?" Marasi asked, lowering her hands.

"NOTHING," Wayne replied. "Come on. We should move, right? If Mister Miles Murderer is still alive, he'll be wanting to shoot us, right? And as good as Wax is at getting shot—he's had lots of practice, you see—I think we best be avoiding more of that sort today."

"He's right," Waxillium said, pulling on his vest, then putting on his shoulder holsters. He winced.

"Are you sure you're all right?" Marasi asked.

"He's fine," Wayne said, holding the door open for them. "*I* got quite near my entire rusted back blown off earlier, if you'll kindly recall, and I didn't hear nearly an ounce of the sympathy you're showin' him."

"That's different," Marasi said, walking past him.

"What? Why? 'Cuz I can heal?"

"No," she said, "because—even after knowing you only a short time—I'm fairly certain that on one level or another, you deserve to get blown up every now and again."

"Oi," Wayne said. "That's harsh."

"But untrue?" Waxillium said, pulling on his coat. It was looking quite ragged.

"Didn't say that now, did I," Wayne said, and sneezed. "Keep moving, slowboy. Rusts! A man gets shot, and he thinks he can take all afternoon. Let's move!"

Waxillium walked past. He forced himself to smile, though he was starting to feel as ragged as his coat. There wasn't much time. Miles had taken off his mask, but had obviously expected to kill Waxillium. He now knew that he'd been outed, and that would make him even more dangerous.

If Miles and his people were going to strike for more aluminum, they'd do it soon. Tonight, probably, assuming there was a shipment. Waxillium expected one soon; he'd read something in the broadsheets about House Tekiel boasting of their new armored freight cars.

"So what do we do when we get back?" Wayne asked softly as

they walked toward the railway car. "We're going to need some-place safe to plan, right?"

Waxillium sighed, knowing what Wayne was fishing for. "You're probably right."

Wayne smiled.

"You know," Waxillium said, "I'm not sure I'd call any place near Ranette 'safe.' Particularly if you are there."

"Better than being exploded," Wayne said happily. "Mostly."

14

Waxillium pounded on the door of the townhome. The area around them was a typical Elendel neighborhood. Vibrant, lush walnut trees lined either side of the cobbled street. Even after seven months back in the city, the trees still made him stare. Out in the Roughs, trees as large as these were rare. And here was an entire street full of them, mostly ignored by the inhabitants.

He, Wayne, and Marasi stood on the porch of the narrow, brick-faced home. Before Waxillium had a chance to lower his hand, the door swung open. A lean, long-legged woman stood inside. Her dark hair was pulled back into a shoulder-length tail, and she wore brown trousers and a Roughs-style long leather coat over a white, no-nonsense laced shirt. She took one look at Waxillium and Wayne, then slammed the door shut without saying a word.

Waxillium glanced at Wayne, and then they both took a step to the side. Marasi looked at them in confusion until Waxillium took her by the arm and pulled her over.

The door slammed back open, and the woman shoved a shotgun out. She glanced around the corner at the two of them, then narrowed her eyes.

"I'll count to ten," she said. "One."

"Now, Ranette," Waxillium began.

"Two three four five," she said in quick succession.

"Do we really have to—"

"Six seven eight." She raised the gun, taking aim at them.

"All right then . . ." Waxillium said, hustling down the steps, Wayne following, hand holding his carriage man's cap in place.

"She wouldn't really shoot us?" Marasi asked softly. "Would she?"

"Nine!"

They reached the sidewalk beneath the towering trees. The door slammed closed behind them.

Waxillium took a deep breath, turning around and looking at the house. Wayne leaned back against one of the tree trunks, smiling.

"So, that went well," Waxillium said.

"Yup," Wayne replied.

"Well?" Marasi demanded.

"Neither of us got shot," Waxillium said. "You can't always be sure, with Ranette. Particularly if Wayne is along."

"Now, that's right unfair," Wayne said. "She's only shot me three times."

"You're forgetting Callingfale."

"That was in the foot," Wayne said. "Barely counts."

Marasi pursed her lips, studying the building. "You two have some curious friends."

"Curious? Nah, she's just angry." Wayne smiled. "It's how she shows affection."

"By shooting people?"

"Ignore Wayne," Waxillium said. "Ranette might be brusque, but she rarely shoots people other than him."

Marasi nodded. "So . . . should we go?"

"Wait for a moment," Waxillium said. To his side, Wayne started whistling, then checked his pocket watch.

The door was flung open again, Ranette holding her shotgun up on her shoulder. "You're not leaving!" she called.

"I need your help," Waxillium called back.

"I need *you* to stick your head in a bucket of water and slowly count to a thousand!"

"Lives are at stake, Ranette," Waxillium yelled. "Innocent lives."

Ranette raised her gun, taking aim.

"Don't worry," Wayne said to Marasi. "At this distance, birdshot probably won't be lethal. Make sure your eyes are closed, though."

"You're not helping, Wayne," Waxillium said calmly. He was sure Ranette wouldn't shoot. Well, reasonably sure. Maybe.

"Oh, you actually want me to help?" Wayne said. "Right. You still have that aluminum gun I gave you?"

"Tucked in the small of my back," Waxillium said. "Without any bullets."

"Hey, Ranette!" Wayne called. "I've got a neat gun you can have!"

She hesitated.

"Wait," Waxillium said, "I wanted that—"

"Don't be a baby," Wayne said to him. "Ranette, it's a revolver made entirely of aluminum!"

She lowered her shotgun. "Really?"

"Get it out," Wayne whispered to Waxillium.

Waxillium sighed, reaching under his coat. He held up the revolver, drawing some looks from passersby on the street. Several of them spun about and hastened in the other direction.

Ranette stepped forward. She was a Lurcher, and could recognize most metals by simply burning iron. "Well then," she called. "You should have *mentioned* that you'd brought a bribe. This might be enough to get me to forgive you!" She strolled down her front walk, shotgun slung up over her shoulder.

"You realize," Waxillium said under his breath, "that this revolver is worth enough to buy an entire *houseful* of guns? I think *I* might shoot you, for this."

"The ways of Wayne are mysterious and incomprehensible," Wayne said. "What he giveth, he can draw back unto himself. And lo, let it be written and pondered."

"You'll ponder my fist, hitting your face." Waxillium plastered a smile on his lips as Ranette stepped up to them; then he reluctantly handed over the revolver.

She looked it over with an expert eye. "Lightweight," she said. "No maker's mark stamped on the barrel or the grip. Where'd you get this?"

"The Vanishers," Waxillium said.

"Who?"

Waxillium sighed. *That's right.*

"How could you not know who the Vanishers are?" Marasi blurted. "They've been on every broadsheet in the city for the last two months. They're all anyone is talking about."

"People are stupid," Ranette said, popping the revolver open, checking the chambers. "I find them annoying—and those are the ones I like. Did this have aluminum rounds too?"

Waxillium nodded. "We don't have any of the pistol rounds. Just a few rifle rounds."

"How did they work?" she asked. "Stronger than lead, but much lighter. Less immediate stopping power, obviously, but they'll still tear themselves apart on hitting. Could be very deadly if they hit the right spot. And that's assuming wind resistance doesn't slow the bullets too much before they reach their target. The effective range would be way down. And they'd be highly abrasive to the barrel."

"I haven't fired it," Waxillium said. He eyed Wayne, who was grinning. "We've . . . er, been saving it for you. And I'm sure the rounds are of a much heavier alloy than the revolver itself, though I didn't get a chance to test them yet. They're lighter than lead rounds, but not even close to as light as nearly pure aluminum would be. The percentage is still high, but the alloy must solve most of those issues somehow."

Ranette grunted. She waved the gun absently toward Marasi. "Who's the ornament?"

"A friend," Waxillium said. "Ranette, people are looking for us. Dangerous people. Can we come in?"

She tucked the revolver into her belt. "Fine. But if Wayne touches anything—*anything*—I'll blow off the offending fingers."

Marasi kept her tongue as they were led into the building. She wasn't particularly fond of being referred to as an "ornament." But she *was* fond of remaining unshot, and so silence seemed prudent.

She was good at silence. She had been trained to it over two decades of life.

Ranette closed the door behind them, then turned away. Shockingly, the locks on the door all *did themselves*, twisting in their mounts and clicking. There were nearly a dozen of them, and their sudden move caused Marasi to jump. *What in the Survivor's Deadly Name?*

Ranette set her shotgun in a basket beside the door—it appeared that she kept it there the way ordinary people kept umbrellas—then sidled past them in the narrow hallway. She waved a hand, and some kind of lever beside the interior door lurched. The door sprang open as she walked to it.

Ranette was an Allomancer. Of course. That was why she'd been able to recognize the aluminum. As they reached the door, Marasi studied the contraption that had opened it. There was a lever that could be pulled, which in turn moved a rope, pulley, and lever arrangement on the other side.

There's one on each side, Marasi realized as they stepped through the doorway. *She can open her doors from either direction without needing to lift a hand.* It seemed an indulgence. But, then, who was Marasi to critique another person's use of their Allomancy? This would certainly be useful if you often walked about with your hands full.

The living room beyond had been converted to a workshop. There were large worktables on all four sides, and nails had been pounded into the walls to hang an impressive variety of tools. Marasi didn't recognize any of the machinery that cluttered those tables, but there were a lot of clamps and gears. A disturbing number of electrical cords snaked across the floor.

Marasi stepped very carefully. Electricity couldn't be dangerous when it was in cords, could it? She'd heard stories of people getting burned, as if struck by lightning, from getting too close to electrical devices. And people spoke of using this power for everything— replacing horses with it, making mills that ground grain on their own, using it to power elevators. Disturbing. Well, she'd keep her distance.

The door slammed shut behind them in response to Ranette's Allomancy. She had to Pull on a lever for it, so that meant she was a Lurcher, not a Coinshot like Waxillium. Wayne was already poking through things on the desks, completely ignoring her threat to his fingers.

Waxillium surveyed the room, with its wires, windows—covered by shutters—and tools. "I assume it's living up to your expectations?"

"What?" Ranette asked. "The city? It's a pit. I don't feel half as safe here as I did out in the Roughs."

"Still can't believe you abandoned us," Wayne said, sounding hurt.

"You didn't have electricity," Ranette said, sitting at her desk in a chair with wheels on the bottom. She waved an absent hand, and a long, thin tool flipped out of a cubby on the wall. It flew toward her and she snatched it, then brought it down and began prodding at the gun Waxillium had given her. From what Marasi understood, gestures weren't needed for Pushing or Pulling, but many used them anyway.

Ranette completely ignored her visitors as she worked. She Pulled a few more tools without looking up, causing them to streak across the room to her. One nearly clipped Marasi on the shoulder.

It was unusual to see Allomancy used so casually, and Marasi wasn't certain what to make of it. On one hand, it was fascinating. On the other, it was humbling. What would it be like, to have a power that was *useful*? Lord Harms had insisted that Marasi keep her ability—such as it was—quiet, calling it unseemly. She could see through him. He wasn't so much embarrassed to have an Allomancer daughter as to have one that was illegitimate. He couldn't have Marasi looking like a better catch than Steris.

Bitter thoughts, she told herself, intentionally pushing them away. Bitterness could consume a woman. Best to keep it at arm's length.

"This gun is good work," Ranette said, though she sounded grudging. She'd donned some spectacles with a magnifying lens on them, and was in the process of staring down the barrel of the revolver while shining a small electric light into it. "You want me to figure out who made this, I assume?"

Waxillium turned to study a line of half-finished guns on one of the tables. "Actually," he said, "we came here because we needed someplace safe to think for a few hours."

"Your mansion isn't safe?"

"My butler failed to poison me, then tried to shoot me, then set off an explosive in my study."

"Huh." She cocked the pistol a few times. "You need to screen these people better, Wax."

"I'll take that under advisement." He picked up a pistol and sighted down its barrel. "I'm going to need a new Sterrion."

"Like hell you will," Ranette said. "What's wrong with the ones you have?"

"Gave them to the aforementioned butler," Waxillium said. "And he probably dumped them in the canals."

"What of your Ambersairs? I made you one of those, didn't I?"

"You did. I lost it fighting Miles Dagouter earlier today."

This made Ranette stop. She lowered the aluminum gun, then turned her chair. "*What?*"

Waxillium drew his lips into a line. "He's the one we're hiding from."

"Why," Ranette said pointedly, "is Miles Hundredlives trying to kill you?"

Wayne strolled forward. "He's trying to overthrow the city or something, dearie. For some reason, he thinks the best way to do that is by robbin' folks and blowing up mansions."

"Don't call me dearie."

"Sure thing, honey."

Marasi watched in silence, curious. Wayne seemed to like taunting this woman. In fact, though he tried to act nonchalant, he kept glancing at her, and had been edging through the room closer and closer to her seat.

"Whatever," Ranette said, turning back to her work. "Don't really care. But you're not getting a new Sterrion."

"Nobody else's guns shoot as straight as yours, Ranette."

She didn't reply. She did glare at Wayne, who had moved up to the point where he was leaning over her shoulder and looking at the gun.

Waxillium smiled, then turned back to the unfinished guns on the desk. Marasi joined him, uncertain what she should be doing. Hadn't they come here to plan their next move? Neither Waxillium nor Wayne seemed eager to get on with things.

"Is there something between them?" Marasi whispered, nodding her head toward Wayne and Ranette. "She acts a little like a jilted lover."

"Wayne could only wish," Waxillium whispered back. "Ranette's not interested in him like that. I'm not certain she's interested in *any* man like that. Doesn't stop him from trying, though." He shook his head. "I'm half tempted to think that all of this—coming to Elendel to investigate the Vanishers, looking me up—was about eventually persuading me to come with him to Ranette's. He knew she wouldn't let him in unless he was with me and we were doing something important."

"You're a bizarre pair, you know."

"We try."

"So what's our next move?"

"I'm trying to decide. For now, if we linger long enough, she might give me a new revolver."

"Either that, or she'll shoot you for annoying her."

"Nah. She's never shot anyone after letting them in the door that I can recall. Not even Wayne." He hesitated. "She'll probably let you stay here, if you want. It would be safe. I'll bet there's a paid Coppercloud rotation going on in one of the nearby buildings, shrouding the area. Ranette *hates* people sensing her Allomancy. I doubt there are half a dozen people in Elendel who know she lives here. Harmony only knows how Wayne tracked her down."

"I'd rather not stay. Please, whatever you're doing, I want to help."

He picked something up off the desk; a small box of bullets. "I can't figure you out, Marasi Colms."

"You've solved some of the most troubling crimes the Roughs have ever known, Lord Waxillium. I doubt I'm nearly as mysterious."

"Your father is very well off," Waxillium said. "From what I know of him, I'm certain he would have provided you with a comfortable endowment for the rest of your life. Instead, you attend university—choosing one of the most difficult programs of study offered."

"You left a position of considerable comfort yourself," she said, "choosing to live away from convenience and modernity."

"I did."

She selected one of the bullets out of the box, holding it up, looking it over. She couldn't see anything distinctive about it. "Have you ever felt you were useless, Lord Waxillium?"

"Yes."

"It's difficult to imagine that of someone as accomplished as yourself."

"Sometimes," he said, "accomplishment and perception can work independently."

"True. Well, my lord, I have spent *most* of my life being politely told I was useless. Useless to my father because of my birth; useless as an Allomancer; useless to Steris, as I was an embarrassment. Sometimes, accomplishment can temper perception. Or so I hope."

He nodded. "I have something for you to do. It will be dangerous."

She dropped the bullet into the box. "To be of use in even a single burst of flame and sound is worth more than a lifetime of achieving nothing."

He met her eyes, judging her sincerity.

"You have a plan?" she asked.

"There isn't much time for a plan. This is more of a hunch with scaffolding." He held up the box of bullets, speaking more loudly. "Ranette, what are these?"

"Hazekiller rounds."

"Hazekiller?" Marasi asked.

"It's an ancient term," Waxillium said. "For an ordinary person trained to fight Allomancers."

"I'm working on ammunition for use against each basic type of Allomancer," Ranette said absently. She'd unscrewed the grip of the pistol and was pulling it apart. "Those are Coinshot rounds. Ceramic tips. When they Push on the bullet as it flies toward them, they'll yank off the metal portion at the back, but the ceramic should keep flying straight and hit them. Could be better than aluminum rounds—those, the Allomancer can't sense at all, so he knows to take cover rather than relying on Pushes. These they'll sense and assume they can beat—right up until they're on the floor bleeding."

Wayne whistled softly.

"Ruin, Ranette!" Waxillium said. "I've never been so glad we're on the same side." He hesitated. "Or, at least, that you're on your own special side that we don't happen to run afoul of too often."

"What are you going to do with them?" Marasi asked.

"Do?" Ranette asked.

"Are you going to sell them?" Marasi said. "Patent the idea and license them?"

"If I did that, then *everybody* would have them!" Ranette shook her head, looking sick. "Half the people in the city would be here, bothering me."

"Lurcher rounds?" Waxillium asked, holding up another box.

"Similar," Ranette said, "but with the ceramic on the sides. Not quite as effective, at least at long range. Most Lurchers protect themselves by Pulling bullets to hit an armored plate at their chest. Those bullets, they explode when Pulled on, and you get a little shrapnel blast of ceramics. Should work at ten feet or so, though it might not be lethal. I suggest aiming for the head. I'm trying to get the range up."

"Tineye rounds?"

"Make extra noise when fired," Ranette said. "And another noise when they hit. Fire a few shots around them, and their enhanced senses will have them cowering on the floor, holding their ears. Pretty good if you want to take one alive, though with a Tineye, you're going to have trouble finding them in the first place."

"And Pewterarm rounds," Waxillium said, studying the final box.

"Not really much special there," Ranette said. "Large bullets, extra powder, wide hollow tips, soft metal—meant to have a lot of stopping power. A Pewterarm can keep going long after being shot a few times, so you want to knock them down and keep them there long enough for their body to realize it should be dying rather than fighting. Of course, the best way to drop one is just hit him in the head the first time."

A Pewterarm wouldn't be like Miles, capable of healing immediately. They had great endurance, and could ignore wounds—but those wounds would still kill them, eventually.

"Huh," Waxillium said, holding up one of the long bullets. "None of these are a standard caliber. You'd need quite the gun to fire them."

Ranette didn't respond.

"This is nice work, Ranette," Waxillium said. "Even for you. I'm impressed."

Marasi expected the gruff woman to brush off the compliment, but Ranette smiled—though she obviously tried to hide her satisfaction. She buried her head in her work, and didn't even bother to glare Wayne away. "So who are the people you said are in danger?"

"Hostages," Waxillium said. "Women, including Marasi's cousin. Someone is going to try to use them to breed new Allomancers."

"And Miles is involved in *that*?"

"Yes." Waxillium's voice was solemn. Worried.

Ranette hesitated, still bent over the disassembled revolver. "Third cubby up," she finally said. "All the way at the back."

Waxillium walked over and reached a hand into the depths. He withdrew a sleek, silvery revolver with a grip that blended onyx and ivory in wavy stripes, separated by silver bands. It had a long barrel, the silvery metal so highly polished that it practically glowed in the even electric lights.

"That's not a Sterrion," Ranette said. "It's better."

"Eight chambers," Waxillium said, raising an eyebrow as he turned the revolver's cylinder.

"That's Invarian steel," Ranette said. "Stronger, lighter. It let me shave the thickness between chambers, increase the number without making it too big. See the lever on the back, below the hammer?"

He nodded.

"Hold it down and spin the wheel."

He did so. The wheel locked on a certain chamber.

"It skips that chamber and the one beside it if you fire it normally," Ranette said. "You can only fire them if you flip the lever."

"Hazekiller rounds," Waxillium said.

"Yeah. Load six ordinary shots, two special ones. Fire them when you need them. You burning steel?"

"I am now."

"Metal lines in the grip."

"See them."

"Push the one on the left."

Something clicked inside the gun. Waxillium whistled softly.

"What?" Wayne asked.

"Allomancer-only safety," Waxillium said. "You have to be a Coinshot or a Lurcher to turn it off or on."

"The switch is embedded inside the grip," Ranette said. "No exterior sign that it's there. With that, you'll never have to worry about someone firing your own gun at you."

"Ranette," Waxillium said, sounding awed. "That's *genius*."

"I call the gun Vindication," she said. "After the Ascendant Warrior." Then she hesitated. "You can borrow it. *If* you bring me a field-test report."

Waxillium smiled.

"This is Nouxil's work, by the way," Ranette said, waving to her table.

"The aluminum gun?" Waxillium asked.

Ranette nodded. "I thought it might be so from the shape of the barrel, but the mechanics inside are distinctive."

"Who is he?" Wayne asked, leaning down further.

Ranette pointedly put a hand to Wayne's forehead and pushed him back. "Gunsmith. Disappeared about a year ago. We had a correspondence going. Nobody's heard from him." She held up a piece of metal from inside the gun grip. "Anyone here speak High Imperial?"

Waxillium shook his head.

"Makes my head hurt," Wayne said.

"I can read it, kind of," Marasi said, taking the square piece of metal. There were several characters scratched into the metal. "Was-ing the where of needing," she read, forming the unfamiliar words. The lofty tongue was used for old documents dating to the time of the Origin, and occasionally for government ceremony. "It's a call for help."

"Well, we know how Miles got his guns," Waxillium said, taking the plate and looking it over.

"Wax," Ranette said. "Miles always had a darkness in him, I know. But this? Are you *sure*?"

"Sure as I can be." He raised Vindication up beside his head. "I saw him face-to-face, Ranette. He spouted some rhetoric about saving the city as he tried to kill me."

"That'll be useless against him," Ranette said, nodding to Vindication. "I've been trying to figure out a gun to use against Blood-makers. It's only half finished."

"This will be fine," Waxillium said, voice even. "I'll need every edge I can get." His eyes were hard, like polished steel.

"I'd heard rumors you'd retired," Ranette said.

"I had."

"What changed?"

He slid Vindication into his shoulder holster. "I have a duty," he said softly. "Miles was a lawkeeper. When one of your own goes bad, you put him down personally. You don't rely on hired help. Wayne, I need shipping manifests. Can you borrow me some from the railway offices?"

"Sure. I can have them in an hour."

"Good. You still have that dynamite?"

"Sure do. Here in my coat pocket."

"You're insane," Waxillium said without missing a beat. "But you brought the pressure detonators?"

"Yup."

"Try to avoid blowing anything up by accident," Waxillium said. "But hold on to that dynamite. Marasi, I need you to buy some fishing nets. Strong ones."

She nodded.

"Ranette," Waxillium began, "I—"

"I'm not part of your little troop of deputies, Wax," Ranette said. "Leave me out of this."

"All I was going to do was ask to borrow a room in your house and some paper," Waxillium said. "I need to sketch this out."

"Fine," she said. "So long as you're quiet about it. But Wax . . . you *really* think you can take Miles? The man is immortal. You'd need a small army to stop him."

"Good," Waxillium said. "Because I intend to bring one."

15

Wax is slippery," Miles said, walking alongside Mister Suit through the dark tunnel connecting the dorms to the forging hall of the new lair. "He has lived so long precisely by learning to avoid being killed by people who are stronger and craftier than he is."

"You shouldn't have revealed yourself," Suit said sternly.

"I wasn't about to shoot Wax without him seeing me, Suit," Miles said. "He deserves more respect than that." The words gnawed at him as he said them. He hadn't mentioned the first shot he'd taken at Wax, the one while the man's back had been turned. Nor had he mentioned the cloth of his mask, pushed back into his flesh by Wax's bullet, making it hard to heal his eye. He'd needed to pull it free.

Suit snorted. "And it's said that the Roughs are the place where honor goes to be murdered."

"It's the place honor goes to be strung up, flayed within an inch of its life, then cut down and left in a desert. If it survives something like that, it'll be stronger than hell. Certainly stronger than anything you have at your Elendel dinner parties."

"That from a man who so readily went to kill a friend?" Suit said. The tone was still suspicious. He thought Miles had intentionally let Wax escape.

He didn't understand at all. This wasn't about the robberies any longer. The paths chosen by Wax and Miles had crossed. The future could only continue down one or the other.

Either Wax would die or Miles would. That would settle the matter. Roughs justice. The Roughs weren't a simple place, but they *were* a place of simple solutions.

"Wax is *not* a friend," Miles said, and truthfully. "We were never friends—no more than two rival kings could ever be friends. We respect each other, we did similar jobs, and we worked together. It ends there. I'll stop him, Suit."

They stepped out into the forging room and climbed the stairs up to the balcony that ran along the north side of the large chamber. They walked to the end and stopped beside a doorway, beyond which was the lift. "You are quickly becoming a liability, lawkeeper," Suit said. "The Set does *not* like you, though—as of yet—I have continued to vouch for your effectiveness. Do not make me regret that. Many of my colleagues are convinced that you will turn against us."

Miles didn't know if he would or not. He hadn't decided. He basically only wanted one thing: vengeance. All of the best motives boiled down to a single, driving emotion.

Vengeance for fifteen years in the Roughs, achieving nothing. If this city burned, maybe—for once—the Roughs would see some justice. And maybe Miles could see a government set up here in Elendel that wasn't corrupt. A part of him acknowledged, however, that seeing them—the lords who ruled, the constables who pandered, the senators who spoke so grandly but did nothing of use to real people—cast down would be the most satisfying part.

The Set was part of the establishment. But then, they wanted revolution too. Perhaps he wouldn't turn against them. Perhaps.

"I don't like being in this place, Suit," Miles said, nodding to the chamber where the Vanishers had set up. "It's too close to the center of things. My men will be seen coming and going."

"We will move you soon," Suit said. "The Set is in the process of

acquiring a railway station. You are still committed to the job tonight?"

"I am. We need more resources."

"My colleagues question that," Suit said. "They wonder why
we went to so much trouble to outfit your men with aluminum, if it
was only to be lost in a single fight without so much as killing one
of the Allomancers who faced you."

It's important, Miles thought, *because I intended to use that aluminum to finance my own operations.* Now he was practically destitute,
right back where he'd begun. *Damn you, Wax. Damn you straight to
Ironeyes' Tomb.*

"Do your colleagues question what I've done for them?" Miles
said, drawing himself up. "Five of the women they wanted are in
your possession, all without a speck of suspicion attached to you and
the Set. If you wish that to continue, my men will be *properly* outfitted. A single Rioter could turn the entire bunch against one another."

Suit eyed him. The slender old man did not walk with a cane,
and his back was straight. He was not weak, despite his age and
obvious fondness for fine living. The door to the lift opened. Two
young men wearing black suits and white shirts walked out of it.

"The Set has agreed to this job tonight," Suit said. "After it, you
are to go to ground for six months and focus on recruitment. We
will prepare another list of targets for you to acquire for us. When
you return to activity, we will discuss whether or not the flamboy-
ance of being the 'Vanishers' is required."

"The theatrics keep the constables from—"

"We will discuss it *then.* Will Wax try to interfere tonight?"

"I'm counting on it," Miles said. "If we try to hide, he'll dig us
out eventually. But it won't come to that—he'll figure out where
we're going to hit, and he'll be there trying to stop us."

"You are to kill him tonight, then," Suit said, pointing to the two
men. "The woman you took yesterday will remain here; use her as
bait, if it comes to that. We don't want to move her while that one
has her trail. As for these two, they are to aid you in making certain everything goes smoothly."

Miles gritted his teeth. "I don't need help to—"

"You *will* take them," Suit said coldly. "You've proven unreliable with regard to Waxillium. It is not open for discussion."

"Fine."

Suit stepped closer, tapping Miles on the chest and speaking softly. "The Set is anxious, Miles. Our monetary resources are very limited at the moment. You may rob the train, but don't bother with hostages. We will take half of the aluminum you steal tonight to fund several operations you need not know about. You can have the rest for weapons."

"Have your two men there ever fought Allomancers?"

"They are among our finest," Suit said. "I think you'll find them more than capable."

They both knew what this was. Yes, the two would fight Wax, but they would also keep an eye on Miles. *Great.* More interference.

"I'm leaving the city," Suit said. "Wax is getting too close. If you survive the night, send someone to update me." He said that last part with a hint of a smile.

Insufferable bastard, Miles thought as Suit walked over to the lift, where a quartet of bodyguards waited. He was leaving on his regular train; he'd probably come back on his regular one too. He probably didn't realize Miles had been tracking those.

Suit departed, leaving Miles with the two black-coated men. Well, he'd find some use for them.

He returned to the main chamber, followed by his new baby-sitters. The Vanishers—the thirty or so of them that remained—were getting ready for the job tonight. The Machine had been brought into the chamber via the far platform, which moved up to ground level in a large industrial lift, a majestic electrical wonder.

The world is changing, Miles thought, leaning down on the railing. *First railways, now electricity. How long before men take to the skies, as the Words of Founding say is possible?* The day might come where every man knew the freedom that had once been reserved only to Coinshots.

Change didn't scare Miles. Change was an opportunity, a chance to become something you were not. No Augur was bothered by change.

Augur. He usually ignored that side of himself. His Feruchemy was what kept him alive—and these days he hardly noticed even that, save for the faint sense of extra *energy* to every step he took. He never got headaches, never felt tired, never had sore muscles, never dealt with colds or pain.

On a whim, he took hold of the banister and swung over, dropping to the floor some twenty feet below. For a brief moment, he knew that sense of freedom. Then he hit. One of his legs tried to break—he recognized the slight pop. But the bone's fractures re-knit as quickly as they broke, and so it never fully snapped, cracks opening on one side but resealing on the other.

He rose from a crouch, whole. The black-coated babysitters dropped beside him, one dropping a bit of metal and slowing a moment before he hit. A Coinshot. Well, that would be useful. The other surprised him, landing softly, but not dropping any metal. The ceiling had metal crossbeams. This man would be a Lurcher; he'd Pulled upon those beams to slow himself.

Miles strode through the room, inspecting the Vanishers as they prepared their gear. Every bit of aluminum they had left had gone for guns and bullets. They'd use those from the start this time. At the wedding-dinner fight, it had taken the men a few moments to switch weapons. Now they knew what to anticipate. Their numbers might be fewer, but they'd be much better prepared.

He nodded to Clamps, who was watching over the men. The scarred man nodded back. He was loyal enough, though he had joined up for the thrill of robbery rather than the purpose of any cause. Of them all, only Tarson—dear, brutal Tarson—had anything resembling true loyalty.

Clamps claimed to be dedicated, though Miles knew otherwise. Well, Clamps hadn't been the one to fire the first shot in the last mess. For all Miles's professions about wanting to change things, his temper—and not his mind—had eventually ruled.

He should have been better than that. He was a man created to have a steady hand and an even steadier mind. Made by Trell, inspired by the Survivor, yet still weak. Miles questioned himself often. Was that the mark of a lack of dedication? He'd never done anything in his life without questioning.

He turned, studying his domain, such as it was. Thieves, murderers, and braggarts. He took a deep breath, then burned gold.

It was considered one of the least of the Allomantic metals. Far less useful than its alloy, which was in turn far less useful than one of the prime battle metals. In most cases, being a gold Misting was little better than being an aluminum Misting—a power so useless, it had become proverbial for one who did nothing.

But gold was not completely useless. Just mostly so. Upon burning it, Miles split. The change was visible only to his own senses, but for a moment, he was two people, two versions of himself. One was the man he had been. The angry lawkeeper, growing more bitter by the day. He wore a white duster over rugged clothing, with tinted spectacles to shade his eyes against the harsh sun. Dark hair kept short and greased back. No hat. He'd always hated those.

The other man was the man he'd become. Dressed in the clothing of a city worker—buttoned shirt and suspenders over dirty trousers with fraying cuffs. He walked with a slouch. When had that begun?

He could see through both pairs of eyes, think both sets of thoughts. He was two people at once, and each one loathed the other. The lawkeeper was intolerant, angry, and frustrated. He hated anything that broke with the strict order of the law, and meted out harsh punishments with no mercy. He had a special loathing for someone who had once followed the law, but had turned his back upon it.

The robber, the Vanisher, hated that the lawkeeper let others choose his rules. There was really nothing sacred about the law. It was arbitrary, created by powerful men to help them hold power. The criminal knew that secretly, deep down, the lawkeeper understood this. He was severe toward criminals because he felt so impotent. Each day, life grew worse for the good people, the people who tried, and the laws did little to help them. He was like a man swatting mosquitoes while ignoring the gash in his leg, an artery open and throbbing gushes of blood onto the floor.

Miles gasped, and extinguished his gold. He felt weary, suddenly, and slumped back against the wall. His two minders watched him with emotionless expressions.

"Go," Miles said to them, waving a weak hand. "Check over my men. Use your Allomancy to determine if any of them accidentally left metal on their bodies. I want them clean."

The two men looked at each other. They didn't behave as if they cared to obey him.

"Go," Miles said more firmly. "So long as you're here, you should be useful."

After another moment of hesitation, the two men walked away to do as ordered. Miles slumped down farther, back to the wall, breathing in and out.

Why do I do that to myself?

There had been considerable speculation about what a gold Misting really saw when burning his metal. A past version of himself, certainly. Was it the person he had actually been? Or was it a person he might have become, if he'd chosen another branching path of his life? That possibility had always struck him as sounding reminiscent of the mythical lost metal, atium.

Either way, he liked to think that burning his gold on occasion helped him—that each time he did it, it let him take the best of what he had been and mix it with the best of what he could be. An alloy of himself, then.

It disturbed him how much the two people he became hated each other. He could almost feel it like an oven's heat, radiating from coal and stone.

He stood back up. Some of the men were staring at him, but he didn't care. He wasn't like the criminal bosses he'd often arrested in the Roughs. They had to worry about looking strong in front of their men, lest they be killed by someone who wanted to seize power.

Miles couldn't be killed, and his men knew it. He'd once put a shotgun to his own head in front of them to prove it.

He walked over to a pile of trunks and boxes. A few were full of things Mister Suit had ordered stolen from Wax's mansion, effects the man hoped would help them fight—or perhaps frame—the former lawkeeper. Suit had resisted killing Wax at first, for some reason.

Miles left them and walked around to the back side, where his own trunks had been deposited following the hasty evacuation of their old hideout. He picked through a few, then opened one. His white duster was inside. He took it out, shaking it, then got out a pair of sturdy Roughs trousers and a matching shirt. He slipped his tinted spectacles into the pocket, then went to change.

He'd been worried about hiding, worried that he'd be recognized and branded an outlaw. Well, an outlaw was what he had become. If this was the path he had chosen, he could at least walk it with pride.

Let them see me for what I am.

He would not turn from his course. It was too late to change one's aim when the hammer was already falling. But it wasn't too late to straighten his back.

Waxillium stared at the wall of Ranette's sitting room. One side was piled with furniture, where she'd put things out of the way to make a handier pathway between her workshop and her bedroom. The other half of the room was strewn with boxes of various kinds of ammunition, bits of scrap metal, and cast barrels for gun making. There was dust everywhere. Very like her. He'd asked her for a way to prop up his paper pad, expecting her to find him an easel. She'd absently handed him some nails and pointed toward a hammer. So he'd just hung it on the wall, wincing as he drove the nails into the fine wood.

He stepped up, using a pencil to scribble a note to himself in the corner. The pile of shipping manifests that Wayne had brought lay to the side. Apparently, Wayne had left a gun he'd borrowed from Ranette in place of the manifests, considering it a fair trade.

It had probably never occurred to him that a group of train engineers would be completely baffled to find their manifests gone and a pistol in their place.

Miles will strike at Carlo's Bend, Wax thought, tapping the paper.

It had been easy to locate a shipment of aluminum. House Tekiel, tired of being robbed, was indeed making a large fuss over their new vault-style railway car. Wax could understand the reasoning; the Tekiels were best known as bankers, and their business relied on security and asset protection. The robberies been become a major embarrassment to them. They were intending to recover in a visible way.

It was almost like a dare to Miles and his Vanishers. Wax made another notation on his paper. The Tekiel shipment would follow a very direct route toward Doxonar. He'd mapped it, noting locations where the railway tracks wound close to one of the canals.

I won't be able to watch where we're going, Wax thought, making another notation. *I need to know exactly how far from the previous stop Carlo's Bend is. . . .*

There wasn't much time to prepare. He fingered the earring in his left hand, running his thumb along its smooth side as he thought.

The door opened. Wax didn't look up, but the sound of the footsteps was enough to tell him it was Marasi. Soft shoes. Ranette and Wayne both wore boots.

Marasi cleared her throat.

"Nets?" Wax asked, distractedly writing the number 35.17 on the paper.

"I found some, finally," she said, walking up beside him, looking over the notations. "You can make sense of this?"

"For the most part. Except Wayne's doodles."

"They . . . appear to be pictures of you. Unflatteringly ugly ones."

"That's the part that doesn't make sense," Waxillium said. "Everyone knows I'm irreparably handsome." He smiled to himself. That was one of Lessie's phrases. Irreparably handsome. She'd always claimed he'd look better with a nice scar on his face, after good Roughs fashion.

Marasi smiled too, though her eyes were on his notations and scribbling. "The phantom railcar?" she asked, pointing to his drawing of a ghostly train coming down the tracks, alongside a diagram of how it had probably been made.

"Yes," he said. "Most of the attacks happened on misty nights, apparently to make it much easier to hide the fact that the phantom 'train' is really just a false front with a large headlamp, attached to a moving rail platform."

"You're certain?"

"Reasonably," Waxillium said. "They're using the canals to attack, and so they need some sort of diversion to keep eyes off what is sneaking up behind."

She pursed her lips, thoughtful.

"Was Wayne out there?" Waxillium asked.

"Yes, he's bothering Ranette. I . . . honestly left the room because I worried she'd shoot him."

Waxillium smiled.

"I picked up a broadsheet when I was out," she said. "The constables have found the old hideout."

"Already?" Waxillium said. "Wayne said we had until dark."

"It's dark already."

"It is? Hell." Waxillium checked his watch. They had less time than he'd thought. "It still shouldn't be in the papers yet. The police found the hideout early."

Marasi nodded toward his sketches. "This indicates that you know where the Vanishers will strike. I don't want to pound a brittle metal, Lord Waxillium, but we really should tell the constables that fact."

"I *think* I know where the attack will happen. If we let the constables know, they'll flood the area and scare off Miles."

"Wax," she said, stepping closer. "I understand that independent spirit; it's part of what makes you what you are. But we're not in the Roughs. You don't have to do this all by yourself."

"I don't intend to. I'll involve the constables, I promise. Miles, however, is not an ordinary criminal. He knows what the constables will try, and he will watch for them. This has to be done at the right time, in the right way." Waxillium tapped his notations on the wall. "I know Miles. I know how he thinks. He's like me."

Almost *too* much so.

"That means he can anticipate you too."

"He undoubtedly will. I'll anticipate him better."

The moment Waxillium had drawn his gun and fired back against the Vanishers, he'd started down this path. Once he got his teeth into something, he didn't let go.

"You are right about me," he said.

"Right? I don't believe I said anything about you, Lord Waxillium."

"You're thinking it," he said. "That I'm arrogant for wanting to do this my way, for not handing this over to the constables. That I'm foolhardy to not look for help. You're right."

"It's not so bad as that," she said.

"It's not bad at all," he said. "I *am* arrogant and foolhardy. I *am* acting like I'm still in the Roughs. But I'm also right." He reached up, drawing a small square on the paper, then an arrow from it toward the precinct building.

"I've written a letter for Ranette to send to the constables," he continued. "It details everything I've discovered, and my guesses on what Miles will do, should I fail to best him. I won't make any move tonight until we're well away from the railway and any passengers. The Vanishers won't take a hostage tonight. They'll try to be as quick and as silent as possible.

"But it will still be dangerous. People might die, innocent ones. I'll try my best to keep them from harm, and I firmly believe I have a better chance against Miles than the constables would. I realize that you are studying to be an attorney and a judge, and that your training mandates you should go to the authorities. Considering my plans, and my promises, will you refrain and help me instead?"

"Yes."

Harmony, he thought. *She trusts me.* Too much, probably. He reached up, squaring off a box of notes. "This is your part."

"I won't be in the train car with you?" She sounded worried.

"No," Waxillium said. "You and Wayne will watch from the hilltop."

"You'll be alone."

"I will."

She fell silent. "You knew what I was thinking of you. What are *you* thinking of *me*, Lord Waxillium?"

He smiled. "If the game is to work the same way, I can't tell you my thoughts. You need to guess them."

"You are thinking about how young I am," she said. "And you're worried about having me involved, lest I be hurt."

"Hardly a difficult guess. So far, I've given you what . . . three opportunities to abandon this course and seek safety?"

"You're *also* thinking," she said, "that you're glad I insist on staying, because I will be useful. Life has taught you to use the resources you have."

"Better," he said.

"You think I'm clever, as you have stated. But you also worry that I get flustered too easily, and worry it will be used against you."

"Do those records you've read talk about Paclo the Dusty?"

"Sure. He was one of your deputies before you met Wayne."

"He was a good friend," Waxillium said. "And a solid lawman. But I've *never* met a man who was as easy to startle as Paclo. A softly closed door could make him yelp."

She frowned.

"I assume the records didn't talk about that," Waxillium said.

"They depict him as very brave."

"He *was* brave, Lady Marasi. You see, many people mistake startlement for cowardice. Yes, a gunshot would make Paclo jump. Then he'd run to see what had caused it. I once saw him stare down six men with guns trained on him, and he didn't break a sweat."

He turned to her. "You are inexperienced. So was I, once. So is every man. The measure of a person is not how much they have lived. It is not how easily they jump at a noise or how quick they are to show emotion. It's in how they make use of what life has shown them."

Her blush deepened. "I'm also thinking that you like to lecture."

"It comes with the lawman's badge."

"You don't . . . wear that anymore."

"A man can take it off, Lady Marasi. But he can never stop wearing it."

He met her gaze. She looked up with eyes that were deep, reflective, like the water of an unexpected spring in the Roughs. He steeled himself. He would be bad for her. Very bad. He'd thought the same of Lessie, and he had been right.

"There's another thing I'm thinking about you," she said softly. "Can you guess it?"

All too well.

With reluctance, he broke her gaze and looked at the pad. "Yes. You are thinking that I should talk Ranette into lending you a rifle. I agree. While I do think that it would be wise of you to train with a revolver eventually, I'd rather you spend this particular encounter with a weapon you use well. Maybe we can find a rifle that will fit those aluminum rounds Wayne grabbed."

"Oh. Of course."

Waxillium pretended not to notice her embarrassment.

"I think," Marasi said, "that I'll go check on Wayne and Ranette."

"Good idea. Hopefully she hasn't discovered that he took one of her guns to trade."

Marasi withdrew, walking to the door in haste.

"Lady Marasi?" Waxillium called.

She hesitated at the door, turning, hopeful.

"You did a good job of reading me," he said, nodding in respect. "Not many can do that. I'm not known to be free with my emotions."

"Advanced interrogation techniques class," she said. "And . . . uh, I've read your psychological profile."

"I have a psychological profile?"

"Yes, I'm afraid. Doctor Murnbru wrote it after his visit to Weathering."

"That little rat Murnbru was a *psychologist*?" Waxillium said, genuinely baffled. "I was sure he was a gambling cheat, passing through town looking for marks to swindle."

"Er, yes. That's in the profile. You, uh, have a tendency to think anyone who wears too much red is a chronic gambler."

"I do?"

She nodded.

"Damn," he said. *I'm going to need to read that thing.*

She left and pulled the door closed. He turned back to his plan once again. He raised his hand and slipped his earring into his ear. He was supposed to wear it when praying, or when doing something of great import.

He figured that tonight, he'd be doing a lot of both.

| 3217 Smelter's Row, 6th Oct. | You decide. Story on the reverse, in the fifth column. | division of the Greater Basin Automotive Conglomerate, and is responsible for the content of this message.

…capable of beautiful …nship.

…dally in the insig-
…Please forgive me; …continues to reel at …ts of this week. For, …believe that I have …been spared death, …ed king of this tribe! …n on the dawn of my …ntioned execution. …ing dragged awake …-too-kind fashion, …myself beneath the …un, trudging across …dusty ground. The …tood in silent lines, …me with beady eyes, …n a darkened blue, …of a fine blue scarf if …en singed by fire and …, Red dust stained …ies, and many wore …bare of clothing.

…my life to Hander-…ithful Handerwym; …e day I pulled him …t lake, sodden and …wned. The faithful …n, though sworn not …r kill, has proved his …hundred times. The …emed to respect him, …and allowed him a …roach to embrace his …oon to be murdered …st bleak of fashions. …hat embrace, I found …—my trusty revolv-…ped into my hand, …behind my back. …how he slipped it …m the koloss, and he …d that he had made …e of his metalminds …a connection to the …t is an arcane art he …explored and un-…nd he wishes for me …very little in the way …ation, as he regards

its power as sacred.

Well, I was armed, but still bound. Connection notwith-standing, the koloss pulled him away, though they didn't seem to realize what he had done. I had never had reason to bless the overly long sleeves of the jacket I received in ex-change from that bandit so many weeks ago, but in this case, they may have proved my salvation.

When I tell you of this shot, I ask that you not think too highly of me. Indeed, it was more chance than skill that proved my friend that day. I had managed to wiggle my way free of the bonds slightly, so that I could move one hand down below the other. I twisted the gun in my fingers and was able to lay it flat against my palm, the barrel pointing upward along my arm. At the last mo-ment before I was to meet the headsman, I ducked my head forward and pulled the trigger.

Preservation prevailed, and though I felt the bullet graze the back of my head, it also passed through my bindings. A quick jerk of my hands freed me at that point, and though I was exhausted, I still had some small amount of tin left inside of me. I burned it, enhancing my senses, and raised the gun to shoot the

executioner between the eyes. Koloss are strong, but even they can fall to a bullet in the right place.

The next shot felled the largest of their leaders. I had hoped this alone would se-cure me with their awe, but while it gave them pause, it did not make them free me. Glint had been loaded with only three bullets when I left her; I looked to Handerwym, and he shook his head grimly. He had not had the ammuni-tion to reload her.

I was left with one bullet and an entire village full of monsters. I will not lie and say I was confident in my chances! However, I should mention to you a curious aspect about the koloss. You

see, ever since their first in-teraction with me, they had been insistent that anyone may join them. Any man they deemed worthy could be made koloss, they claimed. Indeed, several of their most brutish and powerful war-riors claimed to have once been men from the City. Obviously false, but there is something in their mindset that makes them think this way.

And so, with my single bullet, I decided to prove to them that I was worthy to join them. Only a test of the greatest skill would provide this proof, I decided, and so, I raised the gun and—

—*Continued next week!!*—

16

Wayne hobbled through the railway station, supporting himself on his brown cane, walking with a slow, intentionally frail step. There was quite a crowd pushing and shoving one another and gawking at the train up ahead. A group of them surged to the side, nearly toppling him.

Everyone was standing up so tall. That gave Wayne—back bent with age—no hope of seeing what the fuss was about. "No thought for a poor elderly woman," Wayne grumbled. A gravelly tone, nasal and higher-pitched than his normal voice, mixed with a nice Margothian District accent. The district no longer existed, at least not in the same way; it had been consumed by the industrial quarter of its octant, its residents moving away. A dying accent for a dying woman. "No respect at all. A travesty, I tell you. Plain and simple, that's what it is."

A few youths in the crowd in front glanced back at him, taking in his ancient coat—it went down to his ankles—his face furrowed with age, his silvery hair beneath a felt cap. "Sorry, ma'am," one of them finally said, making way for him.

Now, there's a nice boy, Wayne thought, patting his arm and hobbling forward. One by one, people made way for him. Sometimes it took a little fit of coughing that sounded like it might be contagious. Wayne was careful not to look like a beggar. That would draw the attention of constables, who might think he was looking for marks to pickpocket.

No, he wasn't a beggar. He was Abrigain, an old woman who had come to see what the fuss was about. Abrigain wasn't rich, nor was she poor. Frugal, with a meticulously patched coat, a favored hat that had once been fashionable. Spectacles thick as a dockworker's wits. A few very young boys let her by, and Abrigain gave them each a piece of candy, patting them on their heads. Nice boys. They reminded Abrigain of her grandchildren.

Wayne eventually reached the front. There, the Breaknaught sat in all its glory. It was a train car built like a fortress, with thick steel armor, shiny rounded corners, and a massive door on the side. That door looked like the one to an enormous vault, with a rotating wheel lock on the outside.

The door was open, and the chamber inside was mostly empty. A large steel cargo box had been *welded* to the floor at the center of the railcar. In fact, he could see through the door in the railcar that the cargo box itself looked as if it had been welded shut on all sides.

"Oh, my!" Wayne said. "That *is* impressive."

A guard stood nearby, wearing the insignia of an officer in the private security force of House Tekiel. He smiled, puffing out his chest with pride. "It marks the dawn of a new era," he said. "The end of banditry and railway robberies."

"Oh, it's impressive, young man," Wayne said. "But surely you exaggerate. I've seen railcars before—I even rode on one, curse that day. My grandson Charetel wanted me to come with him and meet his bride over in Covingtar, and it was the only way, though I thought riding in a horse cart had *always* worked well enough for me before. Progress, he'd called it. Progress is getting locked up in a box, I suppose, unable to see the sun overhead or enjoy the trip. Anyway, that train car was like this one. Only not so shiny."

"I assure you," the guard said, "this is *quite* impregnable. It will change everything. You see that door?"

"It locks," Wayne said. "I can see that. But safes can be cracked, young man."

"Not this one," he said. "Bandits won't be able to open it because it can't be opened—not by them, and not by us. Once that door is closed, it engages a mechanism tied to a ticking clock inside the doors. Those doors cannot be opened again for twelve hours, regardless of whether or not one knows the door code."

"Explosives," Wayne said. "Bandits are always blowing things up. *Everyone* knows that."

"That steel is six inches thick," the guard said. "The amount of dynamite it would take to blow it open would likely destroy the contents of the car."

"But surely an Allomancer could get in," Wayne said.

"How? They could Push on the metal all they wanted; it's so heavy, it would toss them backward. And even if they somehow *did* get in, we will have eight guards riding inside the railcar."

"My," Wayne said, letting his accent slip. "That's impressive indeed. What will the guards be armed with?"

"A full quartet of . . ." the man began, but then trailed off, looking more closely at Wayne. "Of . . ." His eyes narrowed in suspicion.

"Oh, I'm missing my tea!" Wayne exclaimed, then turned and began hobbling back through the crowd.

"Stop that woman!" the guard said.

Wayne stopped pretending and stood up straight, shoving his way through the crowd with more fervor. He glanced over his shoulder. The guardsman was forcing his way forward in pursuit. "Stop!" the guardsman yelled. "Stop, damn you!"

Wayne raised his cane and pulled the trigger. His hand started wobbling as it always did when he tried to use a gun, but this one only had blanks in it, so it was all right. The pistol-like crack drove the crowd into a panic, people ducking down in a wave like wind blowing through a field of grain.

Wayne darted through the prostrate figures, hopping over some of them, reaching the back of the crowd. The guard raised his gun; Wayne dashed around a corner of the station building. Then he stopped time.

He threw off his coat, then pulled off the blouse underneath, revealing a gentleman's suit: black coat, white shirt, red cravat. Wax had called it "purposefully unimaginative," whatever that meant. He removed the items that, tied to the inside of the blouse, had formed the elderly woman's bust: a small bag, a collapsible gentleman's hat, and a wet rag. He unfolded the hat and stuffed the blouse into the extra space inside it before pulling off his wig and putting the hat on his head.

He ripped the outer layer off his cane, turning it black instead. He tossed the wig aside, then dropped the bag by the wall. Finally, he wiped his face clean of makeup with the rag, discarded it, then collapsed his speed bubble.

He stumbled out around the corner of the building, acting as if he'd been shoved. He cursed, straightening his hat and raising his black cane, shaking it in anger.

The guard puffed up beside him. "Are you all right, m'lord?"

"No!" Wayne snapped, filling his voice with every ounce of aristocratic condescension he could manage. Madion Ways accent, the richest area of the First Octant—where House Tekiel owned much of the land. "What kind of ruffian was that, Captain! The launch was supposed to be handled with poise and care!"

The guard froze, and Wayne could see his mind working. He'd been expecting a random nobleman, but this person sounded like a member of House Tekiel—the guard's employers.

"Sorry, m'lord!" the guard said. "But I chased 'im off."

"Who was he?" Wayne said, walking over to the wig. "He threw this aside as he passed me."

"Was dressed up like an elderly woman," the guard said, scratching his head. "Asking me questions about the Breaknaught."

"Damn it all, man. That must have been one of the Vanishers!"

The guard paled.

"Do you know how embarrassed our house will be if something

happens on this trip?" Wayne said, stepping in, shaking the cane. "Our reputation is on the line. Our *heads* are on the line, Captain. How many guards do you have?"

"Three dozen, m'lord, and—"

"Not enough! Not enough at all! Send for more."

"I—"

"No!" Wayne said. "I'll do it. I have several of my own guards here. I'll send one to fetch another division. Your men are watching the area for more *creatures* such as that one?"

"Well, I haven't told them yet, m'lord. Thought I'd try to get 'im myself, you see, and—"

"You left your post?" Wayne screamed, raising hands to the side of his head, cane dangling from his fingers. "You let him *lure you away*? Idiot! Get back, man! Go! Alert the others. Oh, Survivor above. If this goes wrong, we're dead. Dead!"

The guard captain scrambled back and ran for the train, where people were moving away in a panic. Wayne leaned back against the wall, checked his pocket watch, then waited for a good moment when he had enough space to put a speed bubble. He was reasonably sure nobody was looking.

Off came the hat. He dropped the cane and reversed his jacket, turning it into a brown and yellow military coat, matching that of the guards. He pulled off his fake nose and took a triangular cloth cap out of the bag he'd dropped by the wall.

He put this on his head instead of the gentleman's hat. Always have the right hat. That was key. He strapped a handgun on over the coat after dropping his pants, revealing the soldier's uniform beneath. Then he collapsed his bubble and jogged around the corner, making his way up to the tracks. He found the captain organizing his men, yelling orders. There were some angry noblemen arguing with one another nearby.

The cargo wasn't being unloaded. That was good. Wayne had figured they'd just give up on this run, with all the fuss, but Wax had disagreed. He said that the Tekiels had made such a big deal of the Breaknaught that a hiccup or two wouldn't stop them.

Fools, Wayne thought, shaking his head. Farnsward didn't agree with the decision. He'd been in House Tekiel's private guard for ten years now, though he'd mostly served on the Outer Estates with his lord, who was chronically ill. Farnsward had seen a lot in his time, and he'd learned that there *were* reasons to take risks. To save a life, to win a battle, to protect the house's name. But to take a risk just because you'd said you would? Foolishness.

He jogged up to the captain he'd talked to earlier and saluted. "Sir," he said. "I'm Farnsward Dubs—Lord Evenstrom Tekiel said I should report to you." An Outer Estates accent with a hint of aristocracy, picked up from so long associating with them.

The man was looking frazzled. "Very well. I guess we can use every man."

"Sorry, sir," Wayne said, leaning in. "Lord Evenstrom is excitable, sometimes. I know how it goes; this isn't the first time he's sent me to help someone who didn't need it. Bren and I will stay out of your way."

"Bren?"

"Oh, he was right behind me," Wayne said, turning around, looking confused.

Wax ducked out of the station, wearing a uniform similar to Wayne's. He also had a fake paunch of some size, hiding some specific materials he'd need for the night.

"There he is," Wayne said. "He's a dull-minded lout, sir. His father left him the position, but you could hit his steel against flint all night and not get a spark, if you know what I mean."

"Well, stay here," the captain said. "Guard this post. Don't let anyone approach the train car, no matter what they look like." He left, running over to the batch of noblemen.

"'Ello, Wax," Wayne said, tipping his hat to the other man. "Ready to get swallowed?"

Waxillium glanced back toward the station building. Civilians were still scattering. The ground was littered with hats and handkerchiefs. "You need to make sure they still send the train, Wayne. No matter what, it *must* go forward."

"I thought you said they'll be too embarrassed not to launch it."

"For the first part, yes. Not so sure about this next part. Make it happen, Wayne."

"Sure thing, mate." Wayne checked his watch. "She's late—"

A sudden series of cracks split the air. Gunshots. Even though Wayne was expecting them, they still made him jump. The guards around them cried out, shouting, looking for the source of the shots. Waxillium fell, screaming, blood spraying from his shoulder. Wayne caught him as another guard spotted flashes coming from atop the building.

The guards opened fire as Wayne dragged Waxillium out of harm's way. He looked about, then—acting frantic—shoved Waxillium into the open door of the railcar. Several of the guards looked at him, but nobody said a word. Waxillium's eyes were staring dead into the air. The other guards had probably lost mates to bandits or house skirmishes, and they knew. In the heat of the fighting, you got the wounded to safety, and it didn't bloody matter where.

The firing stopped from atop the building, but it started up again from a rooftop nearby. A few bullets sprayed sparks from the top of a nearby girder. *A little close there, Marasi,* Wayne thought with annoyance. Why did every woman he met try to shoot him? Just because he could heal from it. That was like drinking a man's beer just because he could order more.

Wayne plastered a worried look on his face. "They're comin' for the cargo!" he yelled. Then he grabbed the door to the large cargo car, kicked the counterbalance lever to the side, and ran forward. He slammed the door on the Breaknaught shut—Wax inside the railcar, Wayne himself standing outside—before anyone thought to stop him.

The gunfire stopped. Nearby, the guards cowering behind cover looked at Wayne with horrified expressions. The door to the train clicked into place, settling in.

"Rust and Ruin, man!" one of the nearby soldiers said. "What have you done?"

"Locked up the cargo!" Wayne said. "Look, it made them stop."

"There were supposed to be soldiers inside there!" the captain said, running up to him.

"They were trying to get in before we got it locked," Wayne said. "You saw what they were doing." He looked at the door. "They can't get to the cargo now. We've won!"

The captain looked concerned. He glanced at the noblemen who were picking themselves off the ground. Wayne held his breath as they came storming over to the captain. The captain, however, repeated Wayne's same words.

"But we stopped them," the captain explained, knowing that he—and not Wayne—would bear the blame if it was decided that mistakes had been made. "They dropped their attack. We won!"

Wayne stepped back, relaxing against a pillar as guards were sent to try to find out who had been shooting. They came back with a large number of rifle bullet casings planted on the ground in various locations, though most of the "shots" had been blanks. Several beggar boys had been paid to fire blanks into the air, then plant stories of men getting into horse carriages and riding away in a hurry.

In under an hour, the train was on its way—with everyone at House Tekiel convinced they'd fought off a major Vanishers robbery. There was even talk of giving Wayne a commendation, though he deflected the glory to the captain and slipped away before anyone could begin asking just *which* lord retained him as a bodyguard.

17

Waxillium rode alone in the cold cargo railcar, shoulder wet with fake blood, listening to the wheels thump over the tracks beneath him. A swinging lamp hung where he'd placed it on a hook in the ceiling, near a corner. He'd also secured the webbing of nets on the ceiling, tucked up and held in place by special hooks affixed with industrial tape. It felt good to have all of that removed from wrapping around his legs, thighs, and fake paunch. His guard's uniform, now much too large for him, lay in a heap in the corner, and he wore a utilitarian pair of suit pants and a light black jacket instead.

He sat on the floor, back to the side of the cargo container, legs stretched out. He held Vindication in his hand, absently spinning the cylinder and hitting the switch to lock it on to the special chambers. He had two of each type of hazekiller round in his pocket, and had loaded a Coinshot round and a Pewterarm round into the special chambers.

He still had his earring in.

You wanted me to do this, he thought toward Harmony. Did an accusation count as a prayer? *Well, here I am. I'll expect a little help, if that's acceptable to your immortal plan, and all that.*

The cargo box was beside him. He could see why House Tekiel was so proud of the job they'd done; the welded strongbox would be ridiculously difficult for thieves to steal. Getting it out of the car would require hours spent cutting it free with a gas torch or a large electric saw. That, plus the clever door and the supposed existence of guards, would make for a daunting—perhaps impossible—robbery.

Yes, the Tekiels had been clever. Problem was, they were thinking about this all wrong.

Waxillium pulled a package from beneath his coat. The dynamite and detonator that Wayne had found. He set the package beside him on the floor, then eyed his pocket watch. *Right about now . . .*

The train suddenly started to slow.

"Yup," Wayne said, looking through the spyglass as he crouched against the hillside. "He's right. Wanna see?"

Marasi took the spyglass nervously. The two of them were in position following a hasty gallop out of the city. She felt naked, wearing a pair of Ranette's trousers. *Completely* improper. Every man they passed would stare at her legs.

Maybe that will stop the Vanishers from shooting, she thought with a grimace. *They'll be too distracted.* She raised the spyglass to her eye. She and Wayne were atop a hill along the railway route, outside of the City. It was nearly midnight when the train had finally come chugging along.

Now it was slowing, and the brakes caused screeches and sparks in the night. Ahead of the train, a ghostly apparition was approaching in the opposite direction, a bright light shining in front of it. She shivered. The phantom railcar.

"Wax'll be happy," Wayne said.

"What?" she asked. "About the phantom?"

"No. There's mist tonight."

She started, realizing that it was forming in the air. The mist wasn't like a normal fog; it didn't come rolling in over the ocean. It grew in the air, sprouting like frost on a cold piece of metal. She shivered as it began to envelop them, giving the headlamps below a ghostly cast.

She focused the spyglass on the approaching train. Because she'd been warned what to look for, and because of her angle, she could easily see the truth. It *was* a decoy. A hand-propelled rail wagon behind a wooden engine facade.

"How do they make the light work?" she said.

"I dunno. Magic?"

She snorted, trying to get a good look at what was behind the framework. "Must be some kind of chemical battery. I've read of the work . . . but Rust and Ruin, that's a *powerful* light. I doubt they can run it for long."

As the real train pulled to a halt, some men sprang from its sides. House Tekiel had sent guards. That gave Marasi a smile. Maybe the robbery wouldn't happen after all.

The front portion of the phantom train dropped.

"Aw, *hell*," Wayne said.

"What is—"

She was cut off by a loud series of shots, incredibly fast. She jumped back by reflex, ducking down, though nothing was aimed at them. Wayne grabbed the spyglass, raising it.

Marasi couldn't make out what happened next through the darkness and the mists. And she was glad. The shots continued, and she heard men screaming.

"Rotary gun," Wayne said softly. "Damn, these people are *serious*."

"I have to help," Marasi said, unslinging the rifle Ranette had given her. It was of an unfamiliar make, but the woman swore it would be more accurate than anything Marasi had ever used. She raised the rifle. If she could hit the Vanishers . . .

Wayne took the barrel of her rifle in one hand, gently pushing it down. The rotary gun stopped firing, and the night grew silent.

"There's nothing you can do, mate, and we don't want to draw the attention of that damn rotary. Besides, you really think you can hit one of them from all the way up here?"

"I've hit red at five hundred paces."

"At night?" Wayne said. "In the mists?"

Marasi fell silent. Then she held out her hand and gestured impatiently for the spyglass. Wayne gave it to her, and she watched six men hop from the phantom train. They walked along the sides of the real train, guns at the ready and watching.

"Distraction?" Wayne asked, watching.

"Lord Waxillium thought so. He said to . . ." She trailed off.

He said to watch the canal.

She turned, scanning the canal with the spyglass. Something big and dark was floating down it. Shrouded in mists, it looked like some kind of massive beast—a leviathan swimming quietly through the water. It came up to the middle of the train, then halted. A dark, shadowy leg lifted from the black mass. *By the Survivor,* she thought, shivering. *It's alive.*

But no . . . the leg was too stiff. It moved up, rotated out, then came down. As the thing in the canal stopped, the leg clamped into place on the shore. *For stabilization,* Marasi realized. *That's what made the depression in the ground we saw earlier.*

Once the thing . . . the machine . . . was stabilized, some men moved through the darkness to the vault car. They worked for a few moments. Then a large arm rose out of the dark mass on the canal. It swung over toward the tracks, then reached down, grabbed the entire vault car, and *lifted* it.

Marasi gaped. The car was lifted only a few feet, but that was enough. The machine was a crane.

The Vanishers who had unhooked the couplers helped push the train car over across the narrow strip of land toward the canal. The black mass had to be a barge. Marasi ran some quick numbers in her head. In order to lift the train car like that, the barge must be very heavy and have considerable ballast on the other side.

She lifted her spyglass and was pleased to be able to pick out another crane arm extending in the other direction, holding some kind of heavy weight. The barge sank somewhat into the waters as the vault car was lifted, but not as far as Marasi would have assumed. It probably was designed with some means of bottoming out in the canal, perhaps an extendable section underneath the barge. That, plus the stabilizing arm, might be enough.

"My, my, my . . ." Wayne whispered. "Ain't that somethin'."

The machine dropped the entire vault car onto its barge, and then lifted something else off. Something large and rectangular. She had already guessed what to expect. A replica.

Marasi watched as the duplicate railcar was lowered onto the tracks. The couplings made it *very* tricky. This could ruin their entire plan; lower the car in the wrong way, ruin a coupler, and when the train pulled away it would leave its back half on the tracks. That would make it more obvious what had happened. The Vanishers on the ground guided the process.

Several of the other Vanishers were firing shots through the windows of a passenger car a few places ahead, probably to keep anyone from peeking out. However, the way the tracks bent around a tree-topped hill here, it would be very difficult for anyone inside to get a good view of what was happening. The phantom railcar's light had vanished a few moments ago, and she knew it would be speeding backward along the tracks. Where did they keep it hidden? Perhaps it was loaded onto another barge after getting far enough ahead to be out of sight?

The Vanishers who had been working with the barge were running over to climb back onto their vehicle, which was slipping out into the center of the wide canal, where it was practically invisible in the misty night. It moved as a shadow.

"Wayne!" she said, scrambling up. "We've got to go."

He sighed, standing. "Sure, sure."

"Waxillium is *in that train car!*"

"Yeah. You ever notice how often he gets to be the one who rides in comfort, while I have to do things like gallop or walk all the time? Not very fair."

She slung the rifle on her shoulder, hurrying down the hill. "You know, when I was reading the reports, I never imagined that you'd complain this much."

"Now, that's not fair. I'll have you know that I pride myself on my cheery, optimistic attitude."

She stopped, looking back at him, raising an eyebrow. "You pride yourself on it?"

He raised a hand to his chest, adopting a tone that sounded almost priestly. "Yes, but pride is bad, you know. I've been trying to be more humble lately. Hurry up, hurry up. We're gonna lose them. You want Wax to be cornered and alone? Gosh, woman."

She shook her head, turning and continuing down the hillside to where their horses were tied.

Miles stood with hands clasped behind his back, riding on the front of the Machine as it slid quietly down the canal. The part crane, part barge wasn't exactly what he'd envisioned when he'd explained his plot to Mister Suit, but it was close.

He was proud of what he'd done: not just become a thief, but become one that captured people's imaginations. Suit could say what he wanted about the theatrics, but they worked. The constables had no idea how he was performing the thefts.

"They checked on all six of the Tekiel guards, boss," Tarson said, stepping up to him. His arm was out of its sling. Pewter savants could heal quickly. Not as quickly as someone like Miles, but it was still remarkable. Of course, pewter savants were also likely to run themselves to death, never noticing that their body was exhausted. It was a dangerous art that burned men up as quickly as Allomancers burned metal.

"Engineers too," Tarson continued. "They caught a few more guards in the last passenger car, trying to sneak out to see how we were getting the cargo. We shot them. I think that means we're clean."

"Not yet," Miles said softly, staring forward into the darkness as they sailed through the mists, moving by way of a pair of slow-turning propellers underneath the barge. "Waxillium knows how we're doing this."

Tarson hesitated. "Uh . . . you sure?"

"Yes," Miles said absently. "He's inside the train car."

"What!" Tarson spun, looking at the large car riding in the middle of the barge. Miles could hear members of his team covering it with a tarp, to obscure it as they approached the City. They'd look like an ordinary barge, the arms and ballast hidden under other tarps and the whole thing disguised to look like a shipment of stone from one of the outer quarries. Miles even had a shipping manifest and docking authorization, along with a few tarps that actually hid piles of neatly cut stone.

"I don't know the method he used," Miles said. "But he'll be in there. Wax thinks like a lawkeeper. This is the best way to find our hideout—stay with the cargo you know will be stolen, even if you're not sure precisely how." He paused. "No. He'll have guessed how we're doing it. That's the risk of being as good as he is. As good as I was. You start to think like a criminal."

Better than a criminal, really.

In a way, it was surprising that more lawkeepers didn't end up turning to crime. If you saw something done wrong frequently enough, you'd—by nature—want to see it finally done right. Miles had started planning these robberies in the back of his mind ten years ago, when he'd realized that railway security was focused on the railcars. At first it had been just a thought experiment. That was another thing to be proud of. He had robbed, and he'd done it well. Very well. And the people . . . he'd gone through the city, listening. They spoke with awe of the Vanishers.

They'd never treated him like that back in the Roughs. They'd hated him while he'd protected him. Now they loved him while he stole from him. People were baffling, but it felt good not to be hated. Feared, yes. But not hated.

"So what are we going to do?" Tarson asked.

"Nothing," Miles said. "Wax likely doesn't realize I've guessed he's there. That gives us an advantage."

"But . . ."

"We can't open the railcar here," Miles said. "That's the entire point of the thing. We'll need the workshop." He paused. "Though I suppose we could just dump the entire car into the canal. It's deep enough here to sink entirely. I wonder if Wax has a plan to open the door if something like that happens."

"I don't think Mister Suit would much like us sinking the train car, boss," Tarson said. "Not after what he must have spent to make that replica."

"Yes. Unfortunately, the canal is only about fourteen feet deep. If we dumped the car, we'd never get it back out before another ship's hull collided with it, revealing what we've done. Pity."

Waxillium's death would almost be worth the loss of the cargo. Mister Suit didn't realize how dangerous the man was. Oh, he *acted* like he did. But if he had really appreciated how dangerous, how *effective*, Waxillium was . . . well, he'd never have allowed this robbery. He'd have stopped all operations and pulled out of the city. And Miles would have agreed with the move, save for one thing.

That would have meant no confrontation.

They floated into the City, carrying the train car, its cargo, and its occupant—almost as if Wax were a lord in his grand carriage. His was a nearly impregnable fortress that protected him from the dozen or so men on the barge who would happily have killed him.

Mister Suit's two minders—who called themselves Push and Pull—joined Miles at the front of the barge, but he didn't speak to them. Together, they drifted through Elendel. Streetlights were lines of fire in the mists, bright white, running along the canal. Other lights sparkled high in the sky, the windows of buildings that were shrouded in the mist.

Nearby, some of his men were muttering. The mists were considered bad luck by most, though at least two of the major religions accepted them as manifestations of the divine. Miles had never been certain how to think of them. They made Allomancy stronger, or so some claimed, but his abilities were already as strong as they could be.

The Church of the Survivor taught that the mists belonged to him, Kelsier, Lord of Mists. He appeared on nights when the mist was thick and gave his blessing to the independent. Whether they be thieves, scholars, anarchists, or a farmer who lived on his own land. Anyone who survived on his own—or who thought for himself—was someone who followed the Survivor, whether he knew it or not.

That's another thing the current establishment makes a mockery of, Miles thought. Many of them claimed to belong to the Church of the Survivor, but discouraged their employees from thinking for themselves. Miles shook his head. Well, he no longer followed the Survivor. He'd found something better, something that felt more true.

They sailed down past the outer ring of the Fourth and Fifth Octants. Two massive buildings rose up opposite one another across the canal. The tops disappeared into the mists. Tekiel Tower was on one side, the Ironspine on the other.

The freight dock for the Ironspine was alongside its own branch from the canal. They steered the barge into it, gliding to a stop, then used the dock's stationary crane to lift the hidden train car off the barge. It was supposed to be a big pile of rock, after all. They slowly swung it into the air, then over and gently down onto the platform.

Miles jumped off the barge and onto the ground and walked to the platform, joined by Push and Pull. The rest of his men filed in around him, looking very pleased. Some were joking with one another about the bonus they'd get for the heist.

Clamps looked very disturbed, and he scratched at the scars on his neck. He was a Survivorist, his scars a mark of devotion. Tarson just yawned a wide, gray-lipped yawn, then cracked his knuckles.

The entire platform shook, then began to move, descending one story into the foundry hall. Once they passed through, the doors closed above. The lift lurched slightly as it came to a stop. Miles looked to the side, down the long tunnel that Mister Suit claimed would someday provide train access under the city. It looked hollow, empty, lifeless.

"Hook up the chains," Miles said, hopping off the platform. "Fix the train car in place."

"Couldn't we just wait?" Tarson asked, frowning. "It'll open in twelve hours, right?"

"I plan to be gone in twelve hours," Miles said. "Wax and his people are too close. We're going to crack that car open, deal with whoever's inside, then grab the aluminum and go. Get to work; let's rip the door off."

His men hastened to obey, tying the large train car to the wall with a large number of clamps and chains. Another set of chains was hooked to the Breaknaught's door; these chains wrapped around the same powerful electric winching mechanism that raised and lowered the platform. The platform shook as it was disengaged, the motors instead engaging the chain wheels.

Miles walked to the gun rack, selecting two aluminum handguns identical to the ones in his holsters. He was disturbed to notice that there was only one other gun on the rack. They'd lost a fortune in weaponry. Well, he'd just have to see that Waxillium was duly repaid. Miles strode through the room, chains clinking on the floor and men grunting. The air smelled of coke from the inactive forges.

"Arm up!" Miles ordered. "Get ready to fire on the person inside the moment we open the thing."

The Vanishers glanced at one another, confused, but then unslung or unholstered guns. He had about a dozen of them here, with some others in reserve. Just in case. Never put all your bullets in the same gun when Waxillium was around.

"But boss," one of the Vanishers called, "the report said the train left without the guards inside!"

Miles cocked his gun. "If you find a building without rats, son, then you know that something more dangerous scared them away."

"You think he's in there?" Push said in a near monotone, stepping up beside him. Obviously, he hadn't heard Miles's conversation about Wax on the barge.

Miles nodded.

"And you brought him here."

Miles nodded again.

Push's face darkened. "You should have told us."

"You were given to me to help deal with him," Miles said. "I just wanted to see you boys get your chance." He turned. "Start the motor!"

One of the men pulled the lever, and the chains grew taut. They groaned, pulling against the door. The train car rattled, but was kept in place by the other chains behind.

"Be ready!" Miles called. "When the door opens, fire at anything that so much as *quivers* inside that car. Arm yourselves *only* with aluminum, and don't save ammunition. We can collect the bullets later and recast them."

The train's door buckled in its mountings, the metal groaning. Miles and his men moved out to the sides, away from the path of the chains. Three hastily went to set up the rotary gun, but Miles waved them down. They didn't have aluminum bullets for that, so firing it could be a disaster against a prepared Coinshot.

Miles refocused his attention on the vault car. He stilled his breath and felt his body grow warm as he increased the power he was tapping from his metalmind. He didn't need to breathe. His body renewed itself each moment. He'd stop his heartbeat if he could. A heartbeat was such an annoyance when trying to aim.

Even without breathing, he'd never been able to shoot as well as Wax. Of course, nobody could. The man seemed to have an inborn instinct for firearms. Miles had seen him make shots he'd have sworn were impossible. It almost seemed a shame to kill such a man. It would be like burning a one-of-a-kind painting, a masterpiece.

But it was what had to be done. Miles extended his arm, sighting with the revolver. The door continued to warp, and the links in several of the chains began to show strain. But there were enough of them, and the motor was strong enough, that the door's bindings began to break. Scraps of metal sprang free, bolts snapping. One took Miles on the cheek, ripping skin. The cut regrew itself immediately. No pain. He only faintly remembered what pain felt like.

Then the door gave a final screech of death, ripping free and flying across the room. It hit the ground, spraying sparks and skidding as the man at the lever hastily stopped the engine. The door came to a rest between the Vanishers, who nervously trained their weapons on the dark interior of the car.

Come on, Wax, Miles thought. *Play your hand. You've come to me. Into my den, into my lair. You're mine now.*

Poor fool. Wax never could stop himself if a woman was in danger.

That was when Miles noticed the string. Thin, almost invisible, it led from the fallen door to the inside of the railcar. It must have been tied to the door, then set inside in a loose pile with lots of slack. When they yanked the door off, the string didn't snap, but was strung out along behind. What . . .

Miles glanced again at the fallen door. Tape. Dynamite.

Aw, hell.

Someone inside the train car—hiding behind the box of aluminum—pulled the string tight with a sudden jerk.

18

Outside, the entire room shook. Inside, the train car lurched—though it appeared someone had been kind enough to secure it in place, preventing Waxillium from being thrown about too much. He held on to the rope he'd tied around the strongbox, head down, Vindication up beside his ear.

As soon as the blast wave passed, he threw himself over the top of the box and ducked out into the room. Smoke churned in the air; bits of stone and steel were scattered across the floor. Most of the lights had been knocked out by the explosion, and those that remained were swinging wildly, painting the room with bewildering shadows.

Waxillium scanned the devastation and did a quick count. At least four men down. He probably could have hit more if he'd detonated the explosion earlier, but he'd worried about hurting innocents. He'd needed a moment to glance out and make sure that Steris or others weren't near.

Waxillium Pushed up and backward off a scrap of metal, throwing himself into the air before any Vanishers could draw a bead on him. He aimed Vindication as he flew, shooting one man who was rising and shaking his head. Waxillium landed atop the train car and fired twice more with precision, killing two more Vanishers.

A ragged figure stood up on the side of the room, and Waxillium shot just before he recognized Miles. The left side of his suit coat and shirt had been shredded, but he'd already regrown his flesh, and now was lifting a gun of his own.

Damn, Waxillium thought, dropping down behind the wrecked train car. He'd been hoping to find himself in a more traditional hideout, with narrow hallways and hidden nooks. Not this open stone pen of a room. It was going to be hard not to get boxed in here.

He glanced around the side of the railcar, and was met with a hail of fire from four or five different places. He ducked back around, hastily reloading Vindication with ordinary rounds. He was pinned down already. This was *not* going well.

Another of the room's lights flickered, then went out. Fires started by the explosion illuminated the room with a primal red glow. Waxillium crouched down, Vindication held ready. He didn't bother with a steel bubble; they were all firing aluminum bullets.

It was either get pinned down and killed as they rounded the railcar, or risk getting shot as he broke out. So be it. He kicked up a chunk of metal, then Pushed it in front of him. It drew gunfire as he charged after it, Pushing behind himself to rise soaring through the air. He turned sideways, firing as he flew, mostly to force the enemy to keep their heads down. He managed to shoot one, however, before hitting the ground and sliding into the shadow of some fallen boxes.

He righted himself and reloaded hastily. His side was aching, bleeding through the bandage. The railcar was affixed to the north side of the room. He'd dashed out to the west, and had ended up in the northwestern corner of the room where the boxes were stacked. The western side, a little bit to the south of him, opened on some kind of tunnel. Maybe he could run that way.

He ducked around the side of the boxes and plugged one of the Vanishers in the forehead. Then he rolled into cover behind a larger stack of crates.

Someone was creeping around the boxes to his left; he could

hear their steps crunching on bits of rubble from the explosion. Waxillium raised his gun, stepped to the side, and fired.

The black-suited man raised a casual hand. Tracking the bullet with the blue lines of an Allomancer, Waxillium could see it get flung back and hit the wall above him. *Great. A Coinshot.* He rolled Vindication's cylinder, locking it into place. Unfortunately, fire from the other Vanishers forced him back down before he could shoot the special round.

That Coinshot was close. Waxillium had to move quickly. He grabbed a few of the weighted kerchiefs from his pockets and threw them out with Pushes to draw fire, then worked his way around the right side of the boxes. He had to keep in motion. It—

He came face-to-face with someone moving around the boxes to flank him. The lean man had ashen skin and wore Wayne's hat. Tarson, he'd been called at the other fight.

Tarson's eyes widened in surprise and he swung a fist—never mind that it was holding a revolver. The man was koloss-blooded, maybe a Pewterarm as well, considering how easily he'd recovered from being shot. Men like that often punched first and thought about their guns second.

Waxillium barely pulled back in time; he felt the fist brush past the tip of his nose, then collide with one of the boxes, smashing it. He raised Vindication, but Tarson—moving with supernatural quickness—slapped it out of his hand. Yes, a Pewterarm for certain. Koloss-blooded men were strong, but not nearly that fast.

Reflexively, Waxillium Pushed himself backward. Going hand-to-hand with this man would be suicide. It—

The roof exploded.

Well, not the entire roof. Just the portion above Waxillium, where it looked like the train car had been lowered on some kind of mechanical platform. Waxillium ducked down as pieces of metal dropped; he Pushed some away. Gunfire erupted above, and the Pewterarm ducked back before it, as a few bullets hit the boxes nearby.

A figure dropped from above, wearing a duster and holding a

pair of dueling canes. Wayne hit hard right beside Waxillium, grunting in pain, and the distinctive shimmer of a speed bubble popped up around them.

"Ouch," Wayne said, rolling over and stretching out his leg, letting it heal from fracturing.

"You didn't need to jump down so quickly," Waxillium said.

"Oh yeah? Look up, muffin-brains."

Waxillium glanced upward. While he'd been fighting the Pewterarm, the black-suited Coinshot had advanced. The man was landing in slow motion atop the crates, revolver in hand, a puff of smoke coming out as a bullet slowly left the barrel. That barrel was pointed right at Waxillium's head.

Waxillium shivered, then took a deliberate step to the side. "Thanks. And . . . muffin-brains?"

"Tryin' out better insults," Wayne said climbing to his feet. "You like the new duster?"

"Is *that* what took you so long? Please tell me you didn't go shopping while I was fighting for my life."

"Had to take out three gits what was guarding the entrance up above," Wayne said, spinning his dueling canes. "One of them had this fine garment upon his person." He hesitated. "I'm a little late 'cause I was trying to figure a way to beat him up without ruining the coat."

"Great."

"Had Marasi shoot 'im in the foot," Wayne said, grinning. "You ready to do this thing? I'll try to take our friend with the koloss blood there."

"Be careful," Waxillium said. "He's a Pewterarm."

"Charming. Y'always do introduce me to the most lovely of folks, Wax. Marasi's going to cover us from above, keep the gunmen pinned down. Can you handle the Coinshot?"

"If I can't, it's time to retire."

"Oh. Is that what we're calling 'getting shot' these days? I'll remember that. Ready?"

"Go."

Wayne dropped the speed bubble and rolled forward, surprising the Pewterarm as he came around the boxes. The Coinshot's bullet hit the ground. Waxillium jumped for Vindication, which had fallen onto a nearby box after being knocked from his hand.

The Coinshot moved by reflex, jumping down and Pushing on the gun. Ranette was many things, but rich wasn't one of them—and so Vindication wasn't made of aluminum. The Coinshot's Push threw the gun right at Waxillium's head. He cursed, ducking, letting the gun pass above. He had other guns, of course, but they had only ordinary bullets.

Guessing the Coinshot was trying to slam the gun into the wall and break it, Waxillium Pushed upward with everything he had, sending the gun soaring up through the hole in the ceiling.

Waxillium followed it, dropping a round and launching himself after his weapon. The Coinshot tried to fire on him, but a well-placed shot from Marasi—she was using aluminum bullets herself—nearly took him in the head, causing him to duck away.

Waxillium passed into a wave of mist that was falling into the room like a waterfall. He burst into the dark, misty night sky and snatched Vindication from the air. He Pushed himself sideways off a lamppost as bullets zipped up after him, leaving trails in the mist.

He hit the building beside him and grabbed hold. Something dark soared out of the hole and into the air. The Coinshot. He was joined by a second man wearing black, also some kind of Allomancer, though the trajectory of his flight looked more like that of a Lurcher.

Great. Waxillium pointed his gun downward and drove an ordinary bullet into the ground, then Pushed down on it while decreasing his weight to drive himself into the sky. The other two followed in graceful leaps, and Waxillium rolled the cylinder of Vindication and locked it on to the special chamber.

Goodbye, he thought, firing right at the Coinshot's head.

By sheer chance, the man happened to Push himself to the side just at that moment. It hadn't been a deliberate dodge, just a lucky motion. The bullet streaked uselessly into the mists past the man, who raised his own gun and fired a pair of shots, one of which clipped the side of Waxillium's arm.

Waxillium cursed as his blood sprayed into the dark night, then Pushed himself off to the side to move erratically and avoid their fire. *Idiot!* he thought, angry. *Doesn't matter how good your bullets are if you don't aim carefully.*

He concentrated on staying ahead of the other two, jumping back and forth up the side of the enormous Ironspine Building. The Coinshot moved in graceful leaps after him, while the Lurcher was more direct, Pulling himself on the metal in the building's steel frame in bursts. He'd jump outward, then Pull himself upward and back toward the building, like a strange inverse rappeller.

Both saved their bullets, waiting for the right shot. Waxillium did the same, but for a different reason; he wasn't certain firing on them would do any good. He needed to load another hazekiller round. And, if possible, he needed to split up the two Allomancers so he could deal with them one at a time.

He worked his way upward, pushing off the steel beneath the stone in the ledges he landed upon. He soon ran into the same problem as the first time he'd climbed this building. It grew narrower at the top, and he could go only up and out, not in. This time, he didn't have his shotguns. He'd given those to Tillaume.

He did have that other hazekiller round, the one built to hit a Pewterarm especially hard. He hesitated—should he save it for the man below?

No. If he died now, he'd never have another chance to face the man below. Waxillium reached out, pulling the trigger and thrusting himself backward. It wasn't as powerful as the shotgun, but as light as he was, it did nudge him back toward the building.

The Coinshot blew right past him in the air, looking surprised. The man leveled his gun, but Waxillium fired first. An ordinary round—but the Coinshot was forced to Push against it to keep it away. Waxillium Pushed at the same time, and that shoved him to the building. The unfortunate Coinshot was launched out into the sky away from the tower.

Good, Waxillium thought. Now over a hundred feet in the air, he grabbed the facade. He fired down at the Lurcher, but the man was Pulling carefully. Waxillium's bullet arced and hit the plate on the Lurcher's chest.

Waxillium hesitated for a moment, then let go of the wall, balancing as he pulled his other revolver out of his second shoulder holster.

He emptied it, firing all six rounds in rapid succession. The Lurcher turned, angling his chest toward Waxillium, sparks flying as the bullets hit his breastplate. Luck wasn't with Waxillium—sometimes you could kill a Lurcher that way, as one of the bullets ricocheted toward his face or the plate at his chest got knocked free. Not this night.

Cursing, Waxillium threw himself out into the air and dropped past the man. The Lurcher jumped out into the air after him. They plunged through the mists.

Waxillium fired a shot downward to slow himself right before he hit the ground. He needed to get a shot at the Lurcher at just the right angle to—

A second shot cracked in the air, and the Lurcher screamed. Waxillium twisted, raising his gun, but the Lurcher hit the ground face-first, already bleeding.

Marasi popped up from a shrub next to him. "Oh! That looks like it hurt." She winced, looking concerned for the man she'd just shot with an aluminum rifle round.

"Hurting is kind of the idea, Marasi."

"Targets don't scream."

"Technically, he was a target too." *And many thanks to Wayne for grabbing the wrong bullets back after the wedding dinner.* He hesitated. What was he forgetting?

The Coinshot.

Waxillium cursed, dropping the empty ordinary pistol and grabbing Marasi. He ducked into the opening as a spray of gunfire came from the mists, narrowly missing them. Waxillium carried her down into the room, landing softly.

The lower chamber was a scene of chaos. Men lay broken on the floor, some dead from the blast, others fallen to Waxillium's shots. A large group of Vanishers had set up near the western tunnel, firing out at Wayne—who was in full form, burning through his bendalloy like a madman. He'd appear, draw fire, then vanish into a blur, and appear right next to where he'd been. He called insults as the bullets missed him, then moved again.

The gunmen kept trying to guess where he'd appear next, but that was a fruitless game. Wayne could slow time, see where the bullets were heading, then walk to a place where they wouldn't hit. It took a great deal of luck and skill to hit a Slider who knew you were there.

Impressive as it was, though, it was a delaying tactic. With so many men firing on him, Wayne couldn't risk moving any closer. He had to wait momentarily between creating speed bubbles, and if he was too close to the men, there was a good chance they'd be able to aim, shoot, and hit him in the seconds that he was exposed. The longer Wayne tried to dodge, the better the men shooting at him would get at judging the pauses. If he tried it too long, he'd get hit.

Waxillium took in the scene, then held out a hand to Marasi. "Dynamite."

She handed him her stick.

"Find cover. Try and hit that Coinshot when he comes down for us." Waxillium dashed into the room, firing without looking toward the group of men. They cried out, ducking for cover. Waxillium reached Wayne as a speed bubble went up.

"Thanks," Wayne said. Streaks of sweat ran down the sides of his face, though he was grinning.

"The Pewterarm?" Waxillium asked.

"We fought to a standstill," Wayne said. "Bastard is *fast*."

Waxillium nodded. Pewter burners always gave Wayne trouble. Wayne could heal far more quickly, but the Pewterarm's powers made him fast and strong. In a hand-to-hand fight, Wayne was at the disadvantage.

"He still has my lucky hat," Wayne noted, nodding to where the gray-skinned man stood behind the group of Vanishers, egging them on. "This latest group came from that tunnel. I think there are more down there. Don't know why Miles hasn't brought them in."

"Too many guns firing in a room this size gets more and more dangerous for his men," Waxillium said, looking about. "He'll want reserves, try to wear us down. Where is Miles, by the way?"

"Trying to flank me," Wayne said. "I think he's hiding to the side of the train car there."

Wayne and he stood in the center of the room, train car behind and to the left, boxes and crates behind and to the right, tunnel to the right.

Waxillium could reach the train car pretty easily. "Great," he said. "First plan to deal with Miles is still a go."

"I don't think it'll work."

"That's why we have a second plan. But let's hope this one does work. I'd rather not put Marasi in more danger." Waxillium held up the dynamite. There was no fuse—it was meant to be set off by pulling a detonator. "You go for those men. I've got Miles. Ready?"

"Yup."

Waxillium tossed the dynamite and Wayne dropped the speed bubble right before the dynamite hit the border. Any object—small ones particularly—that left a speed bubble was deflected slightly in an unpredictable way. That was why firing bullets out of one was practically useless.

The Vanishers looked up from their hiding places. The dynamite fell toward them. Waxillium leveled Vindication and fired the last bullet in the cylinder at the falling dynamite.

The explosion shook the room, loud enough to set Waxillium's ears ringing. He spun, ignoring that, to see Miles step out from beside the broken train car. Waxillium grabbed a handful of rounds and ran for the vault car, hastily ducking inside to find cover as he reloaded.

A figure darkened the doorway a moment later. "Hello, Wax," Miles said. He stepped up into the vault car.

"Hello, Miles." Taking a deep breath, Waxillium Pushed against the metal hooks above, which he'd affixed there to hold the nets in place. They sprang free, dropping the nets around Miles.

As Miles jerked about in surprise, Waxillium Pushed on the clasps at the bottom of the nets, shooting them out of the gaping hole where the door had been. That pulled the nets tight at the bottom and yanked Miles's feet out from under him.

Miles hit the floor of the railcar's interior, banging his head against the box that held the aluminum. That probably wouldn't even daze him, but the awkward fall *did* make him drop his gun. Waxillium leaped forward, grabbing it and pulling it out of the nets; then he stood, breathing quickly.

Miles thrashed at the nets. Despite his incredible healing powers, he wasn't any stronger than an ordinary man. The trick wasn't to kill him. It was just to incapacitate him. Waxillium stepped forward, only now finding a chance to bind the wound on his arm. It wasn't bad, but it was bleeding more than he'd have liked.

Miles looked up at him, growing calm. Then he reached into his pocket, got out his cigar case, and pulled a small, slender stick of dynamite from it.

Waxillium froze. He felt an awful moment of realization, followed by a jolt of terror.

Aw, hell! He threw himself past Miles and out of the railcar. The awkward leap left him spinning in the air. He had a brief glance of Miles yanking at the dynamite's blasting cap. The man was enveloped in a bright, powerful blast.

The explosion hurled Waxillium forward like a leaf before the wind. He smashed to the ground, and his vision flashed. He lost a few moments.

He came to, bloodied, dazed, rolling to a stop. His head swam. He was unable to move or even think, his heart thumping in his chest.

A figure stood up in the railcar. Waxillium's vision was too blurry to make out much, but he knew it was Miles. His clothing had been shredded, much of it blown off his body, but he was whole. He'd set off dynamite in his *hand* in order to free himself from the nets.

Rust and Ruin . . . Waxillium thought, coughing. How badly was he hurt? He rolled over, numb. That wasn't a good sign.

"Is there any doubt that I have been chosen for something great?" Miles bellowed. Waxillium could barely hear it; his ears were nearly useless after that blast. "Why else would I have this power, Waxillium? Why else would *we* be what we are? And yet, we let others rule. Let them make a mess of our world while we do nothing but chase petty criminals."

Miles hopped down from the train car, then strode forward, bare-chested, trousers hanging in rags. "I am tired of doing what the city tells me. I should be helping people, not fighting meaningless fights as prescribed by the corrupt and the uncaring."

He reached Waxillium, leaning down. "Can't you see? Can't you see what important work we could be doing? Can't you see that we're *meant* to be doing it, perhaps even ruling. It's almost like . . . like we, with the powers we have, are divine." He seemed to almost be begging for Waxillium to agree, to give him justification.

Waxillium just coughed.

"Bah," Miles said, straightening up. He flexed a hand. "You don't think I realize that the only way to stop me is to tie me up? A little explosion can serve a man so well, I've found. I keep the dynamite in the cigar cases. Few people look there. You should have questioned the criminals I caught back in the Roughs. A few of them tried capturing me with ropes."

"I . . ." Waxillium coughed. His own voice sounded wrong in his ears. "I couldn't have talked to any of the criminals you caught. You killed them all, Miles."

"So I did," Miles said. He grabbed Waxillium by the shoulder, hauling him to his feet. "I see you dropped my gun as you jumped out of the train. Wonderful." He punched Waxillium in the stomach, causing him to exhale with a grunt. Then Miles let him fall to the ground, wandering over toward a gun lying nearby.

Dazed, but knowing he needed to get to cover, Waxillium somehow lurched to his feet. He Pushed against a piece of machinery and sent himself sailing across the room, where he landed beside the boxes. Those had been scattered in the blast, but they still provided some protection.

Coughing, bleeding, he crawled behind them. Then he collapsed.

Wayne spun between two Vanishers. He brought his dueling canes to the side, slamming them into the back of one of the men. He was rewarded with a satisfying *crack*. The man fell.

Wayne grinned, dropping his speed bubble. The other man who had been trapped in it with him spun about, trying to draw a bead on Wayne—but while sped up, he'd inadvertently moved into the path of several of his comrades who'd been firing.

The Vanisher fell to a spray of bullets. Wayne jumped back, erecting another bubble around just him and one confused Vanisher.

Everything outside slowed—bullets stilled in the air, shouts vanished, the waves diffusing as they hit the speed bubble. That did strange things to sound. Wayne spun about and knocked the gun out of the hands of the Vanisher behind him, then lunged forward and rammed the end of a cane into the man's neck. The man gurgled in surprise; then Wayne smacked him on the side of the head, dropping him.

He stepped back, puffing and spinning one of his canes. His bendalloy was running low, so he ate another bit. His last. More worrisome were his metalminds, which were almost completely spent. *Again*. He hated fighting that way. A single gunshot could end him. He was as fragile as . . . well, everyone else. It was most disturbing.

He stepped up to the perimeter of his speed bubble, wishing it would move with him. That Pewterarm was still wearing Wayne's lucky hat; the man had ducked behind cover when Wax had thrown the dynamite, and had only just emerged. He didn't appear to have been injured badly; a few scrapes to his face, the sort of thing a Pewterarm could ignore. Too bad. But at least the hat was doing all right.

The man had begun to charge toward Wayne, moving extremely slowly, yet noticeably faster than the other Vanishers. It was frustrating, but Wayne knew he had to stay away from the man. He'd never beaten a Pewterarm without a lot of health stored up. Better to keep jumping around, keeping the man confused until Marasi or Wax could shoot him a few times.

Wayne turned and scanned the area nearby, choosing where he should stand as he dropped the bubble. With so many bullets being fired, he didn't want to . . .

Was that *Wax*?

Wayne gaped, only now noticing Waxillium's bloodied form hurtling across the room, as if by a Steelpush. Wax was pointed toward a group of boxes on the northwestern side of the room, to Wayne's left. His suit had been shredded and burned along one side. Another explosion? Wayne thought he'd heard something, but jumping in and out of speed bubbles could really play havoc with sounds.

Wax needed him. Time to end this fighting, then. Wayne dropped the bubble and dashed forward. He counted to two, then put up another bubble and dodged right. He dropped it and kept running, bullets streaking through the air where he had been. To the eyes of those trying to track him, he'd have blurred and appeared immediately to the right of where he'd just been. He did it again, dodging back in another direction, then dropped the bubble.

Almost there. Another bubble up, and—

Something hit Wayne in the arm. He felt the blood before the pain, strangely enough. He cursed, stumbling, and threw up a bubble immediately.

He grabbed his arm. Warm blood squirted between his fingers, and in a panic, he tapped the last smidgen of healing in his metalmind. It wasn't enough to fix the gunshot wound; it barely slowed the bleeding. He turned, noticing another bullet about to hit his speed bubble. He jumped to the side just before it touched the perimeter, zipped through the air in a heartbeat, then hit the other side and slowed again, deflected erratically up toward the ceiling.

Damn, Wayne thought, tying an improvised bandage on his wounded arm. *Someone has very good aim.* He glanced about to find the black-suited Coinshot kneeling beside the wall, holding a familiar-looking rifle, sights on Wayne. The rifle was the one Ranette had given to Marasi. *Well, this is going to hell faster than bendalloy burns.*

He spent a moment of hesitation. Wax was down. But Marasi . . . what had happened to her? Wayne couldn't spot her anywhere, though the Coinshot had cover beside some machinery, and he had her gun. That spoke loads.

Wax would want him to go help the girl.

Gritting his teeth, Wayne turned and dashed toward the Coinshot.

Waxillium groaned, stretching against the pain and pulling the small two-shooter from his ankle holster. He'd dropped Vindication in the blast—Ranette was going to kill him for that—and he'd left his other gun up above when grabbing Marasi. He was down to this.

He unsuccessfully tried to cock the tiny pistol with a shaking hand. He didn't dare prod to feel the extent of his wounds. His leg and arm had been flayed.

Mist continued to flood down from the hole above. It had mostly enveloped this side of the room. With despair, Waxillium realized that his two-shooter had been damaged in the blast, and the hammer no longer cocked. Not that it would be of any use against Miles anyway.

He groaned again, leaning his head back against the floor. *I thought I asked for a little help.*

A voice returned to him, distinct and unexpected. *And a little is what you received, I think.*

Waxillium started. *Well . . . could I have some more, then? Um, please?*

I must be careful in playing favorites, the voice inside his mind replied. *It upsets the balance.*

You're God. Isn't playing favorites kind of the point?

No, the voice replied. *The point is Harmony, creating a way for as many as possible to make their own choices.*

Waxillium lay staring up at the swirling mists. The blast had dazed him worse than he'd thought.

Are you divine, the voice asked of him, *as Miles claims that Allomancers are?*

I . . . Waxillium thought. *If I were, I doubt I'd be in this much pain.*

Then what are you?

This is a very bizarre conversation, Waxillium thought back.

Yes.

How can you see things like what has been done by the Vanishers, Waxillium asked, *and not do something to help?*

I have done something to help. I sent you.

Waxillium breathed out, blowing the mists in front of him. What Miles had said bothered him: *Is there any doubt we've been given this for a reason?*

Waxillium gritted his teeth, then forced himself to stand. He felt better in the mists. The wounds didn't seem so bad. The pain didn't seem so sharp. But he was still unarmed. Still cornered. Still . . .

Suddenly he recognized the box right in front of him. It was his own trunk. The one he'd taken with him when first leaving for the Roughs, twenty years ago. The one—now battered and aged—he'd brought back with him to the City.

The one he'd filled with his guns on that night months ago. There was a tassel from a mistcoat hanging out of one side.

You're welcome, the voice whispered.

Marasi hid in the shadows behind the broken train car, anxious, her heart pounding. The Coinshot had come hunting her after what she'd done to his friend. With his Allomancy, he'd have been able to see her wherever she ran, despite the darkness and the mist, so she'd tucked the rifle behind a few boxes and hid elsewhere.

It felt cowardly, but it had worked. He'd shot a few times into the boxes, then walked around and picked up the gun, looking baffled. He'd obviously expected to find her bleeding and dead.

Instead, she was simply unarmed. She had to get to a weapon, had to do *something.* Wayne had been shot; he'd lured the Coinshot away, but he'd been dripping blood when she'd seen him.

The room was chaos, and it left her disoriented. Wayne had told her that the dynamite sticks they had were relatively small ones, but detonating them in close confines was still enormously, painfully loud. The gunshots were nearly so. The air smelled of smoke, and when gunshots weren't sounding, she could faintly hear men groaning and cursing and dying.

Before the Vanishers had appeared at the wedding dinner, she'd never been in any kind of fight. Now she didn't know what to do; she'd even lost track of which direction was which. The room was dark, lit only by flickering flames, and the mists made apparitions around her.

Some Vanishers were huddled together, guarding the mouth of the tunnel with the koloss-blooded man. She could barely make them out when she peered out of her hiding place. They held their guns leveled. She couldn't go that way.

A figure strode from the darkness nearby, and she barely held in a gasp. She recognized Miles Hundredlives from his description. Narrow face, short dark hair. He was stripped to the waist, exposing a powerful chest. His trousers were in tatters. He was counting the bullets in a revolver, and was the only one in the room who wasn't creeping or cowering. His legs kicked up mist, which now coated the floor.

He stopped by the Vanishers at the mouth of the tunnel and said something she couldn't hear. They ducked away, retreating down the passage. Miles didn't follow them, but strode through the room, getting closer to Marasi. She held her breath, hoping he'd pass closely enough to her hiding place for . . .

A rustle of cloth sounded, and the Coinshot dropped into place beside Miles. Miles stopped, raising an eyebrow.

"Pull is dead," the Coinshot said. Marasi could barely hear him, but she could tell that his voice was taut with anger. "I've been trying to end the short one. He keeps leading me on chases through the room."

"I believe I have said before," Miles said, voice loud and bold, "that Wayne and Waxillium are like rats. Chasing them is useless. You need to draw them to you."

Marasi leaned forward, breathing shallowly, as quietly as she could. Miles was almost close enough. A few more steps . . .

Miles snapped his revolver closed. "Waxillium crawled somewhere. I lost him, but he's wounded and unarmed." Then Miles turned and pointed the revolver directly at Marasi's hiding place. "Call for him if you would, Lady Marasi."

She froze, feeling a sharp stab of horror. Miles's face was calm. Icy. Emotionless. He would kill her without a second thought.

"Call for him," Miles said more firmly. "Scream."

She opened her mouth, but nothing came out. She could only stare at that gun. Her training in the university told her to do as he ordered, then run the moment he turned away. But she couldn't move.

The mist-shrouded shadows at the corner of the room began to shift. She ripped her gaze away from Miles. Something dark moved in the mists. A man, standing up tall.

The mists seemed to draw back. Waxillium stood there, wearing a large, dusterlike coat, cut into strips below the waist. A pair of revolvers gleamed in holsters at his hips, and he rested a shotgun on each shoulder. His face was bloodied, but he was smiling.

Without saying a word, he lowered the shotguns and blasted Miles in the side.

19

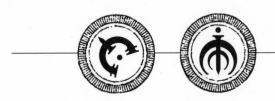

Shooting Miles was, of course, useless. The man could survive a dynamite explosion at close range. He could take a few shotgun blasts.

But the shots caused the Coinshot to Push himself away in alarm. They also left Miles sprayed with metal. Wax increased his weight and Pushed, though he found it hard to get a purchase on the birdshot. Any metal that pierced a person's body or touched his blood was very difficult to affect with Allomancy.

Fortunately, Miles's body obliged him by healing itself and spitting out the birdshot. In the instant before it could drop to the floor, Wax's Push suddenly found anchors, and he threw Miles across the room and into the wall.

The Coinshot landed on the other side of the room. Waxillium dashed forward, mistcoat flapping. Damn, but it felt good to be wearing one of those again. He skidded to a stop beside Marasi, taking cover next to the railcar.

"I almost had him," Marasi said.

"Waxillium!" Miles bellowed, his voice echoing in the room. "All you do is stall. Well, know *this*. My men have gone to kill the woman you came here to save. If you want her to live, give yourself to me. We—"

His voice cut off strangely. Wax frowned as something moved behind Marasi. She jumped, and Wax pointed a shotgun, but it turned out to be Wayne.

"Hey," he said, puffing. "Nice gun."

"Thanks," Wax said, shouldering it, noting the speed bubble around them. That was what had stopped Miles's voice. "Your arm?"

Wayne glanced down at the bloody bandage around his left arm. "Not so good. I'm outta healing, lost some blood. I'm slowing, Wax. Slowing too much. You look pretty beat-up yourself."

"I'll survive." Wax's leg was throbbing, his face scraped up, but he felt surprisingly good. He always felt that way, in the mists.

"The things he's saying," Marasi said. "You think he's telling the truth?"

"He might be, Wax," Wayne said urgently. "The blokes who was set up in front of the tunnel, they charged off a few shakes back. Looked like they had something important to do."

"Miles *did* tell them something," Marasi added.

"Damn," Wax said, glancing around the corner of the railcar. Miles might be bluffing . . . but then again, he might not be. It wasn't a chance Wax could take. "That Coinshot is going to make things difficult. We need to take him down."

"What happened to Ranette's fancy gun?" Wayne asked.

"Not sure," Wax said with a grimace.

"Wow. She's gonna rip out your insides, mate."

"I'll be sure to blame you for it," Wax said, still watching the Coinshot. "He's good. Dangerous. We'll never take out Miles unless that Allomancer is dead."

"But you've got those special bullets," Marasi noted.

"One," Wax said, slipping a shotgun into its holster inside his coat. He pulled out the other Coinshot round. "I don't think an ordinary revolver will fire this. I . . ."

He trailed off, then looked at Marasi. She was raising an eyebrow at him.

"Right," Wax said. "Can you two keep Miles busy?"

"No problem," Wayne said.

"Let's go, then," Wax said, taking a deep breath. "One last try."

Wayne met his eyes and nodded. Wax saw tension in his friend's face. The two of them were battered and bloodied, low on metals, metalminds drained.

But they'd been here before. And this was when they tended to shine their brightest.

As the speed bubble fell, Wax ran out from behind the train car. He tossed the bullet into the air ahead of him, then Pushed on it with a quick snap of power. The Coinshot raised his hand with casual confidence, Pushing it right back at Wax.

The casing and bullet proper broke free and flipped toward Wax, who deflected them easily, but the ceramic tip continued forward. It took the Coinshot right in the eye.

Bless you, Ranette, Wax thought, leaping up and Pushing off the coins in a fallen Vanisher's pocket. That launched him forward, into the tunnel. There were tracks on the ground here, as if this were built for a train.

Wax frowned in puzzlement, but Pushed on them, heedlessly hurling himself through the darkness until he reached a set of stairs leading upward. The ceiling here was wood; a structure of some sort had been built over the tunnel. He charged into the stairwell, which led up to the wooden building, perhaps a barrack or dormitory.

Wax smiled, the pain of his wounds retreating further as he grew more energetic. He heard footsteps on the wooden floor at the top of the stairwell. They were ready for him. It was a trap, of course.

He found that he didn't care. He unslung both shotguns, then Pushed on the nails in the steps and blasted up the stairwell. He passed the first floor and continued on toward the second—he'd rather check up first, then down. If Steris was being held here, she'd probably be up at the top.

Now we're burning, Wax thought, metal flaring, energy rising. He threw his shoulder against the door at the top of the stairs, breaking out into a second-floor hallway. Feet stomped up the steps behind him and men burst out of rooms nearby, fully armed, wearing no metal.

Wax smiled, raising his shotguns. *All right. Let's do this.*

Wax Pushed hard against the nails in the boards under the feet of the men leveling aluminum guns at him. Planks ripped free by their nails, making the floor tremble, throwing off the Vanishers' aim. He dodged right, rolling out of the hallway and into a room to its side. He came up and spun, leveling both shotguns back at the doorway.

Vanishers from the stairwell piled into the hallway after him, and his arms jerked as he fired twin shotgun blasts. He *Pushed,* slamming the men back and sending himself crashing out the window. This building was more an old warehousing shed; there was no glass in the windows, just shutters.

Wax blasted out into open air. There was a lamppost on the dark street, a little bit to his left. He Pushed on that while at the same time dropping his weight to nearly nothing. The Push sent him back against the outside of the building; he landed and half ran, half leaped parallel to the ground along the wall.

Reaching the next room over from where he'd been, he Pushed on another lamppost and crashed through the window feet-first, splinters spraying around him. He landed and came up in the building, then turned toward the wall between him and the room he'd just left.

He holstered the shotguns and grabbed his revolvers, pulling them out in a cross-armed motion. They were Ranette-made Sterrions, among the best guns he'd ever owned. He raised them and increased his weight, then Pushed hard on the nails in the wall before him.

The cheap wood exploded away, the wall disintegrating into a spray of splinters and planks, nails becoming as deadly as bullets as they ripped into the men in the next room. Wax fired, dropping any that the nails had missed in a storm of splinters, steel, and lead.

A click to his left. Wax spun as a doorknob turned. He didn't wait to see who was beyond. He Pushed on the doorknob, ripping it out of its frame and through the door, into the chest of the Vanisher trying to get in. The door slammed open, and the unfortunate man crashed through the wall of the hallway—there were no rooms on the other side, just the wall of the narrow building—propelled out into the misty night.

Wax holstered the Sterrions, barrels smoking, chambers empty. He pulled out the shotguns, rolling into the hallway and coming up in a crouch. He raised a shotgun in each direction. A few straggling Vanishers climbed up the stairs to his right; another group were leveling weapons to his left.

He Pushed on the twin metal levers on the sides of his shotguns, cocking them with Allomancy. The spent casings flipped out into the air above the guns, and Waxillium fired while Pushing, driving birdshot and spent casings into the waiting Vanishers on either side.

The floor next to Waxillium exploded.

He cursed, throwing himself to the left as gunfire from below blasted chips of wood into the air. They were getting smart, firing at him from underneath. He turned and ran, firing shotgun blasts down through the floor, mists creeping in through the broken walls.

There had to be another dozen Vanishers below. Too many to fire at without being able to see them. A bullet grazed his thigh. He turned and ducked away, leaping over the bodies of the fallen and dashing down the hallway. Bullets chased him, the floor splintering, men calling below as they fired everything they had up at him.

He hit the door at the end of the hallway. It was locked. A healthy dose of increased weight—along with some momentum and a shoulder—fixed that. He crashed through and found himself in a small windowless room with no other doors.

A short, balding man cowered in one corner. A woman with golden hair and a rumpled ball gown sat on a bench at the back of the room, her eyes red, her face haggard. Steris. She looked utterly dumbfounded as Wax spun through the broken doorway, mistcoat tassels flaring around him. He Pushed on some of the nails in the floor back in the hall, causing the boards there to ripple, drawing much of the gunfire.

"Lord *Waxillium?*" Steris said, shocked.

"Most of me," he said, wincing. "I may have left a toe or two in that hallway." He glanced at the man in the corner. "Who are you?"

"Nouxil."

"The gunsmith," Wax said, tossing him a shotgun.

"I'm not actually a very good shot," the man said, looking terrified. A few bullets blasted up through the floor between them. The Vanishers had realized they'd been tricked. They knew what he was looking for.

"It doesn't matter if you're a good shot," Wax said, raising his empty hand to the back wall and breaking it open with an increased-weight Push. "It matters if you can swim or not."

"What? Of course I can. But why—"

"Hang on tightly," Wax said as more gunshots erupted around him. He Pushed on the shotgun in the gunsmith's hands, flinging him out the opening, throwing him some thirty feet in an arc toward the canal outside.

Wax spun, grabbing Steris as she stood up. "The other girls?" he asked.

"I haven't seen any other captives," she said. "The Vanishers implied they were sent somewhere."

Blast, he thought. Well, he was lucky to find even Steris. He Pushed lightly off the nails in the floor, propelling the two of them toward the ceiling. As they approached, he took advantage of the fact that it didn't matter how heavy an object was when it came to falling. All objects fell at the same rate. That meant that increasing his weight manyfold would not affect his motion.

Raising his shotgun, he shot a concentrated blast of pellets into the ceiling. Then he Pushed on them sharply, his increased weight meaning the Push didn't really move him much—just as when he was lighter, a Push affected him greatly.

The result was that he continued his momentum upward—but

his Push blasted a hole in the ceiling. He made himself incredibly light and Pushed more strongly off the nails below. The two of them shot up through the hole he'd made, propelled some forty or fifty feet into the air. He spun in the night, mistcoat tassels splaying outward, smoking shotgun clutched tightly in one arm, Steris in the other. Bullets from below left streaks in the mist as it swirled around them.

Steris gasped, clinging to him. Wax drew every bit of weight he had left, draining his metalminds completely. That was hundreds upon hundreds of hours of weight, enough to make him crush paving stones if he tried to walk on them. In the strange way of Feruchemy, he didn't grow more dense—bullets would still cut through him easily if they hit. But with this incredible conflux of weight, his ability to Push grew incredible.

He used that weight to Push downward with everything he had. There were numerous lines of metal below. Nails. Doorknobs. Guns. Personal effects.

The building trembled, then undulated, then *ripped apart* as every nail in its frame was driven downward as if propelled by a rotary gun. There was an enormous crash. The building was crushed down into the railroad tunnel on top of which it had been built.

The weight was gone from him in an instant, compounded upon itself in that moment, his metalminds drained all at once. Wax let gravity take him, and he dropped through the mists, Steris clinging to him. They landed in the middle of the wreckage at the bottom of the railroad tunnel. Smashed lumber and fragments of furniture were strewn across the floor.

Three Vanishers stood in the mouth of the tunnel, openmouthed. Wax raised the shotgun and cocked it with Allomancy, then laid into them with shotgun blasts. They were the only ones that had still been standing. Everyone else had been crushed down into the tunnel.

A small fire flickered in the corner where a lantern had fallen. By its light, he checked on Steris, the mists pouring down around them and filling the tunnel.

"Oh *Survivor of Mists!*" Steris breathed, cheeks flushed, eyes wide, lips parted as she held to him. She didn't look terrified. If anything, she seemed aroused.

You are a bizarre woman, Steris, Wax thought.

"Do you realize that you have missed your calling, Waxillium?" a voice yelled from within the blackened tunnel. It was Miles. "You are an army unto yourself. You are *wasted* in the life you've taken upon yourself."

"Take this," Wax said softly to Steris, handing her the shotgun. He cocked it. One shell left. "Hold it tightly. I want you to run for the precinct station. It's at Fifteenth and Ruman. If one of the Vanishers comes for you, fire the shotgun."

"But—"

"I don't expect you to hit him," Wax said. "I'll listen for the sound of the shot."

She tried to comment further, but Wax ducked down to get his center of mass beneath her, then carefully Pushed the shotgun up into her middle. He used it to launch her up and out of the pit. She landed awkwardly, but safely, and hesitated only a moment before running off into the mists.

Wax scrambled to the side, making sure he wasn't backlit by the fire. He pulled a Sterrion from its holster and fished out some rounds. He reloaded as he crouched down.

"Waxillium?" Miles called from deep inside the tunnel. "If you're done playing, perhaps you'd like to come settle things."

Wax crept up to the tunnel mouth, then stepped inside. The mists had filled it, making it difficult to see—which would work equally against Miles. He made his way forward cautiously until he saw the light from the big workshop at the end, where fires still burned.

By that light, he could faintly make out the silhouette of a figure standing in the tunnel, holding a gun to the head of a slender woman. Marasi.

Waxillium froze, pulse accelerating. But no, this was part of the plan. It was perfect. Except . . .

"I know you're in there," Miles's voice said. Another figure moved, tossing a few improvised torches into the darkness.

With a freezing sense of horror, Waxillium realized that Miles wasn't the one holding Marasi. He stood too far back. The man holding Marasi was the one named Tarson, the koloss-blooded Pewterarm.

Her face illuminated by wavering torchlight, Marasi looked terrified. Waxillium's fingers felt slick on the revolver's grip. The Pewterarm was careful to keep Marasi between himself and Waxillium's side of the tunnel, gun to the back of her head. He was squat and tough, but not very tall. He was only in his twenties—like all koloss-blooded, he'd continue growing taller throughout his life.

Either way, at the moment, Waxillium couldn't get a bead on him. *Oh, Harmony*, he thought. *It's happening again*.

Something rustled in the darkness nearby. He jumped and nearly shot it until he caught the outline of Wayne's face.

"Sorry about this," Wayne whispered. "When she got grabbed, I thought it was Miles. And so I—"

"It's all right," Waxillium said softly.

"What do we do?" Wayne asked.

"I don't know."

"You always know."

Waxillium was silent.

"I can hear you whispering!" Miles called. He walked forward and tossed another torch.

Just a few steps more, Waxillium thought.

Miles stopped where he was, eyeing the creeping mists with what seemed like distrust. Marasi whimpered. Then she tried jerking, the way she had back at the wedding dinner.

"None of that," Tarson said, holding her carefully. He fired a shot right in front of her face, then brought the gun back to her head. She froze.

Waxillium raised his revolver.

I can't do this. I can't watch another one die. Not by my hand.

"All right," Miles called. "Fine. You want to test me, Wax? I'm counting to three. If I reach three, Tarson shoots, no other warnings. One."

He'll do it, Waxillium realized, feeling helpless, guilty, overwhelmed. *He really will.* Miles didn't need a hostage. If threatening her wouldn't bring Waxillium out, then he wouldn't bother with her.

"Two."

Blood on the bricks. A smiling face.

"Wax?" Wayne whispered, sounding urgent.

Oh, Harmony, if I've ever needed you . . .

Mist curled around his legs.

"Th—"

"Wayne!" Waxillium yelled, standing.

The speed bubble went up. Tarson would fire in mere moments. Miles behind him, pointing angrily. Torchfire frozen. It was like watching an explosion in slow motion again. Waxillium raised his Sterrion, and found his arm incredibly still.

It had been still on the day he'd shot Lessie, too.

He'd shot her with this very gun.

Sweating, trying to banish the images from his head, he tried to find a clear shot at Tarson. There wasn't one. Oh, he could hit Tarson, but not anywhere that would drop him immediately. And if Waxillium didn't hit just right, the man would shoot Marasi by reflex.

The head was the best way to drop a Pewterarm. Only, Waxillium couldn't *see* the head. Could he shoot the gun? Marasi's face was in the way. The knees? He might be able to hit a knee. No. A Pewterarm would ignore most hits—if the damage wasn't immediately lethal, he'd stay up, and he'd shoot.

It *had* to be the head.

Waxillium held his breath. *This is the most accurate gun I've ever fired,* he thought. *I can't sit here, frozen. I have to act.*

I have to do something.

Sweat dripped off his chin. He raised his hand with a quick motion in front of him, then pointed the Sterrion to the side, off center from Marasi or Tarson. Wax fired.

The bullet shot out of the bubble in an instant, then hit slower time. It deflected, as bullets always did when fired from within a speed bubble. He watched it go, judging its new trajectory. It moved forward sluggishly, spinning as it cut through the air.

Wax took careful aim, waited several excruciating moments. Then he readied his steel.

"Drop it on my mark," he whispered.

Wayne nodded.

"Go."

Wax fired and Pushed.

The speed bubble fell.

"—ee!" Miles called.

A small shower of sparks exploded in the air as Wax's second bullet, propelled with incredible speed by his Steelpush, clipped the other one in midair and deflected it to the side: behind Marasi, into Tarson's head.

The Pewterarm dropped immediately, gun slapping to the ground, eyes staring dully upward. Miles gaped. Marasi blinked, then turned about, raising her arms to her chest.

"Aw, biscuits," Wayne said. "Did you *have* to hit him in the head? That was my lucky hat he was wearin'."

Miles recovered his wits and raised his revolver toward Wax. Wax turned and fired first, hitting Miles's hand, dropping his gun to the ground. Wax shot it, knocking it backward into the other room.

"Stop *doing* that!" Miles screamed. "You bast—"

Wax shot him in the mouth, driving him backward a step, throwing out chips of tooth. Miles still wore only the tattered remnants of his trousers.

"Somebody shoulda done that ages ago," Wayne muttered.

"It won't last," Wax said, plugging Miles in the face again to try to keep him disoriented. "Time for you to be off, Wayne. Backup plan is still a go."

"You sure you got them all, mate?"

"Tarson was the last." *And I'd better not be wrong. . . .*

"Grab my hat if you get the chance," Wayne said, scrambling away as Wax shot Miles in the face again. This hit barely bothered him, and the half-naked man lurched forward. Toward Marasi. Miles was unarmed, but there was murder in his eyes.

Wax dashed forward, throwing the empty gun at Miles, then fishing out a handful of bullets. He Pushed them toward the former lawman. One sliced him in the arm, one cut through his gut and came out the other side, but none lodged in a way that Wax could push them to shove Miles back.

Wax hit Miles just before he reached Marasi. The two went down in a heap on the dirty ground, under the mists rolling across the floor.

Wax grabbed Miles by the shoulder and started punching. *Just . . . keep . . . him busy . . .*

Miles showed a flash of amusement through the annoyance. He took a few of the punches, Wax's fist growing sore in the process. Wax could punch until his knuckles broke and his hand was reduced to a bloody mess, and Miles would be no worse for the wear.

"I knew you'd go for the girl," Wax said, holding Miles's attention. "You talk grandly about justice, but in the end, you're just a petty criminal."

Miles snorted, then kicked Wax free. Pain flared in Wax's chest as he was thrown back into a muddy portion of the tunnel, cold water splashing around him, soaking his mistcoat.

Miles stood up, wiping some blood off his lip where it had split, then healed. "You know the *really* sad thing, Wax? I understand you. I've felt like you, I've thought like you. But there was always that distant, rumbling dissatisfaction within. Like a storm on the horizon."

Wax got to his feet and rammed a fist into Miles's kidney. It didn't even get a grunt. Miles grabbed him by the arm, twisting it, causing his shoulder to flare with pain. Wax gasped, and Miles kicked the back of his knee, sending him to the ground again.

As Wax tried to roll over, Miles grabbed him by the front of his shirt and hauled him up, then laid into him with a fist to the face. Marasi gasped, though she had been told to stay back. She did her part.

The punch slammed Wax down to the ground, and he tasted blood. Rust and Ruin . . . he'd be lucky if his jaw wasn't broken. He also felt like he'd ripped something in his shoulder.

His wounds suddenly seemed to crash down upon him. He didn't know if it was the mists, some action of Harmony, or simple adrenaline that had helped him ignore them for a time. But he hadn't been healed. His side screamed from where he'd been shot, and his leg and arm had been burned and scraped raw by the explosion. He'd been clipped by bullets in the thigh and the arm. And now, Miles's beating.

It overwhelmed him, and he groaned, slumping down, struggling to merely remain conscious. Miles pulled him up again, and Wax managed to get in one thrashing swing that connected. And did nothing. It was very, very difficult to brawl with a man who didn't flinch when you hit him.

Another punch sent Wax to the ground again, head ringing, eyes seeing stars and flashes of light.

Miles leaned down, speaking in his ear. "Thing is, Waxillium, I know you feel it too. A part of you knows that you're being used, that nobody cares about the downtrodden. You're just a puppet. People are murdered every day this city. At least one a day. Did you know that?"

"I . . ." *Keep him talking.* He rolled onto his back, aching, meeting Miles's eyes.

"People murdered every day," Miles repeated, "and what was it that brought you out of your 'retirement'? When I shot an old, would-be aristocratic wolfhound in the head. Did you ever stop to think of all the other people being killed in the streets? The beggars, the whores, the orphans? Dead because of lack of food, or because they were in the wrong place, or because they tried something stupid."

"You're trying to invoke the Survivor's mandate," Wax whispered.

"But it won't work, Miles. This isn't the Final Empire of legend. A rich man can't kill a poor one just because he feels like it. We've gotten better than that."

"Bah!" Miles said. "They pretend and lie to make a good show."

"No," Waxillium said. "They have good intentions, and make laws that prevent the worst of it—but those laws still fall short. It's not the same thing."

Miles kicked him in the side to keep him down. "I don't care about the Survivor's mandate. I've found something better. That doesn't matter to you. You're just a sword, a tool that goes where it's pointed. It rips you apart that you can't stop the things that you know you should. Doesn't it?"

They met eyes. And, shockingly—despite the agony—Waxillium found himself nodding. Truthfully nodding. He did feel it. That was why what had happened to Miles terrified him.

"Well, someone has to do something about it," Miles said.

Harmony, Waxillium thought. *If Miles had been born back then, in the days before, he'd have been a hero.* "I'll start helping them, Miles," Waxillium said. "I promise it to you."

Miles shook his head. "You won't live that long, Wax. Sorry." He kicked again. And again. And again.

Waxillium curled around himself, hands over his face. He couldn't fight. He just had to last. But the pain was mounting. It was *terrible*.

"Stop it!" Marasi's voice. "Stop it, you monster!"

The kicks stopped falling. Waxillium felt her beside him, kneeling, hand on his shoulder.

Fool woman. Stay back. Unnoticed. That was the plan.

Miles cracked his knuckles audibly. "I suppose I should deliver you to Suit, girl. You're on his list, and you can replace the one Waxillium set free. I'll probably have to track her down."

"Why is it," Marasi said angrily, "that small-minded men must destroy that which they know is better, and greater, than they?"

"Better than me?" Miles said. "This? He isn't great, child."

"The greatest of men can be taken down by the simplest of

things. A lowly bullet can end the life of the most powerful, most capable, most secure of men."

"Not me," Miles said. "Bullets are nothing to me."

"No," she replied. "You'll be brought down by something even more lowly."

"Which is?" he asked, amused, voice growing closer.

"Me," Marasi replied.

Miles laughed. "I'd like to see . . ." He trailed off.

Waxillium cracked his eyes, looking down the length of the tunnel toward the broken ceiling where the building had stood. Light flooded that pit from above, growing brighter at a remarkable rate.

"Who have you brought?" Miles asked, sounding unimpressed. "They won't arrive quickly enough." He paused. Waxillium rolled his head to the side and saw the sudden horror in Miles's face. He had seen it, finally: a shimmering border nearby, a slight difference in the air. Like the distortion caused by heat rising from a hot street.

A speed bubble.

Miles spun on Marasi. Then he ran for the bubble's border, away from the light. Trying to escape.

The light at the other end of the tunnel became bright, and a group of blurs moved down it, so quickly it was impossible to distinguish what was causing them.

Marasi dropped her bubble. The sunlight of full day streamed in from the distant pit, and filling the tunnel—right outside where the bubble had been—was a force of over a hundred constables in uniform. Wayne stood at their head, grinning, wearing a constable's uniform and hat, a false mustache on his face.

"Get 'im, boys!" he said, pointing.

They moved in with clubs, not bothering with guns. Miles screamed in denial, trying to dodge past the first few, then punching at the group that laid hands on him. He wasn't fast enough, and there were far too many of them. In minutes, they had him held down against the ground and were wrapping ropes around his arms.

Waxillium sat up with care, one eye swelling closed, lip bleeding, side aching. Marasi knelt beside him, anxious.

"You shouldn't have confronted him," Waxillium said, tasting blood. "If he'd knocked you out, that would have been the end of it."

"Oh, hush," she said. "You aren't the only one who can take risks."

The backup plan had been straightforward, if difficult. It had begun with eliminating all of Miles's lackeys. Even one of them, left alive, could have noticed what the speed bubble meant and shot Waxillium and Marasi from the outside. There wouldn't have been anything they could have done to prevent it.

But if the lackeys were gone, and if Miles could be distracted long enough while the bubble was up, Wayne could go to gather a large force to surround Miles while he was helpless. He'd never have let it happen if he'd suspected. But within the speed bubble . . .

"No!" Miles screamed. "Unhand me. I defy your oppression!"

"You are a fool," Waxillium said to him, then spat blood to the side. "You let yourself get isolated and distracted, Miles. You forgot the first rule of the Roughs."

Miles screamed, one of the constables pulling a gag over his mouth as he was tied tightly.

"The more alone you are," Waxillium said softly, "the more important it is to have someone you can rely upon."

20

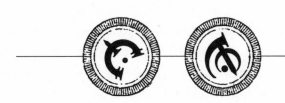

The constable-general has decided not to charge your associate for impersonating an officer of the law," Reddi said.

Waxillium dabbed at his lip with the handkerchief. He sat in the precinct office nearest the Vanisher lair. He felt like slag, with broken ribs and half his body wrapped in bandages. He'd have scars from this.

"The constable-general," Marasi said, voice hard, "should be *glad* for Lord Waxillium's aid—in fact, he should have begged for Lord Waxillium's help all along." She sat beside him on the bench, hovering protectively.

"He actually *does* seem glad," Reddi said. Now that Waxillium paid closer attention, he noticed how the constable kept glancing through the precinct room toward Brettin, the constable-general. Reddi's eyes narrowed slightly, lips turning down. He was baffled by his superior's calm reaction to events.

Waxillium was too exhausted at the moment to bother with the anomaly. In fact, it was nice to hear of something happening in his favor.

Reddi was called over by one of the other constables, and he left. Marasi laid a hand on Waxillium's good arm. He could practically *feel* her concern for him physically in the way she hesitated, the way her brow wrinkled.

"You did well," Waxillium said. "Miles was your catch, Lady Marasi."

"I'm not the one who had to be beaten bloody."

"Wounds heal," Waxillium said, "even on an old horse like me. Watching him attack me and doing nothing . . . I'll bet that was excruciating. I don't think I could have stood it, if our places had been reversed."

"You'd have done it. You're like that. You're every bit the man I thought you might be, yet somehow more *real* at the same time." She looked at him, eyes wide, lips pursed. As if she wanted to say more. He could read her intent in those eyes.

"This isn't going to work, Lady Marasi," he said gently. "I'm thankful for your aid. Very thankful. But the thing you wish between us is not viable. I'm sorry."

Not unexpectedly, she blushed. "Of course. I wasn't implying such a thing." She forced a laugh. "Why would you think—I mean, it's silly!"

"I apologize, then," he said. Though, of course, they both knew what the exchange had meant. He felt a deep regret. *If I were ten years younger . . .*

It wasn't the age per se. It was what those years had done to him. When you watched a woman you loved die by your own gunshot, when you saw an old colleague and respected lawkeeper turn bad, it did things to you. Ripped you up inside. And *those* wounds, they didn't heal nearly as easily as the bodily ones.

This woman was young, full of life. She didn't deserve someone who was basically all scars wrapped up in a thick skin of sun-dried leather.

Eventually, Constable-General Brettin walked over to them. He was as stiff-backed as before, constable's hat carried under his arm. "Lord Waxillium," he said in a monotone.

"Constable-General."

"For your efforts today, I have requested that the Senate give you a citywide deputized forbearance."

Waxillium blinked in surprise.

"If you are not aware," Brettin continued, "this would give you powers of investigation and arrest, as if you were a member of the constabulary, sufficient to authorize actions such as those of last night."

"That is . . . very considerate of you," Waxillium said.

"It is one of the only ways to excuse your actions without drawing embarrassment down upon the precinct. I have backdated the request, and if we are in luck, nobody will realize you were working alone this past night. Also, I do not wish for you to feel that you *need* to work alone. This city could use your expertise."

"With all due respect, sir," Waxillium said, "that's quite a change from your previous stance."

"I have had occasion to change my mind," Brettin said. "You should know that I will soon be retiring. A new constable-general will be appointed in my position, but he will be required to accept the Senate's mandate regarding you, should this motion be accepted."

"I . . ." Waxillium was uncertain how to reply. "Thank you."

"It's for the good of the City. Of course, note that if you abuse this privilege, it will undoubtedly be revoked." Brettin nodded awkwardly and withdrew.

Waxillium scratched at his chin, watching the man. Something decidedly odd was going on there. He was almost like a different person. Wayne passed him, tipping his lucky hat—which was bloodied on one side—and grinning as he approached Waxillium and Marasi.

"Here," Wayne said, covertly handing something wrapped in a handkerchief to Waxillium. It was unexpectedly heavy. "Got you another of those guns."

Waxillium sighed.

"Don't worry," Wayne said, "I traded a real nice scarf for it."

"And where did you get the scarf?"

"Off one of the dead blokes you shot," Wayne said. "So it wasn't stealin'. He ain't gonna need it, after all." He seemed quite proud of himself.

Waxillium tucked the gun into his empty holster. The other holster held Vindication. Marasi had searched through the hideout after Miles was taken and had recovered it for him. That was good. It would have been sad to survive this night, only to have Ranette kill him.

"So," Marasi said, "you traded a dead man's scarf for another dead man's gun. But . . . the gun itself belonged to someone dead, so by the same logic—"

"Don't try," Waxillium said. "Logic doesn't work on Wayne."

"I bought a ward against it off a traveling fortune-teller," Wayne explained. "It lets me add two 'n' two and get a pickle."

"I . . . have no response to that," Marasi said.

"Technically that *was* a response," Wayne said.

"Looks like they fished that gunsmith outta the canal for you, Wax, and he's alive. Not real happy, but alive."

"Has anyone found anything regarding the other women who were kidnapped?" Waxillium asked.

Wayne glanced at Marasi, who shook her head. "Nothing. Maybe Miles will know where they are."

If he'll talk, Waxillium thought. Miles had stopped feeling pain long ago. Waxillium wasn't certain how anyone would go about interrogating him.

Waxillium felt that by not rescuing the other women, he had failed in large measure. He'd vowed to get Steris back, and he had. But a greater evil had been done.

He sighed as the door to the captain's office opened, and Steris stepped out. A pair of senior constables had taken her statement, after taking that of Waxillium and Wayne. The two constables waved for Marasi next, and she went, glancing over her shoulder at Waxillium. He'd told her to be frank and straightforward with them, and to not hide anything he or Wayne had done. Though, if she could, she was to obscure Ranette's role.

Wayne wandered over to where some constables were eating morning sandwiches. They regarded him with suspicion, but—by experience—Waxillium knew that Wayne would soon have them laughing and asking him to join them. *Does he even understand what he does?* Waxillium wondered as Wayne launched into an explanation of the fight for the constables. *Or does he just do it all by instinct?*

Waxillium watched for a moment before realizing that Steris had approached him. She sat down in the chair directly across from him, maintaining good posture. She had fixed her hair, and while her dress was rumpled from her day of captivity, she looked relatively composed.

"Lord Waxillium," she said. "I find it necessary to offer you my thanks."

"I hope the necessity isn't too onerous," Waxillium said with a grunt.

"Only in that it comes . . . is required . . . after an onerous captivity. You should know that I was not touched indecently by my captors. I remain pure."

"Rust and *Ruin*, Steris! I'm glad, but I didn't need to know that."

"You did," she said, face impassive. "Assuming you still wish to proceed with our nuptials."

"It wouldn't matter either way. Besides, I thought we weren't to that point yet. We haven't even announced that we are seeing one another."

"Yes, though I believe we can now amend our previous timetable. You see, a dramatic rescue such as you have effected will be expected to create an outpouring of my emotions. What once might have been a scandal will instead be viewed as romantic. We could plausibly announce an engagement next week and have it be accepted in high society without concern or comment."

"That's good, I suppose."

"Yes. Shall I proceed with our contract, then?"

"You don't mind that I've returned to the miscreant ways of my past?"

"I rather think that I would soon be *dead* if you had not," Steris said. "I am not in a position to complain."

"I intend to continue," Waxillium warned. "Not every day, patrolling a beat or anything like that. But I've received a forbearance—and an offer—to be involved in constabulary business in the city. I plan to take on the occasional problem that needs extra attention."

"Every gentleman needs a hobby," she said evenly. "And, considering the self-indulgences of some men I've known, this wouldn't be problematic by comparison." She leaned forward. "In short, my lord, I see you for what you are. The two of us, we are beyond the points in our lives where expecting the other to change would be realistic. I will accept this about you if you will accept me. I am not without my faults, as my previous three suitors chose to explain to me—at length—in written communication."

"I hadn't realized."

"It is not an issue worthy of your attention, really," she said. "Though I did think that you'd have realized I did not come to this potential union without—no offense—a measure of desperation."

"I understand."

Steris hesitated; then a bit of her coldness seemed to depart. Some of her control, her steely will, fell away. She looked tired, suddenly. Worn. Though behind that mask, he saw something that might have been affection for him. She clasped her hands before her. "I am not . . . good with people, Lord Waxillium. I realize it. I must stress, however, that you have my thanks for what you have done. I speak it from the depths of all that I am. Thank you."

He met her eyes, and nodded.

"So," she said, growing more businesslike. "We progress with our engagement?"

He hesitated. There was no reason not to, but a part of him found that he thought himself a coward. Of the two offers this day—one unspoken, the other blunt—*this* was the one he was contemplating?

He glanced toward the room where Marasi was giving the report of her involvement in this mess. She *was* entrancing. Beautiful, intelligent, motivated. By all logic and reason, he should have been completely infatuated with her.

In fact, she reminded him a lot of Lessie. Perhaps that was the problem.

"We move forward," he said, turning back to Steris.

EPILOGUE

M arasi attended Miles's execution.
    Daius, the senior prosecutor, had counseled against it.
He never attended executions.

She sat on the outer balcony, alone, watching Miles walk up the
steps to the firing platform. Her position was above the execution
site.

She narrowed her eyes, remembering Miles standing in that
underground room of darkness and mist, pointing a gun at her hiding place. She'd had a gun to her head three times during that two-
day span, but the only time she'd really believed that she would die
had been when she had seen the look in Miles's eyes. The heartless
lack of emotion, the superiority.

She shivered. The time between the Vanisher attack at the wedding and Miles's capture had been less than a day and a half. Yet
she felt like during that time she'd aged two decades. It was like a
form of temporal Allomancy, a speed bubble around her alone. The
world was different now. She'd nearly been killed, she'd killed for
the first time, she'd fallen in love and been rejected. Now she'd
helped condemn to death a former hero of the Roughs.

Miles looked with contempt on the constables who tied him to the restraining pole. He'd shown that same expression through most of the trial—the first one she'd helped prosecute as an attorney, though Daius had been the lead on the case. The trial had gone quickly, despite its high-profile and high-stakes nature. Miles had not denied his crimes.

It seemed that he saw himself as immortal. Even standing up there—his metalminds removed, a dozen rifles cocked and pointed toward him—he didn't seem to believe he would die. The human mind was very clever at tricking itself, at keeping the despair of inevitability at bay. She'd known that look in Miles's eyes. Every man had it, when young. And every man eventually saw it as a lie.

The rifles went to shoulders. Perhaps now Miles would finally recognize that lie himself. As the guns fired, Marasi found that she was satisfied. And that disturbed her greatly.

Waxillium boarded the train at Dryport. His leg still ached, he walked with a cane, and he wore a bandage around his chest to help with the broken ribs. One week wasn't nearly enough time to heal from what he'd been through. He probably shouldn't have left his bed.

He limped down the corridor of the lavish first-class carriage, passing handsomely appointed private rooms. He counted off to the third compartment as the train labored into motion. He walked into the chamber, leaving the door open, and sat down in one of the well-stuffed chairs by the window. It was affixed to the floor, and sat before a small table with a long, single leg. It was curved and slender, like a woman's neck.

A short time later, he heard footsteps in the corridor. They hesitated at the doorway.

Waxillium watched the scenery passing outside. "Hello, Uncle," he said, turning to look at the man in the doorway.

Lord Edwarn Ladrian stepped into the room, walking with a whale-ivory cane and wearing fine clothing. "How did you find me?" he asked, sitting down in the other chair.

"A few of the Vanishers we interrogated," Waxillium said. "They described a man that Miles called 'Mister Suit.' I don't think anyone else recognized you in the description. From what I understand, you were hermitlike during the decade leading up to your 'death.' Save for your letters to the broadsheets about political matters, of course."

That didn't answer the question exactly. Waxillium had found this train, and this car, based on the numbers written in Miles's cigar box, the one Wayne had found. Railway routes. Everyone else thought they had been trains the Vanishers had been planning to hit, but Waxillium had seen a different pattern. Miles had been tracking Mister Suit's movements.

"Interesting," Lord Edwarn said. He took a handkerchief out of his pocket and wiped his fingers as a servant entered, bringing a tray of food and setting it on the table in front of him. Another poured him wine. He waved for them to wait outside the door.

"Where is Telsin?" Waxillium asked.

"Your sister is safe."

Waxillium closed his eyes, and fought down the welling of emotion. He'd thought her dead in the wreck that supposedly claimed his uncle's life, but had dealt with his emotions, such as they were. It had been years since he'd seen his sister.

Why, then, was finding out that she lived so powerfully meaningful to him? He couldn't even define *which* emotions he was feeling.

He forced his eyes open. Lord Edwarn was watching him, holding a glass of crystalline white wine in his fingers. "You suspected," Edwarn said. "All along, you suspected I wasn't dead. That's why you recognized whatever description those ruffians were able to give. I've changed clothing styles, my haircut, and even shaved my beard."

"You shouldn't have had your butler try to kill me," Waxillium said. "He was too long in the family employ, and he was too ready to kill me, to have been hired by the Vanishers on such short notice. It meant he was working for someone else, and had been for some time. The simplest answer was that he was still working for the person he'd served for years."

"Ah. Of course, you weren't supposed know he caused the explosion."

"I wasn't supposed to survive it, you mean."

Lord Ladrian shrugged.

"Why?" Waxillium asked, leaning in. "Why bring me back, if only to then have me killed? Why not arrange for someone else to take the house title?"

"Hinston was going to take it," Lord Ladrian said, buttering a roll. "His disease was . . . unfortunate. Plans were already in motion. I didn't have time to search out other options. Besides, I hoped—obviously, without basis—that you'd have overcome your overdeveloped childhood sense of morality. I had hoped you'd be a resource to me."

Rust and Ruin, I hate this man, Waxillium thought, memories of his childhood returning to him. He'd gone to the Roughs, in part, to escape that condescending voice.

"I've come for the other four kidnapped women," Waxillium said.

Lord Ladrian took a sip of wine. "You think I'm going to give them up, just like that?"

"Yes. I will expose you, otherwise."

"Go right ahead!" Lord Ladrian seemed amused. "Some will believe you. Others will think you mad. Neither reaction will hinder me or my colleagues."

"Because you've already been defeated," Waxillium said.

Lord Ladrian almost choked on his roll. He laughed, lowering it to the table. "Is that honestly what you think?"

"The Vanishers are gone," Waxillium said, "Miles is being executed as we speak, and I know that you were funding him. We captured the goods you were stealing, so you have gained nothing there. You obviously didn't have much in the way of funds to begin with. Otherwise you wouldn't have needed Miles and his team to do the robberies."

"I assure you, Waxillium, that we are *quite* solvent. Thank you.

And you'll find no proof that I or my associates had anything to do with the robberies. We rented Miles his space, but how could we have known what he was up to? Harmony! He was a respected lawkeeper."

"You took the women."

"There is no proof of that. Just speculation on your part. A few of the Vanishers will swear to their graves that Miles raped and killed the women. I know for a fact that one of those Vanishers survived. Though I *am* still curious how you found me here, in this particular train."

Waxillium made no reply to that specifically. "I know that you're ruined," he said instead. "Say what you will, I see it. Give me the women and my sister. I'll recommend to the judges that you be shown leniency. Yes, you funded a group of robbers as a means of high-stakes investment. But you explicitly told them not to hurt anyone, and you weren't the one to pull the trigger and kill Peterus. I suspect you'll escape execution."

"You assume so many things, Waxillium," Lord Ladrian said. He reached into the pocket of his jacket and removed a folded broadsheet and a thin, black leather appointment book. He set them down on the table, broadsheet on the top. "Funding a group of robbers as a means of high-stakes investment? Is that *really* what you think this was about?"

"That and kidnapping the women," Waxillium said. "Presumably as a means of extorting their families."

That last part was a lie. Waxillium didn't believe for a moment that it was about extortion. His uncle was planning something, and considering the family lines of those women, Waxillium suspected that Marasi was right. It was about Allomancy.

He harbored a hope that his uncle wasn't involved in the direct . . . breeding. The very idea made Waxillium uncomfortable. Perhaps Ladrian was merely selling the women to someone else.

What a thing to hope for.

Ladrian tapped the broadsheet. The headline was about news that was going around the city. House Tekiel was on the brink of collapse. They'd had too much bad publicity in the robbery last week, even though the cargo had been recovered. That, mixed with other serious financial troubles . . .

Other serious financial troubles.

Waxillium scanned the broadsheet. Tekiel's main house business was security. Insurance. *Rust and Ruin!* he thought, making the connection.

"A series of targeted attacks," Ladrian said, leaning in, sounding pleased with himself. "House Tekiel is doomed. They owe payments on too many high-profile losses. These attacks, and the insurance claims, have devastated them and their financial integrity. Company shareholders have been selling their stakes for pennies. You claimed my finances were weak. That is only because they have been dedicated to a specific task. Have you wondered, yet, why your house is destitute?"

"You took it all," Waxillium guessed. "You funneled it out of the house finances into . . . something. Somewhere."

"We have just seized one of the most powerful financial institutions in the city," Ladrian said. "The materials stolen are being returned, and so while we've assumed Tekiel's debts by purchasing them, the claims for lost goods will soon be nullified. I *always* expected Miles to be captured. This plan wouldn't work without it."

Waxillium closed his eyes, feeling a dread. *I've been chasing chickens this entire time,* he realized. *While someone stole the horses.* It wasn't about robberies, or even kidnappings.

It was insurance fraud.

"We needed only the *temporary* disappearance of goods," Edwarn said. "And everything has worked out perfectly. Thank you."

The bullets ripped through Miles's body. Marasi watched, holding her breath, forcing herself not to wince. It was time to stop being a child.

He was shot again. Her eyes open, her nerves steeled, she was able to watch with horror as his wounds started to heal. It should have been impossible. They'd searched him carefully for metal-minds. Yet the bullet holes pulled closed, and his smile widened, his eyes wild.

"You are fools!" Miles yelled at the firing squad. "One day, the men of gold and red, bearers of the final metal, *will* come to you. And you *will* be ruled by them."

They fired again. More bullets ripped into Miles. The wounds again closed, but not all the way. He didn't have enough healing stored in whatever last metalmind he had hidden. Marasi found herself shivering as a fourth volley struck his body, causing him to spasm.

"Worship," Miles said, his voice failing, his mouth spouting blood. "Worship Trell and wait . . ."

The fifth volley of bullets hit, and this time none of the wounds healed. Miles slackened in his bonds, eyes open and lifeless, staring at the ground before him.

The constables looked extremely disturbed. One of them ran up to check for a pulse. Marasi shivered. Right up until the end, Miles hadn't seemed like he accepted death.

But he *was* dead now. A Bloodmaker like him could heal repeat-edly, but if they ever actually stopped healing—let their wounds consume them—they would die like anyone else. Just to make certain, the nearest constable raised a handgun and blasted Miles three times in the side of the head. This was gruesome enough that Marasi had to look away.

It was done. Miles Hundredlives was dead.

In turning away, however, she saw a figure watching from the shadows below, ignored by the constables. He turned away, black robe rippling, and walked out through a gate leading into the alley.

"It's not only about the insurance," Waxillium said, meeting Ed-warn's eyes. "You took the women."

Edwarn Ladrian said nothing.

"I'm going to stop you, Uncle," Waxillium said softly. "I don't know what you're doing with those women, but I *am* going to find a way to stop it."

"Oh please, Waxillium," Edwarn said. "Your self-righteousness was tiring enough when you were a youth. Your heritage alone should make you better than that."

"My heritage?"

"You are of a noble bloodline," Ladrian said. "Directly back to the Counselor of Gods himself. You are Twinborn, and a powerful Allomancer. It was with great regret that I ordered your death, and I only did so under pressure from my colleagues. I suspected, even hoped, you would survive. This world needs you. Us."

"You sound like Miles," Waxillium said, surprised.

"No," Ladrian said. "He sounded like *me*." He tucked his hand-kerchief into his collar, then began to dine. "But you are not ready. I will see that you are sent the proper information. For now, you may withdraw and consider what I've told you."

"I don't think so," Waxillium said, reaching into his jacket for a handgun.

Ladrian looked up with a pitying expression. Waxillium heard guns being cocked, and glanced to the side, to where several young men wearing black suits stood in the corridor outside. None were wearing metal on their bodies.

"I have nearly twenty Allomancers riding in this train, Waxillium," Edwarn said, voice cold. "And you are wounded, barely able to walk. You don't have a sliver of evidence against me. Are you certain this is a fight you want to start?"

Waxillium hesitated. Then he growled and reached forward with an empty hand to sweep the meal off his uncle's table. Dishes and food spilled to the floor with a crash as Waxillium bent forward, enraged. "I'll kill you someday, Uncle."

Edwarn leaned back, unthreatened. "Lead him to the back of the train. Throw him off. Good day, Waxillium."

Waxillium tried to reach for his uncle, but the men rushed in and grabbed him, pulling him away. His side and his leg both flared in pain at the treatment. Edwarn was right about one thing. This wasn't the day to fight.

But that day *would* come.

Waxillium let them tow him down the hallway. They opened the door at the end of the train and tossed him out toward the tracks that sped by beneath. He caught himself with Allomancy, as they'd no doubt expected he would, and landed to watch the train speed away.

Marasi burst out into the alleyway beside the precinct building. She felt something stirring in her, a powerful curiosity she could not describe. She *had* to find out who that figure was.

She caught a glimpse of the hem of a dark robe disappearing around a corner. She ran after it, holding her handbag in a tight grip and reaching inside for the small revolver Waxillium had given her.

What am I doing? a part of her mind thought. *Running into an alleyway alone?* It wasn't a particularly sensible thing to do. She just *felt* that she had to do it.

She ran a short distance. Had she lost the figure? She paused at an intersection, where an even smaller alleyway cut off from the first. Her curiosity was almost unbearable.

Standing in the mouth of the smaller alleyway, waiting for her, was a tall man in a black robe.

She gasped, stepping backward. The man was well over six feet tall, and the enveloping robe gave him an ominous appearance. He brought up pale hands and took down his hood, exposing a shaved head and a face that was tattooed around the eyes in an intricate pattern.

Driven into those eyes, point-first, were what looked like a pair of thick railroad spikes. One of the eye sockets was deformed, as if it had been crushed, long-healed scars and bony ridges under the skin marring the tattoos.

Marasi knew this creature from mythology, but seeing him left her cold, terrified. "Ironeyes," she whispered.

"I apologize for bringing you like this," Ironeyes said. He had a quiet, gravelly voice.

"Like this?" she said, her voice coming out as almost a squeak.

"With emotional Allomancy. I sometimes Pull too hard. I've never been as good at this sort of thing as Breeze was. Be calm, child. I will not hurt you."

She felt an instant calmness, though that felt terribly unnatural, and left her feeling even worse. Calm, but sick. One should not be calm when speaking with Death himself.

"Your friend," Ironeyes said, "has uncovered something very dangerous."

"And you wish him to stop?"

"Stop?" Ironeyes said. "Not at all. I wish him to be informed. Harmony has particular views about how things must be done. I do not always agree with him. Oddly, his particular beliefs require that he allow that. Here." Ironeyes reached into the folds of his cloak, bringing out a small book. "There is information in this. Guard it carefully. You may read it, if you wish, but deliver it to Lord Waxillium on my behalf."

She took the book. "Pardon," she said, trying to fight through the numbness he had put inside her. Was she really speaking to a mythological figure? Was she going mad? She could barely think. "But why didn't you take it to him yourself?"

Ironeyes responded with a tight-lipped smile, watching her with the heads of those silvery spikes. "I have a feeling he'd have tried to shoot me. That one does not like unanswered questions, but he does my brother's work, and that is something I feel inclined to encourage. Good day, Lady Marasi Colms."

Ironeyes turned, cloak rustling, and walked away down the alley. He put his hood up as he walked, then lifted into the air, propelled by Allomancy over the tops of the nearby buildings. He vanished from sight.

Marasi clutched the book, then slid it into her handbag, shaking.

Waxillium landed at the rail station, dropping as gently as he could from his Allomantic flight down the tracks. Landing still hurt his leg.

Wayne sat on the platform, feet up on a barrel, smoking his pipe. He still had his arm in a sling. He wouldn't be able to heal it quickly—he had no health stored up. Trying to store some now would just make him heal more slowly during that process, then heal more quickly as he tapped his metalmind, ending with no net gain.

Wayne was reading a small novel that he'd picked out of someone's pocket on their train ride out to the estates. He'd left an aluminum bullet in its place, worth easily a hundred times the price of the book. Ironically, the person who found it would probably throw it away, never realizing its value.

I'll need to talk to him about that again, Waxillium thought, walking up onto the platform. *But not today.* Today, they had other worries.

Waxillium joined his friend, but continued staring to the south. Toward the city, and his uncle.

"It's a pretty good book," Wayne said, flipping a page. "You should try it. It's about bunnies. They talk. Damnedest thing ever."

Waxillium didn't reply.

"So, was it your uncle?" Wayne asked.

"Yes."

"Crud. I owe you a fiver, then."

"The bet was for twenty."

"Yeah, but you owe me fifteen."

"I do?"

"Sure, for that bet I made that you'd end up helpin' me with the Vanishers."

Waxillium frowned, looking at his friend. "I don't remember that bet."

"You weren't there when we made it."

"I wasn't there?"

"Yeah."

"Wayne, you can't make bets with people when they aren't there."

"I can," Wayne said, tucking the book into his pocket and standing, "if they *shoulda* been there. And you shoulda, Wax."

"I . . ." How to respond to that? "I will be. From now on."

Wayne nodded, joining him and looking toward Elendel. It rose in the distance, the two competing skyscrapers rising on one side of the city, other smaller ones growing like crystals from the center of the expanding metropolis.

"You know," Wayne said, "I always wondered what it would be like to come here, find civilization and all that. I didn't realize."

"Realize what?" Waxillium asked.

"That *this* was really the rough part of the world," Wayne said. "That we had it easy, out past the mountains."

Waxillium found himself nodding. "You can be very wise sometimes, Wayne."

"It's onnacount of my thinkin', mate," Wayne said, tapping his head, increasing the thickness of his accent. "It's what I do wif my brain. Somma the time, at least."

"And the rest of the time?"

"The rest of the time, I don't do so much thinkin'. 'Cuz if I did, I'd go runnin' back to where things is simple. You see?"

"I see. And we do have to stay, Wayne. I have work to do here."

"Then we'll see it done," Wayne said. "Just like always."

Waxillium nodded, reaching into his sleeve and sliding out a thin black book.

"What's that?" Wayne asked, taking it, curious.

"My uncle's pocket book," Waxillium said. "Filled with appointments and notes."

Wayne whistled softly. "How'd you take it? Shoulder bump?"

"Table sweep," Waxillium said.

"Nice. Glad to know I've taught you *somethin'* useful during our years together. What did you trade for it?"

"A threat," Waxillium said, looking back toward Elendel. "And a promise."

He would see this to the end. Roughs honor. When one of your own went bad, it was your job to see the mess cleaned up.

ARS ARCANUM

METALS QUICK REFERENCE CHART

METAL	ALLOMANTIC POWER	FERUCHEMICAL POWER
C Iron	Pulls on Nearby Sources of Metal	Stores Physical Weight
↷ Steel	Pushes on Nearby Sources of Metal	Stores Physical Speed
⊛ Tin	Increases Senses	Stores Senses
⊛ Pewter	Increases Physical Abilities	Stores Physical Strength
∅ Zinc	Riots (Enflames) Emotions	Stores Mental Speed
↗ Brass	Soothes (Dampens) Emotions	Stores Warmth
⊌ Copper	Hides Allomantic Pulses	Stores Memories
⊌ Bronze	Allows One to Hear Allomantic Pulses	Stores Wakefulness
⊖ Cadmium	Slows Down Time	Stores Breath
⊕ Bendalloy	Speeds Up Time	Stores Energy
⟩ Gold	Reveals Your Past Self	Stores Health
⊍ Electrum	Reveals Your Own Future	Stores Determination
⊛ Chromium	Wipes Allomantic Reserves of Target	Stores Fortune
⊛ Nicrosil	Enhances Allomantic Burn of Target	Stores Investiture
⊋ Aluminum	Wipes Internal Allomantic Reserves	Stores Identity
⟨ Duralumin	Enhances the Next Metal Burned	Stores Connection

ALUMINUM: A Mistborn who burns aluminum instantly metabolizes all of his or her metals without giving any other effect, wiping all Allomantic reserves. Mistings who can burn aluminum are called Aluminum Gnats due to the ineffectiveness of this ability by itself. Trueself Ferrings can store their spiritual sense of identity in an aluminum metalmind. This is an art rarely spoken of outside of Terris communities, and even among them, it is not yet well understood. Aluminum itself and a few of its alloys are Allomantically inert; they cannot be Pushed or Pulled and can be used to shield an individual from emotional Allomancy.

BENDALLOY: Slider Mistings burn bendalloy to compress time in a bubble around themselves, making it pass more quickly within the bubble. This causes events outside the bubble to move at a glacial pace from the point of view of the Slider. Subsumer Ferrings can store nutrition and calories in a bendalloy metalmind; they can eat large amounts of food during active storage without feeling full or gaining weight, and then can go without the need to eat while tapping the metalmind. A separate bendalloy metalmind can be used to similarly regulate fluids intake.

BRASS: Soother Mistings burn brass to soothe (dampen) the emotions of nearby individuals. This can be directed at a single individual or directed across a general area, and the Soother can focus on specific emotions. Firesoul Ferrings can store warmth in a brass metalmind, cooling themselves off while actively storing. They can tap the metalmind at a later time to warm themselves.

BRONZE: Seeker Mistings burn brass to "hear" pulses given off by other Allomancers who are burning metals. Different metals produce different pulses. Sentry Ferrings can store wakefulness in a bronze metalmind, making themselves drowsy while actively storing. They can tap the metalmind at a later time to reduce drowsiness or to heighten their awareness.

CADMIUM: Pulser Mistings burn cadmium to stretch time in a bubble around themselves, making it pass more slowly inside the bubble. This causes events outside the bubble to move at blurring speed from the point of view of the Pulser. Gasper Ferrings can store breath inside a cadmium metalmind; during active storage they must hyperventilate in order for their bodies to get enough air. The breath can be retrieved at a later time, eliminating or reducing the need to breathe using the lungs while tapping the metalmind. They can also highly oxygenate their blood.

CHROMIUM: Leecher Mistings who burn chromium while touching another Allomancer will wipe that Allomancer's metal reserves. Spinner Ferrings can store fortune in a chromium metalmind, making themselves unlucky during active storage, and can tap it at a later time to increase their luck.

COPPER: Coppercloud Mistings (also known as Smokers) burn copper to create an invisible cloud around themselves, which hides nearby Allomancers from being detected by a Seeker and which shields nearby individuals from the effects of emotional Allomancy. Archivist Ferrings can store memories in a copper metalmind (coppermind); the memory is gone from their head while in storage, and can be retrieved with perfect recall at a later time.

DURALUMIN: A Mistborn who burns duralumin instantly burns away any other metals being burned at the time, releasing an enormous burst of those metals' power. Mistings who can burn Duralumin are called Duralumin Gnats due to the ineffectiveness of this ability by itself. Connecter Ferrings can store spiritual connection in a duralumin metalmind, reducing other people's awareness and friendship with them during active storage, and can tap it at a later time in order to speedily form trust relationships with others.

ELECTRUM: Oracle Mistings burn electrum to see a vision of possible paths their future could take. This is usually limited to a few seconds. Pinnacle Ferrings can store determination in an electrum metalmind, entering a depressed state during active storage, and can tap it at a later time to enter a manic phase.

GOLD: Augur Mistings burn gold to see a vision of a past self or how they would have turned out having made different choices in the past. Bloodmaker Ferrings can store health in a gold metalmind, reducing their health while actively storing, and can tap it at a later time in order to heal quickly or to heal beyond the body's usual abilities.

IRON: Lurcher Mistings who burn iron can Pull on nearby sources of metal. Pulls must be directly toward the Lurcher's center of gravity. Skimmer Ferrings can store physical weight in an iron metalmind, reducing their effective weight while actively storing, and can tap it at a later time to increase their effective weight.

NICROSIL: Nicroburst Mistings who burn nicrosil while touching another Allomancer will instantly burn away any metals being burned by that Allomancer, releasing an enormous (and perhaps unexpected) burst of those metals' power within that Allomancer. Soulbearer Ferrings can store Investiture in a nicrosil metalmind. This is a power that very few know anything about; indeed, I'm certain the people of Terris don't truly know what they are doing when they use these powers.

PEWTER: Pewterarm Mistings (also known as Thugs) burn pewter to increase their physical strength, speed, and durability, also enhancing their bodies' ability to heal. Brute Ferrings can store physical strength in a pewter metalmind, reducing their strength while actively storing, and can tap it at a later time to increase their strength.

STEEL: Coinshot Mistings who burn steel can Push on nearby sources of metal. Pushes must be directly away from the Coinshot's center of gravity. Steelrunner Ferrings can store physical speed in a steel metalmind, slowing them while actively storing, and can tap it at a later time to increase their speed.

TIN: Tineye Mistings who burn tin increase the sensitivity of their five senses. All are increased at the same time. Windwhisperer Ferrings can store the sensitivity of one of the five senses in a tin metalmind; a different tin metalmind must be used for each sense. While storing, their sensitivity in that sense is reduced, and when the metalmind is tapped that sense is enhanced.

ZINC: Rioter Mistings burn zinc to riot (enflame) the emotions of nearby individuals. This can be directed at a single individual or directed across a general area, and the Rioter can focus on specific emotions. Sparker Ferrings can store mental speed in a zinc metalmind, dulling their ability to think and reason while actively storing, and can tap it at a later time to think and reason more quickly.

ON THE THREE METALLIC ARTS

On Scadrial, there are three prime manifestations of Investiture. Locally, these are spoken of as the "Metallic Arts," though there are other names for them.

Allomancy is the most common of the three. It is end-positive, according to my terminology, meaning that the practitioner draws in power from an external source. The body then filters it into various forms. (The actual outlet of the power is not chosen by the practitioner, but instead is hardwritten into their Spiritweb.) The key to drawing this power comes in the form of various types of metals, with specific compositions being required. Though the metal is consumed in the process, the power itself doesn't actually come from the metal. The metal is a catalyst, you might say, that begins an Investiture and keeps it running.

In truth, this isn't much different from the form-based Investitures one finds on Sel, where specific shape is the key—here, however, the interactions are more limited. Still, one cannot deny the raw power of Allomancy. It is instinctive and intuitive for the practitioner, as opposed to requiring a great deal of study and exactness, as one finds in the form-based Investitures of Sel.

Allomancy is brutal, raw, and powerful. There are sixteen base metals that work, though two others—named the God Metals locally—can be used in alloy to craft an entirely different set of sixteen each. As these God Metals are no longer commonly available, however, the other metals are not in wide use.

Feruchemy is still widely known and used at this point in Scadrial. Indeed, you might say that it is more present today than it has been in many eras past, when it was confined to distant Terris or hidden from sight by the Keepers.

Feruchemy is an end-neutral art, meaning that power is neither gained nor lost. The art also requires metal as a focus, but instead of being consumed, the metal acts as a medium by which abilities within the practitioner are shuttled through time. Invest that metal on one day, withdraw the power on another day. It is a well-rounded art, with some feelers in the Physical, some in the Cognitive, and even some in the Spiritual. The last powers are under heavy experimentation by the Terris community, and aren't spoken of to outsiders.

It should be noted that the inbreeding of the Feruchemists with the general population has diluted the power in some ways. It is now common for people to be born with access to only one of the sixteen Feruchemical abilities. It is hypothesized that if one could make metalminds out of alloys with the God Metals, other abilities could be discovered.

Hemalurgy is widely unknown in the modern world of Scadrial. Its secrets were kept close by those who survived their world's rebirth, and the only known practitioners of it now are the kandra, who (for the most part) serve Harmony.

Hemalurgy is an end-negative art. Some power is lost in the practice of it. Though many through history have maligned it as an "evil" art, none of the Investitures are actually evil. At its core, Hemalurgy deals with removing abilities—or attributes—from one person and bestowing them on another. It is primarily concerned with things of the Spiritual realm, and is of the greatest interest to me. If one of these three arts is of great interest to the Cosmere, it is this one. I think there are great possibilities for its use.